# AND MORE CRITICAL ACCLAIM FOR LUANNE RICE

"A rare combination of realism and romance."
—*The New York Times Book Review*

"Luanne Rice proves herself a nimble virtuoso."
—*The Washington Post Book World*

"Few writers evoke summer's translucent days so effortlessly, or better capture the bittersweet ties of family love."
—*Publishers Weekly*

"Ms. Rice shares Anne Tyler's ability to portray offbeat, fey characters winningly."
—*The Atlanta Journal-Constitution*

"Rice has an elegant style, a sharp eye, and a real warmth. In her hands, families, and their values . . . seem worth cherishing."
—*San Francisco Chronicle*

"Luanne Rice has enticed millions of readers by enveloping them in stories that are wrapped in the hot, sultry weather of summer. . . . She does it so well."
—*USA Today*

"What a lovely writer Luanne Rice is."
—Dominick Dunne

"[Luanne Rice's] characters breaks readers' hearts. . . . True-to-life characters dealing with real issues—people following journeys that will either break them or heal them."
—*The Columbus Dispatch*

"A joy to read."
—*The Atlanta Journal-Constitution*

"Addictive . . . irresistible."
—*People*

"Rice writes as naturally as she breathes."
—Brendan Gill

## NOVELS BY LUANNE RICE

WITH JOSEPH MONNINGER
*The Letters*

# Secrets
## of Paris

# Secrets of Paris

A NOVEL

# LUANNE RICE

BANTAM BOOKS • NEW YORK

2012 Bantam Books Mass Market Edition

Copyright © 1991 by Luanne Rice

Published in the United States by Bantam Books, an imprint of The Random House Publishing Group, a division of Random House, Inc., New York.

BANTAM BOOKS and the rooster colophon are registered trademarks of Random House, Inc.

Originally published in hardcover in the United States by Viking Penguin, a division of Penguin Books USA Inc., in 1991.

Grateful acknowledgment is made for permission to reprint excerpts from the following copyrighted works:

*Madame de Sévigné: A Life and Letters* by Frances Mossiker. Copyright © 1983 by Frances Mossiker. Reprinted by permission of Alfred A. Knopf, Inc., a division of Random House, Inc.

*Selected Letters* by Madame de Sévigné, translated by Leonard Tancock, Penguin Classics 1982. Copyright © Leonard Tancock, 1982. Reproduced by permission of Penguin Books Ltd.

ISBN 978-0-345-53036-3
eBook ISBN 978-0-553-90817-6

Cover images: © TanMan/Getty Images (sunset),
David Sacks/Taxi/Getty Images (couple), Jan Martin Will/Shutterstock (Seine)

Printed in the United States of America

www.bantamdell.com

9 8 7 6 5 4 3 2 1

Bantam Books mass market edition: April 2012

For Max, Olivier,
and Amelia Onorato,
*with love*

# Secrets
## of Paris

# 1

*What I am about to communicate to you is the most astonishing thing, the most surprising, most triumphant, most baffling, most unheard of, most singular, most unbelievable, most unforeseen, biggest, tiniest, rarest, commonest, the most talked about, the most secret up to this day, the most enviable, in fact a thing of which only one example can be found in past ages, and, moreover, that example is a false one; a thing nobody can believe in Paris (how could anyone believe it in Lyons?).*

—From Madame de Sévigné to Coulanges,
December 1672

Lydie McBride occupied a café table in the Jardin du Palais Royal and thought how fine it was to be an American woman in Paris at the end of the twentieth century. The sun warmed her arms. People strolled along the dry paths, and the silvery dust mingled with the smell of strong coffee. It was one of the first hot spring days. Then something happened—cups clattered on the waiter's tray, or the breeze shifted, and Lydie thought of home.

She felt a keen hankering for it: for her family, for her block in New York City, for the racetrack, for strangers speaking English.

"May I borrow your sugar?" someone asked in a low voice.

Lydie jumped. She had just been longing so hard to hear the English language, she wondered for an instant whether she had conjured the sound out of the May air. But then she regained her composure.

"Of course," she said, passing the china bowl to the woman at the next table. She watched her, a tall woman Lydie's age with dark hair twisted into a chignon, stir two sugar cubes into her coffee. This woman wore red lipstick perfectly; her eyes were hidden behind big sunglasses. Lydie, who never wore much makeup and had the sort of flyaway red hair that always looked uncombed, had the impression of much gold jewelry.

"I need some quick energy," the woman explained. "I just had a fitting at Chanel—an experience that never fails to take the heart out of me."

Lydie smiled at the way she made shopping at Chanel sound like torture—somehow Lydie knew that she lived here.

"What brings you to Paris?" the woman asked.

Lydie hesitated, trying to formulate the short version of a complicated answer. "Well, for work. Michael—my husband—is an architect. He's working on the Louvre, part of an exchange program. And I'm a stylist."

"A stylist? As in hair?"

Lydie laughed. "No, I work with photographers, doing pieces for magazines and catalogues. I set up the shots. The editor tells me what he wants in a photo layout, and it's my job to get all the props."

"I think my husband uses stylists," the woman said. "He's in the jewelry business."

"Yes," Lydie said, nodding. "I work with jewelers a lot. He's French?"

"Yes, but we met in America . . ." The woman trailed off, as if she thought the conversation was going on too long or growing too intimate. "I'll tell you something," she said. "I met my husband one day, he took me to Guadeloupe the next weekend, and then I enrolled in Berlitz, and then he asked me to marry him. You'll think I'm crazy, but it all took place in less than five weeks. The French understand, but Americans never do."

Lydie leaned forward, and she captured the moment, sure as a photograph: the way the sun struck the woman's hair, the blaze of primroses in a jardiniere behind her head, Richelieu's palace casting a shadow on the garden. "I don't think that's crazy," Lydie said. "I believe in love at first sight."

"Well," the woman said. She checked her watch, a tiny gold one with Chinese figures instead of numerals. Then she looked at the sky. "I should go. I'm running late."

Now Lydie checked her watch. She had planned to go to the Bibliothèque Nationale, to look up details of seventeenth-century weddings for a piece in *Vogue*. Then, like the woman, she gazed up. She felt unwilling to leave. The palace against the blue sky looked dark and ancient, as if it had stood there forever. She wanted to stall for time, to prolong this pleasant, casual conversation with another American. "Where are you off to?" she asked after a moment.

"Oh, home," the woman said. "I told my housekeeper she could go online."

"Your housekeeper?"

"Yes. I'm teaching her to use the computer. Didier bought it when personal computers hit Paris in a big way, but it just sits there."

Lydie regarded the woman more carefully. With her jewelry and clothes and slightly regal bearing, she gave the impression of someone who would want distance between herself and a domestic employee. "Are you training her to do your correspondence?" Lydie asked.

The woman smiled, but the smile seemed distant. "Kelly wants to improve her life. She's a Filipino, from the provinces outside Manila, and she's here in Paris illegally. She's just a little younger than I am—she's been to college. She shares a place with an amazing number of brothers and sisters. Her goal is to get to the United States."

"And you want to help her?" Lydie asked, sitting on the edge of her chair.

"Well, it's practically impossible."

"My parents immigrated to the United States from Ireland," Lydie said.

"It's especially hard for Filipinos," the woman said, again looking at her watch. She gathered her bags and stood. "Well. Hasn't this been fun?" she said.

"Maybe . . ." Lydie began.

"We should exchange phone numbers," the woman said, grinning.

And while Lydie wrote out her name and number on a piece of notepaper, the dark-haired woman held out a vellum calling card, simply engraved, with an address on the Place des Vosges and the name "Patrice d'Origny."

⤜⤛

Walking down the rue des Petits Champs, Lydie felt in no hurry to get to the Bibliothèque Nationale. Even though she had hours of research to do for a photo series that was already a week overdue, she felt like playing hooky. The BBS wheels on a red BMW 750 parked by the curb caught her eye. Nice wheels, Lydie thought. She had spent many childhood Saturdays at her father's body shop in the Bronx—a cavernous place filled with smells of exhaust and paint, the flare of welding torches, the shrieks of machinery and metal tearing—without seeing many BBS wheels. Her father was the boss but wore blue overalls anyway. He would leave her in the office, separated from the shop by a glass window, coming back every fifteen minutes or so to visit her.

"What happened to that car?" Lydie had asked once, watching another wreck towed in.

"An accident, darling. He hit a tree off the Pelham Parkway, and he must have been drunk, because he knew how to drive."

"How do you know?" Lydie asked, when what she really wanted to know was what had happened to the man.

"See his wheels?" her father asked, pointing at the car, leaning his head so close to Lydie's that she caught a whiff of the exhaust that always seemed to cling to his hair and clothes. "They're BBS. A man doesn't buy wheels like that if he doesn't know how to drive."

To her father, "knowing how to drive" had covered more than mere competence. It was a high compliment and meant the driver was alert behind the wheel, unified with his car and the road, aware of the difference between excellent and ordinary machinery.

Walking away from the red BMW with its high-performance, nonproduction wheels, down the narrow Paris street, Lydie had the urge to drive fast. In America she raced cars for a hobby, but over here she hadn't had the desire. She had resisted this move to Paris. She had told Michael it was because she didn't want to leave her family, which now consisted of only Lydie and her mother. But Michael had said no, what Lydie did not want to leave was her family tragedy.

Eight months before Michael accepted the position at the

Louvre, Lydie's father had killed his lover and himself. Margaret Downes. Lydie felt a jolt every time she remembered the name. After forty years of what everyone considered a great marriage, Cornelius Benedict Fallon had fallen in love with another woman. Lydie hadn't known and Julia claimed, even now, to have had no clue. Lydie knew there must have been clues, and she often felt furious with her mother for not seeing them. Because right up until the time the New York City detectives knocked on her door, Lydie had believed in her mother's myth of a happy family.

Lydie was her parents' only child; born relatively late in their marriage, she knew she was beloved. They had raised her to feel confident and live like a daredevil. A favorite story of her father's was of how Lydie at eight, watching the Olympics on television, had suddenly stood and done a perfect backflip off the back of the sofa. The second time she tried, she broke her collarbone. During high school she took up whitewater kayaking, tutoring children in a neighborhood few of her convent school classmates would even visit, and hitchhiking to Montauk on Saturdays. One day her father let her take an H-production Sprite for a spin. The intensity of concentration required to speed thrilled her, and from then on she thought of racing as a legitimate way to drive a car fast.

Cutting through the Galerie Vivienne, remembering that Bugeye Sprite and her old fearless self, Lydie felt her eyes fill with tears. The emotion was so strong she stopped in front of a wine shop, pretending to regard the window display while she cried. She thought of the car Michael had given her for Christmas, just before the shooting. They had shopped around together, and Lydie had fallen in love with a showroom stock Volvo 740 wagon. Michael had grinned at the idea of his wife racing a station wagon, the car favored by women living in the Litchfield Hills to ferry kids and groceries around Lime Rock. Secretly, he had bought it for her. Lydie closed her eyes, remembering that Christmas morning: in their apartment on West Tenth Street she had opened a small box containing brown leather driving gloves, a map of Connecticut with "Lime Rock" circled in red, and the keys. She hadn't even driven it since her father died. It sat in Sharon, Connecticut, in a garage behind her crew chief's house.

Michael had told her about the Louvre position as if he were giving her a gift even greater than the car: the gift of adventure, a year in Paris. But Lydie hadn't wanted to come. She had wanted to stay in New York; she couldn't imagine leaving her mother. She couldn't imagine leaving the scene. But in spite of lacking heart, she couldn't say no to Michael, who was incredibly excited about the move. And then, the day had come to pack their things into a crate that would cross the Atlantic on a Polish freighter.

Julia had sat on Lydie and Michael's bed, watching them pack. Lydie knew that although her mother felt abysmally sad at seeing Lydie go, she wouldn't dream of speaking up. Julia would think that by doing so she would spoil Michael's happiness. She was plump, especially in the bosom, with soft, curly gray hair and, even then, a perpetually happy expression in her blue eyes. Lydie could hardly bear to look at her that day; she rummaged through a dresser drawer. Coming upon her driving gloves, Lydie slipped them on, flexing the new leather.

"Can't wait to see you drive at Le Mans," Michael said. "It's only about two hours from Paris."

"I can't wait," Lydie said, doubting even then that she would drive in France.

"Oh, you two will have such a ball," Julia said, grinning. "All the museums and the restaurants. Your aunt Carrie and I spent a weekend in Paris one time. It was lovely."

"Flying to Paris from Ireland is like taking the Eastern Shuttle to Washington," Michael said. From his tone Lydie could tell he felt grateful to Julia for her enthusiasm.

"Well, we took the boat, but yes—distances are so different over there. It's a short trip from Paris to anywhere in Europe. You'll have a marvelous time."

"It'll be great," Michael said, speaking to Lydie.

She said nothing, but smiled at him. He was trying to assemble a cardboard carton. The sight of her tall husband—a whiz on any basketball court but a klutz when it came to anything remotely mechanical—trying to transform a sheet of corrugated cardboard into a vessel that would actually hold their belongings made Lydie laugh.

"Here, let me," she said, folding flaps, slapping on the plastic tape without even taking off her gloves.

"What a woman," Michael said, bending down to kiss her.

"She's one in a million," Julia said. "After she won her first race at Watkin's Glen, her father said she could do anything. Do you remember that nice dinner we all had afterward?"

"Sure," Lydie said, quivering with the memory. They had drunk champagne, and after dinner her father had bought her a cigar. She could picture her parents perfectly: their proud smiles, her mother's girlish smile, the absent way her father reached over to touch Julia's shoulder. It killed Lydie to think Margaret Downes had already brought her car in for its second paint job in six months, that Neil had already fallen in love with her. The happy expression on her father's face that night, so full of love, had been for Margaret.

Lydie crouched, assembling another carton. Michael sat beside her, pulling the tape out of her hands and holding them tight; he knew what the memory meant to her. Julia said nothing, looking on. She had started to cry but stopped herself. Lydie eased her hands from Michael's grasp, ripped off a piece of tape, closed a seam. Every crack she taped, every box she built, brought her closer to leaving. And, somehow, the idea of leaving the scene of her father's death and crime filled her with doom. She felt wild with an abundance of unfinished business.

"A year in Paris," Julia had said. "I can't imagine any couple who could enjoy it more than you."

But it wasn't working out that way, Lydie thought now, entering the Bibliothèque's vast courtyard. With their great luck, she had thought they would be the most frivolous pair in Paris. But Michael's exhilaration had turned to patience; he was waiting for Lydie to get back the spirit he had fallen in love with. So far it hadn't happened. Since coming to Paris, Lydie felt a gulf widening between herself and Michael, and she couldn't do a damned thing about it.

Just before a race, Lydie always experienced a vision. In a flash she saw the crash, the rollover, herself paralyzed in a hospital. And the vision always refined her concentration, made her take great care and drive more safely. Now, walking numb through the streets of Paris, she felt as if the crash had happened, and she hadn't even seen it coming.

◎

"Why didn't anyone tell us it stays light in Paris till midnight?" Michael McBride asked. He was watching Lydie cook dinner. They stood in the kitchen of their Belle Epoque apartment overlooking the Pont de l'Alma. A roasting chicken sizzled in the oven.

"It's nowhere near midnight," Lydie said, smiling. "It's ten-fifteen, and the sun's going down."

"Lydie!" Michael said, feeling impatient but vowing to stay calm. "I think you're missing my point. All I'm saying is that the sun would have set two hours ago in New York. It's something different, and I think it's neat."

"Paris is farther north than New York," Lydie said. "New York is actually on the same parallel as Rome."

Michael let it drop. If he opened his mouth again, he knew Lydie would come back with another rebuttal. They kept just missing each other these days. Sometimes they had full-scale fights. Like yesterday, when Michael had asked Lydie to meet him at Chez Francis for dinner and Lydie complaining bitterly about how she missed Chinese takeout. Then Michael had accused her of deliberately trying not to enjoy their year in Paris and Lydie going on and on about eggrolls.

Still, watching her now, he felt a shock of love for Lydie. She moved around the kitchen with an unconscious grace, a small frown on her face when she concentrated on cooking the meal. He'd seen that same expression on her face when she raced cars. She looked delicate, with her pale skin and fine reddish-gold hair, but Michael had always thought of her as a tiger: strong, always moving, ready for anything.

"I met someone in a café today," Lydie said. "An American."

"Oh?" Michael said.

"We talked for a while, and it made me realize how much I've missed that. Someone to talk to."

"What do you call what goes on between us?" Michael asked. "A silent movie?"

Lydie smiled and laid down her wooden spoon. Taking her hand, Michael led her into the living room. He still felt a jolt when he came upon their furniture, which for seven years had sat in the same New York apartment, here, across the Atlantic, in Paris. There were the low mahogany table, the seascape by Lydie's mother, the sofa covered in a pattern Lydie called "flame-stitch," the ugly lounge chair his father had given him for his thirty-fifth birthday. Lydie, as a stylist specializing in interior design, had great taste, and it had pained Michael to inflict that eyesore on her. But she had said it wouldn't do to hurt the old man's feelings.

"Her name is Patrice d'Origny," Lydie was saying. "She's married to a Frenchman and lives here permanently."

"Why don't you ask them for dinner?" Michael asked.

"Maybe," Lydie said. Although her voice still sounded subdued, her eyes looked happier than Michael had seen them in quite a while. After eight years of marriage, the sight of her smiling eyes, hazel framed with thick blond lashes, made the back of Michael's neck tingle. The feeling of excitement saddened him, because it was the only important thing between them that still felt true. He wanted to kiss Lydie, but she seemed to be concentrating on something.

"Why say 'maybe'?" he asked. "Why not just invite them?"

Lydie cocked her head slightly, as if she was trying to figure out her own hesitation. But the moment passed quickly. "Why not?" she said.

From her indolent tone, Michael doubted that a dinner with the d'Orignys would come to pass. He cursed himself for the disappointment he felt toward Lydie. But he'd been through it all with her: the sorrow, the mourning, the struggle to understand, and there didn't seem an end to it. Maybe he wouldn't feel so deprived if the contrast were not so great. Old Lydie versus new Lydie; he loved the old Lydie better.

He could see her now, one October day at Lime Rock, the old Lydie speeding them around the track. She wore her racing overalls and sunglasses; she gripped the wheel with wicked intensity. "You scared?" she asked, possibly wanting him to be. But he wasn't. He was fascinated. He loved riding with her while she cranked the Volvo wagon up to 135 MPH. Seven miles down Route 112 Michael had pulled off the road and there, behind a red barn, Lydie dropped her overalls, laughing because she wore nothing under them, wanting Michael to be amused. Amusement was not what he remembered feeling. He remembered pulling her close, kissing her, feeling her shiver in the autumn air, making love to her on the cold ground.

And the words "cold ground" made Michael think of Neil

Fallon. He and Neil had gotten along well, more like friends than father- and son-in-law. But Michael laid the blame for Lydie's transformation directly at Neil's feet. The man had lived his whole life as a good husband and father, an average businessman who had cared more about coming home for dinner every night than making a million dollars. He had devilish charm; on a bet he had truly, before witnesses, sold drunken Dennis Lavery his own car. With his elegant profile and wild black hair, Neil was so handsome that even Michael noticed. He was a Lion and a Knight of Columbus, a regular churchgoer who could be seen passing the basket at nine o'clock mass at St. Anthony's. By the time he started spending time with Margaret Downes, he had established himself as such a pillar that Julia and Lydie never questioned his absence or preoccupation. So how could Michael blame Lydie for falling apart when Neil, with his sharp-tongued, gentle-eyed Irish devil act, had turned out to be the Devil himself?

Michael knew that he was the only person Neil had told about Margaret Downes. Two nights before the shooting, Michael dropped his own car off at Neil's shop and hung around waiting for Neil to give him a ride home. Dented or mangled cars filled the six bays. Welding torches roared. An irate customer leaned across the office desk, haggling over the cost of replacing his Ford LTD quarter panel.

"I can't leave yet, but let's get out," Neil said, frowning, leaving his Danish office manager to placate the customer.

They road-tested a Ford pickup, down Zerega Avenue to the Hutchinson River Parkway. Neil drove easily, playing with the wheel and accelerating in a way that reminded Michael of Lydie. They headed north, toward Connecticut.

"What's up?" Michael asked after a long while; he had never known Neil to maintain a silence for more than a minute, and it alarmed him.

"I'm in love," Neil said, staring straight ahead.

"With someone . . ." Michael tried to hide his shock.

"With someone besides Julia," Neil said, finishing Michael's thought for him.

"What are you going to do?" Michael asked, with full Catholic knowledge that Neil could never divorce Julia, that Neil was talking about a mortal sin, that the situation was impossible.

"Not a damn thing. She won't leave her husband," Neil said, his voice bleak. "I want to see Margaret tonight; I'll have one of the fellows drive you home."

"That's okay," Michael said. "I'll take the subway."

"I want you to tell them you left me working at the shop."

"You want me to lie to Lydie and Julia for you?" Michael asked, making it as plain as possible that he thought Neil had sunk very low. Was Neil implying that if Margaret would leave her husband he would leave Julia?

"Yes," Neil said, sounding remote, without a trace of defiance. Then he shot Michael a dark look. "If you ever did this to Lydie, I'd kill you."

That was in Michael's mind now as he stared across his Paris apartment at Lydie: her father telling Michael he would kill him if he ever betrayed her. It had struck Michael odd at the time, for Neil to threaten, even if he hadn't meant it, to kill Michael. It proved that killing was on his mind; two days later he had shot himself and Margaret.

"I know what," Michael said to Lydie. "Get on the telephone, call your new friend, and ask her out to lunch tomorrow."

"Right now?" Lydie asked.

"Sure. Before you forget all about each other," he said, for he doubted she would call on her own.

Lydie went through her briefcase, found Patrice's card, dialed a number on the phone. Turning his back, Michael walked to the window. He heard Lydie speak French, then English. Horns blared on the Avenue Montaigne. The tour boats plied the river Seine beneath their window; their spotlights shimmered across the white walls, a twinkling of pale yellow, peach, and silvery gray.

"She invited me over," Lydie said, coming toward Michael. "Tomorrow, to her apartment on the Place des Vosges."

"That's great," Michael said. He felt a mixture of things: relief, as if this new friend of Lydie's could give to her some of the things Michael found himself increasingly unable to give, and hope. Hope that this could make her happy. He thought of her walking to the Place des Vosges tomorrow, of all the wonderful parks and monuments she would pass. The Grand Palais, the Champs-Elysées, the Place de la Concorde, the Tuileries, the Louvre. Let Paris make you happy, he thought.

"I'd better check the chicken," Lydie said. Michael had often heard her mother's theory that roast chicken was the truest test of a good cook. He went to her then, held the back of her neck. She tilted her head, and he looked into her eyes, golden in the half-light. He kissed her, thinking of the places they had kissed in spring: at the track, underwater, on a peak in the White Mountains, in Florence, on a hot subway platform at Fourteenth Street, now in Paris. The kiss felt right, and so did his arms around his wife. But the rest of it was unfamiliar. He thought the word "wife." It meant possession, love, sex: in that order. Then he thought "Lydie," which had once meant everything in nature and the world, and wished that it did not now only mean "wife."

# 2

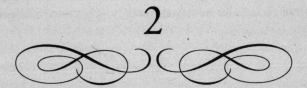

*You have taken my daughter on the most beautiful voyage in the world. She was thrilled with it, but you took her up and down mountains, exposing her to the precipices of your Alps and the waves of your Mediterranean. I am somewhat inclined to scold you, but not until I have embraced you tenderly.*

—To Monsieur de Grignan, June 1672

LYDIE WAS AWAKE at dawn the next morning. Michael slept beside her. His back was tan and muscular, his light brown hair tangled on the pillow. She watched him, trying to tell whether he was dreaming. She pressed closer to him, their bare bodies sticking slightly with sleep's sweat. She kissed his shoulder.

She thought of her date with Patrice today, and for the first time she thought that maybe coming to Paris was the best way to forget. She had resisted coming, to put it mildly, at the beginning. The destination, Paris—imagine!—had paled compared to what she was leaving: one despondent mother and her father's grave. Yet she had always wanted to live in a foreign country. It had seemed her destiny. The pretty accents of her parents and relatives, her mother's stories about Clew Bay and her father's about Dublin had constantly reminded her that the world went beyond her block in New York.

Lydie had visited Ireland, at sixteen, with her parents. Ireland, although beautiful, had frightened her. From her parents' tales she had expected soft edges: verdant pastures, gentle rain, cozy priories, friendly people who earned their livings as farmers and stonecutters. Instead, she was struck by the feeling of danger: by the coastline, steep and intricate as a Gothic steeple, by gray stone churches, grim, in every market square, by an undercurrent her parents had not prepared her for.

There were people who still remembered her parents, people Lydie had heard about her whole life, who seemed at once gentle and fierce. The combination had alarmed her. Her mother's people were intense when it came to their memories, to Ireland, to the Church. Her father's people, in Dublin, no longer attended mass, and they were intense about *that*.

Lying in bed, Lydie remembered the time she and her father had climbed Ireland's holy mountain. The memory, vivid and exact, was one of her most powerful. Croagh Patrick, named for the saint, overlooked Clew Bay and the countryside outside Westport, where Lydie's mother had grown up. The ascent had been fun: a lark. Lydie had pretended to be Maria von Trapp crossing the Alps in *The Sound of Music*. At the various holy points along the way she had interrupted her fantasy to do the requisite Catholic rituals like walking seven times around the statue of Saint Patrick while saying seven Hail Marys.

At the summit she and her father had picnicked on salmon they had caught fishing with her uncle in Sligo the day before. After lunch they had prayed together. Lydie remembered saying the rosary out loud. It was then that Lydie started feeling terrified. The prayers had given her the idea she might fall off the mountain. After all, wasn't the purpose of prayers to shorten your time in Purgatory? To speed you into heaven? But to get to heaven, didn't you have to die first? It was late in the day; they began to descend. She remembered walking through clouds, down the jagged, precipitous trail. Thousands of feet below there were green pastures leading to the rocky shore and the glittering bay, the green and blue as true as colors in the spectrum. With every step Lydie had grown dizzier, more breathless. She stumbled, and in her memory she saw one foot step off the mountain's edge. Her father had hugged her tight, holding her face against his wool coat, damp from clouds and the salt air. "Steady there," he had said. "Are you scared? You know your mother and I climbed this mountain every year when we were young. Everyone in Ireland does. It's the safest place on earth to be—the saint will look after you. Especially you."

Lydie had wanted to believe it was true. Wasn't her uncle a priest in Dungannon? Hadn't her mother washed the cardinal's clothes? But she had a terrible vision of her father falling off the mountain. She saw him hurtling through the air, the father she loved, and not even Saint Patrick could save him.

On that trip, Lydie knew that she wanted to live in a foreign country, but not Ireland: one that was southern, sensual, rich with cathedrals, tapestries, and vineyards. Lydie had wanted to live in a country whose beauty was not rugged and terrible, a country that celebrated its saints' days with fireworks going off in the little villages instead of pilgrimages up the dangerous holy mountain.

Now here she was in France. She snuggled closer to Michael, who stirred. France satisfied her in every way except that it was far from the heart of her family. In spite of the art, beauty, and romance, everywhere Lydie went she felt as though she were missing something back home. She wondered how her mother was getting on without her. It made her sick, really ashamed, when she remembered one day last week. She and Michael had met for a glass of wine. They had sat at a café across the Seine from the Louvre and the Jardin des Tuileries. Michael was silent; he seemed to be thinking about something that had happened at work. Sitting there, Lydie just absorbed the scene.

The sun cast gold light on a row of poplars that must have stood there since the time of Napoleon. Holding Michael's hand, Lydie had gazed at them. She had imagined the great artists who had sat in the same spot. She had pretended to be Monet regarding the poplars; she had just started to see them as an Impressionist would, all light and color, when she had a vision of her home. It was twilight; there was her mother standing alone in the walled garden behind her house. Her mother's face was sad. Lydie blinked hard, to get rid of the image. She wanted to enjoy the present. But the idea of home was a veil, and there were days Lydie couldn't lift it to see Paris.

She had squeezed Michael's hand. "You're a dear man," she had said.

"Who am I?" Michael had said. "Monsignor Mangin?"

"Oh, God," Lydie had said, catching his drift. "I do sound like my mother, don't I?"

"Give it another try," Michael had said.

"You make me weak in the knees, baby."

"Much, much better," Michael had said.

Lying in bed, Lydie remembered that. Her thoughts returned to her parents. Julia and Cornelius, known as Neil, had sailed from Ireland to New York the same year but separately when Julia was nineteen and Neil was twenty-five. They had met at night school, where Julia was a student and Neil a janitor. Julia washed the cardinal's clothes at St. Patrick's by day. One day the cardinal found her crying. "What is the matter, child?" he had asked. Of course Julia cannot remember his exact words, but that is the phrase distilled from years of retelling: "What is the matter, child?"

"I am homesick, Father," Julia had said.

"Ah, do you know the poem, by Yeats, 'Under Saturn'?"

Well, no cardinal would really expect a young Irish washer-woman to know Yeats, but Julia had stood tall, tears running down her cheeks, and recited "'I am thinking of a child's vow, sworn in vain, never to leave the valley his fathers called their home.'"

Then the cardinal had asked where she had learned the poem, and Julia had said "In school, in Ireland, Father."

"Do you miss school?" the cardinal had asked.

"Oh, yes, Father," Julia had said.

And so the cardinal had arranged for her to take evening courses in education at Marymount, where Neil Fallon worked a second job as the night janitor, trying to save enough money to start a business. They fell in love and married by the spring semester. Within four years, after two miscarriages, they had Lydie, and within six Julia had her degree. And now, forty years later, Neil had been dead eleven months.

∽

Lydie and Michael went about their morning ritual. In Paris they had separate bathrooms, but only one person could use hot water at a time. Lydie showered first while Michael shaved; when he heard her shower stop, he stepped into his own. Lydie boiled water for coffee. Since she took longer to dress, Michael went to the *pâtisserie* for croissants. On his way back to the apartment, he bought the *International Herald Tribune*. This early-morning, wordless cooperation was one thing Lydie loved about marriage. They knew each other so well. Lydie knew that Michael liked silence at the breakfast table; he was probably reviewing his schedule for the day.

Their breakfast table overlooked Avenue Montaigne and Montmartre in the distance. The early sun lit the Basilica with white light, and to Lydie it looked holy, the way it might appear in a child's prayer book. She broke off a piece of croissant, savored the flavor of butter and yeast. She drank her *café crème* slowly; when the cup was empty, she would have to leave for work.

"I should go in a minute," Lydie said. "I have a shoot at Tolbiac."

"Tolbiac? Chinatown?"

"Yes. For a young French designer who wants nothing French in the background. He'd love to shoot the ad in Hong Kong, but he can't afford a location outside Paris."

"Where do you come up with your ideas?" Michael asked, laughing. "Chinatown in Paris. I'll be damned."

"And this afternoon I meet Patrice," Lydie said. "I wonder if her husband is d'Origny of d'Origny Bijoutiers. I'm sure it's family-run."

"What is it?"

"One of the super-snazzy jewelry houses in the Place Vendôme. I've borrowed from them. For a layout on Hungarian royalty I used a d'Origny pearl collar made of two hundred pearls. One hundred ninety-eight were white, but one was black, another pink. Baroque. Very beautiful and odd." Lydie grew silent, as she often did when recalling an old layout or planning a new one.

"I remember that piece," Michael said. "I'm glad you're seeing Patrice, you know."

"I know," Lydie said. Michael had never kept watch over Lydie's friendships before, but now Lydie wondered whether Michael wanted someone to take her off his hands.

"Have I told you George Reed is coming from the United States today?" Michael asked.

"No," she said, surprised that he had not. George Reed was Michael's immediate superior at Rothman, Inc., the man who had arranged for Michael to work on the Louvre in exchange for the participation of a French architect on the National Gallery project in Washington, D.C.

"We have a meeting at the Ministry of Culture," Michael said.

Lydie stood, faced Michael. He slid his arm around her neck and kissed her. His neck smelled like soap and powder. His remark about Patrice stuck with her, made her wonder how far apart they had grown. She couldn't even ask him if he meant what she thought he meant: would it be a great relief to him if Lydie found a confidante? They stood there for a few seconds, hugging. Lydie didn't want to let go.

Later, stepping aboard the Métro, she tried to imagine Michael's meeting with George. Michael's contacts in France were not being as cooperative as everyone had hoped they would be. The work was not moving swiftly. It seemed that French architects and designers resented the assignment of an American to turn the Louvre's Salle des Quatre Saisons into an information center. Even Charles Legendre, Michael's assigned liaison, lagged when it came to introducing Michael around.

Lydie knew that Michael planned to create a seventeenth-century atmosphere in the Salle. In spite of the conservatism of his ideas, he was having trouble convincing curators to find him paintings by Poussin and la Tour. He had located a master artisan from Burgundy to build an information desk similar to tables by A.-C. Boulle, cabinetmaker to Louis XIV, but the Ministry had so far refused to approve the work order. One terrific plan for repairing the mosaic floor and another for redirecting the flow of tourists existed only on paper. And Michael's worries were not eased by the knowledge that his French counterpart in the United States had already met the President and First Lady, who admired the new painting gallery he had designed for Washington's National Gallery.

Lydie had a vision of Michael shaking George's hand, grinning a little too earnestly perhaps. His mother had once told Lydie that as a child Michael had suffered stomachaches whenever he felt he had disappointed someone—his family, a teacher, his basketball coach—and Lydie knew he still did. She felt a rush of sorrow and love for him, the man she loved more than anyone in the world.

∽

The photographer, the models, and Jean-Claude Verglesses stood on the sidewalk in front of Chinatown's largest supermarket. Lydie waved, introduced herself to the photographer, and bumped cheeks with Jean-Claude. He wore a blue work shirt and had his blond hair tied back. He's trying to look like a designer for rock stars, Lydie thought. She surveyed the street. Men were hauling carts of cabbages from a flatbed lorry into the store. Five old Chinese women dressed in black passed by; one spoke angrily to the lorry driver for blocking the sidewalk.

"Remember, Lydie," Jean-Claude said in French, "the dresses speak for themselves. Nothing elaborate, all right? I want a squalid backdrop for these things."

Lydie, who rarely did fashion work, nodded. Young designers who could not afford famous fashion stylists would hire her, then try to do the job themselves. "I think we could do something with those cabbages," she said. Everyone entered the supermarket through the service entrance, and Lydie spoke to the man who owned the store. She had worked here before; he gave her permission to use his cabbages in Jean-Claude's advertisement.

The cabbages were round, smooth, cool green and white, and they echoed beautifully the lines of Jean-Claude's pouf skirts. The models perched on the carts while Lydie and the photographer buried their feet and ankles in cabbages. Jean-Claude stood back and smoked. "Cabbages?" he said. "I don't know about this. What is more French than cabbage? I said squalid and exotic."

Street light filtered through the open door. The storeroom had concrete walls; yellowed tape held a faded kung fu poster in place. Lydie smiled at Jean-Claude. "Tell me this isn't squalid," she said. He shrugged. A group of workers gathered to watch. The models tried to look detached, as if they weren't standing in piles of cabbages. The photographer went to work.

Lydie and her entourage moved from the supermarket to the kitchen of Maison de Chine to the warehouse of a Far East importer on Avenue Tolbiac. She had the models squat beside white porcelain statues of the Buddha, a form that, like the cabbages, perfectly echoed the pouf skirts.

"I must wait to see the proof sheets," Jean-Claude said, "but this might work."

Lydie knew he wanted the public to believe the pictures had been taken in Hong Kong; she had tried to avoid any background that would give away the Paris location. This was all part of the image, and Lydie understood it. Financial backing would come easier to Jean-Claude if he gave the impression of success. She wondered how old he was. Twenty-five? She had the urge to tell him his ponytail made him look as though he were imitating Karl Lagerfeld, but she did not. She felt fond of him because he was young and because he was desperate to be successful. She considered telling him not to worry. She considered giving him a sisterly kiss on the forehead. Instead she made her expression serious and shook his hand. "I really hope you like the pictures," she said.

"Do you need a ride home?" he asked.

"Actually, I'm going to the Place des Vosges, if you're heading in that direction," Lydie said.

"It's not far out of my way," he said. "Come along."

# 3

*I wanted my two maids with me so that there would be
someone there whom I knew.*

—To Françoise-Marguerite, May 1675

Waiting for Lydie McBride to arrive, Patrice walked through
the cool rooms of her old house to the bathroom and looked in
the mirror. She powdered her cheeks with a sable brush. Patrice
loved the regality of makeup. She thought it courtly: the powder,
the scents, the brilliant and subtle colors, reminiscent of queens
and another age. She dabbed her finger in a pot of scarlet lip gloss
and rubbed it over her lips.

Turning from the mirror, she walked directly into her bedroom. She couldn't quite fathom why she felt so anxious about
Lydie coming over. Patrice was used to visitors. Since marrying
Didier, Patrice had entertained with a vengeance. Dutch diamond
cutters, Hong Kong gold brokers, Australian gem dealers were always arriving with their wives, expecting to be courted with food
and wine. Patrice had perfected a foreigner's idea of the true

French dinner: paupiettes of sole, then leg of lamb, then cheeses, then petits fours.

For Didier's family and French friends she usually served provincial dishes, the way they themselves did. Sausage and potatoes, pot-au-feu, roast chicken. Didier had known his two best friends since boyhood; his sister Clothilde lived half a mile away. At first they had seemed to embrace her without reservation—telling her all the old stories, making sure she knew where to find the best dry cleaner in Paris, giving her the best seat at their regular tables at Taillevant, La Coupole, Chez Georges. *That* had tipped her off—the way they always treated her with a certain *politesse*. Just last week Patrice had discovered a funky little *salon de thé* in the Place Dauphine, but when she invited Clothilde, Clothilde had insisted they go to her usual spot full of bourgeois matrons in the Rue Royale. Where, of course, she had insisted that Patrice take the seat with the best view.

Patrice had high hopes for Lydie. Although people said Patrice spoke French impeccably, it wasn't the same as speaking your own language: the tongue was only part of it. She looked forward to talking to a married woman her own age, from the eastern United States, with an interesting career. She wondered whether Lydie would find her life frivolous; Patrice lived the life of a housewife and she knew it. In Boston she had managed an art gallery on Newberry Street. Although she had enjoyed meeting the artists, selling their work to appreciative collectors, Patrice had felt happy to give it up. Living in France, Patrice tried to experience everything as the French did—she felt grateful to Didier's friends and sister for showing her the way, even if she also, simultaneously, resented them for it.

Patrice was drawn to things romantic, feminine, and venerable, and for those reasons alone, France suited her. She pulled the tufted chaise closer to the glass doors overlooking the cobbled courtyard, and she settled down to read *Three Women of the Marais*. It was a scholarly work by Anne Dumas, in French, over a thousand pages long, about three noblewomen of the seventeenth century who had lived in the Marais, the quarter of Paris where the Place des Vosges was located, in houses that still stood.

When Patrice read about Madame de Sévigné, Ninon de Lenclos, and the Marquise de Brinvilliers, she left the twentieth century, literally left it: she went back three hundred years. She had the feeling that if a malady happened to strike her while immersed in *Three Women of the Marais,* no modern cure could help her. She couldn't remember ever hearing the telephone ring while she was reading it; if it did, she could imagine the sound being as alien to her as it would to Madame de Sévigné. These were three fabulous women. They knew kings, ministers, and cardinals, and they managed their resources at a time when women rarely did. Telling their stories, which were racy, poignant, and brave, Anne Dumas illustrated the history of Paris at that time. Reading the book, Patrice had come to feel like the fourth woman of the Marais.

Kelly entered the room. She nodded and smiled without saying anything, not wanting to interrupt Patrice. Her silence seemed greater than a courtesy, and it really moved Patrice. She lowered her book. How many people could coexist the way they did? They knew how to stay out of each other's way, yet they also enjoyed talking together. Patrice had found herself relying too strongly on Kelly's companionship lately, another reason she felt glad Lydie McBride was coming over.

"I think I'll go outside for a while," Patrice said.

She was sitting in the Place, reading her book and sunning herself, when she saw Lydie pull up to her building in a car full of what appeared to be high school students. "Yoohoo!" Patrice called, provoking stares from proper French matrons also taking the sun.

Lydie spied her, waved, walked toward her.

"So, how was the malt shop?" Patrice asked.

Lydie grinned. "Aren't they young? They're models and an up-and-coming fashion designer."

"I'm in a Chanel rut," Patrice said, sounding but not feeling sad.

"That's not so awful," Lydie said.

Patrice noticed Lydie's clothes, which were good. A sleek black suit, not haute couture, but well made. Heavy silver earrings and bracelets. Tiffany, probably. Saving her place, she closed her book. "Shall we go upstairs?"

"I'd love to," Lydie said.

Patrice preceded Lydie through the barrel-vaulted arcade that led to her front door. She was composing a little speech in her mind; if she struck the right balance between housewife and tour guide, she wouldn't sound as though she were bragging.

"These houses were built in 1612," she said, "and Didier bought an apartment in one of them ten years ago, from descendants of the original owner. Pity they had to subdivide. Here's the spot where Henri II died after someone put his eye out in a joust. They used to hold jousts in the square until Catherine de Medici called them off. She was Henri's widow." Patrice nodded toward a heavy wooden door whose panels were held together by iron bolts. "That's an original door. A princess lives there."

"The age of Europe knocks me out," Lydie said. "Everything seems venerable and ancient."

"America is practically brand new," Patrice said. Usually people were impressed when she mentioned the princess. It pleased her that Lydie was not. Then she pushed the button beside her front door, and they stepped off the square into a cobbled courtyard. Patrice led Lydie up one flight of stairs. "We don't need an elevator for one flight because Didier and I are spry and youthful, but you should see certain older Parisians who come to dinner. Of course we tell them an elevator would spoil the character of the building."

"Does every Paris building have some excuse for not having an elevator?" Lydie asked. "Our concierge told Michael there's an old man in our building who has blocked an elevator for years because when he dies he wants his pallbearers to carry him downstairs in dignity. He claims if there were an elevator, his pallbearers would use it."

"Poor guy," Patrice said, finding her key and unlocking the heavy door. "He'll probably keel over on the street and never even get to travel dead through the building." She glanced around for Kelly, heard water running in the kitchen.

"This is truly incredible," Lydie said, surveying the interior.

"It's nice, isn't it? Didier already had it when I married him, so I can't take credit." Patrice glanced at the Gobelins tapestry and wondered what a stylist like Lydie would make of it. She wondered whether Lydie would realize that many of the other pieces were copies. Most people could not.

Lydie turned around and around, her gaze lighting on the important pieces in a way that satisfied Patrice. Warm light slanting through the front windows made Lydie's hair look more golden than red. When Patrice knew her better she would suggest a hair salon that specialized in the use of real Luxor henna. "Is Didier a collector?" Lydie asked.

"Well, mainly he just raided his grandmother's attic, but yes, he does enjoy collecting."

"Is d'Origny Bijoutiers . . . ?" Lydie began.

"The family business," Patrice said. She felt so happy to have Lydie over. She had really missed it, the casual visit to or from a friend. "Just wanted to say hi," she used to say to Lynn or Holly, her two best friends in Boston. A conversation of no particular importance would ensue over tea or a drink: some gossip, or perhaps the story of a small disagreement with her boss. Occasionally a lengthy reminiscence about the past. About old boyfriends. Such a conversation with Clothilde would never be possible.

"Let's sit down," Patrice said. "Can I get you something?"

"Not right now," Lydie said. "A couple of hours with those models has shown me the need to starve."

"I think you look great," Patrice said.

They both smiled, recognizing familiar patterns of girl talk.

"Tell me how you met your husband," Patrice said.

"We first met in high school. We grew up in New York."

"High school sweethearts?"

"No, we didn't know each other well. I went to the convent school and he went to the boys' school next door. I was too radical to go for him at the time. He played sports, for one thing. Basketball and soccer. I went for solitary types—I had a mad crush on a priest."

"So, when did you see the light and fall for Michael?"

"We both went away to college. We would run into each other in New York on vacations, but we were seeing other people. Then five or so years later we both ended up working in the city. I was painting, trying to get galleries to show my work. I started working as a stylist to make money. An architectural magazine hired me to do a piece in Washington. Michael happened to be there at the same time . . . that's when we fell in love."

"That's a romantic story," Patrice said.

"Things were really good then," Lydie said, making Patrice wonder how they were now.

"Do you ever feel homesick for America?" Patrice asked.

The smile left Lydie's face, replaced by an expression dark and confusing to Patrice. A few seconds passed before Lydie spoke. "Yes," she said finally. "I miss my mother . . . and father."

"You're an only child? So am I," Patrice said.

"We were a close family."

"'Were'?" Patrice asked.

Lydie nodded but said nothing. She looked so upset, Patrice felt a wave of tenderness toward her. But the moment was awkward; Patrice really didn't know Lydie well enough to press her. So she did what she felt most comfortable doing in these emotional situations: she bulldozed the conversation into something they could laugh over.

"My mother's planning to visit. I've known about it, in an abstract sort of way, for a while now. But now she's set the date—the last week in July."

Lydie looked interested. "Aren't you happy?" she asked.

"Not exactly," Patrice said. "She'll be exhausted the first week, pepping up just in time for August, when Paris closes down and heads for the beach. My mother hates the beach. And Didier and I plan to go to Saint-Tropez for the entire month."

"Can't you talk about it with her? Maybe convince her to change the dates?"

"You are making the obvious mistake, assuming my mother is a reasonable woman. Once my mother makes her plans, they are cast in stone forever. You know, she's just like the meter maid who tells you once her pen starts writing the ticket it can't stop."

"Where does your mother live?"

"Boston."

"How can someone who lives in Boston hate the beach? With all that New England coastline?"

"Oh, she adores the *shore*—it's the beach she can't stand. You know—sand, sunbathing, fun. I'm just imagining the conflict between her and Didier. He goes on vacation to swim and get a tan. So do I, for that matter. But I can just see my mother, trying to drag us to the Matisse chapel at Vence or the ruins in Nîmes.

A trip to Europe doesn't count for her without one cathedral a day."

Lydie laughed. "Put her on a tour bus."

"She doesn't speak a word of French. She learned the language in college, but she feels it's the French's duty to speak English. She considers herself a patriot."

"How does Didier take that?"

"Oh, my God. It's like dueling anthems: she's 'The Star-Spangled Banner' and he's 'La Marseillaise.' You have to realize: my husband feels guilty every day of his life for being too young to join his father and brothers in the Resistance. He truly loves France. Never mind—tell me about your work. Done anything especially interesting lately?"

"Last week a fashion magazine hired me to do a piece on what men carry in their pockets. So I had to think up the types. A businessman, an artist, a tennis player, a priest—and then I went around town borrowing and buying things I thought each one would have in his pockets."

"Tell me what the artist had in his pockets," Patrice said.

"A tiny magnifying glass, eighteenth century. A bird's feather, some pastels in a leather case, a sketchpad from Sennelier."

"I love it. The businessman?"

"An Hermès agenda, a black fountain pen, let's see . . . a bill from Chez Edgard, and a sterling silver pacifier from Bulgari."

Patrice and Lydie laughed. "The pacifier's perfect," Patrice said. "Didier's a great businessman, let me tell you, but he's a real boy. He's in meetings all day long, or on the phone to New York, or wooing someone in the Far East, and I hold his hand."

"Well, it's important to have someone to rely on," Lydie said.

"Yes," Patrice agreed, watching Lydie's eyes cloud over. But Lydie's distraction didn't last long. She smiled, focused on Patrice.

"Today was interesting," she said. "I'm helping that young

designer with his catalogue. I hardly ever do fashion work, and I'm not used to the models. They're so beautiful. But they act so cool—they seem to *want* a blank look in their eyes."

Patrice, who had smoked cigarettes and practiced seeming aloof all through high school, could imagine that Lydie had never had a cool day in her life. All her emotions seemed very close to the surface; her expression changed constantly. "Their only purpose in life is to wear clothes, I'm convinced," Patrice said.

"Right, their makeup never moves. Anyway—" At the thought of what she was about to say, Lydie laughed so hard she had to stop talking. "Anyway, we arranged them in carts of cabbages. Cabbages up to the knees. Oh, the expressions on their faces—"

"Bye-bye blank stares," Patrice said. "So where did all this happen, anyway?"

"Here in Paris—in Chinatown."

"Chinatown is where Kelly goes on her days off," Patrice said. "Your housekeeper, right?"

"Yes. It's the closest she can get to her culture here in Paris."

"How is she doing on the computer?"

"Pretty well," Patrice said. "Though sometimes I feel like such a shit for teaching it to her. Raising her hopes about getting to America, when there's not a chance in hell."

"Like I told you—my parents immigrated."

"Immigration laws are much stricter now," Patrice said. "You know, I started teaching her the computer because I felt guilty employing an intelligent woman my own age to clean my house. Isn't that textbook *noblesse oblige*?"

"I don't think so. I think it's really nice of you. Do you need the computer for your work?"

"Nope. I don't work. I'm just an amateur historian and a damned good cook. Will you excuse me for a minute? I'll get us some iced tea," Patrice said, heading for the kitchen.

Kelly stood by the sink. She peeled carrots with verve, the way she did everything else. If Patrice didn't know better, she might have thought Kelly enjoyed the work. Kelly looked up, smiled, but continued working. Her black hair was full and silky, cut in a perfect line. One or another of her sisters wanted to be a hairdresser and practiced on Kelly and the others when given the chance.

"Hi," Patrice said, going to the refrigerator for the bottle of iced tea and a lemon. "What are those carrots for?"

"For a salad, Mum. I thought it would be too hot for a warm meal tonight."

"Good thinking," Patrice said, pouring the tea. "As soon as you finish, why don't you start on the computer? That friend I told you about is here now."

"Okay, Mum," Kelly said.

Patrice smiled, at she always did, at the name "Mum." It sounded fond, a little funny, coming from a woman not much younger than herself. Kelly had started off calling her "Madame," and Patrice had wanted her to call her "Patrice," considering the slight age difference, but Didier had said it was unseemly for a servant to call the lady of the house by her given name. Somehow they had settled on "Mum."

"Hope you don't mind—I followed you," Lydie said from the doorway.

"No, that's okay," Patrice said, disguising the fact she was taken aback. No one took guests through the house in France the way they did in America. "Here's your tea." She handed the glass to Lydie. "Lydie McBride, I'd like to present Kelly Merida."

"Hello," Lydie said, giving Kelly a big smile and shaking her hand. The gesture made Patrice happy. She leaned against the marble counter, sipping her drink.

"Kelly's a pretty name," Lydie said, making Kelly blush.

"Oh, I'm named for Grace Kelly, Mum," she said.

Patrice laughed, feeling a little jealous that Kelly would call Lydie "Mum," her own special name, right away. "I never knew that about your name," Patrice said.

"Oh, yes," Kelly said. "In the Philippines there are many people named after stars. In my province there are many Elvises."

"And your mother especially liked Grace Kelly?" Lydie asked.

"Well, she liked Myrna Loy better, but she wanted to name me an Irish name, in honor of my saint. I was born on St. Patrick's Day."

"How bizarre," Lydie said, suddenly looking delighted. "I was just thinking of St. Patrick this morning. My family has all sorts of odd connections to him."

"Oh, I hope this will bring us all luck!" Kelly said, clasping her hands together so hopefully it made Patrice's heart ache.

# 4

*I don't think they take it very seriously in Madame de Montespan's circle, but it is true that at least they pay great attention to not separating any woman from her husband or her duties; they don't like scandal unless they cause it themselves.*

—To Françoise-Marguerite, January 1674

Lydie sat in the breakfast nook trying out ideas for the catalogue of a company that sold only antique linens. This company received the bounty of attics, steamer trunks, and dowry chests from Paris, Vienna, Burano, and Cologne. Napkins, tablecloths, doilies, petticoats, collars starched and lacy, bed ruffles. The advertising agent had instructed only that it be romantic, an instruction that Lydie considered wholly unnecessary.

She sighed, laid down her sketchpad. Ideas were not exactly flowing. When she was young and loved cars, mountains, and teaching kids in Harlem, her father used to call her his "radical tomboy." Lydie wondered what he would think of her now, messing around with antique linens. A picture of her father's face came to her, lean and handsome with its crooked smile. How disappointed he had been when she'd given up painting to become a stylist. He had considered it a materialistic business, using her art to sell things.

"I need the money," she had said. "It'll just be for a few years."

"That's what you think now," he had said. "But you'll get used to the money, and you'll never give it up."

He was right, Lydie thought, sitting at her table in Paris. She missed her father and she hated him. She felt a rush of hatred so strong it brought tears to her eyes. Yet once she started crying, all she could think of was how much she had loved him. The telephone rang. She wiped her eyes with the back of her hand and answered it.

"*Allo,*" she said in her best French accent, made more nasal from crying.

"You sound just like a native," her mother said.

"Hi, Mom," Lydie said, thinking, as she often did when she heard her mother's voice, that it conjured exactly the speaker's face in a way voices seldom did. Its low, gravelly hint of Ireland was at once promising and mysterious, and it went along with Julia Fallon's smile, the way she would duck her head and seem to be smiling up at you. As if she had a secret.

"How are you? How's Paris? Are the roses in bloom?"

"The roses are beautiful," Lydie said, still sniffling, glad for the opening to talk about something simple. "Last week I walked through the Bagatelle, which is a little garden in the Bois de Boulogne. Sort of a secret garden . . ." At that second, Lydie had the solution: antique linens draped on rosebushes in the Bagatelle. At dawn, with the mists rising. "There were roses of every color—red, bright pink, yellow. Yellow so pale it's nearly white."

"I don't know why, but when I think of Paris, I think of roses," Julia said. "Our roses are beautiful right now."

"I bet," Lydie said. She envisioned the walled garden behind her parents' ground-floor apartment. She doubted there was another like it in Manhattan: sun shone into the garden all afternoon long. This was the lucky result of the block of buildings just west, none over four stories high, having been granted landmark status. No high-rise would ever replace them, and sunlight came over their rooftops into the Fallons' garden.

"I miss you, honey," Julia said.

"I miss you too." There was silence on the line. "How are you doing?" Lydie asked after a while.

"Oh, I get along. I had lunch with Aunt Carrie the other day. She sends her love. But I just don't have my old get-up-and-go."

"Mom, I think that's normal," Lydie said. "You've been through a shock." Sometimes she wished her mother wouldn't make her worry when she was so far away, but she knew Julia had to talk to someone.

"Are you still homesick?"

Lydie smiled because what came through in that question was Julia's fervent wish that homesickness would overcome Lydie and send her straight back to New York. "Just a little. I met a really nice woman."

Julia Fallon took the news with predictable silence. "That's wonderful," she said after a moment. "I'm sure that makes all the difference."

Lydie knew Julia had little use for friends outside the family, a fairly understandable policy considering all the Fallon and O'Neill relatives who lived in New York. Why should Julia make friends when her sister, brother-in-law, nephews, cousins, and great-aunt all lived within a two-block radius? For Lydie, an only child, that logic didn't apply.

"Is she French?" Julia asked.

"No, American. She's married to a Frenchman and lives here permanently. Can you imagine that?"

"Of course I can imagine it. I left Ireland for good at the age of twenty. On the other hand, I had your father and my sisters with me. I've always needed my family."

Lydie suddenly thought of Kelly, Patrice's housekeeper. Kelly leaving the Philippines reminded Lydie of her mother leaving Ireland: with other members of her family, in search of a better life. While Patrice could be called an expatriate, with all the word's implicit glamour and adventure, Kelly could only be called an immigrant.

"Well, Patrice has no family over here," Lydie said. "But she has a housekeeper she's very close to. I think she considers her a . . ." Lydie groped for the word. "Sister," with its boundless loyalties and resentments, seemed closer than "friend."

"It sounds good for both of them," Julia said, and Lydie supposed she was thinking of herself and the cardinal.

"Kelly wants to go to America."

Julia chuckled. "I can already tell you're thinking of a way to help her."

"No I'm not," Lydie said, surprised.

"Well, you will be soon. That's just the way you are. And America is the place for her to come. It's the only place in the world where the poor can get rich. Whatever else they say about your father, they can't say he wasn't willing to work."

"I know, Mom," Lydie said.

"We're coming up on his anniversary. Can you believe it's been a year?"

"No."

"I still can't get over it. Sometimes I don't believe he's gone," Julia said. Lydie could see her sitting there, that vacant look in her eyes. "Go to church and light a candle for him, will you, honey?"

"I can't do that," Lydie said.

"Oh, Lydie," Julia said, sounding ragged and desperate. "He was your father. Don't you ever forget that."

"I can't forget that, but I can't pray for him either."

"Why not? If I can forgive him, you should be able to."

"I don't see how you can," Lydie said. She was losing her voice. In a moment she wouldn't be able to speak at all.

"I'll tell you how you can. Remember him as he *was*, before he . . . went out of his head."

Lydie knew the family theory of how her father had lost his mind, had killed the woman and himself out of guilt for infidelity. In a way, she wanted to believe that. That his last thought had been for Julia and Lydie. That his last act was meant to punish himself and to spare them.

"I remember him," Lydie said.

"Tell me one of your happy memories, honey," Julia urged.

Lydie didn't have to search far. "Oh, I remember school nights in late June, when it was too hot to study," she said, trying to sound offhand. "We'd take a picnic to Central Park, and Dad would play baseball with me and whoever else was around."

"You were such a tomboy!" Julia said, laughing merrily. "Your father said you could hit the ball a mile, and how you'd *dive* after the ball when it was your turn to go into the outfield. Oh, he was so furious they wouldn't let you play in Little League. Girls do, nowadays."

Tears rolled down Lydie's cheeks as she remembered the sound of cicadas in the trees, the music from other picnickers' radios, the sight of her tall father crouching to pitch a low ball to her.

"Why did he do it?" she asked Julia.

"The guilt . . ." Julia said.

"No," Lydie said. "Why did he do it?"

The line was silent, except for static that might have been the Atlantic Ocean rolling over the wires. "I don't know," Julia said helplessly.

"I'm sorry," Lydie said. "I know you wanted to hear happy memories."

Then, with marked cheeriness, Julia laughed a little. "Oh, honey. I *thank* you. You're the only one I can talk to."

"Anytime," Lydie said.

"That's the spirit," Julia said. "How's Michael?"

"He's fine."

"Of course he is—he's wonderful. He's one in a million. Give him my love, will you?"

"Okay. I miss you, Mom," Lydie said. Back in New York they had talked all the time—sometimes every day.

"And I miss you, sweetheart," Julia replied.

# 5

*Aren't you amazed how people can change and how differ-
ently things come into one's head?*

—To Françoise-Marguerite, March 1680

Michael McBride loved someone new, and she didn't know
it. She was French; she worked at the Louvre. Every morning,
walking along the Seine from his apartment to the Louvre, he had
fantasies about her. When he actually saw her, however, they
barely spoke. Her project was entirely different from his. Her
name was Anne.

Tonight he walked the route with Lydie, on their way to a performance of Molière at the Comèdie Française, and it felt strange;
all the familiar sights reminded him of his feelings for Anne.

"Don't you want to take a cab?" he asked. "It's a long way."

Lydie looked down at her new open-toed shoes. Her feet blis-
tered easily; to accommodate her love of walking Michael kept a
supply of Band-Aids in his wallet.

"Let's walk," Lydie said. "My feet will be fine."

But twenty minutes after leaving the apartment, she was limping, barefoot, carrying her shoes. They walked along the quai, and Michael watched the way she stepped carefully from cobble to cobble, as if they were stepping-stones across a stream. Gentle waves lapped barges moored to the bank; bicycles and pots of spring flowers covered the deck of one, a striped umbrella shaded the table on the deck of another, but the boats were deserted. Many mornings Michael had imagined himself and Anne leaving Paris on one of those barges.

"Would you ever want to take a barge trip?" he asked Lydie.

"Oh, I don't know," she said. "Don't they usually stay on the rivers?"

The answer made Michael sad. He knew Lydie loved the beach, hated taking vacations inland. Now that he had begun facing the flaws in his marriage, it seemed he could see only Lydie's faults. As if he had been blind to them for so long, blindly in love with her, her small faults seemed major. For example, that she couldn't see the romance of taking a barge through Burgundy in the fall. Of bicycling through vineyards each day.

So he brought Anne into the vivid daydream: chilly air, the spicy scent of ripe grapes, crimson leaves and gold grasses, strenuous exercise that would make them feel they deserved the fine dinners those barges were reputed to serve every night. He imagined tasting wines with dinner: wines produced by the vineyards they had visited that day. He could see the wine, its color somewhere between orange and ruby, served in a ballon—a glass as big as a crystal ball. Walking along the quai he felt himself get hard, and he knew why: a dinner like that on one of these barges with Anne would make him feel like loving her all night long.

Michael took Lydie's hand, as if that could make up for the way he felt about Anne. He knew that his marriage would probably end in Paris. He had wanted the Paris year to be special for him and Lydie; he had thought that coming might spark him to love her the way he once had. Instead, it had left him excited, churned up, with no one to share it with. He had loved Lydie so much, and she had loved him back. But now she loved her family's drama more than she loved him; sometimes he considered her attitude overvigilant. Lately, he'd begun to consider it ghoulish.

As a teenager he had thought girls cared more about love than boys did. He had understood that certain trappings were important to them: Valentine presents, birthday presents that could be shown off for their intimacy, a willingness to talk and hug before sex and sometimes instead of it. But Michael cared about those things, wanted to do them. Even before Neil's death Lydie had been more pragmatic than he was, cared less about passion than he did. For him marriage should be romantic, even thrilling and dangerous.

And was it guilt for that thought that made Michael remember Lydie's loyalty? The pride she felt at having him work on the Louvre? She never missed the chance to put his work into historical perspective; the idea made him feel excited and daunted. She would invoke all the artists and architects over the ages who had been commissioned by kings and ministers to work on the Louvre, and say that now he was one of them. He ran the phrase "over the ages" through his mind again. If his ideas were accepted, the Ministry of Culture would direct builders to place stones and glass and information booths according to the specifications of Michael McBride. He had left his mark on museums in New York, Dallas, Cleveland, and Hartford, but to leave it on the Louvre would, for Lydie, ensure real and certain immortality.

"There it is," Lydie said.

The Louvre. They had reached the ramp that would take them up to street level. Regarding the museum, its walls long and massive as a fort's, its niches filled with great, noble statues, Michael was envisioning its blueprint. From the air, its outline was bold and majestic, yet as simple, as symmetrical as a letter of the alphabet.

Michael and Lydie walked past in silence, but something about the way she gazed up the walls let Michael know she was thinking about him and his work. The sun, much higher in the sky than it would be in the States at this time of evening in late spring, threw shadows on the stones.

A barge slid along the Seine, its frothy wake golden in the declining light. Lydie stopped in the middle of the sidewalk and looked Michael straight in the eye. Her expression startled him. She might have been about to set him straight about a major fact of life.

"I'm proud of you," she said, surprising him, standing on her bare toes to kiss him. His eyes were closed, and he heard the voices of people passing by. Many of them spoke English; this was, after all, the heart of the tourist district. And beyond the simple pleasure of kissing her, Michael liked joining the ranks of lovers he had seen around Paris, kissing with abandon, caring more for the moment of passion than for decorum. Not caring who was watching.

∽

Lydie believed in the process of change. She believed that a cataclysmic or benevolent event could effect a change, of course, send you veering in a direction you might not normally have taken, and just as her father's death was one such event, that kiss on the quai was another. She believed it signified healing—of her own spirit. She could envision the moment in her mind the way someone passing in a tour bus might have seen it: in a romantic, photogenic haze. The urge to kiss Michael had come upon her suddenly, raised her up on her toes, made her close her eyes and tilt back her head to meet his lips.

Several evenings later they sat in a noisy bistro in the Seventh, just across the Pont de l'Alma from their building. Trays bearing platters of steak *frites* clattered by, and the patrons were happy drinking cheap red wine bottled in Touraine by the owner's brother-in-law. Lydie watched Michael, who seemed restless. He tapped the pepper mill on the paper cloth, staring at the spilled pepper flecks as if they were tea leaves. Where their dinner hours had once been filled with conversation, for the last eleven months they had been quiet, with Lydie closed off and Michael tired of trying to draw her out.

"What are you working on?" Michael asked when he saw her watching him. He spoke in a loud voice, to be heard.

"My linen project. For that catalogue—remember I told you about it?"

Michael nodded, and Lydie realized that he wasn't paying attention. He was looking over her head, across the crowded room. She followed his gaze to the doorway where a couple stood talking to the waiter.

"Do you know them?" Lydie asked.

"I know her from the Louvre," Michael said.

Lydie looked again. The woman had close-cropped dark hair and eyes black as a raccoon's, and she was so small she had to stand on her toes to whisper something to her escort.

"Should we ask them to join us?" Lydie asked in one of those quick and urgent moments of marital consultation. The table to her right was just being vacated by an elderly man and a small blond boy.

"No, let's not," Michael said. But the woman had seen them and was making her way toward their table.

"Michael," the woman said, shaking his hand. Her French accent made the name sound like "Michel."

"What happened to your eyes?" Michael asked.

"I fell down some stairs," she said. A waiter hurrying past bumped her, making her grab the back of Michael's chair to steady herself. A different waiter, also hurrying, told them to take the empty table beside the McBrides'.

"But we don't want to intrude," the woman said to Michael.

"Please," Lydie said. "You won't be intruding."

Introductions were made. The woman was Anne Dumas. The man was Jean Tavanier. Lydie regarded Anne Dumas and guessed her age at thirty-three. The raccoon eyes were no illusion; not the product of kohl and mascara, they were bruised.

"I haven't seen you around the Louvre for a while," Michael said. "Were you badly hurt?"

"No, not too badly. I was visiting the cathedral at Aix-en-Provence, Saint-Sauveur, and I wanted to examine the baptistry. It's ancient, you know, dating back to the Romans, and the steps are crumbling a little. So my foot went down wrong, and—pow!"

"She has a bruise of the brain," said Jean.

"A concussion," Anne said. "But not serious. However, no wine for me tonight."

"A concussion!" Michael said. "How high were the steps?"

"Oh, just over a meter, which is the part that makes it so embarrassing."

"You fell four feet?" Lydie asked.

"Concussions can be really dangerous," Michael said. Lydie stared at him across the table and felt annoyed by his furrowed brow, which seemed to express excessive concern.

"I'm sure you've seen a doctor," Lydie said.

"Naturally. There was a doctor two streets away. My guide knew him well." She laughed. "We had to bump through a crowd of monks on a pilgrimage from Greece, with my head bleeding like mad. You think working at the Louvre with all the tourists is bad. I'm telling you, it's nothing compared to working in a dry temple bath full of monks."

"What work were you doing there?" Lydie asked. "I've always wanted to go to Aix-en-Provence."

"Aix is very lovely," Anne said. "Of course the south of France is hot this time of year, but the cathedral was cool."

"Did your research take you there?" Michael asked.

"Yes," she said. Anne smiled, and her eyes crinkled. She raised one delicate hand to her bruised cheek and her mouth made an "O."

"Hurts?" Lydie said. Anne nodded. She smiled at Lydie again. "I am not an expert on structures," she said. "Not the way your husband is. I am interested in the cultural story, you know? And my interest happens to lie in the past. Mainly in the person."

"She is a historian," Jean said slowly, enunciating each word carefully.

Lydie and Michael had finished their meal, but they waited for Anne and Jean to eat before ordering coffee. Lydie had to marvel that a woman as dainty and bruised as Anne could eat with such gusto, using her bread to wipe her plate, the knife and fork working constantly. Every so often she would glance at Lydie, give her a wonderful smile. Anne was not precisely beautiful, but she had a quality that made Lydie unable to look away from her. Everything about her was smaller than usual. Her stature, her nose, her mouth, her hands. Only her eyes were enormous, black, at once spirited and sad.

"So, you're working with Michael at the Louvre?" Lydie asked when Anne had laid down her fork, dabbed her mouth with the linen napkin.

"No," Anne said. "I am working on a project of my own, and we just get in each other's way."

"Tell Lydie your project," Michael said.

"Well," Anne said, smiling in a way that indicated she had been waiting for this moment; it reminded Lydie of the pleasure she felt when given the chance to explain her own work to someone new. "I am following Madame de Sévigné around. Forget the fact she has been dead for centuries. She is so fantastic, she lives still."

"I'm ignorant," Lydie said.

"Madame de Sévigné is perhaps the greatest letter writer France has known. Her letters tell the story of the seventeenth century; she was trusted by Louis XIV. A member of his court! She was so solid in the middle of all that scandal. And her letters are very funny, sad, poignant. I can't stop reading them. They are mostly to her daughter. She loved her daughter so much, and once the girl was grown, they lived apart. But Madame de Sévigné told the girl everything in letters."

"I'd love to read them," said Lydie, wondering whether the sound of a distant voice had more value than a letter, which could be held. And saved. "Tell me—what is her connection with the Louvre?"

"I am pursuing her connection with Louis XIV, who lived there before Versailles. You can thank him for commissioning many of your husband's predecessors—architects who have left a mark there."

"Is she the reason you went to Aix-en-Provence?" Michael asked.

"Yes," Anne said. "Because that is where her daughter moved after she married Count de Grignan. I begin to feel as though I know them personally, that I am visiting them in their various dwellings . . ."

"Anne is really crazy," Jean said. "She is so obsessive about Madame de Sévigné, she is researching every single connection. And she has already written a book about her."

"Really?" Lydie asked. "What's the title?"

"*Three Women of the Marais,*" Anne said. "She was born on the Place des Vosges."

"I have a friend who lives there," Lydie said.

"Really? To live there—that would be something," Anne said.

Jean laughed in a scoffing manner. "Anne, if you lived there, you might actually start to believe you are the reincarnation of Madame de Sévigné. It would be the worst that could happen."

Lydie giggled and tried to catch Michael's eye, but he was looking away: his head tilted toward Anne, and he was staring at her, a little smile on his lips, as if he was trying to figure her out.

# 6

*I assure you that these days drag on slowly and that uncertainty is a dreadful thing.*

—To Pomponne, December 1664

Charles Legendre, the Louvre's curator for seventeenth-century art, was a fop. Stickpin, black silk socks, significant tie—obviously from some school, probably in Switzerland. Unfortunately he was Michael's designated Louvre liaison. Michael had sort of liked him, with reservations, at their first meeting. That was back in October, when Charles had walked Michael through the painting galleries, suggesting works Michael might want to appropriate for the Salle des Quatre Saisons.

"That is a magnificent Poussin," Michael had said, facing a large canvas depicting warriors in a scene from mythology.

"Ah, yes," Charles had said, his hands folded as he gazed upon the tableau. "Pierre Dauphin counts that among his favorites. Good luck to you, persuading him to let you have it. But of course you must try. Isn't that a charming Wando?"

"It is," Michael had said. But who had ever heard of Wando?

The card beside the painting identified Giancarlo Wando as a Milanese who came to Paris in 1672. Michael wanted at least two important seventeenth-century works—by the likes of Poussin and la Tour. At the time he had thought Charles's motives were innocent. Months later, however, the scene reminded him of his older brother Jack, of a McBride family vacation on Cape Cod, when Jack had tried to trick Michael into wanting the second-best bike: "That red one's sharp, isn't it? With the chrome mud guard. You want the red one, Mike?" Later, wobbling down the sandy road, Michael had discovered what Jack had seen instantly: the rear wheel was out of whack, possibly run over by a car.

Now, sitting opposite Charles in his third-floor office, Michael was on guard. Charles believed in his own charm. Even while sabotaging Michael every step of the way, he managed to keep a smile on his handsome, tan face.

"Your plans are marvelous," Charles said.

"That's all they are—plans," Michael said. "When can I start construction?"

Charles shrugged; as he did, he noticed a white thread dangling from his right shirt cuff. He frowned. He grabbed it with the thumb and forefinger of his left hand. Then, holding the thread, he used his right hand to open his desk drawer. He extracted a pair of tiny gold scissors. Carefully resting his right hand on his leather blotter, he snipped the thread. He placed it in his crystal pencil tray for later disposal.

Michael watched the operation, growing hotter and hotter. *Fop,* he thought again. "Well?" he said. "Can you explain to me why it's taking so long?"

"The Louvre is a museum of many departments, each with its own methods of operation. Additionally, it is an institution of the government of France. No less than the Assemblée Nationale or the Elysée Palace. You cannot expect to impose your plans on such a place without appropriate scrutiny and discussion." Charles said this with an air of national pride that tightened his nostrils and turned down the corners of his mouth.

"Who's doing the scrutinizing and discussing?" Michael asked.

"I, as curator of seventeenth-century paintings, and as your liaison officer, play a role," Charles said. "The Minister of Culture, of course. Even the Prime Minister. You should be honored that the Prime Minister is considering your plans."

"Why can't I hire the people I need? That way, when the approval is given, they'll be ready to go. I'd like to get a team together."

"Because, Michael," Charles said patiently, as if Michael were an idiot, "you would have to pay these people. Even if your plans are never approved, the members of your team would be on the payroll of the French government. And it would be impossible to ever get them off."

"Okay," Michael said. "I won't actually *engage* anyone. But I've talked to masons and painters, and I'd like to—in a tentative way—ask them to set time aside for me. Just in case I'm told I can proceed."

Charles shrugged. "I cannot stop you. But I cannot permit you to do this in the name of France and the Louvre. You will have to do it in the name of Michael McBride which, without intending offense, may not be enough to persuade artisans to pass up other, certain, projects."

"That's fair," Michael said, wanting to draw Charles's significant tie into a tighter and tighter knot and choke the smug smile off his thin lips. "I have another question for you. Why are you holding up the Poussin?"

"Pierre Dauphin will not give it up. If it were up to me . . ."

"I've been told it *is* up to you. You're the curator of the seventeenth century."

"Yes, but it hangs in Pierre's gallery. He is the curator of the Salle Hubert."

What a racket, Michael thought. One guy was curator of the walls, another was curator of the paintings that hung on the walls. George Reed believed that Charles had ultimate control, but he was not certain because none of the French authorities were positive themselves. One minister had told George that if he wanted to be sure, he would have to read Louis XIV's original charter.

"I've heard you have more clout than Pierre," Michael said. "You can give me that Poussin if you want to."

"And where will you hang it?" Charles asked, leaning forward.

"Good point," Michael said, feeling he'd just been beaten in chess. "But when the time comes, will you give it to me?"

"You'll have to take that up with Pierre," Charles said, closing the subject. Michael stood to leave. "You've been enjoying your time in Paris?" Charles asked.

"It's been swell," Michael said. He shook Charles's hand and left.

Michael had had his share of professional disappointments and setbacks, but nothing had prepared him for this bureaucratic stonewalling. He could understand the tangle of rules and personalities and government agencies; he could even accept it. What infuriated him was a deepening belief that the French authorities were enjoying his dilemma. He felt in some ways hampered by the differences of culture; if Charles were American, Michael could imagine talking to him frankly. Yet wasn't that what he had done? Running over the conversation in his mind, he decided that the problem had been Charles's responses.

Charles wouldn't know a frank response if it bit him in the ass. Michael mistrusted any guy who took as long to dress as Charles obviously did. Could his eyelashes be that dark naturally? Walking the corridor that ran the length of the third floor, Michael knew he was thinking like an asshole. He passed the offices of other curators; glancing into one open door, he saw windows that gave onto the Seine and the Left Bank. Just before he reached the stairs, he heard Anne's voice.

Michael stopped dead. The mere sound of her voice made his heart beat faster. So this was where she worked. Every day she passed him downstairs; they would talk for a minute or two, or wave, and that was all. He tried to see inside, but her door was open only a crack. A male voice answered her. Michael did not think it could be Jean; the accent was too refined. He leaned against the stone wall. It felt smooth and cool, and it stung Michael like an electric shock. He was jealous of a faceless voice. The realization disgusted him, and he hurried down the stairs.

❧

Patrice had harbored a curiosity about Lydie's work since meeting her, so she felt especially eager to watch Lydie in action on what Lydie was calling "the rose project." They strolled together through the Bagatelle. Although it was early morning, the heat flourished. Patrice realized that Lydie had hoped for mist, but what she had was steam. Patrice found the setting relaxing. Songbirds in the trees, roses everywhere. But Lydie moved with such purpose, obviously working, that Patrice didn't want to interrupt her by spouting pleasantries.

"This idea might be a flop," Lydie said, reaching into her bag for an antique doily. She scanned the closest bush for the perfect rose on which to place it.

"Isn't that pretty?" Patrice said.

"Martine!" Lydie called the photographer and her assistant and spoke to them in French. "Will you shoot this, please? No, into the sun—make it hazy."

"Soft focus?" the photographer asked.

"No, sharp," Lydie said. "Let the light soften it for you."

Lydie arranged the linens, and Martine took pictures of them, angling the shots from above or below, depending on Lydie's direction. Patrice reached for a linen napkin, slightly yellow with age. If it had ever been folded, the creases had been pressed out of it. That made her think of Kelly, of the pile of ironing Patrice had left her to do. When Kelly ironed a sheet, her expression looked as solemn, as intent as Lydie's did now. Yet how could she compare Lydie's job with Kelly's drudge work? Days had passed since Kelly's last session on the computer. Patrice sensed, uneasily, that since Lydie's arrival on the scene, she had begun neglecting Kelly.

A rose garden seemed the perfect place for Lydie to be, Lydie with her translucent white skin and fine copper hair. Patrice felt so big beside her, but she was spared a true feeling of insecurity by the knowledge that her own sundress, from St. Laurent, was a bit better than Lydie's, from Tiktiner. She felt that they had just arrived, but Lydie already seemed to be wrapping things up. Yet when she checked her watch, she saw that fifty minutes had passed.

"Four rolls of film should be plenty," Lydie said. "Were you bored?" Martine had moved to the shade of an oak tree, to pack her camera cases and drink some orangeade. Lydie tipped the thermos, handed Patrice a cupful.

"Not at all." Patrice surveyed the scene: napkins and doilies draped over buds and roses and leaves. It suddenly struck her as hilarious, grown women arranging linens on rosebushes. She laughed, and so did Lydie. Lydie downed her orangeade so enthusiastically it left an orange smile above her lips, like a milk mustache. Patrice touched her own lips; Lydie got the message and wiped the orange away.

"How did you get into this line of work, anyway?" Patrice asked.

"I started off wanting to be an artist, but . . ." Lydie said. "This is the closest I could get to it. Sometimes when I'm working I feel like I'm making a collage—but it lasts only until the photographer takes the pictures."

"The pictures last."

"Yes, but they're by the photographer," Lydie said. "As soon as I take these napkins off the roses, that's that."

"I see what you mean," Patrice said.

Now Lydie was walking around, putting the linens away. "Michael and I bumped into someone the other night I think you'd be interested in. She's an historian—working at the Louvre."

"Doing what?"

"Research. It's really extraordinary, and a little bizarre. She's obsessed with one woman in French history. In fact, she's already written about her. Madame de Sévigné. Have you ever heard of her before? Don't say yes, because I hadn't and I felt so stupid."

Patrice smiled, happy in spite of herself to be one up on Lydie in an area besides clothing. "Sorry, honey. I know her well. And she is worth being obsessed by. Most people think she was so loving and sweet, especially to her daughter. I mean, this was long before the days of Freud, and I'm telling you he would have had a field day with those two. Their letters make you cringe—they're more passionate than what I write to Didier when he goes away on long business trips."

"Sounds weird."

"What I find amazing is her influence, which was considerable," Patrice went on. "She had the ear of King Louis, that is for sure. Get this: little Françoise-Marguerite wanted to be a ballerina, so Madame de Sévigné convinces Louis to let her dance the role of Shepherdess in the Royal Ballet at the Louvre, with Louis *himself* dancing as Shepherd. I mean, talk about headline entertainment."

"You're an expert on this," Lydie said. "You have to meet this woman."

"If she's typical of people who love Madame de Sévigné, she probably idealizes the mother-daughter relationship. Which explains why she would want to hang around the Louvre, her feet touching the hallowed ground where little Françoise-Marguerite first went on pointe."

"The daughter moved away, is that right?" Lydie asked. "And they never saw each other?"

"Give me a break—she stayed in France. She moved to Provence."

"In the seventeenth century, that must have seemed very far," Lydie said. "I wonder if they ever visited each other."

"Just tell me the name of her book. When I've finished the one I'm reading now, I might go for the sentimental point of view."

"It's *Three Women of the Marais,*" Lydie said, standing on her toes to reach a napkin dangling from the top of a topiary rose-bush.

"Oh, my God," Patrice said.

"What?" Lydie said, turning.

"That's the book I'm reading! It's fantastic, and not sentimental at all. You actually *know* Anne Dumas?"

"I don't, really. But Michael does."

"Is she pretty?"

"In a *gamine* sort of way. Like the young Audrey Hepburn, only short. She is so intelligent, that's what strikes you. And she's charming, but reserved in a sad way. As if something had happened to her once." Lydie glanced over at Martine, who was ready to leave. "Excuse me a second," she said to Patrice.

Patrice sat on a bench. She could not get over the coincidence, the amazing unlikelihood, that Lydie had met Anne Dumas. Patrice had started thinking of her as "Anne," of the time she spent reading *Three Women of the Marais* as time spent in Anne's company, in a sort of seminar. Patrice slid a pair of gold-rimmed sunglasses from her bag and put them on. She recognized, of course, what she'd been doing: using Anne Dumas the way she used Kelly—to fill a void. She adored Didier; she had adjusted very well to France. But she couldn't deny that until recently, until she'd met Lydie, something had been missing from her life. Lydie was her friend. And as soon as Lydie finished with the photographer, Patrice was going to invite her and Michael for dinner some night soon.

# 7

*You want to know how we live, my child? Alas, like this.*

—To Françoise-Marguerite, September 1689

It was Saturday afternoon, and Kelly was peeling cloves of garlic to scatter around the leg of lamb. Didier liked a lot of garlic. Tonight Lydie and her husband were coming to the d'Orignys' for dinner. Kelly's back ached. She felt a little sad. Tonight would point out to everyone the differences between Kelly and Patrice and Lydie. The differences were, of course, already understood by all, but tonight they would be crystal clear. Kelly had seen the dress Patrice was going to wear because Patrice had laid it across her bed for Kelly to iron. It was beautiful: a sheath of rose silk. Just touching the dress with one hand as she passed the cool iron with the other had brought tears to Kelly's eyes.

"That garlic smells heavenly," Patrice said, startling Kelly.

"Hello, Mum," Kelly said.

Patrice leaned against the sink. She started munching some haricots verts that Kelly had already trimmed. She wore a white tennis dress; her hair was pulled back in a messy ponytail, but her makeup was perfect.

"Did you have a good tennis match?" Kelly asked.

"Yes, we did. We beat the shit out of the Dulongs. And it's so beautiful outside. Nice and hot. Summer's coming on, even if you'd never know it in here. This building holds on to winter until mid-July, doesn't it? Aren't you chilly, Kelly?"

"I'm fine, Mum," said Kelly, who was sweating.

"At least we don't need air-conditioning. Those ancients really knew how to insulate a place. Are there places as old as Paris in the Philippines?"

"Oh, yes," Kelly said, thinking of one street in her province said to be older than Christ.

"When you were born and raised in America, you think a place two hundred years old is practically medieval."

"Is America really modern?" Kelly asked, surprised by how wistful she felt. She would trade old for new any day.

"In some ways, yes," Patrice said. "But the attitudes can be as backward as anyplace else. Listen, speaking of backward attitudes," she said, standing up straight, "I came to tell you that Didier wants you to wear your uniform tonight. It's here, isn't it?"

"Yes," Kelly said. She had already planned to wear it.

"Do me a big favor. Press it and have it on when Didier comes downstairs."

"Okay, Mum," Kelly said, placing the knife in the sink, wiping her hands on the linen towel. Patrice left the kitchen. Kelly could not hear where she went. The massive stone architecture kept sound, like heat, from penetrating the walls. Garments she had yet to iron hung in a small closet off the kitchen. Taking down her uniform, Kelly realized that of all her household chores, she disliked ironing most. And she realized the irony of that dislike, considering the pleasures ironing had given her in her early life.

When she was young, five or six years old, the whole family worked for Pan Am. The great American airline hired Kelly's parents to launder their linen. White napkins, tiny pillowcases, aprons, summer-weight cotton blankets. Kelly's father and brothers would drive to the airport in Manila to pick up the soiled linen and deliver the clean; the women would wash and iron it.

Sometimes they worked inside the house, but more often outdoors, under the hot blue sky. She remembered the three large iron cauldrons boiling over coal fires, steam wisping into the hot air. Annette and Ingrid had charge of stirring the laundry with clean sticks. Marie-Vic, Darlene, and Sophia would wring it out with their bare hands and pin it to clotheslines. In the rainy season they strung lines inside the house and fanned it with paddles.

Along with Pan Am's laundry they washed large white sheets to lay on the dirt—the floor of their house and their entire yard had been dirt then. Kelly's sisters would toss the clean linen on one sheet, and her mother would sit cross-legged on another, a large pillow on her lap. And she would iron on that pillow. Kelly had loved watching her.

Absently Kelly lifted the iron she was now using, to test its weight. How light it felt compared to that iron of her mother's! Her mother's iron was enormous and round, hollow and filled with coal. She had to constantly change hands, because it was so heavy. After work, Annette would rub her mother's shoulders with eucalyptus sap. Everyone would be lying on the sheets then, resting and talking. Her older sisters would tell about college, about nice American servicemen they had met: topics that would please their mother, who would smile and say everyone had to work hard to earn money so they could all move to the States and open a fish market.

Kelly finished ironing her uniform. The white collar was starched stiff as cardboard, just as Didier liked it. Unplugging the iron, she remembered the best part of ironing Pan Am's laundry. At the end of the day, after the iron had cooled, Kelly's mother had let her blow the coal ashes out of it. She remembered blowing into the tube, watching the silver ash fly out the trap door. She remembered the gritty, twinkly feeling of ash on her cheeks and in her eyelashes. And she remembered how, every time she did it, her mother would smile and call her "Tinkerbell."

◦◦◦

Didier d'Origny gripped the champagne cork with a white linen towel, twisted, and let a wisp of vapor escape the bottle. He filled four glasses, turning the bottle as he poured, to avoid spilling a drop. The room was silent except for the sigh of air as the cork was removed, then the bubbles fizzing in the glasses. The evening was off to a festive start. Lydie glanced over at Michael, tried to see him as the others would: lean, thirty-five, curly brown hair that needed to be cut, a mouth that smiled easily, and eyes that took everything in.

"To health," Didier said, raising his glass.

"Health," said Lydie, Michael, and Patrice in unison, smiling, clinking glasses, and drinking.

"So," Didier said, setting down his glass. "Have you explored the Champagne region of France?"

"We spent one of our first weekends there," Michael said.

"I loved those underground caves, where they age the wine," Lydie said, remembering walking down one hundred steps into a dim, damp clay-walled chamber lined with racks of champagne.

"Marvelous caves," Didier said. His expression was kind, but a little distant. His blond hair receded slightly from his broad forehead, and he had the sort of weathered skin that made Lydie wonder if he was a skier.

"So, you two were childhood sweethearts," Patrice said, smiling at Michael.

"Actually, I missed my first chance with Lydie," Michael said. "In high school I cared more about the hoop than girls."

"'The hoop'?" Didier asked, lighting a cigarette.

"Basketball," Michael said.

"I don't know how I missed him," Lydie said. "He looked so great in shorts." She could see him now: driving to the basket, his legs long and muscled, running faster than anyone else. She watched how he grinned at Didier in a way he never would at a woman. One athlete to another, Lydie thought.

"Yes, you know it's a shame," Didier said. "It was the same for me—soccer, shooting, skiing. I went to a boys' school. I didn't know about girls until I was twenty-three."

"Oh, give me a break," Patrice said, snorting. "They'll think you were queer unless you tell them you've already been married twice. I'm his third," she said to Lydie, which Lydie had not known.

"My baby, you may be third, but you are the best," Didier said. "It's not right to talk about my first two wives, so let me talk about myself. They were wonderful women. I was the idiot. I didn't know anything until I met Patrice."

"Wonderful?" Patrice raised her eyebrows. "Both of them are in love with new men, but they refuse to get married because they don't want to lose Didier's alimony."

"It's true," Didier said sadly. "I am supporting four adults. Not to mention my children."

"Oh, you have children?" Lydie asked.

"A boy and a girl," Didier said. "One with each wife."

"Make that *six* adults you're supporting," Patrice said. "I mean, we're not talking toddlers. Would you call people of college age 'children'?"

Didier patted her hand, and they smiled at each other, as if they had agreed to turn this bad situation into a private joke. The moment was intimate and excluded Michael and Lydie. Lydie tried to catch Michael's eye, but he was looking away.

Kelly entered the room, placed a crystal dish of small black olives on the tray table. Kelly's head was bowed, and Lydie ducked her own to smile at her. "Thank you, Kelly," Patrice said.

"Now, I am very interested to see what you Americans do about these olives," Didier said.

"I plan to eat one," Michael said, popping one into his mouth. He made a fist, held it to his lips like a microphone, and spit the pit into it: exactly the way he had seen French people do it.

"Very good technique!" Didier said. "Most Americans think olives are disgusting, and the ones who eat them make a mess of the pits. I was all ready to give you a lesson, but you don't need it."

Why would a man want to set himself up as a master of olive eating? Lydie wondered. She saw it as a way for Didier to establish himself as the oldest person, the only father, the only Frenchman in the room. Her father had behaved similarly about his own fatherhood, his Irishness. Whenever Lydie would mix him a half-and-half—the half beer/half stout concoction he remembered from Dublin pubs—he would sip it with an expression of amused tolerance on his face: letting her know it was well-enough made for an American girl.

"Now," Didier said. "Tell me how you plan to desecrate the Louvre."

"We're going to build a great glass column and fill it with the fish of France," Michael said, deadpan. From previous experience with other French people, Lydie knew why he had said it and what was coming next.

"You joke, my friend," Didier said, "but it is no joke to me. Not after what has been done—that glass pyramid. Imagine! A glass pyramid rising out of the courtyard of the Louvre. It is a monstrosity. It is a fucking scandal. No, it is worse than a scandal. I am not religious, but I believe it is a sin. To ruin our ancient and beautiful Louvre with that vulgarity."

Lydie, who had heard tirades about I. M. Pei's glass pyramid before, was shocked by Didier's vehemence. Since arriving in Paris, she had found two camps: those who loved the pyramid and those who hated it. What shocked her was the change in Didier, now too moved to continue speaking. He ate one olive after another. The fist into which he spit his olive pits looked charged, ready to strike. She believed that this was the real Didier, full of passion for La Belle France; his earlier manner, polite and refined, had been a smokescreen.

"I agree with you," Michael said. "That pyramid doesn't belong there."

"I assumed you would like it," Didier said. "After all, you have been brought from America to work on the Louvre. I assumed your work would be consistent with the recent changes."

"Michael's a preservationist," Lydie said, feeling protective of him. Didier's attack made her bristle in Michael's defense, but what struck her at that instant was how far apart she and Michael were these days, that Didier's nationalistic barbs could make her feel closer to Michael than she had in a long time.

And Michael hadn't even noticed her help. He stared straight at Didier. "My ideas are conservative," he said. "I'm designing an information center in the Salle des Quatre Saisons, and my objective is to remain faithful to the original architecture."

"Don't you love the *main* information center?" Patrice asked, laughing, obviously relieved the tension had been defused. "With that big sign telling you how to get from A to B, where to find the toilets, where to find the gift shop, where to find the *Mona Lisa*? As if those are the only things people come to see."

"In a way they are," Michael said. "According to what officials tell me, most people visit the Louvre to see two things: the *Mona Lisa* and the *Venus de Milo*."

"Neither of which is French," Didier said. "Italian and Greek."

"Oh, *chéri*," Patrice said. "Don't be a poophead."

"I apologize to you, Michael, and to you, Lydie," Didier said. "But every time I think of that pyramid, I want to kill people. It spoils the Louvre for me—I may never visit it again. Imagine how you would feel if a great American monument—the U.S. Capitol, for instance—were to be changed irrevocably. By the whims of some politician! An American Mitterand! Imagine how you would feel if they built towers rising from the tips of the Capitol's east and west wings. Wouldn't that make you sick?"

"It would," Michael said.

Washington: it was where Lydie and Michael had fallen in love. Lydie had to look away from him. He sounded so eager to please Didier: a supplicant. Finding fault with him seemed the only way to stop taking all the blame herself. Things had started going wrong after her father's death, when she had felt too shocked and hurt to let Michael help her. But now she wondered: why hadn't he tried harder? Now they were stuck in a holding pattern of silences and misunderstandings. She didn't want to think it, but was this how it felt to fall out of love?

"You know, I am very glad to talk to you about this," Didier said. "I am very happy we agree." He shook Michael's hand, then reached for Lydie's and held it for a minute.

"Secretly Didier thinks all Americans are a little tacky," Patrice said. "Even me."

Did she mean it? Lydie wondered. She couldn't tell; everyone was smiling.

"I was so happy to bring Patrice to France," Didier said. "Did she tell you we fell in love very fast?"

"She did," Lydie said, full of her own memories.

"So did they," Patrice said.

"After we grew up," Michael said, not looking at Lydie. "She hardly noticed me in high school."

"Because you loved the hoop," Didier said.

‌✑

Dinner was perfect. First they ate oysters, oysters that surprised Lydie by their tangy freshness, considering it was June, a month without an "R," when oysters were supposedly out of season. But Didier assured them that the "R" business was an invention of Brittany oystermen who wanted to make the shellfish seem scarce, thus driving up the price. He had bought these oysters himself from a man who brought them to Paris twice weekly from Arcachon.

Next they ate leg of lamb. "*Pré-salé*"—lamb that had grazed on the salt marshes of Normandy. Didier stood at the head of the table. He clamped a sterling silver instrument to the shin bone and, gripping its handle, held the leg in place for carving.

"What a wonderful thing!" Michael said. He admired the art of carving. His father had always carved the Thanksgiving turkey at the table, unlike Lydie's father, who had preferred to sit at the table's head telling stories while her mother carved in the kitchen.

"Do you like this?" Didier asked when the meat had been neatly sliced onto a china platter. He began unscrewing the instrument.

"It's great. What is it?"

"It is a *gigot*-holder. I will give it to you." Wiping the holder on his napkin, Didier handed it to Michael.

"Thank you," Michael said. He grinned at Didier, who grinned back, and Lydie had to admit that her husband really knew how to accept a gift. Lydie herself would have demurred, going on about how she couldn't possibly accept such a thing. She might have even said "expensive thing."

"Patrice told me you're the stylist who arranged those photos of our pearl choker," Didier said to Lydie.

"Yes, I did." Lydie laid down her fork.

"I liked them very much," Didier said. "Where did you learn so much about jewelry? We have stylists we've used for years who never get it right."

"I really don't know anything about jewelry," Lydie said. "But I'm glad you liked the layout."

"Lydie's family thinks she went through a postadolescent transformation," Michael said. "They claim she loved the outdoors and cars, never cared a thing about clothes or jewelry."

"Why can't a woman care about all of those things?" Didier asked, frowning. "Great women do, all the time. They are passionate about the issues that interest them, they know how to shoot and fish . . ."

"Or sail," Patrice said. "Or drive cars . . ."

Didier nodded. "And they know how to come indoors and make themselves and their homes beautiful."

"Don't Americans just love to categorize?" Patrice asked. "Haven't you realized that since you've been here?"

Michael shrugged. "Maybe about some things, but I wasn't categorizing Lydie. I was just trying to give you an idea of how everyone felt when she went off to college with a backpack and hiking boots and came home with style."

"Maybe you didn't mean for that to come out the way it did," Lydie said, laughing nervously.

Michael gazed at her, a troubled expression in his brown eyes, but Didier was nodding. "Now I have your point. We know the old story about an ugly little duck who grows up to be a swan. In any case, Lydie, I want to suggest a collaboration with you. Would you come to my office next week?"

"I'd love to," Lydie said, smiling, staying in her place as long as it took to be polite. Then, rising, she asked to be excused.

"The bathroom is that way," Patrice said, pointing down the hall. "All the way to the end, on your left. I assume you want the bathroom? Or are you looking for a telephone to call your lover?"

"He lives in New York," Lydie said. "I'll reverse the charges."

"Don't bother, honey," Patrice said in her burlesque voice. "We girls have to stick together."

In the bathroom Lydie leaned against the black marble sink and reflected on Didier's ideal: a woman complete with compassion, athletic skills, and a sensitivity to beauty. She believed in the accuracy of what Michael had said: that she had been transformed. But Didier's swan metaphor was so much lovelier than the idea that she, Lydie, had gone off to college one sort of woman and come back another.

All along she had just been trying things out. Born and raised a city girl, Catholic to boot, she didn't think it strange that as a teenager she would tutor kids in Harlem. Back in the early seventies when the Woodstock legacy had yielded things like Earth Day and Common Cause, Lydie and her friends had cared about working to make things better—praying for special intentions and sending money to children in Bangladesh never felt real, while teaching Miguel Torres, Reggie Davis, and Zenita Hawkins to read did. Half the time they'd sit around talking instead of reading from *Prose and Poetry,* and Father Griffin, the young priest who'd administered the program, never cared.

She'd talk about boys with Zenita, flirt with the boys and impress them with her knowledge of cars, and talk about Father

Griffin with all of them in the lovestruck way of someone whose greatest pleasure comes from contriving to discuss her beloved.

In college she had lost touch with Father Griffin and those kids. But just because she became an art major and started auto racing didn't mean she had really changed. Standing in Patrice's bathroom, Lydie considered that she had just broadened her horizons.

Michael's talking about transformation scared her, because it meant transforming was on his mind. Everything around them was transforming: the language they now spoke most of each day, her family, their marriage. She believed he was falling out of love with her in stages. Unsteadily, she brushed her hair and walked out of the bathroom.

"Well, *here* you are," Patrice said, coming down the hall, handing Lydie a glass of wine. "I thought you'd hightailed it to New York. To meet *him*."

"Sorry I took so long," Lydie said.

"Don't worry—the boys have adjourned to the salon. We thought we'd take a little rest before dessert." She paused, looking straight into Lydie's eyes. "Is something wrong?"

The question was so direct and Patrice looked so concerned, Lydie could imagine actually telling her the truth. Standing there in the d'Orignys' baronial hall, Patrice would be expecting Lydie to say she had her period, and Lydie would give her an earful about murder and lost love. The drama of it made her smile. "Everything's fine," she said.

"I thought maybe Didier had upset you with that spiel about the Louvre."

"No, not at all," Lydie said, startled. "And I was really happy to hear he liked my work."

"Wait'll you hear about his new project. You're going to love it. I have to say, though, when he got on his high horse about that pyramid, a structure that I find *enchanting*, by the way, I could have smashed him. But he did fall for your husband like a ton of bricks. It's male bonding. They're in there talking vintages right now. It's the old port-and-cigar routine. They'd be just as happy if you and I stayed in the kitchen and gossiped." Patrice touched Lydie's arm. "You sure you don't want to tell me what's bothering you?"

Lydie smiled. "Please—don't worry." She wondered what sort of miserable signals she was giving out, that Patrice could see right through her.

"In that case, let's crash the salon. I could use a nice cigar myself."

# 8

*I shall have to tell you in the end: he is marrying, on Sunday, in the Louvre, with the King's permission, Mademoiselle, Mademoiselle de ... Mademoiselle ... guess the name.*

—To Coulanges, December 1670

On Tuesday, when the Louvre was closed to tourists, Michael walked through the empty galleries with a blueprint rolled in his left hand. He envisioned where the information table would stand; in which direction the signs to bathrooms, the *Mona Lisa,* and the Way Out would point; the bold print he had chosen for the signs, copied from a seventeenth-century manuscript. This was not major change.

Back in New York he had imagined doing something wild, a design that would remind everyone that the Louvre had once been a palace. But George Reed had gotten the inside word: stay calm, no surprises, remember that the Louvre is a museum, an institution, not a palace any longer. Michael thought of Didier d'Origny, whose mentality was probably representative of the

French in general; Didier had liked Michael's plans. Yet Michael knew the whole thing was political, that some French architect would probably be tapped to succeed him. He could imagine the French press treating it as the victory of France over America.

Footsteps echoed in a far-off gallery. The fact that they belonged to one person, not the hundreds he was used to hearing most days, made him take notice. He wondered whether it could be Anne. He had seen her earlier, heading up to the third floor. In the week or so since her fall, her bruises had faded. She had smiled, waved to him. She had looked pretty, dressed all in white, a ribbon tied in her hair. Seeing her, Michael had wondered why he never tried to talk to her. But of course he knew the answer: talking to her would be the first step toward giving in to his fantasy.

He was mulling that one over when Arthur Chase, a cultural coordinator from the American Embassy, entered the Salle des Quatre Saisons.

"Hey, Mike," Arthur said, coming forward to shake hands.

Michael noticed his suit, cut in the square, comfortable American style, and felt too informal in his khakis and sports jacket. Arthur was about fifty, a college friend of George's, and Michael knew George set stock in the way men dressed. "Do American diplomats get instant access to the Louvre?" Michael asked, hearing himself sound too jovial.

"It helps if you know the guard," Arthur said. "Actually, I'm here for a meeting with a curator, but I wanted to see you first."

"I'm just pacing out the information center that may never be," Michael said.

"Don't be too sure of that," Arthur said.

"What do you mean?" Michael asked.

"I mean our cultural office is talking tough with their cultural office."

"Listen," Michael said, holding up the blueprint. "I hate to think their arms could be twisted to accept a design they don't like."

"Your plans are not the issue," Arthur said. "Your plans are fine. This is about not wanting an American architect to do this particular project. I thought George explained that to you. It's just the French being macho. *Vive la France,* you see? I think everything would have been fine if the I. M. Pei pyramid hadn't caused such furor. They've been setting you up to take a fall—a very quietly publicized fall, but one that would raise the spirits of legions of young French architects."

"What has changed?"

Arthur checked his watch. "The curators here are starting to cooperate. Slowly but surely."

"Are you positive?" Michael asked, suspicious of how casual Arthur sounded.

"I'm sure. You can get the contractors in here right away. Here's my proof: call George when you get home and tell him what I said."

Michael broke into a wide smile. Arthur, George's old college friend, knew how nervous George was, how he would hang on every word of an explanation and transform it into a promise. "Really?" he asked.

"Really," Arthur said. "Call George. And keep up the good work." He waved and left the room. His footsteps echoed to nothing.

Michael knew where to find a phone. His sneakers made no sound as he ran past the main staircase, past the headless *Victory of Samothrace.* Lydie will like this, he thought, and he called her first. But she was not home. The phone rang and rang, its tone foreign, distinctly French. No phone ringing in the United States made a sound like that, something between a honk and a buzz.

Michael found his international calling card and dialed a lengthy series of numbers. He held the receiver away from his ear, waiting for the circuits to click and connect. The receptionist had just told him George was gone for the day when Anne Dumas walked by.

"Anne!" he said.

"You look happy." She smiled up at him.

"I am. My project is moving along a little better."

"That is good news." She touched his sleeve. "Come talk to me," she said, and Michael knew that she had been waiting for this moment too.

She led him to a staircase in a private section of the Louvre and they sat on the cool steps. Michael's elbows touched the stone wall on one side, Anne's bare arm on the other. He sensed the bareness of that arm right through the fabric of his jacket. She smelled faintly of perfume; she wore no makeup, and Michael noticed the sun had lightened the tips of her short, dark hair.

"How is Madame de Sévigné today?" he asked.

Anne sighed. "She is fine, thank you for asking. It is such a beautiful day out, I think she must be sunning herself in the Tuileries. I sit in my office on the top floor, gazing at the Seine, I envy her for being so free on a summer day." She laughed then, the cutest, most feminine laugh Michael had ever heard. "It is nice of you to play with me."

"Play?"

"Yes, you know—humor me. When I write about history I pretend quite a bit. I pretend to know the person, I pretend to follow her around. Not everyone understands that."

"Does Jean?" Michael asked.

"Oh, Jean." Anne sighed. "He understands, but it makes him impatient. Although we have taken a house in Brittany for August, I am thinking of not going. We are not getting along."

"That's too bad," said Michael, feeling his heart beating hard inside his chest.

"Don't feel too sorry for me. Where will you and your wife go for August?"

"We're staying in Paris."

Anne leaned toward him, touched his sleeve again in a way that seemed to Michael shy and charming. "Ah, my fellow prisoner of the heat. You know that Paris in August is unbearably hot? Do you swim?"

"Yes, but not in the Seine," Michael said, knowing the remark was stupid as soon as he said it.

"Actually one can swim *on* the Seine—at the Piscine Deligny. Do you know it? It's that great barge tethered to the quai, across the Pont de la Concorde."

Michael knew it; Lydie called it the "Floating Pickup Joint" because the one time they had tried to swim there the entire pool had been packed with attractive people standing in chest-high water. None of the lanes were free for swimming. The impression was of bodies slick with suntan oil, a cacophony of voices, the water turquoise and sparkling.

"I don't think it's possible to swim at Piscine Deligny," Michael said. "To wade, yes."

Anne laughed. "Oh, did you go there on a Saturday or Sunday? It's terrible then. Instead you must go early on a weekday, because then it is empty. I go three mornings a week and swim laps. You should try it."

"Maybe I will," Michael said. He stared at Anne, willing her to look at him. If she did, he would kiss her. But she seemed to be gazing at his hand, at the fingers of his left hand. One of which wore a wedding ring.

∽◦∾

Lydie had to pass the Louvre to get to d'Origny Bijoutiers. She glanced up, wishing she had time to stop in to see Michael, but she was nearly late for her appointment with Didier. That sort of unplanned visit was the sort of thing Michael loved, the sort of thing they had done constantly when they were first married. But Lydie didn't berate herself, the way she would have just days ago, before dinner at Patrice's. She felt good, excited about her meeting; she didn't want to waste time feeling sorry for anything. She just hurried along, wondering how the meeting would go.

The d'Origny offices overlooked the Place Vendôme, the view from the front window bisected by the great bronze column. To Lydie, this was the most refined spot in Paris. The architecture was grand and pristine and uniform. Across the Place stood the Ritz. She crossed her legs and imagined her stockings were real silk. Except for the receptionist, Lydie had seen only men so far, and it struck her as funny that a jewelry company would employ no women.

"Madame McBride?" the receptionist said after five minutes. She tilted her head in a discreet manner and led Lydie down a walnut-paneled corridor to an office with an even larger window facing the Place.

"What a view!" she said to Didier, who was coming around his Louis XVI escritoire to kiss her cheeks. He seemed to bend from the waist, he was so tall. His black suit was impeccable, certainly custom-tailored, the perfect garment to wear to an office on the Place Vendôme.

"You know, it is beautiful," Didier said, frowning as he faced the window, "but it is a fucking bore. Nothing happening out there. Just rich Americans going in and out of the Ritz."

Lydie laughed. "Rich Americans crossing the Place to buy baubles from you."

Didier scowled. "You would think so, but they come into the store looking for trinkets—little things like keychains and money clips that would make souvenirs for the people back home." Then his face relaxed into an easy smile. "But some want the big pieces. More Japanese and Arabs than Americans, these days."

"So, how can I help you?" Lydie asked.

"We just fired the man who was going to direct our next series of advertisements, and I would like you to take over."

"What was wrong with his work?"

"Everything," Didier said. "And I'll tell you, we're willing to sink a lot of money into these ads. We want to update the company a little. I've finally convinced the board that our image is too staid."

"Did your father start this business?" Lydie asked.

"My father's great-great-grandfather started it. He was jeweler to the last King of France. Yes—many of the crowns and scepters you see in the Louvre were designed by our house."

"And the offices have always been in this building?"

"Oh, yes." Didier laughed. He motioned Lydie to a tufted satin sofa and sat beside her. He lit a cigarette. "But of course the Place was not always so grand. It was just a swamp, and monks used to come here to bugger each other. They were cruising through the mud for pickups. You know, there were a lot of monks in Paris in those days, and many of them had their dwellings on the Rue de Castiglione, which then was just a dirt path. The intellectual monks on one side, and the brute monks on the other side. They drove each other crazy."

"With lust?" Lydie asked.

"Absolutely," Didier said. "Those guys were always getting it up the ass."

Lydie smiled, a little shocked that Didier would say such rude things about monks. She watched him reach for a black lizard portfolio and spread some photographs across his knees.

"These are the pictures I was telling you about," he said. Lydie examined the photographs, which showed set and unset jewels arranged on abstract forms covered with black velvet. A diamond and ruby tiara; a necklace of important sapphires; two unset diamonds; a brooch of diamonds and sapphires in the unsettling shape of an eye. All were wedged, nestled, or draped within folds of black velvet in a manner Lydie supposed the stylist had intended to be sensual.

"It's a little unimaginative," she said.

"It's a bore," Didier said. "It's like going into a jewelry store and asking to see the rings and watching the salesman hold out the display case."

"I think the stylist wanted the jewelry to speak for itself," Lydie said. "I mean, each piece is so striking." She couldn't stop staring at the eye.

"Of course it's striking—it's fucking diamonds, for heaven's sake. Look, we don't need to sell the jewels. They do that for themselves. But we need to perpetrate creativity, and we need to have a little fun."

"A little fun is good," Lydie said.

"I mean, that piece you did on Bulgarian royalty was fun. That old dutchess with the seven chins and the pearl choker hidden somewhere in there. I liked that."

Lydie smiled. She didn't bother to correct him, to tell him the dutchess had been Hungarian.

"You should know that the magazine editor was responsible for printing that photo," Lydie said. "I had another shot, one that I preferred, of the choker in the dutchess's jewelry chest. At least as boring as black velvet."

"Not so," Didier said, shaking his head. "Everyone wants to look inside a dutchess's jewel chest. That is fascinating. I would consider it a privilege, as long as you didn't rearrange what was there to make it more interesting or photogenic. Did you rearrange anything?"

"Yes," Lydie said.

"Well, that is the illusion. It is disappointing to know after the fact, but no one who read *Vogue* that month would have guessed.

Except maybe another stylist—the rest of us would have been fooled. So, what do you think? Can you put my jewelry into a story?"

"A story?" Lydie asked.

"A tale. Something that will live off the page."

Lydie sat back, thinking of the possibilities. She found jewelry one of the best items to style with; because it could be moved, worn, displayed so imaginatively, it was much easier to work with than, say, brass lamps or crystal animals. Telling a story to show off jewelry would be a cinch. She thought of fairy tales, with queens and princesses wearing sapphire crowns, of a jewel thief escaping on the Orient Express, of a space explorer zooming through constellations of diamonds. Yet Lydie had not accepted a major project since moving to Paris. She had taken on small assignments that might require an hour or two of research and an afternoon of shooting, things that could be wrapped in a day.

She thought back to that evening on the quai when she had stood on her toes to kiss Michael. She remembered feeling a shivery sense of change, a hint of life getting back to normal. She had that same sense now. Didier sat across the desk from her regarding her with—what? She gazed back at him and decided it was appreciation. Lydie remembered his ideal, many-faceted woman, and wondered whether she measured up. She smiled at Didier.

"Yes?" Didier asked.

"Yes," Lydie said. They shook on it.

❧

Michael sat on the terrace, looking over the Seine. It was ten o'clock and still not dark. A barge slid by, its engine thudding gently. Voices, jolly and a little raucous, carried up from the quai, and then they were gone. He stared at his book, not reading it. Lydie moved around inside, cleaning up after dinner.

He looked down the river, wondering where Anne lived. In the kitchen the water had stopped running; that meant Lydie had finished and would soon be out. What did it mean, that he would rather fantasize about Anne than spend time with his own wife? He saw Anne in his mind: so soft and small, nude, instantly responsive to his touch. He imagined his hand resting on the base of her back, where it curved into her ass.

Here came Lydie, pulling a chair close. He thought of touching Lydie, of how she responded to his touch: she tightened. She didn't exactly pull away, but she drew into herself. She didn't want to be touched. Making love, she felt stiff, all bones and joints. Remembering how it used to be, how his secret image at the moment of coming with Lydie had been a mouth—kissing, open, warm and wet—he had to look away from her.

"I'm looking forward to working with Didier," she said.

"It sounds good," Michael said. He felt inflated with desire for Anne; it actually hurt to talk to Lydie.

"He's going to give me free rein. At least he says so now, but you know how people get. I'll come up with something, then just watch. He'll get into the spirit and start taking over. It always happens. Do you think it's a mistake to work for a friend of ours? Remember Billy Jenkins?"

Michael glanced at her. She seemed open, enthusiastic about her work again, quite a counterpoint to the shuttered, introspective Lydie of the past year. "Billy Jenkins?" he asked.

"Yes, remember? He married Oona Lydon, that girl from my high school class. Remember I did a brochure for his motel chain and he refused to pay?"

"I'm sure Didier d'Origny is good for his debts," Michael said.

Lydie snapped to look at him. "Of course he is—I'm not saying that. But the business with Billy has totally ruined my friendship with Oona, and I wouldn't want that to happen with Patrice. What's wrong?"

"Nothing," Michael said. He felt all twisted, deliberately misunderstanding Lydie so she would turn against him, allowing him to justify what he was about to do to her and their marriage.

"Michael," she said, her voice conveying a warning.

He stared into space. Could it be possible that now, just as Lydie was turning a corner, he didn't want her anymore? Lydie, whom he had loved since high school, when she was too high-minded to pay attention to him, a jock?

"Is it my imagination?" she asked. "Or are you mad at me?"

"I'm not mad at you," Michael said. That was true: he was long past being mad at her. He knew that he should try to explain the way he felt, the way his anger had turned into frustration and then into indifference. But talking about it might make things better between them and that would mean giving up his dreams of Anne.

"I wouldn't blame you if you were," Lydie said. "Sometimes I hate myself. I think about what happened: how I'm a grown woman in my thirties and I let my life fall apart just because my father died. I mean, that's not normal."

"He didn't just die, Lydie." Michael glanced at her, watched her tuck her hair behind her ears, felt tender in spite of himself.

"Sometimes I think I had a nervous breakdown," she said. "The way I just stopped functioning."

"Well, except for the first couple of weeks you didn't stop functioning."

"No, I have. I just haven't been *feeling* things. I mean, I get up in the morning and do my work, but that's about it. I'm in a daze all the time."

"I guess maybe coming to Paris was a mistake," Michael said. "I thought getting you out of New York would be the best thing. But you weren't ready to leave."

"It's not really fair to say we came to Paris because of me, because you wanted to get me out of New York," Lydie said. "We came because of your work."

"That's true," Michael said grudgingly, because that certainly wasn't all of it. But did she know how hard he had pushed to get it, thinking a year in Paris would be just what she needed to forget?

"I used to think coming here was a mistake," Lydie said. "But I'm changing my mind. I'm starting to feel better. I feel like . . ."

She laughed.

"What?"

"I feel just fine," she said. The way she smiled at him he could tell she thought the tension between them had lifted. He smiled back, then pretended to read his book. He thought of Lydie in her school uniform, the skirt a muddy purple tartan he'd never seen since. She had carried her books in a khaki knapsack and worn hiking boots to school every day, somehow managing to look more beautiful and sexy than any of the other girls. It still hurt to recall that he had asked her out twice and been turned down both times.

Michael remembered how she had followed Father Griffin around. Her crush on him was so blatant, the way she hung around his office, took up any cause he espoused. The way she'd follow him anywhere and tutor so-called kids. Half of them were older than Lydie. Most of them had been kicked out of school and many of them were criminals. Michael remembered the time one guy grabbed Lydie's purse—while she was sitting right there, trying to teach him fractions—and took all her money. The news of it had circulated quickly through the school.

Michael had stopped Father Griffin in the hallway a couple of days later. He had the heaviest beard Michael had ever seen;

Michael remembered thinking it unseemly for a priest to look as though he needed a shave at ten in the morning. "Teaching the hoods anything new these days, Father?" Michael asked.

"They don't have the advantages you do, Michael."

"No, but I hear they've got a new pair of boots, thanks to Lydie Fallon."

"Maybe that boy really needed that money—maybe his family was hungry."

"Probably starving."

"We weren't put on this earth to judge him," Father Griffin said. "Why don't you come with us next week? Maybe you'll learn something."

"You didn't even call the cops, did you?" Michael asked.

"Lydie didn't want to," Father Griffin said.

Because you didn't want her to, Michael remembered thinking. Now with hindsight, he could recognize his resentment for what it was: jealousy that Lydie loved Father Griffin instead of him. He gazed at her. She stared across the Seine, the *Herald Tribune* folded in her lap.

"Remember when your student stole your money?" Michael asked.

Lydie turned to him. "I haven't thought of that in ages," she said.

"Why didn't you turn him in?"

She frowned. "I don't remember. I guess because I felt sorry for him."

"I've always thought it was because the priest told you not to."

"Father Griffin? Oh, I don't think he'd have done that. But I have to admit, when I think of the sixties, I think of him. Peace, love, brotherhood, all that."

"He was hot for you," Michael said.

"I know," Lydie said.

"You do?" Michael asked, surprised.

"I used to imagine seducing him—all the time. We'd be alone in a subway car and the lights would go out, and I'd close my eyes and will him to kiss me."

"Did he?"

"Never. The most he'd do was touch the back of my hand when he was trying to make a point. My father never trusted him."

Michael smiled. "That's perfect. Neil seeing the dark side of a priest. I'll bet he saw right through him, realized your virtue was at stake."

"He said he thought Father Griffin shaved with a rusty razor so he'd always have five o'clock shadow. My father thought anyone with five o'clock shadow was suspect. He called Father Griffin a ladies' man, said he'd quit the priesthood before he turned forty."

"I wonder if he did," Michael said.

Lydie nodded. "Sally Quinlan saw him once with his wife and two kids. Twin boys. At Playland, can you imagine?"

"Perfect," Michael said, laughing. He looked over at Lydie, thought about taking her hand. He wondered whether Father Griffin knew she'd married him.

"So," Lydie said. "Tomorrow I'll start Didier's project. What's on your agenda?"

"I have a meeting tomorrow morning. With some guy who's expert at repairing mosaics. And I planned to swim before work."

"Swim?" Lydie asked.

"At that pool on the river. I've been thinking I need exercise," Michael said, feeling sad and excited by all it implied.

❧

The next afternoon, Lydie walked along the quai toward Notre Dame. She was thinking about the ad series. What if they photographed the jewels worn by people at a fancy dress ball? She had her eyes open for props: gowns, feathers, masks, medals, anything festive and gaudy.

In the heart of Paris, thrilled by her new assignment, she suddenly remembered the night Michael had told her he had been chosen to work on the Louvre. Her first reaction, before she realized it meant leaving her mother, was delight. She remembered holding each other, dancing in circles like lunatics, Michael saying "I can't believe it" over and over again, Lydie saying "I *knew* you were a great architect." Michael had brought home champagne. They had drunk the bottle, drinking toasts that were silly, pompous, and serious. "To the Eiffel Tower," "to great architects everywhere," "to a graffiti-free Métro," "to the most romantic city in the world," "to our year in Paris." That's when she had realized that it meant leaving.

In spite of what she said to Michael last night, she knew that he had intended their Paris year to cheer her up. Did Michael have any idea how hard it was to rearrange her mind, to start thinking of her father as a murderer? Neil the good father, the family man, the jolly Irishman, the adulterer, the murderer. If Lydie shared Didier's opinion that complexity was desirable, why couldn't she accept the fact that her father had had a hidden side? For no matter how she tried, she couldn't find any hint, in anything her father had ever said or done, that he could be capable of killing himself and someone else.

And her mother. Where widows were respected and looked after by family and old friends, allowed to reminisce mistily about their husbands, Julia was shunned. In a way she brought it on herself; she felt so ashamed, she assumed people wanted nothing to do with her. She stopped going to the retired teachers' luncheons; she quit the St. Anthony's Ladies' Auxiliary. The saddest part was that she still loved Neil, couldn't bear to hear anything

bad about him. Well-meaning friends might say she was better off
without him, but she didn't see it that way.

For the first time, Lydie thought that maybe coming to Paris
*was* the best thing. If she were in New York, Julia wouldn't be
forced to go out on her own. She would rely on Lydie to comfort
her. She would eat dinner with Lydie and Michael, as she had
nearly every night in the months before they left for France, sometimes drinking so much wine that she would fall asleep on the sofa
and stay there all night, fully dressed, under the blanket Lydie
would spread over her.

Walking along, Lydie felt happy to be free of all that, distracted
by the sights of Paris. She passed shops that catered to tourists,
purveyors of T-shirts imprinted with images of the Arc de Tri-
omphe, duty-free perfume, ashtrays in the shape of Notre Dame,
last year's scarves from Dior, St. Laurent, and Givenchy. Then she
came to the Quai de Megisserie, the animal market, where cages
of swans, peacocks, Rhode Island Red chickens, grouse, quail, and
Canada geese lined the sidewalk. The cages seemed cruelly small.
She stopped before a pair of swans.

"How much to rent these swans?" she asked the proprietor.

"These are beautiful swans," the man replied.

"Yes, but how much?"

While the man considered, Lydie imagined holding the fancy
dress ball at Fontainebleau or Versailles, with swans and peacocks
in the background. What if she rented the birds and never
brought them back? They looked so sad in their cages, and Lydie
believed they would probably die soon. Perhaps Didier's budget
would cover the cost of buying them. She imagined Didier and
Patrice at an estate with a lake and swans, and the image made her
smile.

The man named a price. Lydie thanked him and walked along.

"Don't forget me!" the man called. "Come to me when you need swans."

At the corner Lydie calculated that she had already walked halfway to the Place des Vosges. She had a sudden, compelling urge to talk to Patrice. She thought of the alarm she'd begun to feel about Michael, their marriage. She imagined visiting a doctor, presenting her symptoms, listening to the diagnosis. She wanted not friendly advice but reassurance. So she turned away from the Seine, onto a crooked street that would lead to the Marais.

∽

"She asks that you wait while she finishes her phone call," Kelly said after she had announced Lydie to Patrice. "Would you like a glass of tea?"

"Yes, please," Lydie said. "Patrice tells me you want to get to the United States."

Kelly stopped still. "Yes, I do," she said.

"How do you plan to do it?" Lydie asked.

"There are many ways," Kelly said. "Some girls marry American servicemen. Or find Americans to sponsor them."

"How does that work?" Lydie asked.

"Oh, you must work for an American, and if you are lucky she will bring you to the States with her. I think she must swear to be responsible for you if you are sick or commit a crime. But the rules are very strict, and even with an American sponsor you do not always get in."

Lydie's mother had left Ireland at the age of twenty-one. Her father had been twenty-four, and that year he had started the business. "How old are you, Kelly?" she asked, knowing she would never ask that question to someone who was not a maid.

"Twenty-seven."

"I mentioned you to my mother," Lydie said. "She immigrated to the United States a long time ago."

"Did she arrive with nothing? Does she live there still?" Kelly asked, seeming to hang on every word.

"She arrived with nothing and she lives there still," Lydie said.

"Did she marry an American?"

"No. My father was Irish. Why do you want to get there so badly? Are the Philippines that bad?"

An expression so devout that it could have been a prayer-book illustration of a child in thrall to a vision had crossed Kelly's face. "The Philippines are terrible, but they are our home. So we love them. But everyone wants to get to the States."

"Why? If everyone loves the Philippines so much?"

"The States are the only place you can make money. Filipinos are ambitious. Filipinos dream of a house, fully furnished, a refrigerator, and a freezer full of foods."

"Is your family very poor?" Lydie asked.

"Oh, yes," Kelly said.

They stood there for another minute, but Lydie suddenly felt awkward. "Well, keep trying. At least Patrice is teaching you the computer, so you'll have a skill when you get there."

"Oh, thank you, Mum," Kelly said.

"Why don't you call me 'Lydie'?" Lydie said.

❧

Patrice found Lydie waiting in the living room. She felt keyed up, exactly in the mood to talk. The timing of this visit was just perfect. She wore her black hair swept back with silver combs and a thin cotton caftan instead of her usual shorts or jeans, as if she had had a premonition of this visit.

"Surprise, surprise!" she said.

"I was in the neighborhood," Lydie said.

"This is so great! I was just wishing to see you, and you appear. Didier already called, to tell me he hired you."

"It's fantastic," Lydie said. "I already have ideas . . ."

"Fill me in?"

Lydie shook her head, smiling shyly. "Not quite yet," she said. "On a project like this, I like to keep them to myself at first . . . I'm really thrilled. He gave me absolutely no restrictions."

"That's my Didier," Patrice said. "Patron to the artists, a regular Lorenzo de Medici. He does the same thing with his jewelry designers. Well, I have something to tell you. Today is T minus six and counting."

"What?"

"'T' means 'Tyrant,' alias 'Mother.' She arrives in six days."

"It's that bad?" Lydie asked.

"You'll meet her soon enough," Patrice said, sipping her iced tea. "I suppose you get along great with your mother."

"We have our ups and downs," Lydie said. "But yes, in general."

"Did she give you a hard time about coming to Paris?"

"Not really," Lydie said. "She'd prefer for me to be in New York but she didn't make a fuss."

"God, she sounds eminently reasonable. See, my mother can only understand events in relation to herself. Like, I didn't get married and move to Paris. I left *her*."

"I'm the one who didn't want to come to Paris," Lydie said. "My mother didn't have anything to do with it directly."

Patrice didn't say anything. This was as close as Lydie had ever gotten to telling her anything really personal. She was afraid of saying the wrong thing, spooking Lydie back into privacy.

"I didn't want to leave New York because of . . . a tragedy."

Patrice had never actually heard someone refer to a personal event as a "tragedy" without sounding pompous or maudlin, but she could believe a tragedy had happened to Lydie, who sat across the room, gripping her glass, trying very hard to keep her voice steady and well modulated.

"Are you going to tell me what happened?" Patrice asked.

"My father killed himself. And someone else."

"Oh, Lydie!" Patrice said.

"It came as a big shock," Lydie said. "We were never a dramatic family, in any way. I never heard my parents fight. My father went off to work every morning and came home every night."

"Do you know why he did it?" Patrice asked, fascinated and horrified.

"Well, she was his lover," Lydie said. "Much younger, married herself. With a two-year-old child."

"When?" Patrice said.

"A year ago. It just . . . changed everything. Poor Michael. He's married to a zombie."

"You? You're not a zombie."

Lydie shook her head. "You don't really know me. I'm different around you—it's easy to be. But Michael knows everything. He's been through it all with me. He and my father were very close."

"Well . . ." Patrice said, not knowing what to say.

"I can't make sense of what happened. Michael wants me to. Things have gotten pretty bad between us." She paused, took a breath. "Michael was wonderful to me at the time. Well, he still is. My parents loved him, and he loved them. Michael was the only person my father ever told . . . about the woman."

"Did Michael know what your father planned to do?"

Lydie shook her head.

"What's gotten so bad between you? I thought everything

seemed fine when you came for dinner that night," she said, lying. Afterward she had mentioned to Didier how tense Lydie and Michael had seemed toward each other.

"I let it get in the way of *everything*. I feel numb all the time. I look at Michael and it all comes back to me. I hear my mother's voice on the telephone and I feel guilty for leaving her and for feeling *glad* I left her."

"Doesn't she have friends? Family?"

"Everyone handles this differently," Lydie said. "Her sisters can't quite bear to talk about it."

"Michael is your family too," Patrice said. "He needs you."

"I know," Lydie said, her expression blank. "Isn't it awful? I can take care of my mother, make allowances for her behavior, and I want Michael to do that for me. If I don't feel like going to bed with him, I expect him to understand it's because I'm feeling sad. Or depressed. Or scared."

"I'm sure he does understand," Patrice said.

"I hope so," Lydie said, smiling for the first time since the conversation had begun. "It's a relief to talk about this."

Patrice felt surprised by how happy she felt that Lydie would confide in her. She herself was an only child; only children grew up without anyone to talk to, with barriers of privacy intact without even knowing they existed. So she understood what it took for Lydie to spill such a terrible secret. She wondered whether Lydie had worshiped her father the way Patrice had worshiped hers. Not that he had deserved it: he had left Patrice and her mother when Patrice was four, leaving Eliza hurt and eventually bitter. Patrice knew she gave her mother a bad rap. But when she thought of her father she thought of presents and hugs, and when she thought of her mother she saw a frown. Just a frown, hanging in the air. Like the Cheshire Cat, only upside down and without teeth.

"I feel better," Lydie said.

"I still feel rotten," Patrice said. "It's still T minus six, and counting."

"Maybe things will go wonderfully."

"Let's face it: they never do," Patrice said, full of warmth toward Lydie. It felt so comfortable, talking to her. Was this how it felt to have a sister? That thought just popped into her mind. It must be all this talk about families, she thought.

# 9

*One goes completely naked into a small subterranean
chamber where there is a pipe of hot water controlled by a
woman who directs the flow to whatever part of the body
you wish.*

—To Françoise-Marguerite, May 1675

Michael swam three times before he saw Anne Dumas at the
Piscine Deligny. On his fourth visit he sat in a folding chair reading *Le Monde;* the sun, startlingly hot for such an early hour,
warmed his thighs. His bathing suit was baggy, a red tartan
bought by Lydie at the Tog Shop one summer on Nantucket. The
other men at the nearly deserted pool wore tight spandex suits in
glittery colors: lavender, orange, red. The suits left nothing to the
imagination, and Michael wondered whether his cock would look
so impressive in a suit like that. Michael thought them vulgar, too
obvious, like the mating plumage on peacocks or the scarlet
rumps of great apes. Did women find the style attractive? Only
two women were at the pool so far this morning, both wearing

scanty bikinis. The narrow strips of fabric were a tease, but alluring, not like the men's suits.

Michael stared at one of the women. She was tan, a little plump, so pretty. She smiled at him, and he looked away. God, when had he started ogling sunbathers? His head spun, as if from heatstroke, but Michael knew it was from desire. He felt dirty, as though he were doing something illicit. And wasn't he? He had told Lydie about his plans to swim, much the way a businessman tells his wife the clean details of a business trip: the hotel where he will stay, the meetings he will attend, the presentation he will deliver. Omitting, the way Michael omitted his real reason for coming to the pool, any mention of the female colleague who will be taking the same trip.

Last night, lying beside his sleeping wife, Michael had imagined swimming alongside Anne, reaching for her underwater, kissing her as they sank to the bottom of the pool. He had imagined her breasts, so round and full under the light summer dresses she wore; in the pool the tips would harden to points. He had imagined his erect penis magnified underwater, entering her as she lay on the cool tile. All this action was happening at the bottom of the pool, and Michael found it interesting that the fantasy made him feel so guilty that he was drowning himself and Anne in it.

Yet here he was, back at the pool. And there was Anne, real, in the corner of his eye. His heart raced. He squinted, concentrating on an article about the political right in Lyon.

"Hey, there," she said. "You came."

"Hi," Michael said, trying to sound surprised. He shaded his eyes. She wore a yellow caftan over her bathing suit, green espadrilles on her feet. She grinned; she looked so happy to see him that he rose and kissed her cheek.

"Come on, let's swim," she said. The caftan dropped to the

floor, revealing a turquoise maillot. Michael thought of his fantasies about bikinis and skintight swim trunks, and he laughed. Anne tilted her head, inquisitive, but Michael just smiled. She dove into the pool.

What had seemed so sexual, so unbearably erotic in his fantasy, turned into merely a vigorous workout. Michael swam in the lane beside Anne. Turning his head to take a breath, he glimpsed her legs kicking. A flash of pale thigh, muscular calf; he pulled ahead. He heard his heartbeat echo in his head, unbelievably, slower than it had been when she had first approached on dry land. He was out of shape. He hadn't the energy or strength to think about what could happen, or to make it happen. Instead, he swam as if his life depended on it. As if his ship had sunk a mile out of the harbor and he was fighting against an ebb tide and an undertow to reach the shore.

He couldn't swim anymore. He stopped, treading water, gasping for air. His eyes stung from chlorine, but he scanned the pool, looking for her. There she was, halfway to the other end, stroking steadily. She touched the pool's rim, then kicked off, coming toward him. Easy. Without looking up, she knew exactly where to stop.

"Had enough?" she asked.

He spoke with deliberate smoothness, to give her the idea he had his breath back. "For now."

"It is good for you to start off slowly," she said. "Swimming is the best exercise there is."

"You were right," Michael said. "This place is practically empty."

"Isn't it nice?" Anne said. "Now, let's get out of the water before you die."

They dried their faces on towels, then lay side by side on chaise longues. Michael was silent, his eyes closed, enjoying her closeness. She was right there, the woman he had fallen in love with. He wished the day stretched ahead without appointments. What time was it? Eight-thirty? Nine? He wished that his Louvre project would lead to another, so that he could stay in Paris forever. He felt her take his hand.

He opened his eyes, turned his head to look at her.

"Hi," she said, watching him. She held his hand lightly, as though she wasn't quite sure she wanted him to notice.

He said nothing, only looked.

"We could go somewhere," she said. She smiled, ducked her head. "Oh, it's embarrassing to ask . . ."

"No," Michael said. "It's not. I want to."

"Will you come to my house? It is not far . . ."

Michael wondered whether this was how it felt to be hypnotized. He stood, gathered his towel and newspaper, followed Anne to the bathhouses. If she had told him to bark like a dog, he might have dropped to his knees and howled. She disappeared into one bathhouse, his signal to find his own and get dressed. He moved in slow motion, as though injected with a muscle relaxant. He noticed, with great clarity, the details of his clothes. The waistband of his boxer shorts, his blue boxer shorts, coming apart now, trailing filaments of elastic. His white broadcloth shirt bearing laundry marks from Wong's in New York and the Blanchisserie Clement Marot here in Paris. The madras tie, a gift from Julia.

His trance evaporated the instant he stepped from the dark bathhouse into the bright sunlight. Anne stood there, glowing, the sun on her hair. He went to her, held her face between his hands, kissed her. The kiss was white-hot, fire. Then she touched a cool hand to the back of his neck, making him shiver.

She pulled away. Her smile was gentle, forgiving: it gave him one last chance to get away. He thought of Lydie. He thought her name, "Lydie," and an image of her collarbone, elegant and delicate, came to him. Then Michael, whose romance with Anne had so far taken place in his dreams and imagination, willed his mind to be empty.

"Is it too far to walk?" he asked.

᠃

She lived in an apartment on the second floor of an old, impeccably restored building in the Sixth Arrondissement. It overlooked the rue Jacob, a street so narrow it afforded exquisite intimacy with the building just opposite. Anne walked to the window, to draw the curtain, but Michael stopped her. He stepped onto the balcony, looked up and down the street.

"You must know your neighbors well," he said, gazing across the street into the boudoir of one, the living room of another. He was stalling for time, and he knew it.

"I know everything about every one of them," Anne said. "For example, the man who lives there." She pointed at a window to the left. "Every night at eight o'clock he appears on his balcony in white pajamas. He unwraps a cigar, bites the end off it, and spits it into the street. Then he disappears. And the man who lives there . . ." She pointed at the window exactly opposite. "He is a doctor. On weekdays he lives with his wife, who is fat and blond, but on weekends, when she goes to visit her mother, his mistress, who is fat and blond, moves in."

Michael stared at the doctor's apartment. He kept a red plastic garbage can on the balcony. Also a collection of brooms and mops. Then he noticed the apartment above, which had laundry hanging on a line between two windows. "You'd think the doctor would put a tree or something there instead of cleaning supplies," he said, thinking "mistress."

"That building is a slum," Anne said. "The inhabitants are all well-to-do, but look: laundry hanging out, mops and garbage cans on every balcony." She frowned, perhaps assessing the impression the building made on Michael. He noticed the tension in her shoulders, her neck. She probably wondered what they were doing, standing in front of her window, talking about her neighbors. He hated to think of them living so close, looking in at her.

He put his arms around her, felt a thrill that reminded him of the first time he had touched a girl. Her smallness excited him, and why? Because it symbolized the difference between men and women? Because it reminded him of the year he shot up six inches, discovered sex, had to bend nearly double when dancing with girls in the gym? He lowered his head, kissed her deeply. Her lips felt soft; she tasted so delicious. Everything slid away except the kiss, their mouths, his and Anne's. He wanted the kiss to go on, not stop; exactly the way that other times, during sex, just before coming, he would wish for the feeling to last, or at least recur on demand.

Anne stepped back. She held his forearms, smiled up at him. "I'm glad we are here," she said.

"Yes," Michael said. He glanced around, realized he was looking for the door to her bedroom.

"Would you like a tour of the house?" Anne said, teasing him.

"Okay." He lifted her into his arms. Laughing, she pressed her cheek against his chest. He kissed her hair, which was damp from the pool and smelled of shampoo and chlorine. "Tell me where to go," he said.

"Let's start in that room," she said, pointing to a closed door.

Michael actually held her with one arm as he turned the knob with his other hand; she weighed nothing at all. He felt dizzy, breathless. The room was dark as a cave; heavy curtains blocked the light, and Michael stumbled. Anne clutched his neck; he steadied himself.

"It's an adventure," she said. "We go in there."

"In there?" They stood before what appeared, in the darkness, to be a tent. He brushed the fabric with the back of his hand, found an opening.

"It is my great folly," Anne said, laughing. She tumbled out of his arms. "My bed, can you believe it?"

"Are we playing 'Arabian Nights'?" Michael crawled in after her. It was snug, fantastic. He began to unbutton her blouse. She rolled away from him.

"Not 'Arabian Nights,'" she said, "but there is a fantasy, certainly. This is a canopy bed from the seventeenth century." Anne giggled. "Sometimes I think about it: how many people living at that time could have afforded such a thing? Not many, and one of them was Marie de Sévigné. What if this belonged to her? I don't dare tell you what I paid for it; you would think I am crazy. The curtains are not old; I had them made." She sat erect, handling a fold of the silk damask drapery. The stiff fabric rustled between her fingers. She seemed absent, her mind gone back to the court of Louis XIV.

"It's beautiful," Michael said, lying back.

He sensed, rather than saw or felt, Anne. And he felt sad, because he knew that, although he was about to make love with her, the great moment of romance had passed. He was wide awake. His own mood had slammed into Anne's. There she was, upright, conjuring characters who had died centuries ago. He still wanted her, even though she was crazy. She unzipped his pants, lowered her mouth to his erection. Shivering, Michael closed his eyes. He reached for her shoulders; five minutes ago, this would have been exactly what he wanted.

# 10

*I hear that there is a constant round of pleasure, but not a
moment of genuine enjoyment.*

—To Françoise-Marguerite, June 1680

The ball would be magnificent, Lydie decided. She had located a château in the Loire Valley, whose owners, a titled though
impoverished elderly couple, rented it to paying guests by the day,
weekend, or week. The eighteenth-century château stood in a
park, surrounded by a moat, at the edge of a forest. It overlooked
a swanless lake.

"It's up to you," she said over the phone to Didier. "It's rather
expensive, but I think it's the perfect backdrop for our ball."

"You say they will rent it for the weekend?" Didier asked.

"Yes."

"Then let's take it from Friday night through Sunday and make
a country-house weekend of it. Hold the ball on Saturday night
and shoot the ads then. We justify the expense of the château by
using friends as guests instead of paid actors."

"That's clever," said Lydie, who had been thinking the same thing. "When do you think we should stage it? After August, when people are back from vacation?"

"Absolutely. After the *rentrée,* at the end of September. Give people something to look forward to." Lydie heard him clucking at his end of the wire. "Especially Patrice," he said. "I suppose she has told you about her mother? Last night I had to give a tranquilizer to the poor girl."

"I know she seems to be under a strain," Lydie said. She had not yet met Mrs. Spofford, and although she knew that some women did not like their mothers, she thought Patrice's bad reaction to her mother's arrival petulant and mean. Patrice had said her mother didn't travel easily. Lydie wondered how Mrs. Spofford must feel, coming to Europe to visit her only daughter and finding her furious. Patrice had said to Lydie, "I'm in a killing rage anytime she's in the room."

"I am mad about your ideas," Didier said. "In marketing meetings I tell my managers, 'Take a look at *this* plan, you assholes.' Listen, we will divide the guest list in two. You invite half, I invite half."

"Michael and I don't know that many people in Paris," Lydie said. "We'll ask ten guests, you can have the rest. Will Patrice's mother still be here?"

"God willing, no," Didier said.

When she hung up the phone, Lydie took notes on ideas for the ball. If the weather was fine, perhaps they could hold it outdoors. She would have to arrange for a sumptuous banquet. She envisioned oysters, spider crabs, a roast capon, something *en croute,* platters of *tartes,* Paris-Brest, and petits fours. Every guest would be required to come in costume, and she needed a theme. Eighteenth century? Subjects of famous paintings? The court of Louis XIV?

She left a question mark after the word "theme." She would have to visit the château again, to get a feel for the possibilities.

This project would take the place of Lydie's August vacation, and it was just as well, considering that Michael's work on the Louvre had shifted into high gear. Just as the rest of Paris was winding down, preparing for the great exit when every minister, cabdriver, waiter, executive, and concierge took off for Ile de Ré, Saint-Tropez, Arcachon, Biarritz, or Deauville, Lydie and Michael would be digging in. Paris would be a ghost town, like New York on a hot Sunday in July. The blare of horns on Avenue Montaigne would cease; the few restaurants that remained open would be quiet and relaxed. She could stroll through the garden at the Musée Rodin and find an empty bench. They could stand directly in front of Manet's *Déjeuner sur l'herbe* for as long as they pleased without being jostled. The idea of it made Lydie feel luxurious, and she put down her pen and stretched.

She knew that Patrice and Didier planned to spend all August at Saint-Tropez with Mrs. Spofford, and for the first time Lydie wondered about Kelly. Would she go with them? Or would Patrice give her August off? Lately the thought of Kelly had made Lydie frown, and she wasn't sure why.

The telephone rang, and Lydie answered on the third ring. "Come out to lunch with us," Patrice said, an edge of desperation in her voice. "I need you."

∽

They sat beneath a red umbrella in the courtyard of the Hôtel Diaz de la Peña. Ivy covered the four walls and cascaded from romantic, asymmetrically positioned iron balconies and stone balustrades. Lydie saw red everywhere: the umbrella, the pots of geraniums, the lipstick worn by Patrice and her mother.

"This was always my favorite hotel in Paris," Mrs. Spofford said in a voice that was at once warm and regal. She appeared much too young to be Patrice's mother. Her skin was unlined, powdered white, and her hair was honey-blond. Where Patrice was dark-haired and large, even robust, her mother was fair with a delicacy that bordered on frailty. Lydie could not take her eyes off the woman's wrists, which were thin, elegant, graceful as a ballerina's. The way Mrs. Spofford moved them made Lydie think she too was aware of them. And Patrice as well. How could they support the weight of those bracelets? All three women were captivated by Mrs. Spofford's wrists. It hurt Lydie to look at Patrice, whose anger was a mask blazing with too much eye shadow and lipstick. Like her mother, Patrice wore an armful of gold bracelets. Mother and daughter wore Chanel suits. "Patsy's father thought this hotel flashy, but I adored it."

"She calls me 'Patsy,'" Patrice said. "Didier just loves that."

"Well, dear, your name is 'Patricia.'" A subtle emphasis on the "is."

"Mother, has it ever crossed your mind that 'Patricia' in French is 'Patrice'? When a 'Pierre' moves to Boston he is called 'Peter.' Get it? You have to conform to the culture."

"Whatever," Mrs. Spofford said, turning to Lydie. "Where are you from, dear?"

"New York City, originally. Still, I guess. My husband and I are only here for a year."

"A year in Paris! How marvelous! I spent a year in Paris my junior year abroad. But how much better to have the additional perspective of being an adult. You appreciate more, don't you? I see it in Patsy: she has absolutely melted into France. Her accent is flawless."

"How was your trip, Mrs. Spofford?" Lydie asked.

"Oh, call me Eliza. You make me feel so old. It was fine, thank you for asking. So much easier, now that Air France flies out of

Logan. I only wish we had more time in Paris, instead of going straight to the Riviera."

"Imagine," Patrice said. "Having to spend a month at a house built into the cliff overlooking the sea. With a saltwater pool. Torture."

"Darling," Eliza said. "Saint-Tropez is lovely. But there is so much I want to do in Paris—I want to see that ghastly pyramid, I want to spend a day at least in the Musée d'Orsay, sitting right in front of those Degas horses. And I want to visit dear Sainte Chapelle, which has been closed the last two times I visited you. Is that unreasonable?"

"How do you know it's ghastly if you haven't even seen it?" Patrice asked, lighting a cigarette. At that moment the waiter brought their first course, *salade de langoustines;* Patrice gave him a dirty look, as if she thought his timing was deliberate, and put out the cigarette.

"Patrice loves the pyramid," Lydie said.

"Didier tells me your husband was chosen out of an enormous field of architects to work on the Louvre," Eliza said. "I think that is stunning. I don't know anyone who's worked on the Louvre."

"Thank you. I'll tell him you said so," Lydie said.

"This is delicious, isn't it, Patsy?" Eliza said.

Patrice said nothing. She prodded a *langoustine* with her fork. Lydie felt her stomach tighten as Patrice craned her neck, looking for a waiter. Don't do it, Lydie thought, willing her friend to behave.

"This fish is not fresh," Patrice said to the waiter. "Send over the maître d'."

"Madame, I shall take care of it myself," the waiter said, gathering the plates. Eliza Spofford wore an expression of pure astonishment.

"Put those plates down and send me the maître d'," Patrice said, her voice rising.

"Right away, madame," the waiter said. He hurried away.

"My dear, they are fine," Eliza said. "Maybe a tinge of iodine, but that's par for the course with crustaceans. Now, don't spoil a nice lunch."

Patrice no longer looked angry, but she looked bold, as if she had a mission. "How can we have a nice lunch if the fish is bad? You know what happens if one eats bad fish? One vomits, and one has to spend the day in bed." To the maître d', who had been standing by, she said in a cool tone, "We don't come to a restaurant like this to eat rotten *langoustines*. Bring us something different."

"What would madame desire?"

"Don't give me that shit," Patrice said. "Look in your larder and bring us whatever is fresh."

Lydie looked away. Although the red umbrella blocked direct sun, it absorbed the heat, and Lydie felt sweat on her brow. The atmosphere was airless.

"I think I'll take this opportunity to powder my nose," Eliza said, pushing back her chair, striding with dignity into the hotel lobby.

"Those *langoustines* were perfectly fine," Lydie said. "I think you're acting like a jerk."

"Fuck you. Didn't you see the expression on her face as she said how delicious it was? Pure distaste. Believe me, she would have suffered through it, and tonight she would have told Didier it tasted like iodine."

"It was delicious. Why did you invite your mother to visit you if you're going to be mean the entire time?"

"Listen, I know you love your mother, and I think you're lucky. But all my love goes to Didier, not my mother. You don't know her. She is perfectly capable of being pleasant at a little luncheon. I know what's happening—you'll leave here thinking I'm cruel, one of those parent abusers they're starting to write about in *People* magazine."

"I don't think that," Lydie said. She was silent, looking across the wide table at Patrice. "I know it's hard for you. She seems really nice, but I believe you if you tell me she's not."

"She's not."

"She's beautiful. She looks so young."

Patrice snorted. "She's been face-lifted to within an inch of her life. And before you start thinking she's so wonderful, let me tell you what she's going to say about you when we get home. She'll say you're 'cute' in a way that makes it clear you're not beautiful. And she'll say you're 'youthful' in a way that makes it clear you're not sophisticated. And she'll ask me where in New York City you're from, because she knows it's not the East Side."

Lydie laughed. "You're convincing me. She's not nice."

"Keep that in mind."

"Okay, but *you* act nice. I mean it. It's only a month out of your life, and someday you'll regret it if she leaves on bad terms."

"Lydie, I'll do it for you," Patrice said.

"It's only fair," Lydie said. "I want to give back a little of what I've learned from you."

"That's me, a fountain of knowledge," Patrice said, lifting her eyebrows in puzzlement. "What am I missing here?"

"I'm thinking about you and Didier. You two are really on your own. Where I come from, a marriage comes complete with two entire families. Especially when there's a problem, like in my family. It seems to take up so much time."

Patrice smiled. "You mean we're good influences on you and Michael."

"On me, anyway," Lydie said. "Michael didn't have any trouble breaking away, coming to France."

"Of course not, my dear," Patrice said. "Over here he gets you all to himself."

Lydie laughed. Wasn't it nice to think that way? Then Eliza

returned, excited, saying that she had just run into an old business
acquaintance of Patrice's father in the lobby, a handsome man visiting Paris with the wife to whom he had been married for forty years:
so unusual for a marriage or the parties involved to survive so long!
Then the waiter brought plates of *coquilles St. Jacques,* warm, on a
bed of sauteed leeks; the maître d' poured wine and offered his
deepest apologies; Patrice began to relax. She smiled at her mother.
She inquired about her aunts and about her godmother, Eliza's best
friend. Lydie watched Patrice, knowing she would miss her terribly
when she went to Saint-Tropez. Patrice had a different way of looking at the world, and Lydie was happy to absorb some of it. Mainly,
she was happy to have such a good friend in Paris.

⌒

Michael stood behind partitions that roughly defined the space
that one day would be the Salle des Quatre Saisons, making a list
of people to call: cabinetmaker, stonemason, electrician. He had
lined up workmen and artisans, and the French government had
finally issued papers authorizing the work to be done. He yawned;
the pen felt heavy in his hand. The sleepless exhilaration that
came with being in love was taking a slow toll. At night he would
lie awake beside Lydie, thinking of Anne. Remembering what had
passed between them that day, and not only lovemaking: the
expression in her eyes when she smiled up at him, the thrill he'd
felt at lunch yesterday when she'd reached under the café table to
take his hand.

A guard came around the partitions. His navy blue uniform
looked vaguely military, with its insignia and silver buttons, and it
reminded Michael of what Charles Legendre had said, that the
Louvre was not only an art museum but an institution of the
French government. He knew, also, that the guard would never

wear his uniform on the street. No one did in France. Nurses, sanitation workers, gendarmes, waiters all wore street clothes to work, changing into their uniforms upon arrival. Thus, on the Métro, it was impossible to tell doctors from street sweepers, bourgeois matrons from waitresses. Perhaps that was why the French set such stock in distinguishing marks: Légions d'honneur rosettes, school ties, Orders of Merit, all signs indicating that the wearer belonged to a certain class.

"Monsieur d'Origny wishes to see you," the guard said.

"Show him in," Michael said.

Didier entered a moment later, grinning, shaking Michael's hand warmly. "Hello, my friend," he said.

"What's a busy guy like yourself doing at the museum on a Wednesday morning?" Michael asked.

"You know I'm the *patron*," Didier said with an exaggerated patrician accent. "I do whatever I please. I want a backstage tour before I leave for the Midi. My wife and your wife keep telling me how splendid this place is going to be."

Michael cocked his eyebrows. He waved his arm in a half-circle. "What do you think so far?"

Two walls had been torn out and makeshift partitions erected; the floor had been taken up. A pile of slate rested in one corner. Cartons holding tiny mosaic squares were stacked at Michael's feet. A dropcloth covered a nondescript oak desk. Plaster dust was everywhere.

"Well, it's not splendid yet," Didier said. "I hope you don't mind honesty."

"Actually, it's a relief to hear some," Michael said. "So far I've been impressed by how much the French can bullshit. They are great smilers. I've been promised things you wouldn't believe that never materialize—I have the feeling the Minister's main function is to say 'yes' to your face while saying 'no' behind your back."

"Yes, that is true," Didier said. "We are extremely diplomatic, aren't we?"

"Extremely," Michael said.

"What problems are you having?"

"Name it. Finding contractors everyone agrees on. For example, I interviewed a carpenter who seemed fine. He's worked in museums before—the Marmottan and the old Jeu de Paume. He had good references. I submitted his name to the ministry for review, and Charles Legendre takes a walk down to tell me the guy is a bum, a neighbor of some deputy minister's cousin. His wife divorced him, and he never sends her alimony."

"So, they forbid you to hire him?" Didier asked.

"No, but the message is there. I'll make an enemy of the deputy minister if I do," Michael said.

"I see," Didier said.

"Another thing is the infighting that goes on here," Michael said. "It's more complicated than the U.N. Do I answer to Charles Legendre or Pierre Dauphin . . ."

"I know Pierre," Didier said. "What's your problem with him?"

"He's curator of the Salle Hubert, and he has control of a painting by Poussin that I'd like to hang in here. Legendre supposedly wants me to have it, Dauphin wants to hang on to it. They're playing Capture the Flag. Do you know that game?"

"No, but it sounds simple," Didier said. "I was a boy when the Germans occupied France, remember. Possession is power. Yes, I can see Pierre playing the game."

"That's just one example," Michael said. "I want two major paintings for the Salle; also a tapestry and several less important works. No one will part with anything. The easiest thing I've done is commission a cabinetmaker to build a table. He lives a quiet life in Burgundy, so no one here knows him or has a bone to pick with him."

"To you, this business with the Poussin symbolizes the troubles you are having," Didier said. "I am a peace-loving man, but to achieve peace, you must think like a general. The Poussin is France. Legendre is DeGaulle. Pierre is Hitler. You, my friend, are Eisenhower. I, of course, am Churchill."

"How do we get the Poussin, Winston?"

"You must ask yourself one question," Didier said, leaving no doubt that he was about to present a brilliant strategy. "Who will be curator of the Salle des Quatre Saisons?"

Michael frowned. His exhaustion made him feel amazed and thick. He realized that he didn't know the answer. "I have no idea. Its period is the seventeenth century, so I suppose Charles. On the other hand, it adjoins the Salle Hubert . . ."

"Then consider it unclaimed turf. Come, let us put a bug in Adolf's ear."

On the way to Pierre Dauphin's office they met Anne. She was hurrying down the stairs, her gaze directed at her feet. She banged into Didier.

"*Excusez-moi,*" she said, blushing. Glancing around Didier she caught sight of Michael and beamed. Michael introduced them. Forming a little triangle on the stairs, they made polite small talk.

"My wife admires your work," Didier said.

"How delightful!" Anne said. "I am so pleased." Although speaking to Didier, she kept looking at Michael. She stood on the step above him. Even so, she had to tilt her head up to look into his eyes. His longing for her was so great, and hers for him, that it had to be obvious to Didier. Michael didn't care. He was glad for the secret to be out, proud to have a lover as beautiful and brilliant as Anne.

"I'll see you later," Michael said as Didier continued up the stairs. Anne squeezed his hand and stood there, watching Michael go.

"She is lovely," Didier said.

"Yes," Michael said, wanting to talk about her but feeling a warning coming from Didier.

"Be careful. I had my head turned more than once in my first two marriages. Lydie is a wonderful girl."

Michael said nothing. He couldn't think of Anne and Lydie at the same time. He didn't want to leave Lydie, but he couldn't imagine giving up Anne. He felt drunk on her, unable to sleep, never hungry, as if all his needs were sexual and romantic and only Anne could fulfill them.

Michael knocked on Pierre Dauphin's office door, and was bid to enter.

"Didier!" Pierre exclaimed, coming around his desk to shake Didier's hand. Pierre, stout and bald, came midway up Didier's chest. He dressed like an academic in tweed; he wore an ascot instead of a necktie.

"Giselle is well?" Didier inquired. "And your mother?"

"Both are fine," Pierre replied. "I will be passing the Place Vendôme one of these days with Giselle's necklace—the sapphire one? The clasp seems to be broken."

"Be sure to ask for Boris personally, eh? I shall tell him to expect you," Didier said.

"So good of you, Didier." Pierre had noticed Michael the second they entered the room; for some reason, however, he pretended not to have seen him until this instant. "Our young American!" he said.

"Hi, Pierre," Michael said.

"What is this excellent news about your appointment as curator of the Salle des Quatre Saisons?" Didier asked.

Pierre flushed and opened his mouth, gaping like a fish. Michael stared him straight in the eye, to avoid looking at Didier. "But that is not definite, not by any means," Pierre said. Then, as the idea dawned on him that someone as well-connected as Didier might have inside information, his eyes lightened. "Where, might I ask, have you heard that?"

"Well, isn't it a foregone conclusion?" Didier asked.

"You are the Salle's architect, Michael," Pierre said. "Was it you?"

"I just do my work and hope someone will give me a Poussin," Michael said. "I keep out of politics."

"Was it Jacques de Vauvrey?" Pierre asked Didier fervently, naming the Minister of Culture. "I know he is a member of your club . . ."

Didier held up his hand. "I've said too much, obviously. In any case, I wish you the best. *Au revoir,* Pierre."

In the hallway Michael laughed, but he also felt irritated at Didier for interfering.

"This will work out perfectly," Didier said, chuckling. "Pierre will think he is about to be named curator of your Salle, and so he will give you the painting, thinking he is bringing it along with him."

"Unless he isn't named," Michael said. "He's not going to let that painting go until his appointment is definite."

"Pierre Dauphin is a pompous little fellow," Didier said. "His grandfather was a baron with no money. Pierre bought a necklace for his wife for their fifth anniversary, and every spring he comes to have it fixed. It is a very nice piece of jewelry, but he thinks that because he patronized my office twenty years ago, we owe him great fealty." He shook his head. "I would like to see him give you that painting."

"So would I." Michael appreciated the sentiment, but he still felt annoyed. Didier had barged in, as if his Frenchness gave him the right to take over. In that sense, he was no different from Charles Legendre or Pierre himself: they figured their nationality gave them a natural superiority within the Louvre.

In the back of his mind, however, was the knowledge that Michael was really angry at Didier for what he had said about Lydie and Anne earlier. Things with Lydie had been going downhill for so long; now that Michael had found Anne, he had stopped caring so much about reversing them. But back there in the stairway for just a moment, Didier had reminded him that he had to put on the brakes, and now an image of Lydie's sad smile came to him. So Michael walked through the Louvre with Didier, trying to think of neither Lydie nor Anne, overwhelmed by both of them.

# 11

*Trust me not to waste a moment's time. It is my bad luck to encounter delays where others do not. Sometimes, I feel the impulse to smash china, just as you do!*

—To Françoise-Marguerite, August 1680

Patrice wondered how it was possible to be sitting beside her mother in her own house and feel homesick. Or was it loneliness she felt? The feeling was familiar but distant to her; she hadn't felt it for years, since moving to France. It reminded her of the years before she met Didier, nights when she would eat a pint of ice cream just to fill herself up. She glanced at her mother, the half-spectacles perched at the tip of her nose as she read *Paris-Match,* and knew the empty feeling would go away when her mother returned to Marblehead. Lydie would certainly never feel this way with her mother.

No American had ever adopted France and the French more willingly, more immediately than Patrice had; she felt sure of it. Arriving in Paris with Didier, she felt she had come home. She remembered that flight from JFK, with Didier at her side. Watching Jamaica Bay give way to the Atlantic, Patrice felt as though someone had untied the ropes that held her down, each rope representing some unlovely aspect of her life and American culture: pointless television, lonely nights with Chinese takeout, her mother's voice, the silver flatware her parents had bought on the occasion of her birth for the occasion of her wedding. She had imagined that flatware as ballast, and she felt the plane rise as each fish fork, butter knife, gravy ladle was jettisoned. "We don't *need* that flatware," Patrice had been thrilled to tell her mother, who for at least six years had despaired of Patrice's finding a husband. "Didier has the *ancestral* silver."

"They're saying Princess Caroline is pregnant again," her mother said, reading the magazine. "I wonder if she loves her husband. I wonder what Grace would think of him."

"Did you know Kelly is named for Grace Kelly?" Patrice asked, feeling a mean little thrill, knowing that this would get her mother's goat.

"Kelly? The maid?"

"Yes. She's nice, isn't she?"

"She's fine." Eliza Spofford's thin mouth looked set, as if something was causing her pain.

"Do you think I'm too familiar with my help, mother?" Patrice asked.

"I didn't say that. But I could do without her chattering about Boston versus New York versus Los Angeles. She's a regular gazetteer. Has she made the demography of the United States her life's work?"

"Actually, her life's work is cleaning toilets," Patrice said. "And she has a college degree. Without splitting hairs, she is more highly educated than you are."

"I hate that expression—'splitting hairs.'"

"Well, mincing words, then. I'm trying to work out some way for her to get to America, where she can get a decent job."

"They all want that. And the trouble is, there aren't enough jobs to go around—not even for our own citizens."

"What about America's origins? It was founded by immigrants, wasn't it? I think it's strange that you're from Massachusetts, just a few miles up the coast from Plymouth Rock, and you have that attitude. I was hoping you might sponsor Kelly. She needs someone who lives in America to petition for her."

Eliza took off her glasses. She looked pale, a bit tired. For an instant Patrice was struck by her age, and she felt sorry for her. "Patsy, are you baiting me?" Eliza asked. "You know how I feel about this issue—I've always said America has left the door open for too long. I think Kelly is nice. I like her well enough, but America can't keep doling out. Can't you respect my political views?"

"Not that particular one."

"I came all the way to France to visit my daughter, and this is what happens."

"The only problem with that is, your daughter happens to be me," Patrice said.

"Where do you get that idea? I love you."

"You just hate my life."

"My darling, I just wish you'd married someone closer to home. Is that so terrible?"

Listening to her mother's words, Patrice could almost believe them. But the discrepancy between the message and the truth was so great, it made Patrice dizzy trying to figure it out. Patrice and Eliza had never gotten along; if Eliza wished Patrice lived closer to Marblehead, it was only for selfish reasons. For example, if Didier's family owned Shreve, Crump and Low in Boston instead of d'Origny Bijoutiers in Paris, well, Eliza could be proud of that. Or if Patrice and her husband owned a great house on Beacon Hill instead of their apartment on the Place des Vosges, Eliza could inform Patrice about Boston's best designers, antique dealers, linen shops, domestic employment agencies. Eliza could come to Patrice's parties. Eliza could receive Patrice and her husband on weekends.

Patrice thought of Lydie and her mother, of the great devotion they had for each other. Then she thought of Madame de Sévigné, of the true sorrow she had felt when Françoise-Marguerite had married Count de Grignan and moved to Provence. Patrice found many of the letters written by mother to daughter unreadable: too sad, too sweet, too raw. Now, recalling those letters, facing her own mother, made her realize what they, Patrice and Eliza, did not have. And she despised Eliza for it.

"I think I'm going to go home," Eliza said in a shaky voice.

"Oh, that's predictable," Patrice said. "I'm such an ogre. I'm so mean to my mother. Am I supposed to beg you to stay?"

"Where did you get the idea that I'm so horrible?" Eliza asked, rising from her chair, holding out her hands. "What did I do to deserve it? I came all the way to Paris to see you . . ."

Patrice started to feel uneasy. Her mother sounded dreadful. Her voice broke; it sounded like the voice of an old woman.

"Listen, I really am sorry," Patrice said. "Please stay."

"I don't know," Eliza said. Sun streaming through the tall windows lit her from behind; it shined through the diaphanous green silk caftan she wore. Her body, in silhouette, looked incredibly thin and young. "I'm tired. Maybe it's jet lag—I don't recover from travel the way I once did. I think I'll lie down."

"Would you like Kelly to bring you something? Some tea, maybe?"

"No, thank you." But she stopped at the door, turning to face

Patrice. She was smiling. "On second thought, I'd like some as-pirin. That fizzy kind that dissolves, the kind you can only get in Europe."

"I'll get you some," Patrice said.

On her way to the pharmacy, she considered the innuendo. On the one hand, her mother might have been making a concession to Patrice's decision to live in France, to her Frenchness, by asking for a specifically French brand of aspirin. On the other hand, it signified that Patrice had given her a headache.

"Aspirine Upsa," Patrice said to the clerk. She dropped the green box into her bag and headed home. The sun blazed; she wished she were already lying on a beach in Saint-Tropez, work-ing on her tan, her head empty. She was tired of second-guessing, of analyzing every exchange she had with her mother. She re-membered how, as a child, she would hear her mother reply to her father's inquiries about her well-being in any situation: her posi-tion at a restaurant table; the number of ice cubes in her glass; her reaction the time she had to cancel her trip to visit her sister in Cleveland because Patrice had contracted mumps. "I'm perfectly fine," Eliza would say, in a way that made it crystal clear that she was not. The woman was impossible to please; she was a martyr to her own cause.

When Patrice arrived home, she knocked gently on her mother's door. Hearing no reply, she pushed it open. Eliza sat on the edge of her bed, her back straight, talking on the telephone. She was inquiring about flights to Boston. Patrice placed the green box on the bedside table and, leaving the room, quietly closed the door behind her.

She found Kelly in the kitchen. Kelly, wearing the black uni-form she had been instructed to wear for the duration of Eliza's visit, stood at the sink, shelling peas.

"You may not believe this now," Patrice said, eating a raw pea, "but you are lucky your mother lives halfway around the world."

Kelly said nothing, but smiled.

"Did you buy salmon for dinner?" Patrice asked.

"Yes, Mum. It will be such a pretty meal, with pink salmon and bright green peas. I hope your mother will like it."

"I'm not sure whether I care about that." Patrice felt her eyes fill with tears.

"What is it?" Kelly asked, sounding alarmed. "What is wrong, Mum?"

Kelly's voice was so kind, so concerned, that Patrice began to cry. She covered her eyes with her hands and sobbed, and she felt Kelly touch her shoulder.

"Everything will be all right," Kelly said. "You haven't seen your mother in such a long time. When I finally see my mother I know we will have to get used to each other again."

"She is so difficult," Patrice said. "No one can please her."

"She is very far from her home."

"You've been so nice to her," Patrice said, sniffling. "I really appreciate it."

"It is my pleasure. She is so nice to me! Yesterday she told me all the places your relatives live in the United States. Boston, Cleveland, Palm Beach, and Farmington."

Listening to Kelly gush, Patrice felt sorry for her. Eliza had made a fool of her, telling her a few pitiful facts about the United States while holding her in contempt. It reminded Patrice of the loyalty she had felt for Lydie at lunch, listening to Lydie talk on about her job, about Michael's, as though Eliza actually took her seriously. Knowing that Eliza would dismiss Lydie from memory ten minutes after leaving the restaurant, Patrice had felt protective of her friend.

Eliza valued people from families of good social standing, preferably from Boston's North Shore, certainly not maids or second-generation Irish from New York. The two ironies, of which Patrice was dimly aware, were that Eliza herself came from a nonexalted background, from a family who had owned a small textile mill in Fall River, and that Patrice, in spite of her democratic taste in women friends, had inherited her mother's respect for old-line names and anything prestigious. Still, in spite of that, Patrice knew she was quite different from her mother. She could appreciate any fine, decent person regardless of background. Wasn't she standing in her kitchen, spilling her guts to Kelly?

"Do you feel better now, Mum?" Kelly asked.

"A little."

"Hello, hello," Eliza said, shaking the box of aspirin. "I've come for a glass of water."

In one swift motion, Kelly reached for a glass, filled it with Evian water from the refrigerator, and handed it to Eliza. "You're so efficient, dear," Eliza said.

"Are your travel plans set?" Patrice asked. She felt peculiar. She felt like crying, shouting, belting, and hugging her mother all at once.

"Now, don't be hurt, Patsy, but I think it is best that I leave a little early. We've had this lovely week in Paris. I've had such a good time. You know I don't care too much for the Riviera, and this way I can get back to Boston and you and Didier can have a nice vacation alone together."

"The trouble is, we'll always remember this. That you came for a month and left after a week because we couldn't stand each other." Patrice remembered what Lydie had said the other day: "Be nice to your mother, it's only a month out of your life."

"That's not true," Eliza said. "I not only can stand you, I love you. I simply want to give you and Didier a nice time alone together. Don't forget, your father was a businessman; I know how hard those men work, how they need their time off. And he is just so in love with you!"

And Patrice knew that Eliza had deemed that tale to become the reality. Eliza was expert at reinvention; it would go down in history that Eliza had left France early not because mother and daughter hated each other but because Eliza did not want to intrude on Patrice and Didier's vacation. On their little love nest in Saint-Tropez. Patrice tried to feel relieved. Wasn't this exactly what she wanted? Instead, she felt sick.

Eliza dropped two aspirin tablets in the water, and the three women stood silent, listening to them dissolve. "Why they don't market this stuff in America is beyond me," Eliza said.

"The aspirin in America is very different?" Kelly asked after a moment. Patrice thought it brave of her; she knew it was one thing for Kelly to have a conversation with her, quite another to give Eliza the impression that she considered herself an equal part of their trio. But such was the strength of Kelly's desire to know everything, no matter how minute, about the United States.

"Oh, in America they have these horse pills, impossible things to swallow." Eliza sipped her aspirin as if it were a cocktail. "You are a very lucky girl, dear, to have Patsy as your employer."

"Yes, Mum. I know," Kelly said.

"She is so concerned for your future, she has been trying to recruit me to take you home with me."

Kelly gasped, beamed at Eliza, then Patrice. "Oh, really? Really?"

"I tried," Patrice said.

"I'm sorry to say, it won't be possible right now," Eliza said. "For one thing, I employ a girl whom I am absolutely devoted to.

And for another, I don't understand all the red tape. But let me send a letter to my congressman, he's a good friend, and maybe sometime in the future . . ."

"Your congressman! Thank you, thank you," Kelly said, twisting her hands.

God, it's pathetic, Patrice thought. The lie cost Eliza nothing at all, and it made Kelly so happy. It gave Kelly hope, and it made Patrice a hero. Kelly wore an expression of pure gratitude. Doesn't this solve everything? Patrice thought. Eliza would feel she had helped Patrice out; Kelly would idolize Patrice for her efforts. If only Patrice had her mother's talent for reinvention. Then she could stop feeling guilty. She could convince herself that she had truly, vigorously helped Kelly fulfill her dream of getting to the United States.

# 12

*You probably know about our defeat at Gigeri, and how
those who gave the advice now seek to throw the blame on
those who carried it out.*

—To Pomponne, November 1664

It surprised Lydie to realize how much she missed Patrice.
Daily things would occur, and she would wish she could call
Patrice to tell her about them. Small things, really, such as the dis-
covery of a new restaurant with a quiet, shady terrace; the infernal
humidity; the frustration Lydie was feeling about Michael's late
hours. Yes, the construction of his project had finally started, and
each day brought new milestones of ineptitude: a door incorrectly
hung, a batch of new mortar that didn't match the old. If Patrice
were in Paris, Lydie believed she wouldn't feel so abandoned. She
would have someone to call; she and Patrice could have lunch or
tea together. In New York she had confided in Julia, but over here
she had Patrice.

Postcards arrived from Saint-Tropez. Lydie felt a little surprised, a little thrilled by the vulgarity of Patrice's cards. Many

were sexual, all featured breasts, as if Saint-Tropez's greatest fea-
ture were its well-endowed female inhabitants. But Patrice's mes-
sages were serious, kind. It seemed she missed Lydie as much as
Lydie missed her. "I haven't spoken a word of English since arriving," she wrote. "All of Didier's friends are French with a
vengeance." On another she wrote: "When are you coming? Get
down here, and fast! You are my only American."

That phrase, "my only American," struck Lydie. In writing it,
Patrice had named something Lydie had been trying to define.
What would happen to Patrice when Lydie returned to the United
States? Lydie had grown so fond of her. She had a private store of
memories based on that luncheon with Patrice and her mother
and on the time Lydie told Patrice everything about her father and
Michael. Lydie couldn't help seeing herself and Patrice with
poignant overtones: two only children in a foreign country.

When Lydie told Michael about it that night, he laughed.

"Patrice can fend for herself," he said. "I think she's a tough
cookie."

"She gives the impression of being tough," Lydie said. "But a
lot of it is an act. You should have seen her with her mother—the
combination of bulldozer and baby. She wanted to act so compe-
tent, make sure the visit ran like clockwork. But when she'd look
at her mother her eyes would get all anxious, because she was
afraid her mother wasn't having a good time. Which she obviously
wasn't."

"It's a long way to come to have a bad time," Michael said.

Lydie picked up on something in his voice. She looked at him
for a long time without speaking. She had the feeling he was
talking about her, Lydie—not Patrice's mother. It didn't seem to
matter to Michael that she felt better, was working hard on the
d'Origny project. "Why don't you say what's on your mind?" she
asked.

"The phone bill is on my mind. How often do you have to call Julia?"

"I hardly ever call her more than once a week!" Lydie said. "I thought staying in touch with her was part of the bargain."

"I guess so," Michael said. "But when you put it that way, you make it sound as if you and I are on opposite sides. That I dragged you here against your will."

"I don't feel that way," Lydie said, taking Michael's hand. He squeezed hers back, but he wasn't smiling. This was a perfect example of how Lydie missed Patrice. She wished she could talk with her friend about Michael's distance. She was in the mood to trade crabby husband stories with Patrice, but Patrice was on vacation.

Lydie crossed the days of August off the calendar. As the days fell away, a warehouse in Neuilly filled with objects for the ball. Every day Lydie walked miles, searching for props. Her outings took her up the funicular to Montmartre; through covered passages, all frosted glass, wrought iron, and tile, off the rue des Petits-Champs; into the leafy village square behind the Panthéon; along the crowded market streets of Mouffetard and Cité Berryer. So many shops were closed for August, the façades blank with lowered steel shutters.

An air of laziness pervaded Paris; Lydie noticed but did not feel it. She walked fast, urgently, as though the next destination was the most important one. She tried to keep the ball in mind. She thought of the countryside and pictured guests dancing to an orchestra outdoors. She saw the ball as a play, herself as the director. In this vision, she stood off to the side, not dancing. She was watching everyone, even Michael, whirl across grass wet with the night's dew.

She felt uneasiness coming from Michael. Sometimes she caught him watching her. Quiet, holding something back, as

though he had a secret or a gripe and was waiting for her to whee-
dle it out of him.

Stopping in her apartment between forays to the warehouse she
would relax. She would sit on her terrace, tilt her face toward the
sun, drink a glass of iced tea. She would think of her frenzy of activity, wonder what she wanted it to obscure.

"We haven't even gone away for a weekend," she said to
Michael when he came home one night. It was late; work had kept
him at the Louvre and they had eaten separately.

"This is my busiest time—yours too," Michael said.

"Somehow I had thought our summer in France would be a
little more fun," Lydie said. "We bought all those guidebooks
back in New York, and we've hardly even used them."

Michael laughed.

"What?" Lydie asked, her feelings hurt.

"It just sounds funny—as if we can't have fun without a guide-
book. I can just see us, on a train through France, reading about,
I don't know, World War II battles, instead of looking out the
window."

"I didn't mean it that way," Lydie said, and she thought
Michael's comment was strange, coming from a man who went
through museums reading the information cards tacked to the
wall before standing back to look at the paintings. "You sound
grouchy," she said. "Are you mad at me?"

"No."

"That's all you have to say? 'No'?"

"I'm not mad."

"But you don't seem exactly happy."

"I'm fine, Lydie," Michael said in a tone that infuriated her. She
imagined that he sounded amused that she would be so worked up
over, apparently, nothing. She stared at him, reading some report.
His brown hair looked lighter, as though it had been bleached by

the sun. When had that happened? she wondered. She looked away, blinded by the halogen lights of a passing tour boat.

"Patrice keeps inviting us to Saint-Tropez," Lydie said.

"I know—Didier sent a note to my office."

"You didn't tell me!"

Michael smiled at her. "I just received it. I'm telling you now."

And suddenly Lydie had the terrible, electric feeling that she was not only nagging him, but turning into a *nag:* a harpy with a perpetually downturned mouth, with frown lines between the brows, with a caw instead of a voice.

"Let's go to Saint-Tropez," she said, lowering her voice an octave. "I'll go topless on the beach."

"You don't have to," Michael said. Lydie, who had so far been too modest to bare her breasts or even wear a bikini at any French beach, suddenly smiled and began to slowly roll up her T-shirt. They lived on the top floor; who besides Michael could possibly see her? She walked around the table toward him and sat facing him on his lap. Michael held her away, so he could look down at her breasts. Then his hands covered them and he kissed her lips. Lydie began to shiver. His kiss was soft and lazy, off to a slow start, and his arms went around her as Lydie began to unbutton his shirt.

He was pressing against her so hard she couldn't move her fingers. The kiss stopped; they rested their heads on each other's shoulders. It took some time for Lydie to realize that they were no longer hugging, but clutching each other. Michael whispered "Lydie," but he didn't seem to want her to reply.

⁂

The atmosphere in Paris turned close, unstable. Every morning the sky was white, and nothing relieved the heat until late afternoon when thunder would rumble east from Brittany, rain would pour down, and lightning twice struck the Eiffel Tower. Lydie caught a summer cold. She spent two days sitting in her living room, a washcloth and a bowl of ice water on the floor beside her, watching the weather change. The tableau of blank sky replaced by violet storm clouds seemed malevolent, biblical, like an Old Testament scene painted by Géricault.

Michael would call to see if she was okay. "I'm fine," she would say, and that was all, even when her fever was 104. Something had passed between them, that night on the terrace, and now his solicitous inquiries for her health reminded her of a man calling his ailing ex-wife: it cost him little and meant nothing.

Or was she delirious? She didn't really know. Her throat was parched, her skin dry. She didn't have the energy to get to the bottom of anything. She was a cool, uncurious observer. Lying on her back she let herself drift into a trance where she and Michael didn't love each other. What was "falling out of love," anyway, but a mystical phrase for something painfully mundane: you stop caring about each other. You no longer ache for each other. You don't mind being alone; perhaps you prefer it. Falling out of love: it didn't happen overnight.

Then the shock of the notion roused her from her trance. Do you really have to work so late? Why don't we make love? Why had she never asked the questions? She knew why: Lydie did not want to hear the true story. She had been raised in a house where you kept your troubles, no matter how awful, to yourself, where you were told to stop crying, where things, bad and even sometimes good, were willfully ignored until they went away or blew up in your face.

Patrice called. The sound of her voice made Lydie cry, but she did not let Patrice know.

"In less than an hour someone will appear at your door bearing gifts," Patrice said.

"What are you, the Delphic Oracle?" Lydie asked.

"No, I'm a fortune cookie. How are you?"

"Sick. I have a cold."

"You poor thing! I must have gotten vibes, because I'm having Kelly bring you a little something."

"Really? What?"

"You'll see."

"Well, thanks in advance. How's the beach?"

"Fantastic. I'm tan, and I mean *all over*. No bikini lines. Why haven't you and Michael come yet?"

"Work. They've started construction at the Louvre. Michael is thrilled."

"I'm very proud of him," Patrice said. "Why don't you come alone?"

Lydie didn't answer for a second. "I'm busy too. Getting everything ready for the ball. By the way, I had invitations printed. Will you ask Didier to send me his guest list?"

"You sound strange. What's wrong?"

"Nothing. Don't worry about me. I always get sick in August. It's an annual event."

"Well, if you say so," Patrice said, sounding unconvinced. "Get yourself some decent medicine and sleep around the clock."

"Okay. I miss you."

"Kisses!" Patrice said, and broke the connection.

Hanging up the phone, Lydie had the strangest feeling that nothing bad would be happening if she and Michael had not left the United States. They would be happy together, she would not be sick, he would not be acting like a jerk. Her mother's guardian angel was punishing her for transferring loyalties to Patrice. She closed her eyes and saw the angel, an avenger: hooded, black-winged, straight from God. She knew she was superstitious, but then, she had been raised by Catholics from Ireland. She fell asleep.

∽

Kelly stepped off the number thirty-two bus carrying the present for Lydie. This was the moment she had been waiting for! All August she had worked alone at the d'Orignys'—polishing silver, cleaning closets and cupboards, wishing for a chance to speak with Lydie. She had Patrice to thank for it. Her lips moved, rehearsing the words she would say. Her palms sweated. She wiped them on a tissue. She wanted them to be dry, because she knew Lydie would shake her hand in greeting. She looked around.

Lydie's neighborhood was so different from Patrice's: every single woman on the street looked like a fashion model. The shops and restaurants had brilliant red awnings with gold lettering: Chez Francis, Bar des Théâtres, Marius et Janette. The Place des Vosges was so drab, so ancient, in comparison. And Kelly's own neighborhood, behind Clichy, could not even be compared. It was dirty, grimy, full of Arabs. The shops sold rice and beans, cheap shoes, sex toys. She wished her sisters and brothers could see her now, walking through the Place de l'Alma, ringing the bell of an American who was not her employer.

"Hello, Lydie, hello, Lydie," Kelly said to herself, walking up the stairs. She remembered to wipe her palms.

"Kelly!" Lydie said, standing in the foyer of her apartment. She was wearing a robe. In the middle of the day! Kelly was so surprised by this, she forgot her greeting. But then Lydie stepped forward, shook her hand. "I'd give you a kiss," Lydie said, "but I'm sick and probably contagious. Come on in."

Kelly remembered to hand her the present, some homemade strawberry preserves that had actually been sent as a thank-you present to Patrice from her mother.

"My favorite kind," Lydie said, examining the jar.

Kelly stood in the entranceway and looked around. Tall windows overlooked the river. The furniture was beautiful! Very contemporary! The couch was covered in a wild pattern; there was an entertainment center complete with TV, VCR, and stereo; pole lamps were everywhere. She thought of Patrice's lamps: old things covered with gilt that flaked every time you touched them.

"Is that a Barcalounger?" Kelly asked, unable to help herself. She had seen pictures of reclining chairs in Patrice's magazines.

Lydie laughed. "Yes. It's not my favorite thing, but Michael's father gave it to him for his thirty-fifth birthday. Why don't we sit over there? You can try it out."

The sweat behind Kelly's knees bonded with the vinyl. "I'll get us some iced tea," Lydie said. Before leaving the room, she showed Kelly how to work the levers. Kelly made her feet go up and down and her head go back. She made herself comfortable, with her feet about six inches off the ground and her head back, not far, just a little.

Lydie rejoined her. At that moment, Kelly realized what she had done: allowed Lydie to serve her.

"Oh, Mum!" she said, scrambling to get out of the chair. This wasn't what she had planned! She had intended to offer to work a little for Lydie, for free, before proposing her idea.

"Sit back and relax," Lydie said. She smiled at Kelly, then sat on the sofa. "Are you enjoying August without the d'Orignys?"

"Oh, yes," Kelly said, holding her head up. Her comfort put her at a disadvantage. She wished she could trade places with Lydie.

"I really miss Patrice, that's for sure," Lydie said. "I don't know what I'll do without her when I return to New York."

"Will that be soon?" Kelly asked, forcing her voice to be steady.

"In October. Has Patrice done anything about helping you to get there? To the United States?"

Kelly could hardly believe it; Lydie was making it so easy for her. "No, not really. It is very hard for her to do, living forever in Paris, married to a Frenchman. It would be much easier for someone who was returning to the United States—to take me with them."

Lydie's head turned fast. Kelly knew then that Lydie realized exactly what she was after. She watched Lydie, generally so soft-looking, with her pretty reddish hair and white skin, even whiter with sickness, and thought she looked shrewd, even a little hard. Kelly felt afraid.

"Oh, I wish I could help you," Lydie said.

"You do? You do?" Kelly asked.

"But how can I, Kelly? This is between you and Patrice. If I brought you to the States, I would be taking you away from her."

Kelly had expected her to say that. It only strengthened her will. She used the levers to lower her feet to the ground, raise her head up straight. Now she felt she was in a chair of power, as substantial as a throne. "I would never want to hurt Patrice," she said. "She has done so much for me. It is *she* who most wants me to get to the United States. She has been teaching me the computer, to give me a skill. She has told me about the Filipino community in Queens . . ."

Lydie moved her mouth without speaking, as though she feared the next words would be painful. "I know she started off doing that, but I believe she feels too attached to you. It's just a sense I have—she hasn't said anything to me. But I think she would miss you terribly if you left."

"And I would miss her."

"Please understand, Kelly. I want you to get to the United States. But I can't go against the wishes of my friend."

Kelly grinned. She could scarcely conceal her triumph. "She tried to get her mother to take me with her."

"She did? She didn't tell me that." Lydie looked astonished.

"Yes, but Mrs. Spofford already employs a person she is devoted to. Patrice was very disappointed, even though Mrs. Spofford promised to talk to her congressman."

Lydie frowned a little. She pulled a loose thread on the sleeve of her robe. The hem of the sleeve was coming down. "I can fix that for you," Kelly said. She rose from the Barcalounger, smiling at Lydie.

"That's okay," Lydie said. "I can sew . . ."

"Please," Kelly said.

Lydie had confusion in her face. It derived from more than Kelly's proposal, Kelly felt sure. "It's awfully nice of you," Lydie said. She handed Kelly a tin box which held needles and thread. Kelly glanced at the robe, a pale shade of yellow, and began matching the thread. Lydie took off the robe, laid it on the Barcalounger. She had a T-shirt on underneath. "I'll be right back," she said.

When she returned, she was wearing a maroon silk robe that could only be her husband's. "Isn't it very hard to get a visa, even if an American is sponsoring you?" she asked.

Kelly stitched busily. "Yes, it is difficult. But they say it is easier if the American says you can do a special job."

"Maid's work is not a special job," Lydie said. "What else can you do?"

"In the Philippines I was an accountant," Kelly said, not looking up from her work. She had finished the drooping sleeve. She tied a neat knot, bit off the thread, and began to strengthen the hem of the other sleeve.

"I do have my own business in New York, but I don't have enough work to keep an accountant busy," Lydie said.

"I want to open a fish market," Kelly said. "My family owned a fish pond in the Philippines, and I know all about fish."

"Fish?" Lydie asked, sounding dazed.

"Yes," Kelly said. She finished the second sleeve. She feared looking into Lydie's face. She felt that she had never been so close to making her dream come true. Her palms were very sweaty. Her fingers trembled.

"Kelly, listen," Lydie said. "I'm sick today. I don't know what to think. I have to talk this over with Michael and Patrice."

Kelly, who believed that all would be lost if Lydie talked with Patrice before making up her mind, looked at her. She looked straight into Lydie's hazel eyes. "What about your mother?" she asked.

"My mother?"

"Did you not tell me that she immigrated to the United States? That you talked to her about me and that she said I should try to go also?"

"Yes, I did."

"Do you believe that your mother had help along the way? That someone helped her to get there?"

"Many people helped her. I know what you're saying, and I appreciate it. I do. Let me think about it." Some of the confusion had left her face, and Kelly knew that she had won.

"Thank you so much, Lydie," Kelly said. "No matter what you decide, thank you for thinking about it. Will you let me do something for you now? I could go to the market for you, or do your laundry. I could go to the pharmacy . . ."

"No," Lydie said, sounding tired. "There's nothing at all. Maybe I'll just take a rest now."

And so they said good-bye.

That night Michael came home with ice cream from Berthillon. It had melted in the heat; the package had sprung a leak, and his hands were sticky. He dumped a pile of contractors' reports on the counter and washed his hands at the kitchen sink while Lydie poured liquid double-chocolate into soup bowls. She felt better after her nap, no longer feverish. She wore a fresh white nightgown, knowing that Michael preferred it to the T-shirt.

"I have the most interesting thing to tell you," Lydie said. "I had a visitor today. Kelly Merida—you know, Patrice's cleaning lady?"

"Should we leave it in the freezer for a few minutes, to get it cold?" he asked.

"Let's eat it just like this. It seems more sinful," she said. She wanted to sound lighthearted, wicked. She wanted to erase whatever had turned bad between them.

"I brought it home to cool you off, for your fever . . ."

"My fever is gone. I'm fine," Lydie said.

"Ah," he said. He stared at her. He didn't touch her. His look was steady, nearly expressionless, but it chilled Lydie, and only someone who knew him as well as she did could understand what it meant. She knew that they were about to have a conversation, and she knew what the conversation would be about. It would not be about Kelly. She put one hand over her eyes, then took it down.

"I love you," she said.

"Not enough," he said.

"What are you talking about? What's bothering you?" She felt a little frantic. She glanced around for the kitchen chairs, but Michael seemed to want to stand.

"Lydie." He placed his hands on her shoulders, guided her to the sideboard and propped her against it. It reminded her of the time, in their kitchen in New York, when he had told her that her father was dead. The overhead light was harsh and yellow; the loudspeaker of one of the tour boats broadcast a distorted message.

"How can you say I don't love you enough?" Lydie asked.

"Because I don't feel it. I haven't felt it for a while. Since before we came to Paris."

"You're the one who's different, Michael," she said. "You've acted strange ever since we got here, and I can't blame you. Your project was up in the air for so long . . . Is there another hitch at work?"

"This isn't about work." His voice rose, his anger freeing something in Lydie. She hit his chest with the heel of her hand.

"God, if I had known this when I agreed to come to Paris—" she said.

"That's right—you 'agreed' to come to Paris. Funny, I'd always imagined my wife would *love* to come to Paris with me. Some people think Paris is the most romantic city in the world."

"I think it's romantic—I love it here." Lydie felt shocked by what he was saying. But she found herself trying to remember the last time they had had sex.

"You don't seem to love me, or at least *being* with me, if there's a difference. You know what stands out in my mind about our time here?"

"What?"

"That time on the quai, when you kissed me. It seemed so nice, so unusual."

Lydie remembered; they had been walking to the Comédie Française that early summer night.

"I felt more like coming home to bed instead of going to the performance," she said.

"Then why didn't you tell me?"

"I don't know. Because we had tickets."

Michael grabbed a contractor's report and tore it in half. "This is what I would have done with the tickets," he said.

"That's really great, ripping up your report," she shrieked.

"Why should you care about my fucking report if I don't?" Michael threw the pages down; they skidded across the sideboard into the wall.

"When did this start? How long have you felt this way? Can you tell me exactly?" Her ears rang, making the words echo.

"I think it hit me when we got to Paris. Back in New York I just blamed it on your family. I thought you were giving them everything you should have been giving me."

"Like what?" Lydie asked.

Michael leaned toward her, grabbed her upper arms so hard she gasped. "Words, Lydie. Your mother's the one you call to talk about your father. I loved him too—do you ever think of that? When he died . . ." Michael closed his eyes and stepped back. He swallowed hard.

"What?" Lydie asked, suddenly terrified.

"When your father died, all I wanted was to comfort you, to help you through it."

"But you did, Michael."

"I wanted the same from you. Remember how he used to say I was like the son he never had? We were close too, Lydie—apart from you. But you were the one who brought us together."

"He loved you," Lydie said, reaching out to stop a tear from rolling off Michael's cheek.

"That ride we took? The day before he died? I saw how unhappy he was. I should have known. I've always believed that— that he was trying to tell me what he was going to do."

"You couldn't have stopped him," Lydie said.

"No?" Michael asked, looking at her. "You know, you've never said that to me before."

Because we don't talk about it, Lydie wanted to say but couldn't. She held her face in her hands and wept.

"You always turned to your mother," Michael said. "I understood that, or I tried to. At least at first. You two were always together; you left me out of it. You didn't care how I felt, and you never let me take care of you."

"That's not true," Lydie whispered, knowing as she said it that it was.

"It is," Michael said. "It is." Having said that, he let out a long sigh that sounded to Lydie like relief.

"Then what happened?" Lydie asked, dreading to hear.

"Well, we moved to Paris. And over here you have Patrice."

"That's different," Lydie said.

Michael stared at her. "You don't even know. This is coming as a big shock to you, isn't it?"

Suddenly his tone was tender. Lydie nodded, and tears filled her eyes again. "You're talking about togetherness?"

"I've been thinking of it as—I don't know. Romance."

Romance, Lydie thought. Wasn't it ironic that her greatest fear before marrying Michael was that marriage, years of it, would dull romance? The heart-in-the-throat sort she had felt while courting? Then, after marrying him, she discovered that what she had called "romance" was, in many ways, fear. Fear that he wouldn't call. Fear that he would love someone else. Fear that he would leave. Marriage had taken all that away.

"What are you going to do?" she asked, the clear realization spreading like an anesthetic. It gave her strength and made her mean. "Are you saying you want to fix it or you want to end it?"

Michael stared at her. "I don't know," he said.

Then it came to her: his sun-lightened hair, his absences, everything. "Are you having an affair?" she asked.

"I care about someone," he said.

"Michael," Lydie said. She had always believed, even before knowing Michael, that her husband would always be faithful, that she would leave him if he were not. She would do what her mother should have done: leave the bastard before it was too late. She gazed into his eyes, which were sad, full of pain. "Brown eyes" did not begin to cover them. Their color was so warm, chestnut or sienna, flecked with black and gold. They made all his expressions seem more dramatic. His excitement appeared more vivid than other people's, his sadness hurt more. "How did it happen?" Lydie asked, hesitant, the way she had inquired about the details of her father's accident.

"I fell in love with her," Michael said.

It was the worst thing he could have said. When she heard the word "love," Lydie imagined she had lost him. She turned her back, walked out of the kitchen. She heard Michael coming after her, his footsteps right behind her. She was remembering the day he had fallen in love with her. It was Easter, eight years ago. They had been working together a few weeks when they were sent to Washington, to study the Hirshhorn sculpture garden.

They had stayed at a little hotel in Foggy Bottom. Separate rooms. She remembered the cherry trees blooming outside. She had lain in bed, smelling the blossoms, propped up on one elbow to look down the Potomac at planes in their landing pattern for National Airport. After a while she had calculated: one plane per minute. She remembered being disappointed that the sculpture garden had too much direct sun, that it was often too hot, that the main shade came from the shadow of the museum, not from trees. After two days of study they were supposed to return to New York, in time for Easter.

"Would you like to stay one more night?" Michael had asked. "Would you like to see Mount Vernon?"

With work behind them, they fell in love. Instantly, Lydie loved everything he said. Every single thing. He couldn't stop touching her, kissing her. They went to bed; she could see Michael's face beside hers on the pillow, his brow damp. He said, "I love you," after they both came in a rush unlike any Lydie had ever felt.

"Turn around," Michael said now in a low voice.

"Leave," Lydie said. "I don't want to look at you." And she meant it. She couldn't stand to know another thing about it. It would be easier if she never had to see Michael again, if she could begin to cure herself of him starting now.

He grabbed her arm, hard, yanked her around. "Is this how you want it to go?" he asked. "Do you really want me to leave?"

"If you love her," Lydie said, choking on the word "love." "Yes. I want you to get out of here."

He stared at her, still holding her arm. She felt his energy, imagined that he wanted to throttle her. But his silence gave her hope. "Or don't you love her? Tell me what you want. Make up your mind!"

Still he said nothing. After a while he shook his head, took away his hand. "I don't know what I want," he said. "That's the rotten thing. I've loved you for so long, Lydie, but I don't trust it much now."

She saw that he was crying. She thought, Why couldn't he have had a secret affair? Why couldn't he have kept it to himself, a fling in Paris to see him through middle age? But that bloodless thought cleared her mind. Suddenly she knew what he was saying about her. By wishing she didn't know about his affair, she was wishing for a happy little marriage. Something pretty, unreal. The kind of marriage her mother wanted for her.

Lydie stood close to Michael, not touching him. She couldn't quite move. Do you love her instead of me or in addition to me? she wanted to ask. Love. She had always loved Michael; perhaps the problem was that "love" had become a state of being rather than action.

"I'm going to leave now," he said calmly.

"To go where? Will you be . . . ?"

"I'll be alone," Michael said. "I'll be at a hotel. This is between you and me, Lydie. We have to decide whether we still want each other."

She sat down heavily on the sofa. "I can't believe this is happening. I never thought this was possible, that it could happen to us."

"Maybe that's the problem," Michael said. "It can happen to anyone."

"Michael . . ." Lydie said.

He looked at her for a long time. "Do you know how much I loved you?" he asked. Then he left.

# 13

*The King laughed very much at this trick, but everyone thinks it is the most cruel thing one can do to an old courtier. Personally I always like reflecting about things, and I wish the King would think about this example and conclude how far he is from ever learning the truth.*

—To Pomponne, December 1664

Lydie's dreams and days became interchangeable. When asleep, she dreamed of the mundane: reading the newspaper, washing her hair, wondering whether to cook for dinner or to go out. She wakened exhausted, as though she had actually spent the past eight hours washing and rewashing her hair; meticulously planning a dinner for two, shopping for the food, cooking it, then at the last minute abandoning the meal to meet Michael at an Alsatian brasserie. Awake the mundane was blurred, thus dangerous. Twice she forgot appointments. Twice she nearly walked into traffic. After the second near miss she steadied herself by leaning against a light pole. She walked along rue du Boccador, not even glancing at the restaurant she and Michael had made their *can-*

*tine*—their regular hangout. She thought of her two brushes with death and figured the first time she had wanted to kill Michael, the second time herself.

She made sure to arrive home every night before dark. She told herself that coming home alone, late, to an empty house was dangerous. But had she always felt that way? When Michael was away on business trips? When he had a late dinner with George or clients and she had the chance to see a movie with Julia or a friend? She had never before felt menaced by an empty house. But now it seemed safer to install herself early, before night fell, when the simple transition from daylight to darkness signified less than to walk in late, after dinner, and realize that she was the only one there.

She told no one that Michael had moved out. She told herself that the reason for this was to prove him wrong, to show that she didn't need to tell her mother and Patrice everything. In fact, she felt ashamed of the situation and she feared that talking about it would make it more real. Although Michael called often, six days passed without her seeing him. But she came awake, wide awake, on the morning of the seventh day, when he invited her to a cocktail party at the American Embassy.

"Arthur Chase invited me," Michael said. "Would you like to go?"

"Yes. That would be nice," Lydie said, shocked. She had expected that their first meeting would be private, a chance to talk about their troubles during dinner or a long walk. How weird this felt, being asked out, as if on a date, by Michael. What would she wear? Would he pick her up or meet her there? In the end, they decided to meet in the bar of the Hôtel Crillon, across the street from the embassy.

"Hi," Lydie said when he entered. She felt happy when he kissed her.

"You look pretty," he said, taking in her black linen suit, the silver necklace he had given her for their fifth anniversary, her hair held back by tortoiseshell combs. His face was set, grave, as though he was afraid of what was about to happen. He called the waiter, ordered two Lillets.

Drinking, she began to relax. She began to remember other cocktail hours with him. He was telling her about his day, a truly familiar topic. She listened avidly about the project, how construction was making a mess of the Louvre, how he expected to see a finished information center in three weeks.

"It's just wonderful," she said, meaning his work. If he would only look at her, into her eyes instead of at her hands, she would smile in a way that would make him love her.

"Thank you," he said. Then, before the drinks were half gone, "Shall we go? We shouldn't be late."

"It's just across the street . . ."

"I know, but I think we should go."

She sensed that he felt confused, was perhaps having a better time than he had expected to. She went along with him. Just ride it out, she said to herself, suddenly feeling superior, more adept. Bear with him, he'll get over this. She wore a secret smile. She stood behind him as he paid the waiter, noting the cut of his suit. His body was so trim, like that of a twenty-year-old athlete instead of a nearly forty-year-old architect. She longed to touch the small of his back.

She knew few people at the party, but Michael seemed to know everyone. He introduced her to an American painter, some American businessmen, an editor from a French publishing house, representatives of the French Ministry of Culture, embassy personnel. The editor was young, pretty. Lydie wondered: is that the one? But nothing special passed between her and Michael. Just hellos, the introduction of spouses.

"How do you know all these people?" she asked him, bristling at the reminder of his secret life.

"I don't know anyone well. I've met them along the way, through work, I guess."

A woman the age of Lydie's mother seemed to want to speak to them. She caught Michael's eye, and he turned to her. "Are you the fellow who's redoing the Louvre?" she asked.

"Is that what they're saying about me?" Michael asked, sounding fake, hearty, the way he sometimes did with women that age.

"Absolutely. Absolutely—it's the talk all through the embassy." She took a long drink of her whiskey; from the pouches under her eyes and the red patches on her cheeks, Lydie deduced that she liked whiskey a lot.

"We're Lydie and Michael McBride," Lydie said, shaking her hand. "Do you work at the embassy?"

"How do you do? I'm Dot Graulty. I'm an old-timer in the consular section—twenty-five years. Art Chase was just pointing you out to me. He comes to me for special favors. Little things that need doing, everyone comes to me." She took another drink. She looked overweight, a little uncomfortable in her tight red jersey dress. She wore two strands of pearls at the throat.

"What sort of things?" Michael asked.

Dot laughed, touched his arm. "Anything! Any nitpicking when it comes to the government—the U.S. government, not the French one. If it's legal, I know the loophole." She frowned. "Does that sound terrible? Like I'm trying to put something over on Uncle Sam?"

"Not at all," Michael said. "Why have you stayed in Paris for so long?"

"My husband is with the *Herald Tribune*. Listen, I'm so happy to have met you." Her gaze had fixed on the bar; her glass was empty. Her fingers wiggling in a distracted sort of wave, she walked away.

"What do you think she really does at the embassy?" Michael asked, watching her go.

"She's probably special deputy to the ambassador," Lydie said. One of her and Michael's favorite pastimes at large, impersonal parties was inventing stories about everyone they met. "She's his trouble-shooter. She finds the loophole that will let him take fresh foie gras home to the States for Christmas."

"She finds the loophole that will let her drink that entire bottle of scotch tonight," Michael said. "She does have that motherly way, though. Doesn't she? Kind of like Julia."

"Yes," Lydie said, touched that he would mention Julia. It seemed a peace offering. She regarded him, thought that she had never seen him so handsome. Perhaps time apart had been exactly what they needed. She warned herself about putting it in the past tense, but she hoped that he would come home with her tonight.

"Now, here she is," said an unfamiliar voice.

"Lydie, I'd like you to meet Arthur Chase," Michael said.

"I've heard so much about the lovely Lydie McBride," Arthur said, shaking her hand. "And I didn't want to wait until Michael's great unveiling party to meet you."

Lydie grinned. "I've been wanting to meet *you*. And to thank you—for helping Michael's project get off the ground."

"It was the least I could do. It was my pleasure. Michael is making up for lost time, working night and day. I'm sure he wouldn't have come here tonight if I hadn't insisted on finally meeting you."

Lydie turned to Michael. By his expression and the blush that was spreading across his cheeks, by the way he continued to look at Arthur and not her, she knew that he had invited her to the party because of Arthur. Tears sprang to her eyes; she couldn't help it. She felt like a fool. She hated her husband. When she could speak, she let out a little laugh. "He's a workaholic," she said.

Arthur had noticed her tears; he looked from Lydie to Michael, worried. "My wife used to say that about me, and don't think I don't know how rough it can be on a wife. Poor Sylvia. It's better, now we're in Paris. Being cultural attaché to India, living in Bombay—that was rough. Make him pay for it, Lydie! Go shopping!"

She knew he had intended it as a joke, to be kind, but Lydie couldn't laugh. The tears spilled down her cheeks. "I'm sorry," she said, turning away.

"I'm sorry." Arthur patted her shoulder. She knew he had walked away when she felt Michael's hand on her back.

"Lydie?" he said. "Lydie?"

"I hate doing this," she said, truly humiliated, feeling pathetic.

"I wanted you to come," he said. "The truth is, I hadn't planned on coming myself, but Arthur kept badgering me about taking the night off, bringing you to this party. I wanted you to come. I've been having a good time . . ."

Lydie gulped until she stopped crying. She wiped her face with the napkin the bartender had handed her with her drink. "If I've just learned a lesson, it's to never make the first date with your husband after he's moved out a cocktail party at the American Embassy."

"It was a bad idea," he agreed.

"Why did you invite me?" Lydie asked. "I don't get it."

Michael looked blank. "Because I wanted to. I had to come— for business, to be political. But I thought it might be fun; I thought you might enjoy it."

So it really was a date. Lydie supposed she should feel happy he had asked her. But after eight years of marriage, how worked up could she get over another courtship?

"I'm going home now," she said.

"Let's go out to dinner," Michael said. "That's what we should have done in the first place."

Lydie was silent, considering. She wanted to go. Earlier in the evening, she had imagined dinner with Michael after leaving the party, a bistro dinner within walking distance of their apartment. She shook her head; she felt too mistrustful of him. She felt ugly and disheveled, the way someone would feel who had just had the rug pulled out from under her before an audience she had once hoped to impress. "I can't," she said.

"Oh, come on, Lydie," Michael said in a sweet tone that made Lydie want to cry again. "Don't we have to start somewhere?"

"I just can't tonight."

"Then we'll do it soon. We should talk," Michael said.

She didn't kiss him good-bye. "We should talk," she thought, walking past the armed police. It sounded like something he would say to an insurance agent. It sounded earnest and casual. Lydie had intended to walk home, but her feet hurt and she felt tired. She changed her mind, headed toward the taxi stand in front of the Crillon. She stood alone for a few minutes before anyone else came.

"Hello there," said Dot Graulty, leaning against a man who appeared as drunk as she did.

"Hello," Lydie said, wondering if the man was her husband. It had to be; how could a lover be enticed by her? She was so tipsy, what could there be to look forward to?

"Lost your fellow?" she asked.

"He's staying late. I'm a little tired." Lydie scanned the Place de la Concorde for a cab. She saw one coming and planned to let Dot take it, even though Lydie had been there first. Suddenly she thought of Kelly. "Do you handle visas at the embassy?" she asked Dot.

"I'm not in the visa section, no, but after twenty-five years I know a thing or two about visas," Dot said.

"Because I might want to take my assistant to the United States when I go back," Lydie said. The cab drew to the curb; the passenger inside was arguing about the fare. "And she'll need a visa."

"She's French?" Dot asked.

"Filipino."

"Oh, the U.S.A. is tough on them. Call what's-his-name. The one from Baltimore . . . Bruce Morrison."

"Thanks, Dot," Lydie said. "Why don't you take this cab?"

"No, honey, you take it," Dot said, leaning against the man with her eyes closed. "We'll get the next one. We're enjoying the air."

Lydie said good-bye and climbed in. She gave the driver her address, then removed a notepad from her purse and wrote down the name "Bruce Morrison." By the time she glanced up they had already driven out of the Place de la Concorde, one of her favorite night sights: she loved the fountains, the obelisk, the way the spotlights made all the stately buildings look gold. Driving along the dark, tree-lined Cours Albert Premier, she was picturing the Place, festive even tonight. It wasn't until the car stopped in front of her building that she realized that she was coming home alone after dark. It was the first time. As she paid the driver, she wondered whether Michael would have preferred to invite that other girl to the party. The one he did or didn't love. The one Lydie hated. She wondered whether he was on his way to her now.

~~∽~~

It felt bizarre to waken in Anne's canopied bed. Light barely filtered through the heavy silk draperies, which, Michael saw that morning, were deep green. He felt swamped by the heat, the closeness. It was the first time he had spent an entire night there. Anne lay beside him, already alert, smiling.

"*Tu as dormi bien?*" she asked, one hand lazily mussing her own hair.

"*C'était un peu trop chaud,*" Michael said, rolling onto his back.

"It's hot, yes," she said. She laughed at her double meaning. "And we'd better make love now, because I don't know when I'll have this chance again, to have you in my bed in the morning."

He had not told her that he was living in a hotel. That was something between himself and Lydie; he wanted time to consider the state of his marriage. Telling Anne would proclaim something to the world, to himself, which he wasn't ready for. Yet here he was in bed with Anne; he felt he had spent half the night with an erection. He had called to invite her to dinner after Lydie had gone home from the embassy. As soon as Anne accepted, Michael had known how the night would go.

She lay on her back, pulling him close, directing his fingers to her *doudounes,* her *zizi.* She wanted him to call their genitals by name, something Lydie had hated. Saying the words in French made it at once easier and more forbidden.

"*Je suis bien obsédé de ta verge,*" she said, regarding his erect penis as if she were, in fact, obsessed with it. She produced a condom, part of their ritual, and rolled it on. She treated his penis a little strangely, as though it had its own life, separate from Michael. Lying back, watching her pay attention to it, Michael figured she considered it a third party. When she left it to kiss his lips, she was giving him equal time, ignoring it, but surreptitiously reaching down every so often to stroke it, to reassure it. Just a little secret between her and it.

He could not be sure, but last night he thought she had whispered "Louis" at the moment of orgasm. He knew she had fantasies of herself as Madame de Sévigné; perhaps, making love in this antique bed, she could pretend Michael was the Sun King. She did research the way other women conducted friendships, love affairs: with passion and intimacy. This was obvious to Michael when he watched her at the Louvre. She blocked out everything but herself and the person she was studying. Her fantasy world carried into real life, and that was strange. Now, entering her, he wondered whether she was making love to him, Michael McBride, or to his penis. Or to Louis XIV. But the thought was brief and faded soon enough.

❧

An hour later, sipping coffee in her living room, all was proper, even demure. She wore a yellow dress with matching yellow sandals. Her hair, lighter than ever, looked curly and full. He had watched her after their shower, stiffening her wet hair with white foam, blowing it dry until it looked the way she wanted. The process was ritualistic, so feminine. He had never seen a woman pay that sort of attention to her appearance. In his mother's case it was unfortunate, because she hadn't much natural beauty to start with. Lydie looked beautiful, in spite of what she did not do; she washed her hair with shampoo thriftily bought by the gallon, then let it air-dry. He had never seen her wear lipstick or nail polish. She disliked any perfume except something called "Water of Struan" that smelled like hay. Thinking of Lydie, he had to look away from Anne.

"There's the doctor," he said, gazing across the street. A tall, stooped old man deposited a dripping tea bag in the garbage can on his balcony. A mangy German shepherd stood at his heels.

"What a pig," Anne said. "Why can't he keep his garbage out of my sight?"

"How do you know he's a doctor?"

"Because he has doctor plates on his car. It's that little red Mini down there. Also, he used to see patients. I'd watch him examining them in his library, which was then a consulting room. They had the most terrible ailments! Shingles, liver tumors, hemorrhoids."

"What did you do? Watch with binoculars?"

Anne's mouth thinned. Michael's joke did not amuse her. "No. It was obvious from their spots, and from the way he palpated their bodies. Sometimes I would see the patients in the rue Jacob, and I could tell what was wrong by the way they walked."

"Don't get mad," Michael said, "but you do have an active imagination."

"I know you intend that as a compliment," Anne said, beaming.

"I do." Just then he remembered George Reed predicting that Michael would find a mistress in Paris. "All men do it," George, who knew Lydie well, had said. "It's the national pastime." The memory was unpleasant.

"I don't like to ask this," Anne said. "But what will your wife think about last night? Did she not expect you to come home?"

"Don't worry about that," Michael said, feeling protective of Lydie. He would never discuss her with Anne.

"I liked her," Anne said. "That time I met her. And I feel funny telling you this, but I have gotten several letters from that friend of hers. The wife of that friend you introduced me to at the Louvre."

"Patrice?" Michael asked, hiding his shock.

"Patrice d'Origny. She has read *Three Women of the Marais*."

"Have you written back?" Michael asked. This information made him dislike Patrice, instead of just feeling jealous of her. Patrice corresponding with Anne seemed disloyal to Lydie. He realized, of course, that he was being unreasonable; how could Patrice know about Anne and him, since even Lydie didn't know Anne's identity? And if Patrice didn't know, why shouldn't she write to Anne?

"Yes. I always answer my fan mail. And her letters were, I don't know . . . different. Sort of dreamy." Anne looked dreamy herself, remembering Patrice's letters. "She really lost herself in the material. I can well understand how that can happen, considering she lives on the Place des Vosges. You know that Marie de Sévigné was born in a house there, don't you? Her grandfather made a fortune collecting the salt tax . . ."

"Patrice's husband makes a fortune selling jewelry," Michael said, wanting to bring Anne back to the present day.

"D'Origny Bijoutiers. I know it well. It is the house where my family has always bought commemorative jewelry. For example, my grandfather acquired a rough diamond in South Africa and had it cut and set by d'Origny—my grandmother's engagement ring. Those particular grandparents were terribly Anglicized. All the silver timbales given by my family to newborn babies come from there. Also, the diamond earrings my father gave to me when I turned eighteen."

Anne had never previously spoken of her family. In fact, Michael realized, she usually treated the people she researched with the familiarity accorded to one's family. Now she was talking about her real family as if they were rich, somehow noble. He thought of applying words like "Anglicized" to his own family or Lydie's: it didn't work. "Immigrant Irish," "middle class," and "New Yorkers" came closer. The McBrides, like the Fallons, were a close Catholic family. The highest praise they could bestow was to call someone "down to earth." He thought of their professions: firemen, police officers, small-business owners, plant managers, teachers, maids. He was the first architect in either family, and all four parents had been so proud. He knew that Julia, and Cornelius before his death, loved him like their own son, and that his parents loved Lydie like one of their daughters. What would the parents think if he left Lydie? If he came home with Anne?

Or if he never went home, lived in Paris for the rest of his life?

"Why do you look so grave?" Anne asked. "What are you thinking?"

"We're going to be late for work," Michael said.

"We are our own bosses," Anne said. "That is what is so wonderful."

"The builders expect me," Michael said. "The table will be delivered today."

"*C'est pas vrai!*" Anne said, sounding delighted. "I cannot wait to see it! You are terrible for not telling me sooner, but I forgive you."

He had known she would love his idea for the information kiosk: a copy of one of Boulle's tables from the King's state chamber in the Palais du Louvre, the chamber planned by Lescot and Scibec de Carpi. In one of those perfect coincidences, that was the time of Madame de Sévigné. Although most of the plans had been formed before he knew her, lately she had been trying to influence him to fill the Salle with paintings and a tapestry actually purchased by Louis XIV.

Now that he had told her about the table, she insisted that he finish his coffee and prepare to leave right away. They walked to the Louvre in five minutes, when it usually took ten.

"It's getting cooler. You can tell fall is coming," Michael said as they crossed the Pont du Carrousel. He gazed upriver, at the great glass dome of the Grand Palais. He tried to pick his apartment house out of those that lined the banks, but it was around the bend.

"Hurry up," Anne said, walking ahead of him.

Although the museum was an hour from opening, the first tourists trailed toward the glass pyramid, where they would enter. Michael and Anne used a more convenient, VIP entrance nearer the street.

"*Patron!*" called Gaston, the project foreman. He came toward Michael, shook his hand. He spoke to Anne. It didn't exactly bother Michael that the workers knew she was his lover, but it made him uncomfortable. Anne herself did not seem to mind.

"So, where is it?" she asked Gaston.

"Downstairs. We waited for Monsieur McBride before bringing it up. It is in four pieces, wrapped, in boxes. I saw them off the truck myself."

"Big boxes!" called Prosper, a toothless Greek whose working papers had just come through.

"Let's bring them up," Michael said. He led Anne, Gaston, and twelve workers down an interior staircase.

"You are Charles Lebrun," Anne whispered to him in English, so the others would not understand. "Architect to the King of France. You are directing this band of workers, from Reims, to install a great and marvelous table of the King's choice. It must be perfect, because guess who's coming to dinner?"

"The court's greatest gossip?" Michael asked.

"Hush, don't spoil it," Anne said, sounding hurt. "Think of her as a reporter, a chronicler of that age."

"Okay," Michael said. Why had he called Madame de Sévigné a gossip, intending to be mean? He felt exhilarated; the installation of the information table meant more to him than any other part of the project. He had found the artisan, ordered it commissioned. Michael remembered all the cajoling he had done to convince the maker to abandon his other work to have it ready on time. It galled him that Anne would tell him to pretend he was Lebrun. That was it. Michael admired Lebrun's work; who wouldn't? But why would Anne suggest that Michael, at his moment of triumph, pretend to be an architect who had lived centuries ago?

Yet when the table was carried in four sections to the second floor and the protective wrapping taken away, when it was centered in the Salle des Quatre Saisons, she gasped.

"As Marie de Sévigné said of Louis the XIV's apartment," Anne said, "'the furnishings are divine, utter magnificence everywhere.'"

"It is perfect," Gaston said. "The best information center in the Louvre."

The table was enormous: stately, simple, and long enough to hold a banquet for the court or all the brochures, maps, and booklets necessary to guide modern tourists through the vast Louvre. He would have liked to order a copy of the one gilded and carved with heads of dragons. The Ministry of Culture had balked at that, citing time and cost, chiding Michael to remember there had been a revolution.

"Now you must turn your attention to the paintings," Anne said. "Poussin's *Sacrament of Extreme Unction must* hang there." She indicated the long north wall. "Settle for nothing less. Remember, Louis XIV's Director of Fine Art would have made Poussin president of a French Academy in Rome if Poussin had not been old and about to die. It is imperative that you hang one of his finest works in here."

Michael said nothing; *Sacrament of Extreme Unction* was the painting Pierre Dauphin guarded so zealously. Michael wanted it for his own reasons. First, because it was a prime example of Poussin's work. Reminiscent of Michaelangelo in its foreshortening and the sculptural heft of its people, it had been painted by Poussin during his long sojourn in Rome. Michael felt moved by its subject—the ministration of last rites. Also, he liked the woman in it. Leaving the room, she glanced over her shoulder with a sad, secret smile that alternately reminded him of Lydie and the St. Pauli girl.

"I have a feeling I'll wind up with *Apollo and Daphne*," Michael said after a while.

Anne shook her head vehemently. "It is too late an example.

Exquisite in its way, but not representative. Poussin died before it was completed. Fight for the *Sacrament*."

Barricades kept tourists out of the hall, but the workers' activity attracted a certain amount of attention.

"Everyone wants to see what is happening," Anne said. "I want to tell them: history is being made!"

Hearing that, Michael thought of Lydie, of how she should be here. He looked around, noting change: restoration of the mosaic floor; two walls, nearly complete, to redirect flow through the French painting galleries; signs done in words, not glyphs, hung where Michael thought they would best be seen. The workers swept shreds of paper into small piles. It was nearly twelve, time for their lunch break. Michael felt relieved they had finished the hard part before lunch, knowing they would return at two drowsy from red wine.

"I have to make a phone call," he said to Anne.

"And I must go upstairs to work," she said. She stood on her toes to reach her arms around his neck. She collapsed against him, pressing her pelvis against his. "My *zizi* remembers this morning," she whispered. When he didn't reply, she nudged him. "Say it," she whispered.

"My *verge* remembers."

She giggled. "You are so cute and embarrassed. So American!"

Walking toward the pay phone, Michael wondered whether his embarrassment was particularly American, whether Didier or Gaston would feel ridiculous calling their body parts cute names in the middle of the day. In bed was a different story. Then that made him wonder whether he had created the embarrassment as punishment for thinking of sex with Anne before calling Lydie.

In any case, Lydie was not home.

# 14

*Never had Paris seen such a crowd of people. Never has the*
*city been so aroused, so intent on a spectacle.*

—To Françoise-Marguerite, July 1676

"It might be possible," Lydie said to Kelly. They sat in a café
overlooking the Beaubourg Center. Lydie drank tea, Kelly drank
Coke. "Mr. Morrison was nice on the phone, very sympathetic
when I told him about you."

"What did you tell him?" Kelly asked.

"That you are a Filipino, in Paris illegally, that I want to take
you to the United States. I told him that you are my assistant."

"Your assistant? How do I assist you?"

"That's what we have to discuss." Lydie spoke softly, in case
some of the Americans jamming the café were embassy spies.

Kelly stared into her Coke, trouble evident in her eyes. "Lydie,"
she said. She glanced up at Lydie, then averted her eyes again.

Lydie waited, holding herself back. She knew she could make
this too easy for Kelly. She could imagine taking over, devoting
herself night and day to Kelly's cause as if it were a religious mis-

sion. It would distract her from Michael, and when it was over, she would feel like a hero. But it was Kelly's cause, not Lydie's, and Lydie could only help her along with it.

"Lydie, what about my fish market?" Kelly asked after a moment.

"I don't really expect you to *be* my assistant," Lydie said, smiling. "It's just something I thought up for the authorities. You can still have your fish market." She withdrew some papers from her briefcase.

"Is that the petition?" Kelly asked.

"Yes," Lydie said, handing it to her. A green-haired boy stood before them, juggling shoes. Four high heels and a man's sneaker. Lydie couldn't take her eyes off him, but Kelly was mesmerized by the petition. Her thumb traced the words "United States Department of Justice." When he passed the sneaker, Lydie fished some francs out of her pocket.

"We have to fill that out," Lydie said.

"It's just four pages long," Kelly said, sounding perplexed.

Naturally she would expect more, Lydie realized, watching her. A document that could change her life's course, make her wish come true, should be many pages long. "Did you know that you have to be interviewed by someone from the embassy?" Lydie asked.

"I have heard that."

"Mr. Morrison said that your being illegally in France causes problems. If you show up at the U.S. Embassy without a proper visa to be here, they have an obligation to report you to the French police."

Kelly looked at her helplessly. "And they would deport me to the Philippines?"

"It's possible," Lydie said. "One option would be for you to return to the Philippines on your own, to file the petition there."

This seemed impossible to Lydie; she hated to even suggest it, but Morrison had said it might be the best bet.

"I would do that," Kelly said, a smile spreading across her face.

"What would happen if you went back?" Lydie asked, shocked by Kelly's happiness.

"I would see my home and the rest of my family. But I would have hope of going to the United States. I would be a star in my province!"

Lydie regarded her. She rarely thought of Kelly as a daughter. In the back of her mind, she thought of Patrice and Didier as Kelly's family. But seeing Kelly grin at the thought of her family made Lydie realize how far Kelly was from home, and how far she had to go.

"Kelly," Lydie said. "Tell me how you got here—to Paris—in the first place."

"I obtained a visa to visit Germany. It is much easier for Filipinos to visit Germany than any other country."

"A tourist visa?" Lydie asked.

"Yes. Did your parents get to the States on tourist visas?" Kelly asked.

"No, immigration laws were much more liberal then. It was thirty years ago." She watched Kelly, sensed that she was nervous, hesitant about going on with the story. "Don't you want to tell me what happened?" Lydie asked.

Kelly shrugged, looked away. "Well, my brother, who was a chauffeur for the Philippine ambassador to France, smuggled me across the border in the trunk of his car." She sipped her Coke, as if that were the end of the story.

"And then?" Lydie asked.

Kelly shrugged. "The ambassador was returning from a vacation in Bavaria. Paul Anka was driving him and his family in the limousine. We had planned the whole thing by letter, when I was in the Philippines, waiting for my visa. So, I landed in Berlin and found the bus to the Black Forest. And Paul Anka was waiting for me at a certain hotel."

Kelly spoke in her usual shy voice, without any obvious emotion, as though the story embarrassed her. The way she told it seemed designed to prevent Lydie from feeling sympathy for her.

"How far did you ride in the trunk?" she asked.

"Many miles," Kelly said. "Don't feel sorry for me, Lydie. I did it because I wanted to—to get to Paris, it was worth it."

At that moment, sitting in the café, Lydie wanted more than anything else for Kelly to get to America. She added it to the list of what she had always wanted most in her life: a happy family, an Alfa Romeo, the cover story in *House & Garden*, Michael.

"I didn't mean to make you so sad," Kelly said.

"It's not just you," Lydie said. "I'm having a hard time myself right now. Is your brother still the ambassador's chauffeur?"

"Yes, but there is a new ambassador, who flies whenever he leaves France. So Paul Anka no longer crosses the border. Also, he works only part-time because there is not so much driving. Before, under the old administration, his duties included doing errands for President and Mrs. Marcos."

"Like what?"

"Many things to buy in Paris!" Kelly said, giggling, perhaps relieved to change the subject. "Boxes and boxes of handkerchiefs from Nina Ricci. One box per week! One hundred socks each month from Charvet."

Lydie laughed along. "I'm going to file you as an H1—an alien of distinguished merit and ability," Lydie said.

Kelly smiled, suspicious. "What do you mean?"

"The other categories cover unskilled laborers, and there are already plenty of those in the United States. If we want to succeed, we must be creative. I have to file an affidavit stating why you have distinguished merit and ability, why you are the only person suitable for this job. Otherwise, the government will tell me to hire an American. I have to swear to it under penalty of perjury."

"You could go to jail. Are the jails bad in the United States?"

"Not as bad as some places, but I don't want to go to jail anywhere," Lydie said. "Besides, by the time we complete the petition, we won't be lying. We must discover your specialty, the thing no one else can do as well. Something that I would be willing to pay you for."

"I know fish," Kelly said seriously.

"Unfortunately, I don't. So we'll say you are indispensable to me. You'll have to learn my tastes. When a magazine editor gives me an assignment, I send you out looking for props. You'll have to learn what I like."

"How will I do that?"

"I'll give you some clippings, of pieces I did in the past. And maybe you can help me with the ball for Didier."

"Patrice will return to Paris soon," Kelly said sadly. "She is my only worry."

"Well . . ." Lydie said. "I'll talk to her."

After she finished her Coke, Kelly stood to go. Her eyes darted from the vicinity of Lydie's head to the ground. Could she be waiting to be dismissed? Sometimes she acted like a servant; other times she seemed comfortable as Lydie's equal. It bothered Lydie to think Kelly would play a subservient role in order to get what she wanted. Or did she really believe that her manner pleased people?

"What is it?" Lydie asked.

"May I go now?"

"You don't need my permission to leave," Lydie said. She wanted disappointment to come through in her voice; she wanted Kelly to drop the act.

Kelly's face went white. "I'm sorry . . . I didn't mean . . ."

"That's okay," Lydie said quickly. "I didn't mean it to come out that way. 'Bye, Kelly."

"'Bye, Lydie." Kelly took a few steps backwards, then turned toward the Métro.

Lydie was going haywire. She chewed an ice cube, watching a turbo Saab back into a parking spot. She replayed the last scene in her mind, listening to her own cold, haughty words: "You don't need my permission to leave." Ten minutes ago she had been on the verge of weeping for Kelly and her hardships, seconds ago she had practically accused her of manipulating Lydie to get what she wanted.

After her father died, people kept telling her she should cry more. Michael, her mother, her aunts. Lydie had listened to them, numb. "Don't you feel like it?" her mother had asked. "No," Lydie had replied. Then, "What will happen if I don't?" Her mother had had no answer for that; no one had. But now Lydie knew. All the sadness she should have felt for her father, whom she had loved, was now coming out of her in a torrent. For her marriage, for the image of Kelly in the trunk of a car, for Patrice, who would be lonely in Paris after Lydie and Kelly moved away.

Sadness overshadowed her anger. The fury she had felt toward Kelly as she left had already evaporated, leaving her with only the vaguest sense that she was really angry at Michael and her father for leaving—not Kelly. It hurt to breathe. She had never felt so sad in her life. Sitting at the edge of a Paris square on a brilliant August afternoon, Lydie didn't think it possible to feel lonelier.

As if she had forgotten how to live on her own, Lydie tried to envision what Patrice would do in her situation. She certainly wouldn't sit idle, feeling sorry for herself. She might very possibly focus some attention on Kelly, helping her get to the United States. She would also try to fix her marriage.

But Lydie couldn't see Patrice and Didier falling apart the way she and Michael had. And why not? She played with her wedding ring, trying to figure it out. For one thing, Patrice was too matter-of-fact. Lydie couldn't picture her putting up with any nonsense in Didier. Patrice kept track of things too closely; she did it with Lydie, Kelly, certainly Didier. If Didier ever had a notion to fool around, Lydie could imagine Patrice knowing about it before he did.

The other, more important reason was Lydie's profound belief that no two people could ever love each other the way she and Michael did. It went so deep, she actually groaned—out loud—to think she could have lost it. She had trusted Michael to love her forever because she had known she would love him forever. She hated herself for turning it into something banal: taking him for granted. She remembered how she had signed notes to him in the first years of their marriage: "Yours till the butterflies . . . yours till Niagara Falls . . . Lydie." The memory made her cringe.

She forced herself to remember the day. She and Michael were cooking in their kitchen on West Tenth Street. He had been ominously upset ever since the night before, when Lydie's father had taken him to some lumberyard in Yonkers.

"Tell me what happened," Lydie said. She and Michael knew little about family intrigue, but he had been hinting about trouble with Neil ever since he'd come home.

"I think your father's having a midlife crisis," Michael said.

Neil Fallon was an extravagantly emotional Irishman, so this theory did not sound at all far-fetched to Lydie. "I'm sure he'll survive it," she had said.

Now, looking back at it from the Carré des Innocents in Paris, she couldn't believe those had actually been her words. Had they? She wracked her brain, trying to remember. As if it mattered! Detectives had rung the bell just half an hour later. On a little card in his wallet, Neil had listed Michael and Lydie as the ones to notify in case of emergency. In a different case—an accident, or a heart attack—the police would have acted differently. Lydie could practically see and hear those other policemen: lowered heads, a sympathetic tone of voice. But Neil had murdered a young woman.

The detective had spoken harshly, asking strange questions that made Lydie think that she herself was suspected of a crime. After three or four questions, Michael had put his arm around her shoulders and whispered that she shouldn't answer. "Tell us what happened," Michael had said to the detective.

"Cornelius Fallon is dead," the detective had said, almost as an afterthought. "It was a murder-suicide."

The possibility of her father as a murderer was so impossible that Lydie had gasped and asked who had killed her father. When the detective told her the truth, she had turned to Michael. She remembered how carefully he watched her, as if he knew she was going to break and he knew he couldn't do anything to stop it. She remembered the feeling of his arms around her shoulders and his voice calmly telling the detective he couldn't ask her any more questions. And Lydie remembered knowing, even before the detective left her kitchen, that her father had given her up, had deliberately bargained her away. Because he would know, by his actions, that for the rest of her life Lydie would first think of him as a killer, second as her father.

# 15

*This conversation lasted an hour, and it is impossible to re-
peat it all, but I certainly made myself very pleasant
throughout this time and I can say without vanity that she
was very glad to have someone to talk to, for her heart was
overflowing.*

—To Coulanges, December 1670

"SURPRISE!" Patrice stood in Lydie's doorway, holding out
the magenta cotton parao she had brought as a gift. Keeping secret her return to Paris had not been easy; twice last night she had
nearly called Lydie even though she had decided, on the plane
from Saint-Tropez, that it would be more fun, more festive just to
show up. She had given fifteen francs to Lydie's concierge to let
her up unannounced. But Lydie was not exactly taking it as
Patrice had hoped. For one thing, she was frowning. For another, she looked as though she had just been roused from deep
slumber.

"You're back," Lydie said. "I didn't expect you until Monday."

"Didier decided the office couldn't survive another day without him."

"Come in," Lydie said, standing aside. "God, you look great—so tan!"

That's more like it, Patrice thought. That's the sort of greeting she wanted from her best friend. She stood in the middle of the room, looked out Lydie's big windows at the Seine, then turned, beaming, to wrap Lydie in a big hug.

"How was your vacation?" Lydie asked.

"And I missed you too!" Patrice said, stepping back.

Lydie gave her a smile, the first one Patrice had seen. "I missed you," she said.

"Which do you want to hear about first? The seclusion experience or the Paris-by-the-sea experience? This is for you."

Lydie took the parao, wrapped it around herself. "It's beautiful. I'll wear it at the beach next summer and think of you. Let's sit out on the terrace," she said. "That way you can update your tan."

"This time yesterday I was lying on the beach, those little cups over my eyes . . . oh, well." As she spoke, Patrice tossed back her head, looked at the sky. "Two days ago, however, we had lunch at Club 55, which is more Paris than Paris. The only people we didn't know we recognized from films."

"The best of both worlds."

"In many ways, Saint-Tropez is *our* Paris concentrated into one small area. Like frozen orange juice before you add the water. Didier has a bunch of pals from the old days—from school, college, his first marriage, his second marriage, a regular rat pack. They all were there."

"Do you like them?"

"Yes, *but* . . ." Patrice said, smiling slyly. "A little goes a long way. You should have come. I'd have had a great time, filling you in on the intrigues. Who's sleeping with whom, who's slept with whose wife."

"That sounds sordid," Lydie said, shocking Patrice with her bitterness. She sat on the deck chair, knees drawn up, scowling.

"It *is* sordid. That's the point," Patrice said quietly, trying to get the lay of the land. "That's why I wish you had been there."

"I didn't think Didier went in for that sort of thing," Lydie said.

"Of course he doesn't. He's a big prude. But I'm telling you, his *friends* are like a fraternity—they have the average mentality of twenty-year-olds. All they think about are their penises and their wallets." Patrice stared at Lydie. "Maybe we should talk about seclusion instead. Let's see . . . our house was very secluded. Days went by when we saw no one but each other. The sky was very blue. The sea was even bluer. Most of the time, Club 55 was just a bad memory. Do you like me again?"

Lydie nodded. She opened her mouth to say something, then closed it. Patrice noticed shadows under her eyes. She looked terrible. "What?" Patrice said, touching the back of her hand.

"Michael is staying at a hotel."

From the look in Lydie's eyes, Patrice knew the hotel wasn't in Dubrovnik. "He's moved out?" Patrice asked. When Lydie didn't answer, Patrice squeezed her hand. "I'm so sorry. I never would have thought . . ." She shook her head. "I know you said there was trouble, but I never would have thought . . ."

"Neither would I," Lydie said. Suddenly she seemed unblocked. Her eyes went wild. "I didn't realize how extreme things had gotten. He's moved out. Patrice, he's in love with someone else!"

"Oh, that's terrible," Patrice said. The only word for Lydie's expression—for the dazed look in her eyes and the way her shoulders slumped—was "devastated." To come to Paris married—in love with your husband—and to have him leave you for another woman must be the worst thing in the world.

"It's terrible," Lydie echoed.

"When did you find out about this?"

"A few weeks ago." Lydie glanced up, a slightly fearful cast to her eyes—as if she thought Patrice would feel offended that Lydie hadn't called to tell her.

"Don't worry," Patrice said. "I understand you had to keep it to yourself."

"It's not that," Lydie said. "I'm thinking of what I just said— that it's been weeks. At first I thought he'd come home after a few days."

"Have you seen him? Do you talk to each other?"

"We talk a lot. We tried to see each other, but I wound up feeling worse. It's awful to say good night at the end of the night and go our separate ways."

Patrice had a guilty pang for two things she was thinking. The first was that without Michael she had Lydie's friendship all to herself. She could imagine doting on Lydie, helping her through this. And her second guilt-provoking thought was that she had at least one thing that Lydie did not have: a happy marriage. She felt her heart overflowing. Patrice had always known she had a generous spirit, but until Didier she hadn't had anyone to give her love to. Demonstrations of love had never been encouraged by her mother. She had the urge to hug Lydie, then make her a nice hot cup of tea.

"Is it possible you could ever fall out of love with Didier?" Lydie asked.

In another instance Patrice might have lied to make Lydie feel better, but this was too important. "No, I can't. Not in a million years. Why? Are you falling out of love with Michael?"

"That's what I don't know," Lydie said.

"Lydie, that's not falling out of love," Patrice said. "Who was it who said, 'It's a thin line between love and hate'? Freud?"

Lydie half smiled. "I would have said Cole Porter. Did you say Freud to cheer me up?"

Patrice, who hadn't, smiled enigmatically. "The point is, if you lie awake thinking of Michael, you're not falling out of love with him."

"I feel as if everything good in me is leaking out. It has been, ever since my father died."

"There's a lot of good in you," Patrice said. She wanted to list the things she loved in Lydie, but Lydie's face had shut down.

"I used to think I was the most passionate person I knew," Lydie said. "I made a project out of *everything*. I couldn't just fall in love—I had to fall *madly* in love. I made Michael an obsession."

"Like how?" Patrice asked.

"Like the beginning of our romance. We were staying in Washington, and one afternoon Michael took me to the Freer, to look at Japanese art. He especially loved the lacquered boxes. The second he told me that, I knew what I was giving him for Christmas. After we got back to New York I took a day off to find the perfect box—a mahogany chest."

"You mean like a blanket chest?"

"No; it's about the size of a large dictionary. Then I found a book on the history of Japanese lacquer. I followed the tradition to the letter—applying coat after coat of black lacquer, which I got from the body shop—sanding between coats. At first I used a brush, but when it got to be November and I had only applied ten of the—I think it was eighteen—coats, I broke down and used a spray can.

"Then I chose the design—a plum tree standing on a riverbank. When the last coat dried, I used the traditional method of 'painting' the design in talcum powder, then brushing on the glue, then applying the gold leaf." Lydie traced a pattern on her knee. "I was thinking of Michael the whole time. I felt as though I had him with me every minute."

"Did he like the box?" Patrice asked.

"Yes," Lydie said. "I gave it to him Christmas morning, and he proposed Christmas night. We wrote each other letters, even though we saw each other constantly, just so he'd have love letters to keep in it."

"That's lovely," Patrice said. One of her few regrets about falling so swiftly in love with Didier was that they had very few love letters. She thought of how pleasant it would be for Lydie and Michael, when they were old, to read through their old letters. But here was Lydie saying they might not be together. "Why not make a project of getting him back? You have it in you."

Lydie shook her head. "It has to come from him," she said. "He's the one who left. I can't 'win' him back."

"No," Patrice agreed sadly.

"And when the ball's over, I'll go back to New York," Lydie said stonily.

"Lydie . . ." Patrice didn't know what to say.

Lydie looked up at her. "I do have a 'project,' though. If that's what you want to call it."

"You do? You mean the ball?"

"No. You're going to have mixed feelings about this."

Patrice could already feel her spine stiffening. She could just hear her mother's voice: "Now, I know you're not going to like this, Patsy . . ."

"I'm going to help Kelly get to America."

"What do you mean? How?"

"I'm filing a petition for her."

Patrice felt rage growing inside her. It wasn't so much that Lydie had taken up Kelly's cause without a word to her: Patrice resented Lydie's defiant tone, as if she were daring Patrice to get upset. Considering the loving thoughts she'd just had for Lydie, it seemed a rank betrayal. "A petition," she said.

"Now, don't get mad," Lydie said.

"I don't know why you think I'll be mad about this," Patrice said coolly. "I have the strangest feeling that you *want* me to be."

Lydie shook her head. "Maybe I'm not thinking straight. I was afraid you'd think I was interfering."

"You plan to take Kelly home with you when you leave? After the ball?"

"If her petition goes through."

Patrice's first thought was that she'd have two people to write letters to. She realized instantly that she was thinking just like her mother, twisting a situation around and planting herself in the middle of it. She tried to imagine how happy Kelly must be. "How far have you gotten?" she asked.

"I've spoken to someone at the embassy. That's all. I know I should have talked to you first . . ."

"Don't be silly," Patrice said. Although she believed it too, she knew how petty it sounded. To say that Lydie should have consulted her before starting the process seemed so selfish. Lydie was acting selfless—*noble,* even. Patrice could actually see the words "HUMAN RIGHTS," weighty as a headline, printed in the air above Lydie's halo of golden hair. "Is this a throwback to your days as a social activist? Isn't that what Michael told us you used to be?"

"I just feel sorry for Kelly," Lydie said.

"So do I," Patrice said, finally feeling calmer. Now that she had composed herself, she laughed. "There must be feasting and merriment *chez* Merida. One of their pilgrims actually found the road to Mecca. Thanks to you."

"You don't want her to go, do you?" Lydie asked.

"Of course I do."

"But you'll miss her."

"Look, I miss a lot of people," Patrice said, thinking of Lydie herself, who would be gone from Paris in just a couple of months. "It's the way of the world."

"You've always mentioned her college education and said how wrong it is for her to be doing housework. But I know that you rely on her, that you're fond of her . . ."

"Look, I just spent a month without Kelly Merida making my bed, so I think I can manage. I think it's great. I really do," Patrice said. She leaned toward Lydie to kiss her cheek, to prove she meant it.

∽

But when Patrice returned home, when she was safe in her bedroom overlooking the Place des Vosges, she saw red.

"It's *treachery*," she said out loud. Kelly, with her simpering manner, her "Oh, thank you, Mum" for any little favor, her false naïveté, while all the time plotting, the wheels clicking, getting what she could out of people. And Lydie! Who would have thought she could be capable of such subterfuge? Acting so *big* about the whole thing, as if she was saving Kelly from a fate worse than death. And all that business about Kelly's education: Patrice was willing to bet Kelly's first years in New York would be spent cleaning Lydie's house or taking care of Lydie's sainted mother in her declining years. She swept around the bedroom, fast and faster. She didn't know what to do with herself.

The bags, still unpacked, stood by the bedroom door. When she had called Kelly last night, to tell her she was home a few days early, Kelly had given her some song and dance about not being able to work until late in the day. She had expected to hear some sort of welcome in Kelly's voice, but there had been nothing. In retrospect, Patrice supposed Kelly, like Lydie, had been dreading Patrice's return. The thought brought tears to her eyes.

Patrice did what she never did: called Didier at his office. She had to make polite small talk about Saint-Tropez with his secretary, Solange. But she kept her cool—she remembered to inquire about Solange's ill husband and the two Chihuahuas they treated like children.

"Hello, baby," Didier said.

"I am ripping mad," Patrice said. "You know what Lydie did? She stole Kelly right out from under my nose."

"You mean she kidnapped the maid?"

"Don't start with the jokes, Didier. I'm not in the mood. She waited until I left town, then she moved in on Kelly. She promised to take her to New York with her."

"But that's good, no? At the beach you were telling me you wanted a better life for Kelly . . ."

Patrice fought to control her temper. Sometimes men, Didier, could be so dense. She remembered the exact conversation: it was after an especially lovely lunch. She had felt so close to him, it had seemed like a good time to enlighten him on the topic of Kelly. Specifically, to chide him gently about the way he treated her like a servant. She had been feeling expansive, and Didier had taken it well. "Didier," she said now, patiently, into the phone. "Imagine training a gem cutter. Some guy from the provinces, a mec, a diamond in the rough, so to speak. Say you treated him like a little brother, taught him to operate in the business world, showed him how things were done in Paris. How would you feel if Léonce came along, took your little gem cutter—now a little more sophisticated, able to tell the difference between Haut-Brion and *vin ordinaire,* for example—and took him off to Geneva?"

"What difference would it make? One man can't own another, can he?"

Patrice screamed, did not bother to cover the mouthpiece. "Thanks for trying to understand!" she said.

"Listen, my baby," Didier said. "I do understand. It is very obviously you care a great deal for Kelly—and for Lydie. But how can you do for Kelly what Lydie can? How can you take her to the United States?"

"What's so wonderful about the United States?" Patrice asked.

"Patrice," Didier said patiently. "Get ahold of yourself. Think about what you are saying."

Patrice took a breath, deep, deeper; the breath filled her, forcing the tears up and out. "It just *gets* me," she said, "down there in Saint-Tropez, missing them both . . . buying them presents. And they've been planning their escape to the good ol' U.S.A."

"They're not escaping you," Didier said. "Leaving you will be their profound regret."

Patrice snorted. "You know just the way to talk to me, don't you, honey?"

"Imagine," Didier said. "Your two girlfriends leaving you all alone in France with me."

"The big bad wolf," Patrice said, laughing now. "But it's not you I'm thinking about. It's your snooty sister and your rat pack. Do you blame me for wanting allies?"

"Well. You must think about it," Didier said. "Just don't be too quick to turn on Lydie. You know she is your best friend."

"That's true," Patrice said, suddenly struck with real and deep sympathy for her. "Didier, something awful happened. Michael moved out."

"Ah . . ." Didier said.

"Why don't you sound surprised?" Patrice asked, instantly suspicious.

"It was a moment between men," Didier said. "But Michael did confide in me about someone else."

"And you didn't tell me?" asked Patrice, convinced that Paris was full of betrayal.

"You know I couldn't have done that," Didier said.

"I hear the little pilgrim now," Patrice said, listening to the sound of Kelly's key in the lock. "I think I'd better have a talk with her."

"Be gentle," Didier said.

"I'll try," Patrice said, already feeling her heart beat faster.

∽

Twenty minutes later, reclining in her bedroom chaise, Patrice reread her favorite section of the Dumas book and tried to breathe evenly. She had not yet spoken to Kelly; she heard Kelly moving through the rooms, presumably removing the sheets that had covered the furniture during the d'Orignys' absence. She wondered what was running through Kelly's mind. Perhaps she was rehearsing what she would tell Patrice: "I am sorry, Mum, but I must leave you." Or "Thanks to your supreme generosity in introducing me to Lydie, I have found passage to the States." Something contrite and humble, Patrice was sure. What a relief it would be if, instead, Kelly held her head high, thumbed her nose, said, "See you later, toots, my ship has come in . . ."

Patrice realized that leaving Kelly alone, not confronting her with what she already knew, was a form of torture. But she couldn't bring herself to seek Kelly out, greet her, lay it on the line. Her skin tingled as she heard Kelly advancing, room by room. Willing herself to concentrate, she read a letter from Madame de Sévigné to her daughter:

"*Are you really afraid that I prefer Madame de Brissac to you? Do you fear that her manner pleases me more than yours? That her mind has found the way to appeal to me? Is it your opinion that her beauty eclipses your charms?"*

Women really know how to stick it to each other, Patrice thought. We know how to play one off another, we use jealousy as a trump card, we fight to be number one in the affections of each other. Madame de Sévigné did it with her own daughter! Poor young Françoise-Marguerite, newly married and miles from home, tortured by the idea that her mother preferred another young woman to her. And, of course, Madame de Sévigné was shrewd enough to know exactly what she was doing. Not like Patrice's mother, who loved her sister in Cleveland more than anyone—more than her husband, more than Patrice. There was no game, no guile about it; nothing could have been clearer.

Was Lydie being shrewd? Patrice would not have thought so, yet she could not deny the jealousy Lydie had caused her to feel. It was an odious, three-cornered jealousy, a triangle, and Patrice wanted to sit at the triangle's peak. This triangle was different from the one she had shared with her mother and Aunt Jane because sitting at the top of this one had seemed possible. In the reverie she always occupied while reading the Dumas book, she envisioned the triangle's sides as the arms of Kelly and Lydie, reaching up toward her. Without Patrice, where would they be? They surely would never have met . . .

"Welcome home, Mum," Kelly said, startling Patrice.

Patrice carefully closed *Three Women of the Marais*. She nodded at Kelly, and the sight of her was a stab in the heart. Did Lydie think Patrice had been blind to Kelly's plight? Did she think Patrice was unaware that in Kelly's plan Paris was just a way station on the way to America? Well, she was not. "Hello," she said, trying to be calm.

"Shall I unpack your bags?" Kelly asked. Nervously, Patrice thought.

"That would be lovely," Patrice said. "In the pocket of that black one you'll find a plastic bag. Take it out, please."

Kelly fumbled with the zipper, then withdrew a small bag. She came toward Patrice, the bag in hand.

"It's a gift for you," Patrice said.

"Oh, Mum . . ." Kelly's face twisted with confusion. Patrice could imagine her wondering whether to confess her secret before opening the gift or afterward. For her part, Patrice knew that it would be kind to divulge her knowledge of Lydie's petition now, but she said nothing. She just stared at Kelly's brown hands, holding the bright plastic bag.

"Open it," Patrice said.

Kelly obeyed. She pulled out a package, wrapped in pink tissue paper. Inside was a black felt bag that contained a coral necklace.

"Thank you, Mum!" she exclaimed, obviously thrilled with it. Patrice had chosen it for the color, an unusually vivid shade of rose, and for the refined craftsmanship. The clasp was made of 14K gold. Didier had checked with his jeweler's eye. Kelly held the necklace close to her face, examining each individual bead. With one hand Kelly held aside her thick black hair; then she fastened the clasp around her neck.

"It's very pretty on you," Patrice said stiffly.

"Thank you, Mum. Thank you very much."

Kelly jiggled her necklace the way Patrice, once as a lark having tea at the mosque, had seen Arabs handle worry beads. "I know about Lydie petitioning for you," Patrice said.

"You do?" Kelly asked, looking worried.

"She told me. I'm happy for you." As she said it, Patrice realized that it was true. On the other hand, she still felt an overwhelming sense of loss and betrayal. Didn't she mean anything to Kelly? They had coexisted—harmoniously, Patrice had thought—for a long time.

"My only regret will be leaving you," Kelly said. The pain in her eyes made the words ring with sincerity and was all Patrice needed to make her throat tighten.

"I will regret that also," Patrice said. "But I know your dream has always been to get to the States. Paris was just a pitstop, right?"

"Excuse me?"

"A stopping-off place. Your halfway point between Manila and New York."

"Yes, that is right," Kelly said.

"I do have one fear," Patrice said. "Our government sets limits on how many people of any one nationality it lets in. Such as eight thousand Brazilians, two thousand Egyptians, one thousand Swedes. The Filipino quota is one of the lowest—because so many Filipinos are already there."

"I know," Kelly said glumly.

"That's not to say you won't get lucky. But you should have a backup plan. Why don't we try to make you legal in France first?"

Kelly looked skeptical. "I don't think . . ." she said.

"I'm not saying you should stay here forever," Patrice said gently. "But French working papers could give you security. Think of them as insurance—in case Lydie's petition falls through."

∽

On the bus home, Kelly felt miserable. Americans had so many ideas. It was because they knew what was possible in the world. Become legal in France, Patrice had said, and now Kelly would have to go along with it even though it was the worst idea she had ever heard. It would make her feel like a traitor to the United States. For eighteen months she had lived in Paris, refusing to learn the French language.

"Think how much easier it would be for you at the market if

you knew French," her sister Sophia would say, but Kelly did not care. She could not help learning a few words and useful phrases, but when it came to conversation, she wanted to speak English and only English.

She knew Patrice would probably move fast. One thing she had observed about Patrice and Lydie was that Patrice set her mind to something and did it right away while Lydie drifted a little. In many ways, she wished it was Patrice filing her petition for immigration to the States. That way it would be granted sooner. On the other hand, she liked Lydie more. Although she felt loyal, even sort of devoted to Patrice, she prefered Lydie's company. She could imagine the day when she could tell Lydie true stories of the Philippines, of her dreams. With Lydie she felt like a woman; with Patrice she felt like a servant.

She disembarked at the Place de Clichy and walked quickly past the Quik-Burger and souvenir shops, turning right into the rue Biot. She ignored the men who spoke to her; she just walked straight ahead, her eyes on the ground. She stopped at the small *café-tabac* where Sophia was employed as a waitress.

Sophia stood behind the bar, brewing espresso into gold-rimmed green cups. Kelly went to her, wordlessly arranging the cups on a brown plastic tray.

"*Bonjour, mademoiselle,*" the café proprietor said to her. Kelly smiled and nodded. He was always friendly to her, and why not? Whenever she stopped in to see Sophia, he had her labor for free.

"What did your employer say?" Sophia asked.

"She was very angry, but she pretended to be glad for me," Kelly said.

"Over there," Sophia said, gesturing to a table where four tourists sat. They must have wandered off the Place de Clichy; they chattered happily, examining the souvenirs they had bought. Kelly set down the cups amid brass ashtrays stamped with the word "PARIS," porcelain salt-and-pepper shakers shaped like the Moulin Rouge, and guidebooks.

Laborers dressed in blue overalls lined the bar, drinking *café* or *pipperment get*, arguing about everything imaginable. Sophia liked to flirt. Kelly watched her now, speaking French to a cluster of them.

"I guess you're too busy to talk," Kelly said to her.

"No, stay," Sophia said. She finished telling her story in rapid French, then joined Kelly by the cash register.

"Patrice wants to get French working papers for me."

"Good—then you'll stay here!" Sophia said, grinning. Sophia and her illegitimate baby were both legal. Sophia, alone among the Meridas, loved France, had lost her will to get to the States.

"Never!" Kelly said, scowling, helping Sophia set up the next trayful of cups.

# 16

*The King burst out laughing and said, "Isn't it true that whoever wrote this is a conceited puppy?"*

—To Pomponne, December 1664

THE ANNOUNCEMENTS CAME nearly simultaneously. Charles Legendre had been appointed curator of the Salle des Quatre Saisons, and a party celebrating its opening would be held two weeks hence. With Charles as curator, all foot-dragging ceased. He proved to be meticulously aware of schedules, of deadlines. Where Michael had once hounded Charles for help in getting things done, Charles now hounded Michael.

"An opening in two weeks?" Michael asked. "That's too soon. I still haven't gotten the paintings I wanted . . ."

Charles leaned against his Marie Antoinette writing desk, managing to express immeasurable self-assurance in his slouch. He cocked one eyebrow. "You know the press has already criticized us for lateness in this matter. The Salle should be open to the public by now. Everyone wonders what has gone wrong, whether there has been a design fiasco. Don't you want to kill those rumors?"

His eyes seemed focused on a point just above Michael's head; Michael figured he was envisioning an imaginary plaque listing his curatorships. With a few more, maybe he would be Minister of Culture one day.

"First I want to get *The Sacrament of Extreme Unction,*" Michael said.

"That is out of the question," Charles said, his lips narrowing, reminding Michael of their original positions, with Michael asking and Charles saying no. "You may hang *Apollo and Daphne* in the Salle. It is an equally wonderful example of Poussin's work."

"Shit," Michael said. Through Anne he had come to learn that in the chess game he and Charles played, *Sacrament* was king and *Apollo* was a rook. He knew that for the Salle des Quatre Saisons to attract serious attention, it needed first-tier paintings by Poussin, who had had Louis XIV's support, and by la Tour, who had had Louis XV's. *Apollo and Daphne,* lovely and moving as it was, was not strictly representative of Poussin's style. For one thing, it was set outdoors. For another, with its flocks and herds and nymphs, it had a more amiable feel than most Poussins.

"I do understand your displeasure," Charles said. "But it is out of my control."

"You have a lot riding on this," Michael said. "What are the critics going to say if we don't have that painting—or one like it?"

Charles nodded solemnly. But then a little blush crept up his neck, and a smile touched his lips. "It's Pierre, you see. He is so furious. You know, he really expected to be named curator of the Salle des Quatre Saisons. I said to him, 'Pierre, if the tables were turned, I would give you the painting.' He is holding on to it—just for spite! Can you imagine, he told some people that his appointment was a foregone conclusion?"

So, Didier had done more harm than good, Michael thought. It was never wise to flatter the ego of a pompous man. Neil Fallon had taught him that. Michael remembered a story Neil told about a funeral director with a fleet of limousines and hearses.

The man smoked Havanas and drove a silver Cadillac and bored everyone with tales of his sons in medical school and his daughter the nun. He was taking bids from repair garages for the chance to service his vehicles. Neil, then a young man, hoped to befriend him and win his favor. He and Julia took the mortician and his wife to Patricia Murphy's for dinner several Friday nights. He sent ebony rosary beads to the man's daughter. He and Julia sat though each dinner listening to the mortician brag about his children and his business. Neil had subjected Julia to dinner conversation about coffins, embalming, hairdos for the dead, bereaved family members unwilling to part with a buck. He had felt confident he was winning the man's trust; years later he told Michael, laughing, that he had believed the mortician was beginning to consider him a son—one who had gone into business instead of medical school. Neil lost the bid.

"Gaston will come with his men tomorrow," Charles said. "To hang *Apollo and Daphne*. Don't despair—it is a magnificent painting."

"Right," Michael said. He said good-bye and left the office. Usually while visiting the Louvre's third floor he stopped in to see Anne. But today he took the back stairs to the street and began to walk west along the Seine. He remembered coming along here, but in the opposite direction, with Lydie last spring. She had gotten a blister. He reached for his back pocket, where he kept his wallet. He was about to check whether he still had any Band-Aids for Lydie's tender feet, but he let his hand drop. This was the spot where she had stood on her toes to kiss him. Sometimes Michael imagined Lydie kissing someone else. If he ever actually saw her with another man, would it drive him home to her? He pondered the concept of "possession." If another man kissed her, would Lydie be more lost to Michael than she had been for the past year?

He cut through the Tuileries and walked up the rue Royale toward the Madeleine. Its Corinthian columns and clean lines gave it the look of a temple, more properly set in the Roman hills than this glitzy shopping street. He turned into the rue de l'Arcade and found his hotel.

"Bonjour," he said to the surly Algerian desk clerk, who handed him his key without a word. He mounted the stairs. Room 320 looked over a quiet, thoughtlessly landscaped courtyard behind the hotel. Michael loosened his tie, took off his shoes, and lay down on the bed. The voices, now familiar, of two neighborhood concierges drifted up. Michael closed his eyes and tried to block them out.

What was he doing, lying on a hotel bed in the middle of the afternoon? He hadn't slept last night. He had lain beside Anne, blinking into the canopy-swagged darkness, sweating. Yet seconds after he'd thrown off the covers, he'd begun to shiver. This had gone on all night. Somehow he had known he wouldn't get *Sacrament*. Let it be Charles's problem, he tried to tell himself. Soon Michael would return to New York, where everyone would know him as the American who had worked on the Louvre. They wouldn't realize, as the French would, that his authority was insufficient to command the best Poussin to hang in his Salle.

The room was too bright. Michael propped himself up on his elbows, considered closing the room's metal shutters. He felt acutely aware of the fact that he was lying in a hotel room. Everything proclaimed it: the cheap furniture, the thin walls through which he could hear a maid cleaning the adjacent room, the extra towels stacked on the bureau. Michael had never thought he was the kind of guy who would end up living in a hotel. He had thought he was the kind of guy who would end up married to Lydie Fallon until one or both of them died.

Until Anne, Michael had never loved any woman but Lydie. His unrequited love for her had grown, secretly, in high school and ruined him for anyone else. It was a fact he hadn't realized until after he'd left her. Michael had dated many women and even lived with one: Jean-Marie Fitzgibbon. He had considered asking Jean-Marie to marry him. But then he and Lydie had met through work and taken that trip to Washington. Michael had then realized what he had been missing all along: Lydie. Not that Jean-Marie wasn't a great girl—she simply wasn't Lydie Fallon.

By sleeping with Lydie, falling in love with her, he had betrayed Jean-Marie. He remembered feeling that he had won something he had wanted for a long time. Lydie loving him made up for all the times she had turned him away in high school. So, on top of the euphoria of new love, Michael had felt like a victor. It was all false; he saw that now. He felt baffled and exhausted, defeated by the simple truth. For as much as he had loved Lydie then, he had wound up betraying her.

෨

Late one afternoon the urge to clean set upon Lydie. She was sitting on the living room sofa, trying to write a letter to her mother, when it hit her: things were in piles all around her. Piles of unanswered and even unopened letters lay on the desk; piles of magazines tilted on tabletops; a pile of unfolded laundry covered the Barcalounger. She gathered the laundry into her arms and carried it into the bedroom.

It had been a white load: sheets, towels, and underwear. Folding it, she noticed straight off that all of the underwear was hers. Her skimpy silk bikini pants, a more substantial cotton pair, her underwire push-up bra—when she had worn *that* last, Lydie couldn't begin to remember, figured that it must have been thrown into the wash accidentally. It had been a long time since she had folded white laundry without any of Michael's underwear in it. Yet surely she had washed clothes in the weeks he'd been gone? Suddenly she missed him so acutely she felt dizzy.

Placing the clean, folded things into her dresser drawer, her gaze lit on Michael's letter box. It sat on the dresser top. She couldn't resist tracing its glossy, lacquered surface with her finger-tip. She found a couple of drips she hadn't sanded down. She touched the crescent moon and the plum tree, its blossom-stippled branches spreading across the river, and her fingers came away dusted with gold leaf.

It was full of love letters they had written to each other. She shuffled through them, all postmarked "New York." Some en-velopes bore letterheads of the company she had worked for then. She opened one from Michael and read it with her heart in her throat.

"*Making love last night made me wonder what kind of thrills you get driving a fast car. Is it at all the same? A sense of being nearly out of control while meanwhile staying very steady and alert? But as I write this, I'm answering my own question. It's not the same at all. Racing, you start out fast and stay fast and you have to keep control of the car every second. Last night, the way I remember it, we started out slow and didn't speed up for a long time—and while I remember stay-ing sort of steady, I was at no time in control. But it was definitely more fun than I ever have at the track. All my love, Michael.*"

Lydie folded the letter, put it back into its envelope. She opened another, this one to Michael.

"*It's great writing you a letter while knowing I'm going to see you tonight. Not that I've written any* [here a letter that might have been an *m* had been erased just before the "any"] *love letters before, but I'll bet there's usually a certain sadness in them. Because if you're writing a letter, it means your beloved is far away, right? I love knowing you're just six blocks uptown. Dad called me at work this morning and asked if I'd bring you home for dinner tonight. I told him no, I'm keeping you all to myself. He obviously thinks you're swell—a factor that has gone against many a boy, but not you! See you tonight—I hope you like our journey to Spain via my experiment in paella. But by the time you receive this, we'll know, won't we? Love, Lydie."*

How shallow she sounded, Lydie thought, reading the words she'd written nine years ago. That cheap trick of turning "many" into "any"—she and Michael had been courting back then, and although she had certainly loved him, she had made him wait and wonder. And that business about her father. While it was true that any time he approved of a boy Lydie liked, Lydie would instantly lose interest, she couldn't believe she had tormented Michael with it. And yet, she had to admit, she liked the girl who had written that letter: confident and full of pizzazz.

Lydie had adored beards and long hair on men; her father wanted everyone to look like the Beach Boys. Lydie had a weak spot for unorthodox Catholic priests or men who had abandoned the faith. Her father saved his highest regard for men seen every Sunday at church with their families—as children with their parents, as adults with their wives and children.

Michael had fit none of those categories. He had long hair but no beard, he was a run-of-the-mill Catholic who went to church when he felt like it. Anytime he heard a song with an even slightly sad or wistful melody, he told Lydie it reminded him of her. Most of the songs were about things the singer wanted but couldn't have. "What Is Love" by George Harrison and "I Want You" by Dylan came to her mind. Sitting on their bed in Paris, Lydie smiled as she remembered taking Michael's hands, looking him straight in the eye, and telling him in a serious tone that the only song that reminded her of him was Billy Preston's "That's the Way God Planned It."

She closed the lid of Michael's letter box and replaced it on the dresser. The urge to clean had left her. Suddenly she wished she could get her hands on a race car. She imagined pulling up at the Hôtel Grande Madeleine, honking her horn, opening the passenger door for Michael. Whipping out the Boulevard Haussmann to the Périphérique, and from there—who cares? Instead she reached for the phone and dialed the hotel's number. It was rather early in the evening, and she didn't actually expect Michael to answer.

"Hello?" came Michael's voice after a delay.

"Did I wake you?" Lydie asked, suddenly feeling that unpleasant and recently familiar sense of shyness.

"No," he said. Then, "Yeah, you did. But that's okay. I should be getting up."

Lydie glanced at her watch. "Are you sick or something?"

"Just tired. I've been busy at work. How are you? Is something wrong?"

"No. I just wanted to . . ." To what? she wondered. "Talk," she finished awkwardly. After a pause she said, "Actually I wanted to take a drive—in a hot car. But I have no idea where to get one."

"You could probably rent one," Michael said.

Lydie laughed. "I can just imagine calling Hertz—'Hi, do you have a regulation Chevy for hire?'"

"Right. 'Forget the unlimited mileage, just point me toward the nearest track,'" Michael said, sounding as if he were waking up.

"Can you believe Le Mans is just about an hour away and I haven't even been?" Lydie said. "I should at least make a visit, to pay homage."

"You should. It would be like a psychiatrist visiting Vienna without a stop at Freud's house in the Berggasse."

"How would you know where Freud's house is?" Lydie asked.

"Didn't you see the article about Vienna in the *Tribune*? I thought you'd like the part about the Habsburg balls. You know, I thought it might inspire you for Didier's."

"I didn't see it," Lydie said.

"Well, I'll send it to you."

Lydie was silent, digesting the fact Michael had said "send" instead of "bring." On the other hand, she had been rejecting his invitations all along. "That would be nice," she said after a while.

"How's it coming—the ball?" Michael asked.

"Really well. But there's still a lot to do for it."

"What'll you do when it's over? Do you have other projects lined up?"

"I'm going back to New York," Lydie said. "I'm taking Kelly Merida with me."

"My time here isn't up till mid-October," Michael said sharply.

What does that have to do with anything? Lydie thought with a certain bitterness. "I'm tempted to say 'So what?'" she said.

"I don't know," Michael said. "Never mind."

"I wasn't even sure you planned to leave," Lydie said. "With your big success at the Louvre and everything else."

Michael laughed. "My big success is not so big. Everything has turned out 'okay,' but *just* okay. I didn't get the paintings I want, the new curator is grabbing all the credit and trying to take over the final details. It's a big mess." He laughed again. "After that great lead-in, I have something to ask you. Will you come to the opening? It's in a week."

"The opening party?" Lydie said. She felt excited to be asked—how could she miss it, after all? But it was another official event, like the embassy party, where she'd be appearing as a figurehead wife. "I don't think so."

"I wish you would," Michael said. "I really want you to be there. Come on—"

Lydie hesitated because he sounded like he meant it. "I don't think so," she said again.

"I really thought you would," Michael said. "You call me up talking about a fast car—I really thought you'd go for it."

"Go for what?" Lydie asked.

"I thought you might take a chance. Take a chance and spend an important night with your husband."

"Who walked out on who here?" Lydie asked, her temper rising. "What about the *un*important nights?"

"Listen, Lydie—" Michael said. "I thought you'd *want* to come to my opening. I suppose you're not going to invite me to the ball."

"I haven't decided," Lydie said, although until that moment she had intended to invite him.

"Thanks, Lydie." Long pause, then, coolly, "Are you asking someone else?"

"That's your style, not mine," Lydie said.

"Shit," Michael said.

"I have to go now," Lydie said.

"This Kelly Merida thing—" Michael said. "I suppose you're investing all your energy in her now?"

"Not really," Lydie said, surprised by his vehemence. "But what if I were?"

"Your father used to say your own grades went downhill when you started spending all your time tutoring."

"My father was full of shit," Lydie said, hanging up on Michael. She sat there, staring at the phone, all the confidence and good feeling draining out of her, and she knew she was right back where she had been before she opened Michael's letter box and started reading.

# 17

*I am off to take my little girl to Livry. Don't worry about her at all, I look after her extremely well and I'm sure I love her much more than you do.*

—To Françoise-Marguerite, July 1672

PATRICE STUDIED THE place card Lydie had just lettered. Now, why was it so much better than the ones Patrice had done? Lydie's had flair, the way her letters swooped and flowed. They weren't nearly so neat, so symmetrical, as Patrice's, but they were undeniably more distinguished. What a waste, that stupid calligraphy class Patrice had taken on Saturday mornings at the Boston Y all during seventh grade. "It will come in so handy, all through your life," Eliza had said, obviously having graduation and wedding invitations in mind. Yet this was the first chance Patrice had had to use the so-called art.

Well, she wasn't creative; she had never claimed to be. She sat back in the armchair at the head of Lydie's dining table, watched Lydie hunched over the little cream-colored card. They had been tentative with each other since Lydie had made her announcement about Kelly's petition. Patrice wanted very much to overcome her hurt feelings and open her heart to Lydie. "I want to *be there* for you," she imagined best friends saying to one another, soulfully, in California. But she and Lydie were just two East Coast girls transplanted to Paris. She thought of the invitation she and Didier had received to Michael's opening and wondered why Lydie hadn't mentioned it.

"Mind if I smoke?" Patrice said.

"Go ahead," Lydie said, not looking up. "This is the third countess I've made a card for."

"Don't I know it," Patrice said. "Didier's inviting all the big guns to this thing. And of course they're all so excited about the *media* attention. I mean, I think Didier has led them to believe the photographers will be from *Women's Wear Daily* instead of an ad agency. They're bringing their own hairdressers and makeup artists. Give me a break."

"Actually, that will make my life easier," Lydie said. "I won't have to hire a beauty crew." She set Countess Abelard's card aside, started another.

"You're a regular handwriting factory," Patrice said.

"Only two hundred more to do," Lydie said, laying down the crow-quill pen. "I thought we were going to keep this down. How is Didier's insurance company going to feel about flashing his jewels around all these people?"

"You know only a *select few* will be chosen to actually wear the d'Origny baubles. Everyone else will mill attractively about in the background."

"I know, but still. I'm getting nervous I won't order enough food."

"Well, make sure," Patrice said. "It isn't like America where the chic party girls just pick at their food—over here they actually eat it."

"Okay."

"Have you heard how Michael's project is coming along?" Patrice asked. It seemed the only delicate way to learn whether he had invited Lydie to the opening.

"It's nearly done," Lydie said. "I'm surprised he hasn't invited you to the opening."

"Well, he did," Patrice said, relieved to have it off her chest. "I've been wondering why you haven't mentioned it. He did invite you?"

"Yes," Lydie said. "I told him I wasn't going, but now I want to. I change my mind every ten minutes."

"What's the problem about going? Why wouldn't you want to?"

"Because I've been to it a thousand times—in my mind. Sometimes I go, and everyone whispers about me because Michael and I are separated and he's there with his girlfriend. Sometimes he's there with her, but I walk in wearing something new by Sonia Rykiel, and everyone scorns him for leaving such a gorgeous creature as myself."

"That's a good one," Patrice said, giggling. She thought of her own favorite fantasy: the moment when President Mitterand pins the Légion d'honneur to her bosom in recognition of her enlightening study, *The Fourth Woman of the Marais,* with Didier's sister Clothilde looking on. If Liz Taylor could win one, why not Patrice?

"The reason I'm not going is because of what I really hope will happen," Lydie said. "That I'll walk in and see him with her and at that moment he'll realize who he really loves: me."

"That could happen," Patrice said.

Lydie shook her head. "I doubt it."

"Are you still leaving France after the ball?" Patrice asked. "Have you told Michael about that?"

"That's my plan," Lydie said. "I think Michael was shocked to hear it. It's strange, though—for a long time, I couldn't wait to leave. To go home to New York. But I don't feel it so strongly anymore. The other day, for the first time, I noticed that when I look at my watch, I don't calculate the time difference between here and New York. I'm living on Paris time now."

"You mean to say that you would look at your watch, see that it's noon here, and automatically think it was six A.M. in New York?"

"Yes," Lydie said. "Didn't you do that when you first arrived?"

"Never," Patrice said. "I was very happy to abandon my previous time zone forever. But maybe Kelly does it too. Sometimes, she'll be doing the breakfast dishes and suddenly say, 'Now they're sleeping in the province.'"

"It's a way of staying connected to people at home."

"When you and Kelly flee the continent, I wonder whether you'll ever think of me, automatically calculate my time of day."

"I'm sure I will," Lydie said, seeming not to notice the edge Patrice permitted to sound in her voice. But it was obvious, after all, that she had: she propped her chin on her hand, leaned forward, said, "You're still upset about that?"

"Oh, I don't know," Patrice said. "At first I thought it was a little . . . well . . . sneaky. The way everything just fell into place the minute I left Paris."

"But it wasn't," Lydie said. "Kelly and I talked about it that time you sent her over with the strawberry jam. Then I met someone from the embassy, and it took off from there."

"It just seems mighty odd that Kelly couldn't have mentioned it to me—and that she had to wait until I was out of the picture before she mentioned it to you."

"I think it was her first opportunity. She's always working when I go to your house, and she probably figured you'd feel compromised if she asked you to get me to take her to America. She did say you tried to get your mother to take her."

"That was a lie," Patrice said sadly. "My mother disapproves of the whole thing. She lied to Kelly just to make me look good. And I went along with it. Isn't that rotten?"

"I don't think it was rotten," Lydie said. "I also don't think you had to lie."

This type of frankness was not Patrice's typical style, and it exhilarated, even frightened her. Saying what was on her mind without veils of subterfuge and Lydie talking right back, neither of them overly fearful of the consequences, was so different from her mother's untruthful approach to life. Eliza had taught Patrice that history could be rewritten on a whim. Patrice remembered her mother's visit in July, of the disaster it had really been and the pleasant little twist Eliza had given it for posterity. Perhaps if Patrice hadn't been an only child, perhaps if she'd had a sister with whom to compare notes . . .

"That guy from the consulate is going to interview Kelly soon," Lydie said. "Bruce Morrison."

"Good," Patrice said. "I'm behind her one hundred percent— whether you believe me or not."

"Is Didier serious about wanting to stage a hunt at the ball?" Lydie asked, perhaps wanting to change the subject as much as Patrice did.

"Yes, only call it a 'shoot,' dear. In France, it's very top-drawer to go shooting. They talk about the old days when a safari was really a safari, when you could hide in the brush and kill elephants and tigers instead of circling them in a bus with a bunch of other tourists."

"Why would anyone want to kill an elephant?" Lydie asked. "What kind of sport is that? They're as broad as barns."

"I don't know. They just did. Isn't it revolting?"

"Yes," Lydie said.

"Now, the French, myself included, I'm sorry to admit, take it out on little things like grouse and rabbits."

"I hadn't intended to rent any hunting—'shooting'—costumes or equipment. But Didier does seem very keen on it."

"He is, but don't worry. It'll all be a stage set. Just a chance for you and me and a few selected others to dress for the occasion. Tumner carries this adorable line of shooting clothes for women—calf-length khaki skirts like the ones Meryl Streep wore in *Out of Africa,* flat brown leather boots, vests with little compartments for shotgun shells, mosquito repellent, your compact . . . Didier thinks they'll look so funky with brooches and pendants."

"We've already planned one shot—a woman with the rifle raised, looking through the scope, wearing an enormous marquise-cut diamond ring on top of her leather-gloved trigger finger."

"I told you—" Patrice said.

"Let's take a break," Lydie said. "I have a cramp in my hand, and these cards are getting sloppy."

"Yours are great," Patrice said.

Lydie glanced up, surprised. "Mine are terrible, compared to yours. Your calligraphy is beautiful. Where did you learn it?"

"From a master in Tibet," Patrice said.

"No, really. I'm serious," Lydie said.

"So am I." Why couldn't Patrice accept Lydie's compliment? She wished she knew. The moment someone singled her out for something, noticed an accomplishment, Patrice ceased to value it. Five minutes ago she had been wishing her lettering was as fine as Lydie's, and here was Lydie telling her it was even better. Patrice handled it by coming up with a compliment to give Lydie.

"Your cheeks look pinker than I've seen them in a long time. Pretty. I think you should go to Michael's opening with him."

"Well, thanks for the advice," Lydie said. Something told Patrice she was trying to be sarcastic. Lydie trying to be sarcastic was pretty funny. She thinned her lips and blinked her eyes. But her tone of voice stayed exactly the same as ever. By first grade Patrice had known more about sarcasm than Lydie would learn in a lifetime.

"You are very welcome," Patrice said earnestly, as if she thought Lydie's thanks were genuine. "You come to me anytime and I mean *anytime* you're wondering what to do, how to behave, which fork to use. Don't hesitate to ask."

"Patrice?" Lydie said, grinning.

"Yes, sweet pea?"

"Piss off."

# 18

*What you might call a bolt from the blue occurred yester-
day evening at the Tuileries, but I must start the story further back.*

—To Coulanges, December 1670

"This is really too emotional," Bruce Morrison said. Although
he was no older than forty, he wore half-spectacles to read Lydie's
petition. She wondered why someone so young and attractive
would want to affect such a curmudgeonly persona. He also wore
a bow tie and a green tweed vest. She bet that under the vest he
wore suspenders instead of a belt. "You see," he continued, "the
government doesn't care about Miss Merida's hardships. It doesn't
care that you are extremely fond of her. It cares only that she is indispensable to your business and that her position cannot be filled
by a United States citizen."

"I see," Lydie said. Her situation here was delicate; she wished
to get as much advice from Bruce as possible without telling him
the whole truth. His easy manner made her want to talk freely
about her connection with Kelly, but she knew there was a line she

must not cross: he was employed by the United States government. They sat in his office overlooking the rue Cambon.

"For example," he said, tapping the petition. "This section
here, where you talk about the economy of the Philippines . . ."
He looked up, removed his spectacles, and laughed. "That's not
news to us. Why do you think so many Filipinos want to emigrate
to America? The living condition there is atrocious. It's not a case
for you to make—it's a given."

"Should I concentrate on why my business can't run without
Kelly?"

"You don't have to go that far. You must submit evidence that
she is indispensable. The paragraph where you say that she knows
your taste in objects, that you can send her out to shops and museums to search for props—expand on that."

"Okay," Lydie said, making notes. She thought of Kelly walking into Bulgari, asking to see tiaras. It was an impossible image.

"Have you decided where you want her to be interviewed? Paris
or Manila?"

"What do you think?" Lydie asked. She glanced up, saw him
stuffing tobacco into a pipe.

"She'll run into trouble either way. The consular section here is
very tough on Filipinos in France illegally. We have an arrange-
ment with the French authorities . . . even if I put in a good word,
I'm not sure it would help. But I'll give it a try. France, then?"

Lydie felt touched that he would say that. She hardly knew
him, after all. "France," Lydie said. "I really appreciate the help
you've given me."

"No problem," he said. "Dot told me to take care of you." He
puffed a cloud of smoke from his pipe, then another.

"Is Dot's office near here?" Lydie asked. "I'd like to thank her."

"Let me walk you over," Bruce said, coming around his desk to hold the back of Lydie's chair as she stood. His hand brushed her shoulder.

"Have you lived in Paris long?" Lydie asked.

"Three years. I'm a bachelor," he said. Cleverly working it in? Although everything had been businesslike between them, Lydie had been waiting to feel sexual tension. They were practically the same age; she wanted to test whether he found her attractive. She had hoped for it, yet the waiting put her on edge, made her feel almost angry.

But that accidental brush was all. He didn't even meet her eye. Naturally a guy who wears spectacles and a bow tie would be gallant, Lydie thought. Pulling back her chair went along with the Scottish country-house decor of his office: sporting prints of water birds and steeplechasers, the pipe rack, the tattered Persian rug. She bet he had a first edition of *Ivanhoe* somewhere around.

At the door of Dot Graulty's office he shook her hand.

"Let me know if you need more help," he said.

"Thank you for everything," Lydie said.

Dot, sober, rose to greet her. Today she wore a trim navy blue suit that still managed to look matronly.

"Lydie McBride, isn't it?" she said.

"You have a good memory!" Lydie said, shaking her hand. "I just want to thank you for putting me in touch with Bruce Morrison. He's been so helpful."

"He's a peach, isn't he?" Dot said. "Knows everything there is to know about visas."

"Well, he certainly gave me good advice," Lydie said. "I made my affidavit much too personal."

"That is such a common mistake," Dot said. "Just between you, me, and the wall, we have a good laugh over some of the sob stories we get here. There's always a sick child or a poverty case or persecution by the dictator. When we get to the word 'scurvy,' we're rolling on the floor."

Lydie, who found the confidence offensive, laughed politely. She thought of Kelly riding through the Black Forest in the trunk of a limousine, and tried to maintain a pleasant expression.

"Let me take a look at your petition," Dot said.

"No, really—" Lydie said.

"I promise not to laugh. I shouldn't have said anything to you—you'll think we're terrible. But you do get hardened. Give me a peek."

Anything for the cause. Lydie handed it over. "Um, what do you do here, Dot?" she asked.

"I'm in charge of all the secretaries. I used to be personal secretary to Ambassador McGovern." She scrutinized the petition.

"It *is* a little excessive," Lydie said, embarrassed.

"Not so bad," Dot said. She looked up. "I notice you're filing individually. Your husband's not cosigning."

"Well, that's true," Lydie said. Was it her imagination, or did Dot wear an expression of sympathy? The world of Americans in Paris, at least those connected with the government, was a small one, and she supposed it likely that people would have heard about the separation by now. "Kelly is my assistant—I figured I should file alone."

"Oh," Dot said, continuing to watch Lydie's face. "It's just that an additional signature can carry weight. Two people taking responsibility for the alien instead of one. This is one of my little tricks of the trade."

"I think it's better this way," Lydie said.

"Whatever you say," Dot said. "By the way, I sneaked in to see Michael's work at the Louvre. Brilliant! Everyone will say so."

"Thank you," Lydie said.

"I tell you what," Dot said. "Leave this petition with me for an hour or so, and I'll punch it into shape."

"Dot!" Lydie said, at once grateful and uncomfortable; she felt sure the only reason Dot would volunteer was because she knew about the separation and felt sorry for Lydie.

"It's a formula, honey. That's all it takes to fill this out, and no one knows it better than I do."

※

Killing time, Lydie decided to buy a book and have tea at W. H. Smith. But walking down the vaulted colonnade of the rue de Rivoli, she changed her mind, crossed the street, and headed through the Tuileries toward the Louvre.

She hadn't yet seen Michael's information center. She knew it was nearly finished, but she hadn't been able to force herself into the museum to look at it. How could she stand to view it amid tourists instead of alongside its architect? If she didn't see it today, she knew she never would. Dot had made it possible. Because somehow Michael was responsible for Dot volunteering to do Kelly's petition. Either out of pity for what he had done to Lydie or awe for the mark he had left on the Louvre: it didn't matter which it was. All Lydie knew, walking through the forest of chestnut trees, was that she had a burning desire to see her husband's work.

Coming into the sunlight by the stone pond, she stopped dead. There was Michael, sitting in a metal lawn chair, his feet propped up on the pond's rim. He was reading the newspaper. And beside him, writing in a notebook, was Anne Dumas.

※

Michael believed in neither the powers of darkness, nor the powers of suggestion, but it seemed a combination of the two that made him turn around. He had to pivot nearly 180 degrees to see

Lydie disappearing into the chestnut woods. He caught just a glimpse of her: red-gold hair, blue linen jacket, big straw bag. But the same powers that had made him turn around told him that she had seen him and Anne.

"Hell," he said.

"Hmm?" Anne said, continuing to write.

He did not reply. He stared at the spot where Lydie had been, wondering whether she stood just out of sight, behind a tree trunk, watching them now.

"I cannot do my work with you saying 'hell,'" Anne said.

"Why not?" Michael asked.

She rested her forearm on his knee. "Because if something upsets you, you should tell me what it is."

"Oh," Michael said. "What are you working on?" He knew it had to be historical; he had learned that Anne was easily distracted from the present by anything in the seventeenth century, the period in which she wished she dwelled and actually, it seemed to Michael, sometimes believed she did.

"My articles for *Figaro*. You know, their Sunday magazine is so popular, this project is really a headache. Six articles, two lectures. Will all those readers care anything about my work? They are not scholars."

"Anne, French people love their own history. The entire country was practically raised on it."

"Exactly my point. What can I tell them that is new without seeming pedantic? So I've decided to write about the rivalry between Madame de Sévigné and Ninon de Lenclos."

"You hardly ever mention Ninon de Lenclos."

"She discovered Voltaire. Also, she screwed the husband *and* the son of Madame de Sévigné. It will be a dramatic tale."

"I'm sure," Michael said.

Anne's eyes crinkled as she smiled into the sun. Her streaked hair had grown since Michael had known her. It curled softly around her ears. "She was the sexiest one in *Three Women of the Marais,*" Anne said. "I always have fun writing about her. Let me tell you a story . . ."

Michael turned away, to stare at the hole in the trees. His romance with Anne felt like homework. He had begun to be diligent about it: see her at work, sleep with her now and then, talk dirty to her, take her to dinner. What had been breathtaking as fantasy was boring, even oppressive, as reality.

The truth was he loved Lydie.

But could he say he was still in love with her? "In love," he had learned during his time away from her, covered more than a state of long-term commitment. It covered more than gentle contentment. Michael still wanted passion and lust, and he had learned that he wanted them with his wife.

"*Chéri,*" Anne said. "Why aren't you listening?"

"I'm a little distracted," Michael admitted.

"The separation has been hard for you. I have seen that."

"Yeah." Michael, who had told Anne about leaving Lydie one night when he had really needed comfort, hated to talk about it. He saw how happy it made Anne. Then he felt guilty for leading her on. Was he using her? He didn't exactly know what she wanted from their relationship, but he had some idea. The last night he had stayed at her apartment, she had whispered that she loved him.

"It is always like that," Anne said. "No matter how bad the problems are, it is always hard to leave a person you once loved. My friend Jean called me last night, and ah!"

"He's back from Brittany?" Michael asked. He wondered where Lydie was now. Probably shopping for props in the rue de Rivoli. Didier's ball was just two weeks off.

"Yes. Of course he claims to have been miserable there without me. I adore Bretagne."

"Do you wish you had gone?" Michael asked, hoping for her to say yes.

"Not with Jean. With you, perhaps. Yes, I think I would see a different Michel in Bretagne." She giggled. "Maybe next year. When the critics review your construction, they will never allow you to leave France."

"I leave in six weeks," Michael said.

"We shall see when the time comes."

&#8198;

Michael planned his meeting with Lydie carefully. He would show up at the apartment, unannounced, so she would not have the opportunity to decline. If she refused to let him in, he would use his key.

Climbing the stairs to his floor, he felt as nervous as a boy on a date, or a slasher. The key in his hand felt like a weapon. He rang the doorbell.

"Who is it?" came Lydie's voice.

"Me."

She opened the door instantly, surprising Michael. Seeing her face-to-face for the first time in—how long? Days? Weeks? He noticed her pallor, normal for Lydie in the middle of winter, but not the end of summer. A black velvet headband held back her burnished hair. She wore the dangling gold earrings their friend Holly had brought her from Egypt. But to counteract the elegance of her headgear, she wore a baggy T-shirt over jeans.

"Can I come in?" he asked.

She stepped aside, glaring, saying nothing. He wasn't used to seeing her wild, out of control. The look in her eyes alarmed him. He thought that look was the last thing you'd see in the forest as the panther tore your throat.

It felt strange and good to be back in his apartment. Michael looked around the living room, saw nothing had changed. Lydie stood behind him, her back against the door; he wondered whether he should wait for her to invite him to sit down or to just take his regular chair.

"I want to talk to you," he said.

"I want to kill you," she said, and Michael flashed, not to the panther, but to Neil Fallon.

"Lydie—" he said, stepping toward her.

She held out one hand, like a traffic cop. He stopped dead.

"You saw me in the park?" he asked. Maybe she nodded; he couldn't quite tell. "Can we straighten this out? Do you want me to tell you about it?"

"Go to confession if you want to talk," Lydie said.

"Lydie . . ." Michael said.

"You just can't stop yourself—the sins feel so good, right?" Lydie asked.

Well, she's right about that, Michael thought, feeling disgusted with himself and with Lydie for pointing it out. "I love you," Michael said. "I'm sorry about everything."

"I thought you loved her. Anne Dumas," Lydie said. For the first time, her tone seemed less aggressive, a little quizzical.

"No. I don't love her," Michael said. He felt dizzy. He wished they could sit down.

"I knew you were seeing someone, but Anne *Dumas?*" Lydie said, her voice trembling. "Watching you with her. In the sunshine, you both looking so tan, so comfortable with each other. You haven't even known her that long . . ."

What difference does that make? Michael wanted to ask, although he already knew the answer. Lydie set great stock in longevity. She believed the person you loved longest you loved most.

Birthdays and anniversaries overjoyed her; they represented the accumulation of affections. But right in the midst of her sentence he reached for her, drew her against his chest. In such a little time Anne had become his measure, and Lydie felt tall, unfamiliar.

"I forgot what I was going to say," she said.

"That's good," he said.

"Everyone knows about you and Anne Dumas, I suppose?" Lydie said, stepping away. "Arthur Chase? Dot Graulty?"

"Who's Dot Graulty?" Michael asked.

"That woman from the embassy. The one who can accomplish anything."

Michael remembered. He had seen her recently, at a press reception at the Louvre. She had carried on about his project—how wonderful it was, how proud Americans could be of him, her eyes constantly clicking between him and Anne. Later Anne had called her *la maternelle*—the mother figure. "She doesn't know anything about it," Michael lied. "Why do you care about her?"

"She's been wonderful to me. Today she helped me file that petition for Kelly," Lydie said.

Michael had to admit that Lydie really knew how to stick with something. Better, perhaps, than he did: look what he had done to his marriage. For weeks, since leaving Lydie, guilt had been booby-trapping him left and right. What had once made sense, his desire for happiness, now mocked him. Especially now, in the presence of Lydie, whom, he realized, he wanted more than anything else. He grabbed her wrists, held them hard. Their eyes locked and they stared at each other for a few seconds until Lydie closed her eyes, tilted her head back, and let him kiss her.

But when the kiss ended, Lydie stepped back. "Just go," she said.

∾

"I think I've blown it," Michael said to Didier. They sat on a bench in the Tuileries just paces from where Lydie had stood when she'd spied him and Anne.

"You've made a mess of things with Lydie," Didier said.

"How do you know?" Michael asked, irate because he hadn't even started to talk yet.

"Because I could see this coming a mile away. You weren't in love with that girl at the Louvre, you only thought you were. But of course it has complicated everything with your wife. Has Lydie found out?"

"She *saw* me with Anne. She was coming through these trees"—Michael waved his arm—"and saw me sitting with Anne over there." He pointed. Doing so, he realized he had chosen this spot to meet Didier as a way to punish himself. He could relive the pain of that day and imagine how horrible Lydie must have felt.

"It is so much worse when they see with their own eyes. My first wife caught me in bed with my mistress. Yes—it is true. Can you believe what a jerk I was? I wanted her to catch us, of course. I left a trail an idiot could follow. She never forgave me. We were divorced less than eighteen months later."

"Thanks for the moral support, Didier," Michael said, feeling worse than ever. At least Lydie hadn't seen him in bed with Anne. He ran that day in the park through his mind: had he been touching Anne when Lydie saw them? Holding her hand? Or had she been stroking his forearm or knee, as she often did when they read together? He didn't think so, but he wasn't sure.

"The point, Michael, is this: I didn't love my first wife. I *wanted* her to find me, as I told you. Somewhere down deep I wanted to be rid of her, so I arranged for her to hate me. God, does she hate me! But, you see, I hate her too. It is different for you. You love Lydie, but you needed to have a fling."

It was times like this that Michael saw how far apart the French and American cultures were. Didier was talking about the need for adultery as if it were absolutely normal and understandable. "She'll never forgive me," he said.

"She will," Didier said. "Because she really loves you. I know because Patrice told me."

Michael knew it too, but he wasn't sure it would be enough to let her forgive him. Also, what if he couldn't forgive himself? "I'd better go," he said to Didier, starting to rise.

"Where? Your hotel room?" Didier asked. "Sit down for a little longer. Calm yourself, then come home for dinner with me."

Michael smiled, thinking of what Patrice would do if Didier unexpectedly brought home a dinner guest. "Thanks anyway," he said.

"Give Lydie the chance to forgive you," Didier said. "You'll have a stronger marriage when it's done. I guarantee it."

"How?" Michael asked. "How do you know that?"

"Because I've seen a thing or two. I'm a little wiser than you are, you know. I am older and I am French, and both those facts make me wiser than a young American. *Tu comprends?*"

"Yes, I understand," Michael said. But all he really understood was that Didier was trying to cheer him up.

⁓

Lydie received a letter from her mother replying to the one Lydie had sent. In her bewilderment, her resolve to not upset Lydie further, Julia had managed to execute a postal soft shoe. "*Dear Lydie,*" (she read) "*I am shocked by your news. You do not say how you are feeling about everything. I just cannot imagine Michael moving out, and you don't quite explain why he has done this. I know, the heart has its reasons. But still, some further details would be appreciated. Are you speaking at least? Never forget: your father and I never stopped speaking. The fact that you so rarely call worries me. With love, Mother.*"

Could Julia be serious, holding her own situation up as something Michael and Lydie could learn from? It amazed and saddened Lydie to see how blind Julia remained—wished to remain—to Neil's betrayal. Perhaps it was true, that her parents had never stopped speaking. Lydie remembered her mother's tearful recount of their last conversation: Neil had asked if she needed anything from the store. Julia had said yes, a quart of whole milk and some Ritz crackers. She had reminded him to wear his hat, it was raining. "You always do take care of me, don't you?" Neil had said. When Julia repeated his last words, describing his smile and the glint in his eyes, she would dissolve into tears, as if their fond good-bye was the end of the story. Of course it wasn't: Neil had gone from there to the store to Margaret Downes's. In her kitchen he had filled her child's bottle with the milk he had bought. Then he had taken Margaret into the bedroom and shot her.

For a long time afterward Lydie, like her mother, had concentrated not on the story's end, but on an earlier aspect. Had her father really bought that milk for Julia? A quart of whole milk seemed a stupid thing to bring his lover. Unless she had asked him to, but the police had said there was plenty in the refrigerator. For weeks after his death Lydie had spent many nights keeping Michael awake, trying to answer that question, as if solving the mystery could push away the truth. But one night Michael put an end to it, to her thinking out loud. "If he bought the milk for Mom, he must have been intending to come home," Lydie said.

"Lydie, he also had a gun. Why would he take the gun with him if he didn't intend to use it?"

"Maybe he was afraid of being robbed." Neil and Julia had been mugged twice within six months, and his office had been robbed. They had lost two thousand dollars altogether.

"He didn't believe in carrying guns. He didn't even keep one at work. The police said he bought it the day before the shooting."

"But what about the *milk*?" Lydie asked, convinced that the milk was the clue. She thought Michael was willfully ignoring it. "What if he bought the gun to protect himself, started carrying it that day? I think what he probably did was stop by her place on the way home from buying milk for Mom. Something happened—I don't know. A fight, or something. He went out of control, and he shot her." The idea of such a loss of control washed over Lydie, leaving her weak. In those first weeks when she knew she would never see him again, all memories of him, even bad ones, were dangerous.

"Lydie . . ." Michael said. Now, sitting in Paris, Lydie could see the desperation in his eyes, hear the sadness in his voice. She could believe that Michael imagined he had lost his wife to a cause, like one of those people who believe in the Kennedy conspiracy and spend their lives trying to prove that Oswald did not act alone. Lydie kept replaying imaginary events over in her mind the way some people watch the Zapruder tape. Her father's rain hat, a clerk slipping a quart of Sealtest into a bag, Margaret Downes smiling as she answered her door. Lydie remembered Michael taking her left hand, forcing her to look him in the eyes. "I think your father bought that milk for the baby. He couldn't be absolutely sure there would be any in the house. I think he wanted the child to have a bottle when—"

"Shut up," Lydie said then, yanking her hand free to cover her ears. But Michael took hold of them, eased them down.

"When he fired the shots. It was a kind thing to do, Lydie. Think of it that way. Your father was crazy, but he thought enough of that baby to make sure she had a bottle."

Now, remembering, Lydie felt tears sliding down her cheeks. She knew that Michael was right. Her father had cared enough about his lover's child to make sure she had a bottle, yet he hadn't even said good-bye to Lydie. She realized that she was being ridiculous, but she couldn't stop crying. She tried to think of the poor baby hearing gunshots. Had she understood what was happening? The baby's mother, Lydie's father, dead in the next room. Back in New York she hadn't let herself think too often about that baby: it would have seemed disloyal to Julia's stubborn interpretation of her husband's intentions. But here in Paris, Lydie was beginning to let herself see things she hadn't seen before.

Lydie wished she hadn't promised to take Patrice to the warehouse in Neuilly. They were going to look at props for the ball and discuss Kelly. Ball gowns, peacock feathers, jewelry . . . suddenly Lydie saw her career the way her father would have—frivolous, an empty enterprise. He had had such high hopes for her. He had been convinced that one day her paintings would hang in museums. He had been right to doubt her when she said her work as a stylist would last only a few years. Some days she loved what she did, thought she had the most interesting job in Paris. Other days, when she thought of Kelly or of what her father would think of her, she felt materialistic and vacant.

Patrice picked her up in Didier's Citroën. They drove up the Champs-Elysées, around the Etoile, toward Neuilly. Lydie saw a slash of scarlet at the top of a maple tree and she remembered late spring, when the roses were new, that early morning with Patrice in the Bagatelle. Now they drove to the warehouse, a dreary windowless building. "This is the place?" Patrice asked doubtfully. "This is where you're storing all the treasures of the universe?"

"You've got it," Lydie said, pulling out the key. "Are you and Didier excited about the ball?"

"Are you kidding? Every night Didier checks the mail before he kisses me—to see who else has accepted."

"Thanks for everything you're doing about the banquet."

"Oh, I know," Patrice said. "Our little oyster man from Arcachon is bringing oysters, spider crabs, and *langoustes*. Our friends from Deauville have a cheese man who's going to supply Camembert, Livarot, and Pont l'Eveque. Terribly photogenic cheeses, I've been assured."

"Plus roasted grouse, a few *gratins* . . ."

"Brown and bubbly, click those shutters," Patrice said. "This is going to be d'Origny's best ad series by far."

The warehouse was vast. Lydie attacked a tall crate with the claw end of a hammer.

"Voilà!" Lydie said. "Ball gowns . . ."

"They are gorgeous," Patrice said. Most were shades of red: crimson, garnet, deep rose. Buried in the red were two of deep green.

"I want some people in period clothes—eighteenth century," Lydie said. As she forced herself to focus on the ball, she noticed that she began to feel better. "Some of the women will wear red. And the ones wearing rubies will wear green. I'll need a list of guests from Didier, with suggestions on who should wear the jewels. Also, an inventory of jewels he wants photographed. I'll have to call him when I get home." She felt like she was talking to herself, not Patrice. She made notations in a spiral-bound book.

"Can I have first pick?" Patrice said, running her hands across the skirts of taffeta, velvet, damask, satin.

"Of course. Do you plan to wear rubies?"

"I hate rubies—they bring bad luck. I told Didier to drape me in diamonds the size of Mont Blanc. They will look *fabulous* against this." She chose a dress whose fabric shimmered even in the dim warehouse: scarlet in a certain light, purplish-black in another. She loved the tight bodice and full skirt, and she couldn't wait to see herself in it.

"Your cleavage will look great in that," Lydie said.

"Won't it, though?" Patrice exclaimed with delight. "Where did you get these from?"

"They're antique," Lydie said. "The reason I'm able to rent them for so long, at such a good price, is that they've been in storage at the costume museum. The curators have to rotate all their exhibits because they have so little space."

Patrice looked around. "Is there anyone else here?" she asked.

"I don't think so," Lydie said.

Patrice dropped her black leather skirt to the floor, pulled her pink angora sweater over her head. "I wish there was a mirror," she said, standing there in her demi-bra and bikini panties. "Which one are you going to wear?"

"I don't know," Lydie said. "I might not dress up. I might just help the photographer."

"You damned well *are* going to dress up," Patrice commanded. "Now choose a dress." When Lydie wasn't fast enough, Patrice grabbed a green one off the rack. Forest-green satin, it was supple and liquid and dark as the woods. "Put it on," Patrice said.

Light filtered through the skylights; several fluorescent lamps running the length of the warehouse were burned out. Others cast diffuse light through the enormous space, making it even gloomier.

Patrice tugged the zipper gently, and the dress closed around Lydie's body. When Lydie turned around, Patrice gasped. "Michael is going to die when he sees you," she said. "You might just wear that little number to his big opening as well."

All the big moments, the turning points of Lydie's life were suddenly parties. The embassy party, Michael's opening, the ball. She could almost believe, though she had never thought such a thing possible, that the outcome of her marriage hinged on whether or not she attended Michael's party.

"Michael came to see me," Lydie said. "After I saw him in the Tuileries with his girlfriend."

"His girlfriend?" Patrice asked. "You saw her? Who is she?"

"Anne Dumas." Lydie felt reluctant to say the name: it carried such weight for Patrice. But Patrice took the news in silence. She reached for Lydie's hand and held it.

"You know," Patrice said after a while, "one of Anne Dumas's 'three women' was the Marquise de Brinvilliers. Does that name ring a bell?"

Lydie shook her head.

"A murderer. She poisoned anyone who got in the way of her happiness. She used to volunteer at Paris charity hospitals so she could practice poisoning patients in order to perfect her technique. She knocked off her father, her brothers, her husband . . ." Patrice trailed off.

"What does that have to do with Anne Dumas?" Lydie asked.

"She wrote that section best," Patrice said. "She devotes more space to Madame de Sévigné, but she really got inside the head of the murderer."

"I hate her," Lydie said.

"I don't blame you," Patrice said. "What happened when Michael went to see you?"

Lydie shivered as she recalled the kiss. "I'm all stirred up. I think about Kelly, because at least there's something I can *do* about her."

"I don't get it," Patrice said, frowning.

"I don't know how to act with Michael. I just don't. Sometimes

I want him back so badly . . . then I remember he left me to be with Anne Dumas. But with Kelly . . . I can help her get to the United States. I'm doing it—I've filed a petition for her."

"How you can compare the two is *way* beyond me," Patrice said. "I want what's best for her too. But Kelly is no substitute for Michael."

"No kidding," Lydie said, feeling impatient with Patrice. "Of course Kelly and Michael are separate. But it feels good to help Kelly."

Patrice and Lydie took off the ball gowns, dressed in their own clothes. They stepped out of the warehouse into bright autumn sunshine.

"Bright out here," Patrice said, shielding her eyes. She dug into her bag for the car keys.

"This is a nice car," Lydie said, leaning on its hood as she waited for Patrice to unlock it.

Patrice had been concentrating on fitting her key into the lock, but her head snapped up and she grinned at Lydie across the car roof. "Want to drive it?"

"You're kidding," Lydie said, but already she felt the adrenaline start to flow.

"I know it's not a Maserati or whatever you're used to, but Didier makes it fly. Why not give it a go?"

Lydie and Patrice crisscrossed in front of the car, Patrice handing her the keys. The keys felt solid in Lydie's hand. She felt confident unlocking the door, strapping on her seat belt.

"Seat belts?" Patrice asked from the passenger seat. "Race car drivers wear seat belts?"

"Safety first," Lydie said, smiling. She switched on the ignition, felt satisfied by the engine's soft murmur. It sounded nothing like her car, whose engine noises at optimal performance resembled a mutter or a hacking cough. Backing out of the space, then pulling forward onto Avenue Guérin, she drove the car slowly, with care, getting a feel for it.

"Floor it," Patrice urged. "I want to see you in action."

"Not here," Lydie said. "Too residential." She could easily believe, however, that Didier could make this car fly. She barely touched the gas, restraining it. When had she last had the urge to drive? It seemed like years ago. She had been behind the wheel, but only for errands; it hadn't given her pleasure for a long time. Now she drove through Neuilly, braking at stop signs, training her eyes on the horizon and whatever stood in its path. She felt the car, its big six-cylinder engine, wanting to get away from her, but she held it back.

"Is this a tank compared to your car?" Patrice asked.

"Yes, but this car is lovely," Lydie said, barely hearing Patrice. She was one with the road, and not only the one on which she drove. In a flash she saw past and future exit ramps, stop lights and race tracks. She held the leather steering wheel lightly, but as surely as she had at the start of races at Lime Rock. "Gentlemen, start your engines," the announcer always called. She smiled now, as she always did when she heard that. Didn't he realize there was a woman racing? Racing she would hold back, part of the pack, until that instant when she saw her chance and pulled ahead. She hadn't won so far. She loved to compete and wanted to win for many reasons. But she lived for the day when she would pull across the line first, drive to the winner's circle, take off her helmet and show the announcer her long hair, let him know that a woman had started her engine.

She felt that way now: as though she had started up after a long sleep. She entered the Périphérique at Porte Maillot, glanced at Patrice. The engine sounded good, the traffic was light. Shifting into overdrive, she pressed down the gas pedal.

"Here we go," she said. But where, exactly, were they going? She sped along the highway that circled Paris, but she kept her eyes on the road. As a passenger she would sit back, enjoying the vista full of Parisian monuments: the Eiffel Tower, Montmartre, Notre Dame. She could imagine driving until she ran out of gas. Driving around and around Paris on the Périphérique, her mind on the road but the thought of Michael tingling in the background, with nowhere special to go, Lydie felt as if she had never had so specific a destination.

# 19

*There will be plays at Court and a ball every week.*

ON THE DAY that the Salle des Quatre Saisons would be un-
veiled, Michael leaned against the great table, watching workmen
adjust the lighting on paintings by Georges de la Tour and Nicolas Poussin. He thought they set a fine seventeenth-century mood
to carry tourists through the painting galleries. Although it
had been his second choice, Michael found Poussin's painting
*Apollo and Daphne* deeply moving. There was Apollo, baffled in
his love for Daphne, tricked by Mercury, frustrated in friendship by Hyacinth, who lay slain at Apollo's feet. It seemed
benevolent to have a painting of Apollo—god of poetry and
painting—hanging in his Salle. Nicolas Poussin had died before
finishing it.

Michael felt baffled in his love for Lydie. He thought back to
springtime, when he had felt so sure he wanted someone new. Instead of trying to understand the dark things moving his wife, he
had fallen for Anne. But his feelings had changed over time. Liv-

ing apart from Lydie, he remembered how it had felt to fall in love with her. Not the second time, in Washington, but the first, in high school. Then it had seemed he saw her only from a distance. Across the room in French class, with other boys at dances, with Father Griffin, their heads together as they discussed matters of obvious importance—ostentatiously, Michael had thought.

Caterers from Lenôtre arrived, asking Michael where to set up the hors d'oeuvres. "Not on that table," he said, because he thought the information table was a prime attraction. Its maker from Burgundy had been invited, along with his wife, their children, and members of the preceding generation on both sides of the family. Curators from museums all through France, members of the American community in Paris, and government officials had been invited. Lydie had been invited.

The caterers set out platters of canapés, a goose sculpted out of foie gras, open-faced sandwiches of smoked salmon. Charles had insisted that champagne be served, regardless of cost. Michael felt pretty sure the budget wouldn't cover it, that Charles was making up the difference with his own money. But with the ministers and officials who were coming, this was a perfect opportunity for Charles to start lobbying for his next curatorship.

"Michel," Anne said, startling him. He turned fast. She wore a wig, the hair piled high on her head, and an ancient dress that looked as though it would fall apart if you touched it. She pirouetted slowly.

"It's . . . extraordinary," Michael said, spellbound. Anne looked exactly like a woman from the seventeenth century; she might have stepped out of the portrait of Madame de Sévigné hanging in her apartment. The dress was quilted brown taffeta trimmed with what once had been silver thread. The wig appeared to be new, with chestnut tendrils curling around the face and two large bouquets of hair on each side.

"Isn't it magnificent?" Anne asked, her dimples deepening. "I had the wig made."

"But why? Where will you wear it?" Michael asked. She made him think of women dressed in period costumes at Sturbridge Village and Williamsburg. He'd seen waitresses dressed that way at the 1964 World's Fair.

"I'm wearing it now, *chéri*," Anne said. "What a silly question. I shall wear it to the party."

Suddenly there was a commotion behind the partition blocking the Salle from tourists. A very small and wiry man, dressed in a tailored black suit, burst through.

"Mademoiselle Dumas!" he said angrily, catching sight of her.

Anne glanced around, as if looking for an escape, then turned to face him. "What do you want?" she asked.

"Give me that dress," he said.

"It doesn't belong to you," she said.

"It belongs to the Musée du Louvre!" he said, stepping forward. "Look! Filaments are falling to the floor!"

Anne and Michael looked at the ground, and it was true; fragments of thread and fabric lay there.

"That dress is *three hundred years old*," the man said, growing red in the face.

"I repeat," Anne said calmly. "It does not belong to you."

"What happened?" Michael asked her.

"This man was *kind* enough to assist me in my research, by showing me, at my request, some antique clothing," Anne said.

"Then it's true?" Michael asked. "That the dress is three hundred years old and belongs to the Louvre?"

"Yes," Anne said. "To the Louvre, not to *him*."

"I work in the Department of Material Culture," the man said. "Here at the Louvre. Now, I *insist* . . ."

"He is just an assistant," Anne said. She faced the man, who was approximately her height. "I am doing important research. I need this dress."

"Oh, my God," the man said, wiping sweat off his brow. "I should never have let you into the storeroom. It is absolutely against regulations . . ."

"He'll get into trouble, Anne," Michael said. "Give him the dress."

"This—from you?" she said, glaring at Michael. Then her lower lip began to quiver. "Fine, I will take off the dress."

"Oh, thank you," the man said, clasping his hands.

"Wait in your office," Anne said haughtily. "I shall bring it to you as soon as I am ready."

"Okay," the man said, still nervous but now hopeful, backing out of the room. Michael felt amused and embarrassed. He had never seen Anne play-act so publicly before. She stood before him, pouting slightly. The contrast between her skin—smooth and pink, so healthy, and the fabric—stiff and decaying—seemed almost obscene.

"I had thought you would admire it," she said.

"I do," Michael said. "But I also see his point."

She waved her hand, dismissing the man. "He is a functionary. Don't worry about him."

"Anne, you are going to return the dress, aren't you?" When she didn't answer, Michael touched her cheek. "Where would you wear it?" he asked.

"I wish I could wear it all the time," Anne said, two big tears spilling out of her dark eyes. "I have never felt so *whole* as I do now. Or *did*, before he spoiled it. Standing here, in the Salle des Quatre Saisons . . ." She looked around, taking in the paintings, the table. "This room is truly a masterpiece, and I wanted to pay homage to you—its creator. On this, the day of its opening." Standing on her toes, she kissed his lips. Michael stood stiff, afraid to touch the dress. Was that his imagination, the sound of it tearing?

"I'm glad you like the Salle so much," Michael said, wondering how Anne's mind worked, whether at that instant she *was* Madame de Sévigné.

"How I would love to see you dressed in clothes of the day," she said, smiling again, drawing herself to her full height, as she always did when preparing to quote from Madame de Sévigné, "'Find out something, my *bonne,* about what the men will be wearing this summer. I shall ask you to send me a pretty fabric for your brother, who implores you to turn him into a fashion plate at minimum cost . . .'"

Michael chuckled nervously. Had Anne already found him a seventeenth-century suit? He could imagine her begging him to dress up with her, how difficult it would be to say no. But he would say no. He had made up his mind; he wanted to be with Lydie. At that moment he felt a bizarre reversal of guilt, for being with Anne when he wanted to be with Lydie.

"Wouldn't it be wonderful to live in the Louvre, even for one night?" Anne asked. "I think of how it must look in the middle of the night, in the darkness, with moonlight coming through the windows . . ." She lowered her voice, took Michael's hand. "Let's do it! Let's spend tonight right here in the Salle."

"Anne, there are guards . . ."

She waved a dismissive hand. Her eyes glittered with excitement. "We'll be quiet as mice. We can stay upstairs, in the attic storerooms. Beds are there—even nightclothes from every epoch, including our own . . ."

"No, Anne," Michael said, knowing that "our own" epoch meant the seventeenth century.

"Oh, you are too rigid," she said, smiling up at him. "Don't you know that in France we value a lack of discipline? It is so important to forget the rules sometimes, to let your spirit be free."

Standing there, listening to the woman who had been his lover, Michael thought he deserved an award for lack of discipline. He had an impulse to run out of the Louvre, leaving behind everything venerable and ancient, into the bright sunshine. At that moment, gazing at Anne in her wig and crumbling dress, he wanted twentieth-century noise: traffic, loud music, loudspeakers blaring from the tour boats. Standing there with Anne, he felt that the air in the Salle des Quatre Saisons had not moved since the seventeenth century.

༄

"What a trouper you are," Patrice said, turning to speak to Lydie in the backseat. "It's really big of you, making an appearance at this thing."

Lydie smiled, then resumed staring at the back of Didier's head. He drove his Citroën toward the Louvre in fits and starts, using the brake twice as often as necessary.

"Why do you say it's big of her?" Didier asked. "She is going because she wants to see the Salle des Quatre Saisons."

"She is giving Michael his due," Patrice said. "She's keeping her personal feelings out of it, and I commend her."

"I'm just staying long enough to say hello," Lydie said, uneasy about the whole enterprise.

Now Didier was searching for a parking spot. For some reason Patrice felt personally responsible for Lydie's decision to attend Michael's opening. It put Lydie in mind of a story her father had told her about a boy who convinced a pagan to attend Christmas mass and felt as if he had given Jesus a nonbeliever's soul for his birthday.

Curiosity, not Patrice, had made Lydie decide to come. She wanted to see Michael's work, and she wanted to see his response when he caught sight of her. She had not told him she was coming. She didn't want him on his best behavior, trotting her around, introducing her to people as "*my wife.*" She wanted to slip in with the crowd, catch his eye, and see what would happen. Dressing as she had, however, she could not pretend she didn't want him to notice her at all. She wore a black dress by Azzadine Alaia, form-fitting to say the least, with a deep "V" in back.

She and the d'Orignys presented their engraved invitations to a guard and he pointed the way. "I know where it is," Didier said importantly. "We know Monsieur McBride."

Suddenly Lydie felt charged with anticipation. The event was gala, after all. The man just ahead of them used an ebony walking stick although he had no limp. Women wore their best dresses. People chattered, craning their necks. Everyone looked important, although Lydie could not say why. Perhaps the occasion gave importance to the crowd, the way it would at ballet premieres, first nights on Broadway, presidential inaugurations.

They entered the Salle and Lydie blocked the door, taking everything in. Her gaze lit on a beautiful long table—it could only be the information table Michael had commissioned. A mosaic floor glinted here and there with tiny gold tiles. Beneath the smell of perfume and hot food, she detected the scent of new plaster. A tapestry covering an entire wall depicted men returning from a hunt. But above all, her eye was drawn to a painting between the doors.

She stared at it and tried to place the story: a scene from Greek mythology? There was Mercury—she recognized his winged feet. A dead boy lay on the ground before a god at once handsome and tortured. Herds of cows, a magnificent tree, Cupid, nymphs.

"It's called *Apollo and Daphne,*" Patrice said, coming over with a printed guide. "I can't tell who's supposed to be Daphne unless she's the one in the tree."

Now that Lydie knew the painting's title, she remembered the story. "That's her—in her father's arms," Lydie said, pointing. "It hasn't been working out for her and Apollo."

"What's not to work out?" Patrice asked in her burlesque voice. "Check out Apollo."

Now Lydie began to look around, subtly she hoped, for Michael. There were Arthur Chase, Dot Graulty, Dot's husband. Her head averted, Patrice said, "Look over my right shoulder. See the tall guy?"

"Which one?"

"The one who looks like a Minister."

"Yes?"

"He's Jacques de Vauvray, the Minister of Culture. The guy he's standing with—the stumpy one? He's Pierre Dauphin, a sort-of friend of Didier's."

"I think I've heard Michael mention him," Lydie said. She could see Michael now, talking to a man covered with war decorations. By the way he edged back, she knew he had seen her and was trying to end the conversation. "Here he comes," she said.

"Did I say I need to use the ladies' room?" Patrice asked diplomatically, but Michael had already joined them.

"Hello," he said. The moment was awkward. He should have kissed Patrice's cheeks, but how could he do that without kissing Lydie?

"It's wonderful," Lydie said of the Salle. "I love that painting." Michael glanced up at *Apollo and Daphne*. He had had his hair cut for the occasion. Was it Lydie's imagination, or was that hair oil? She had never seen him use it before, but she thought he looked handsome, his wavy hair slightly slicked back, like someone from the Lost Generation. "The painting was my second choice," he said.

He wore a double-breasted pinstriped suit that looked extremely European compared to his usual single-breasted blazers from Brooks Brothers or J. Press. His shoes were not shoes at all, but *boots*. Ankle-high black boots with slightly pointed toes: Italian jodhpur boots. Lydie could hardly believe it. She had a clinical urge to engage him in conversation—like a graduate student doing research to learn how deeply he had changed—but she felt speechless.

"This is the most fantastic information center I have ever seen," Patrice said. "It's beautiful *and* informative. I do have one question, though: where's the ladies' room?"

"Through that door," Michael said, pointing.

As Patrice walked away, Lydie resumed watching Michael.

"So, you like it?" he asked.

"Yes—a lot," she said. She knew she should tell him *what* she liked and *why,* but she felt totally captivated by his personal affects: hair, clothes, shoes.

"Didier's kept me up-to-date on the ball," Michael said, "but what's happening with Kelly?"

"She'll be interviewed at the embassy soon," Lydie said. "Can I ask—is that hair oil you're wearing?"

"Greasy kid stuff," Michael said, grinning.

"No kidding," she said. "It looks good."

"There'll be pictures later, and I didn't want to look too American. Give the journalists fuel for their fire."

Now Lydie looked around. She found the Salle very comfortable and harmonious, the paintings well positioned, the information table solid and authentic. "Why are you worried?" she asked. "This place does just what it should do: it provides information in a gallery atmosphere. If there's a long line at the information desk, people can look around at the paintings."

"That was the idea," Michael said. "I'm glad you think it works."

Under cover of social pleasantries, passionate looks were passing between Lydie and Michael. She felt a burning desire to touch his hand. She wanted him to bend her over backwards in a long kiss. It hit her hard, the fact that everything that had happened might be worth it if they could fall in love all over again. How many couples, after all this time, had the chance to feel the intensity of new love?

"Can I get you something?" Michael asked. "How about a glass of champagne?"

"Sure," Lydie said. "That would be fine."

As he walked away, Lydie surveyed the room. There, in the corner, was Patrice talking to Anne Dumas. The sight of them, her tall friend and the dwarfish home-wrecker, brought Lydie out of the romantic mist. She watched them, chatting like two old friends, and felt a variety of things: hatred for Anne, fury at Patrice for being civil to her, curiosity for what they were talking about. Michael came back with the drinks.

Lydie accepted the champagne and drank a sip of it. She had known this would likely happen, that the possibility of running into Anne Dumas was strong. She felt her teeth against the glass.

"Don't let it upset you, Lydie," Michael said, following her eyes. "She works here. I couldn't tell her not to come."

"I know," she said.

"I wanted you to come," Michael said. "You know I did."

"Yes," Lydie said. Here she stood in the Salle des Quatre Saisons, at a celebration of Michael's work—their reason, after all, for coming to France—and she could speak only in monosyllables.

"Let's go over there," Michael said. "I'd like to introduce you to Charles Legendre."

Lydie smiled at him. "I'd rather not meet him right now," she said. "In fact, I'm about to leave." She felt tempted to stay, but sticking to her original plan made her feel more in control.

"Aw, Lydie," Michael said.

She smiled again, at the idea that such a dashing guy, so elegant and European in style, could say "Aw, Lydie." "You sound just like a country boy," she said.

"I have to stay," Michael said. "I'd like to come with you . . . where are you going?"

"I'm going to walk home. Will you tell the d'Orignys for me?"

"Yes," Michael said. And although it had been too awkward to kiss her hello, he kissed her good-bye.

Exiting the Louvre, Lydie knew she wouldn't have left if she thought there was a chance Michael would go home with Anne. She wondered what Patrice had been talking to her about. The history of the Marais, probably. Turning right to walk home along the Seine, she discovered that she didn't care. Hardly at all.

∽

Patrice had the uncomfortable sense of not simply praising Anne Dumas's work, but of gushing. "I'm positively captivated," she said, for measure. She cast a sidelong glance at Michael and Lydie, felt unhappy to see that they were looking in her direction.

"What 'captivates' you?" Anne asked, dimpling.

"Oh, the way you make those seventeenth-century women seem so modern. I feel absolutely *d'accord* with them."

Now Anne frowned. "You cannot possibly feel *d'accord* with all three. When they were at such obvious odds."

"It's true," Patrice agreed. "The noblewoman, the courtesan, and the murderer. Which is your favorite?"

"Madame de Sévigné, of course. Though I admit to a certain

fascination with Ninon de Lenclos. By the age of thirty, Ninon was famous as an intellectual and as an advocate of women's rights. Her opinions in matters of sex and religion were totally avant-garde. Members of the King's court frequented her salon."

"But Ninon stole Madame de Sévigné's husband," Patrice said, watching for Anne's reaction. She could not stop imagining Anne in bed with Michael. She was so adorable, with those tiny features that all seemed somehow upturned: her nose, the smiling corners of her eyes, her bow mouth with the sensual lower lip. Her full hair, brushed up and held in place with a silk headband, was expertly tinted to look sun-lightened. Her rose suede miniskirt was too short for this season, but Anne had the girlishness to carry it off.

Anne waved her small hand in a scoffing manner. "She could have had any lover," she said. "Men were terribly suspicious of Ninon, you know. Louis XIV had her watched by spies—a feminist in seventeenth-century France was dangerous, indeed. Especially one with as many eminent lovers as Ninon had."

Patrice recalled an anecdote presented by Anne in *Three Women of the Marais*. Cardinal Richelieu offered Ninon nearly a million dollars to become his mistress. She declined "because if he pleased me, the sum would be exorbitant, and if he displeased me, the sum would be insufficient." Patrice felt somewhat daring, like a spy herself, engaging Anne in a conversation about love in the seventeenth century while Lydie was over there talking with Michael. She glanced across the room, to see how it was going, but Lydie was gone.

"Oh," she said, frowning.

"Pardon?" Anne said.

"Wasn't Ninon racy?" Patrice asked.

"I see that you are watching the McBrides," Anne said bluntly. Patrice looked around, in case she had missed them. But they definitely had left. No, there was Michael, without Lydie, talking to Didier at the buffet table. "I was thinking of joining them," Patrice said, now feeling awkward. With her uncanny perception, Anne reminded Patrice of a cross between a mind-reader and a schizophrenic.

"Isn't he a talented man!" Anne said, dimpling again.

"Well, she's just as talented," Patrice said forcefully, leaving no doubt. "She's staging an incredible ball at Château Bellechasse, which, as you must know, is a gem of eighteenth-century archi-tecture."

"Well, eighteenth century," Anne said, scoffing. Her gaze en-veloped the Salle, taking everything in. "Now, *this* is a marvel. I feel all of the seventeenth century in this room, as concentrated as bouillon. I feel that I can almost drink it."

"It is superb," Patrice agreed. At that instant she made a wish: that Lydie's ball would be superb, that it would outshine Michael's triumph. Where Patrice had once thought of it only as the "d'Origny ball," she found herself thinking of it more often as "Lydie's ball." What did that mean? Lydie was the artist, but Di-dier was putting up the money and the jewels. As an only child, Patrice had long found it hard to turn the spotlight on someone else. But she felt she was doing it now: making Lydie shine. She felt like a magician doing sleight of hand. Illuminating Lydie for Michael and the public while at the same time shielding her from Anne.

Thus, it shocked and dismayed Patrice when, twenty minutes later, Michael reported that Lydie had left. Patrice ate some hors d'oeuvres and made small talk with Pierre and Giselle Dauphin. As soon as she and Didier arrived home, she telephoned Lydie.

"You couldn't even say good-bye?" Patrice asked, trying to keep the hurt out of her voice.

"You were talking to Anne Dumas," Lydie said. "I'm really sorry. I told Michael to say good-bye for me."

"Well, he did," Patrice said, unable to define the source of her disappointment. "You didn't have to leave, you know. It was obvious Michael wants to be with you."

"I couldn't stand seeing her. What were you two so intent on?"

"The seventeenth century," Patrice said. "I was keeping her out of your hair." Then it dawned on her: she had been distracting Anne Dumas, a woman whom she had admired for longer than she had known Lydie, in order to protect Lydie. And she felt annoyed with Lydie for not acting appropriately grateful.

"The seventeenth century, well . . ." Lydie said. "She must be crazy about the Salle des Quatre Saisons. Isn't it great?"

"Great," Patrice said. "What did you and the architect have to say?"

Lydie was silent, but Patrice could almost hear her smiling. "It's getting better," she said after a moment.

"Lovely," Patrice said, now even more annoyed with Lydie for keeping her conversation with Michael such a big secret. "Should we plan tomorrow?"

"Tomorrow?"

"Isn't tomorrow our little pilgrim's big day? Her interview?"

"Of course," Lydie said. "Two o'clock? Near Smith's?"

"See you there," Patrice said. She felt deflated. She felt herself collapsing inward, like an empty corn husk. She hadn't harbored a mean thought toward Kelly for quite some time, but here she was wondering what embarrassing thing Kelly would choose to wear tomorrow.

She stretched out on her chaise longue. *Three Women of the Marais* lay open across the tufted arm. She tried to close it, but it had lain there for so long it seemed permanently divided at page

340 into two sections. Lydie, no, *events,* had taken away her pleasure in reading it. She thought of Lydie, alone in her apartment, a
thrilling little smile on her face. She could imagine Lydie reliving
her meeting with Michael, her imagination listening for what he
had said, fathoming what he had not. Lydie, Patrice felt sure, was
in the throes of love.

"Hello, my baby," Didier said in his soft, low voice. He sat at
the end of the chaise and commenced rubbing Patrice's feet.

"Hi," she said.

"You look so far away," he said. "What is bothering you?"

"Nothing," Patrice said, then, "Do you think I'm interesting
enough?"

Didier frowned. He stopped rubbing her foot, held it lightly in
his hand. "What do you mean?"

"I mean, am I boring because I don't have work like Lydie's?"

Didier resumed his massage, and his face relaxed. "If you were
any more interesting, I would have to quit my job. You are the
most fascinating woman I know."

He had said that before, but Patrice had never quite believed it.
Now, at his obvious sincerity, she felt her throat tighten. Here
with her husband in their ancient house, in a foreign country, for
the first time in her life, Patrice felt secure. She didn't believe that
she was fascinating, but she knew that Didier believed it. She
could see it in his eyes, eyes that tended to smile even in repose.
She gazed at him, her Frenchman, whose tan and weathered face
gave him more the look of a mountaineer than a businessman,
and she let him rub her foot.

∽

Lydie and Kelly stood on the rue de Rivoli, scanning the Tuileries.
Lydie wore her most businesslike blue suit. Kelly wore a plaid

wool skirt and white blouse and a black jacket Patrice had loaned her to go on top.

"Don't be so nervous, Kelly," Lydie said. "She'll be here in a minute."

Kelly glanced over her shoulder, at the armed soldier who stood at the corner of rue Cambon. "But we must go. We should be in line."

Lydie laughed, touched her shoulder in an attempt to calm her. "There will be no line. You have an appointment. We're thirty minutes early." She checked her watch. She herself was beginning to feel a little anxious; Patrice was ten minutes late. But here she came, waving, breaking into a run.

"Whew," Patrice said, kissing Lydie's cheeks.

"Hello, Mum," Kelly said shyly.

"Hi, Kelly."

"Shall we run though the routine?" Lydie asked. "Let's sit on that bench."

"I think we should go," Kelly said. "We can't be late."

"It's a two-minute walk," Patrice said, smiling gently, the way a parent might smile at a nervous child. "Relax, okay? Lydie and I want to rehearse with you."

Kelly smiled. "I have always rehearsed for this day. When I was thirteen my sister and I played American Embassy."

"Let's rehearse," Patrice repeated.

Kelly pursed her lips, but she relented. Lydie had known she would, but it worried her instead of pleasing her. If Kelly could be assertive with Lydie and Patrice, perhaps she would have a better chance with the consular officer.

"Pretend I'm the interviewer, okay?" Patrice asked. She cleared her throat and made her expression very cross, making Kelly laugh a little.

"Tell me, Miss Merida," she said. "What do you do for a living?"

"I am the assistant to Mrs. Lydie McBride," Kelly said proudly, her spine erect.

"And what does Mrs. McBride do?"

"She is a shopper. I mean, she is a stylist." Kelly reddened at the mistake, glanced apologetically at Lydie.

"That's all right," Lydie said.

"What do you do for Mrs. McBride?" Patrice asked.

"I . . . shop." Kelly slumped a little, and her voice was softer, less confident since her mistake.

"Kelly," Lydie said carefully, not wanting to spook her. "Tell the lady what we discussed. Tell her I have very specific tastes, that I get assignments from important magazines, that major companies hire me to do their catalogues and advertisements. Tell her that you are an *integral* part of my business."

"Integral," Kelly said almost sternly, trying to commit the word to memory. "Integral, integral."

"Tell her that I trained you, that it would take months for me to train someone new."

Kelly nodded fast, staccato, like a short-circuited robot.

"You'll be fine," Patrice said. "Maybe we should knock off the rehearsal, do some deep breathing." Looking over Kelly's head at Lydie, she raised one eyebrow.

Lydie could see Patrice feared that Kelly would bomb in the interview. Perhaps Lydie did too, but she tried to have faith. The three of them walked up the rue Cambon. At the gate to the American Embassy, Patrice spoke to the guard. She proffered the three passports. This was the first time an official had examined Kelly's since her arrival in Germany. Lydie examined her fingernails, then gazed up at a flock of pigeons—deliberately nonchalant. The guard stared from Patrice's face to Kelly's to Lydie's, then let them pass.

"Go through that door, take a left, take a quick right," he said to Patrice. He cast a cold glance at Kelly.

"My enemy," Kelly whispered to Lydie.

"You can't think like that," Lydie said. "This is the most important hour of your life." She sensed Kelly shaking, saw a line of sweat above her lip. "Listen to me," she said sharply. "You were not convincing back there. You sounded frightened, and you sounded like a liar. Keep your back straight, hold your head up. Think of how far you've come. Remember you're as good as anyone else."

"Oh, thank you, Lydie," Kelly said.

At the door to the office, Lydie and Patrice said good-bye to Kelly. She smiled at them but said nothing; wordlessly, she followed the tall American soldier who led her inside, closing the door behind her.

"What if it doesn't work?" Patrice asked.

"We're doing everything we can," Lydie said.

"We're throwing her to the wolves," Patrice said. "You and I can walk out the door, have tea, do anything. But Kelly could be arrested just for breathing the Paris air."

"That's about to change," Lydie said with more confidence than she felt.

"When I hired Kelly, I knew she was illegal in France. I was glad, at the time, because it meant I could pay her lower wages. Isn't that sick?"

"You didn't know her then," Lydie said.

"What kills me," Patrice said, "is the thought of Kelly playing American Embassy when she was thirteen. Remember being thirteen?"

Lydie remembered. You had the greatest dreams and absolutely nothing to hold you back. You believed you could be a movie star, or President, or just plain rich. You didn't know how the world worked. You were blessed with a total lack of perspective. At thirteen, you thought you were *it*. "What did you want when you were thirteen?" she asked, watching the door that had closed behind Kelly.

Patrice stared at Lydie. "A checking account. My best friend got one, with her name on the checks, so I wanted one. How about you?"

"Oh, some boy, I'm sure," Lydie said, trying to remember. "Thirteen—what was that, seventh grade?"

Patrice nodded.

"Then it was Damon Stackpole. That's all I wanted—for Damon to kiss me in the coatroom. I hadn't been kissed before."

Patrice raised an eyebrow. "Let's get the hell out of here and have a drink. Or go shopping. Chanel's half a block away."

"Not shopping," Lydie said, wondering whether Patrice was kidding.

"Come on—a good bout with Chanel will do us good. We'll duke it out with some snotty French salesgirl and walk away with a couple of new handbags. We'll feel much better. We could be back here in twenty minutes. She'll be at least that long."

"Let's just take a walk in the park," Lydie said. "I could use a lemonade, couldn't you?"

"I could use a new jacket," Patrice said, sighing with mock exasperation. Then a sly expression crossed her eyes. "Are you going to tell me about Michael?"

"There's nothing new," Lydie said.

"The park, eh?" Patrice said. "Well, okay."

So Lydie slid her arm through Patrice's and they walked, arm in arm, into the Tuileries, her heart beating a little slower every step she took away from rue Cambon.

∽

Standing in an office in the American consular section, Kelly felt her eyes flood with tears. For the first time in her life she was standing on American soil. It scarcely mattered that it was in France. Here, American laws applied. The carpet was brown, worn thin. How many hopeful aliens had passed through here? How many of their dreams had come true? How many had gotten to the States? The American flag stood in one corner. Old Glory! Unframed portraits of Presidents Washington and Lincoln hung on the wall. She had time to notice every object in the office before the man at the desk beckoned to her.

"Have a seat," he said.

"Thank you, sir," Kelly said. And at that moment, as she lowered herself into the torn vinyl chair, magic entered her. A spell was cast, and Kelly knew: one of her sisters had slipped something, a potion, into her coffee that morning. Something to give her the courage to convince her interviewer of her worth. Her fingers quivered with the power; it shot through her spine the way lightning strikes a tree. Her sisters were good at magic. She remembered the time Annette had put a hex on Boy Bilido's sister, how when the doctors cut her open they found her full of bugs.

The man studied Kelly's petition. He tapped his finger up and down it. "Let's see," he said. "You are twenty-seven years of age, born in Cavite province in the Philippines."

"Yes sir," Kelly said, trying to place his accent. She had never heard one like it. A banner on his wall said "Miami Dolphins." Was he from Florida?

"Ever been arrested?" he asked.

"No sir," Kelly said.

"You finished college? Majored in accounting?" He spoke too

fast for her to respond. "Worked at a bank in Cavite? You're a Catholic? Never married? With no children?"

"I have no children," Kelly said, a bubble of panic rising. She fought it down, forced herself to breathe normally.

"What I don't understand, Miss Merida," said the man, smiling slightly, looking at her for the first time, "is how your education and past work experience prepare you to assist Mrs. McBride."

"I have a flair for the work," Kelly said, earnestly. "And I am an integral part of her business."

"So, tell me just what you do."

Kelly leaned forward, to read the Formica nameplate on the man's desk. It said "Mr. Wright." She felt better, knowing his name. "Mrs. McBride is a stylist," Kelly said. "She is hired by magazines all over the world to create photographs." Kelly remembered several of the examples Lydie had invented for her. Lydie had told Kelly to remember the examples, then use her imagination. "Right now Mrs. McBride is directing advertisements for d'Origny jewelers. We are putting on a banquet. Everyone will be there!"

"A banquet to advertise jewelry?" Mr. Wright asked skeptically.

"Oh, yes," Kelly said. "Beautiful guests will be photographed wearing the jewels. We had to rent ball gowns, foods . . ." What else would you have at a banquet? She tried to picture fiestas in the Philippines, like the feast of St. Mary Magdalene on July 22. "Beautiful tablecloths, embroidered with flowers, birds, and dancing ladies," she said. "Also centerpieces of fruits and flowers. With a twenty-piece band playing music for dancing. Also men to carry statues, very festive, to swing in tune with the band." Kelly had no idea how close this image was to what would happen at a French banquet. She hoped the American Mr. Wright would have no idea either.

"And Mrs. McBride can't arrange that on her own?"

"Oh, no! It takes both of us to do it right. We must have at least twenty different foods on the table—many noodles, beef *and* pork, oysters, mussels, shrimp, crabs, boiled chicken, and some desserts."

"So you order the food, that sort of thing?" Mr. Wright asked.

"Yes, and Mrs. McBride is very picky about the way the foods look. Not everyone can do it right! Because the magazines and companies are paying a lot of money, so she insists it be perfect."

"How long have you worked for Mrs. McBride?" Mr. Wright asked.

"One year," Kelly lied, sitting even more erect. "And she has trained me to know exactly what she likes. And we have the same taste in everything! Imagine how difficult it would be for her to train someone new, someone very different from her."

"Hmmm . . ." Mr. Wright said, making notations.

So far all was going well, Kelly thought. But she must not relax or let him trick her.

"Would you be willing to accompany her to the United States?" Mr. Wright asked.

Kelly took her time. Was this the trick question? Her brother Paul Anka had warned her there would be one. "Yes, I am willing," she said after a minute.

"You have family in America? Your mother and two sisters?"

"That is true."

"Can you tell me the first President of the United States?"

"George Washington, followed by John Adams, Thomas Jefferson, James Madison . . ." Kelly said proudly. She knew them all; she wished he would ask her to name them.

"Have you ever been to Russia?" Mr. Wright asked.

"Never!" Kelly said. "It is the Evil Empire."

Mr. Wright smiled a little, making Kelly very happy. Then he looked very stern, leaning on his elbows in a way that warned

Kelly he was possibly about to ask the trick question. "How did you get to France? Your passport shows no French visas."

Everyone in her family and Lydie had told her not to mention her brother or the Philippine ambassador. "I crossed the German border," she said.

"How?"

"On a bus."

"That seems unlikely. They check passports on buses."

"They didn't check mine. It was nighttime, very late . . . all the passengers were asleep." She said exactly what Paul Anka had told her to say.

"On most buses the passengers give their passports to the driver upon boarding, and he gives them to the border guards," Mr. Wright said, watching her carefully.

"It was a local bus, from Fribourg to Colmar," Kelly said, willing herself to not avert her gaze. She felt the bones in her jaw would crack. "I think perhaps the driver knew the guards."

"Hmmm," Mr. Wright said, making more notations. He wrote silently. Then, "Why Colmar? What was there to see in Colmar?"

The trick question! And Kelly was ready! "Oh, the museum, of course. It is so very beautiful, with the medieval altarpiece depicting scenes of heaven and hell. Have you seen it, Mr. Wright?"

"No, I haven't," he said wryly. He gazed at her for a long time. At that moment, Kelly had hope. Lydie had told her the decision would be made later, after Kelly left the embassy, but just then Kelly could imagine him telling her on the spot: "Welcome to the United States."

But he just looked down, wrote a few more words. "Do you realize that you are in violation of French law, Miss Merida?" he asked.

"Yes," Kelly said, her pulse quickening. She listened carefully for approaching guards.

"In most cases, I would have to report you directly to the French authorities. But someone has intervened on your behalf. Mr. Morrison, of this office, has okayed your release pending consideration of this petition."

"Oh, thank you, thank you," Kelly sputtered. Her body let loose one great shiver, and she felt a tiny trickle of urine escape. There were tears just behind her eyes. She was all fluid, ready to flood.

"You may go," Mr. Wright said.

Kelly bowed her head, rose, backed out of the room as if she were taking leave of a bishop.

In the waiting room she looked around for Lydie and Patrice. Not seeing them, she walked outside and there they were, coming toward her through the park. All of a sudden she thought of leaving Patrice and felt a pang. Kelly understood it. In her province, people accepted the great emptiness that accompanied loving someone, because ultimately you would separate in the search for a better life. Even when it meant leaving family, loved ones behind. This was accepted as destiny. When the chance came to get to the States, you were propelled forward by a nameless force. You didn't stop to think, or to worry, about whom you would miss. In this life, missing people you loved was inevitable. Nothing could be simpler, Kelly thought, watching Patrice come toward her with an expectant look in her eyes. Kelly would pack her bags when the time came.

❧

All the Meridas in Paris came to the apartment behind Clichy to honor Kelly. Colorful streamers hung from the ceiling and music played on the radio. Delicious smells of ham, chicken, and milkfish filled the air. Everyone had questions about the interview. "What was the trick question?" Paul Anka asked. "Something about the German border?"

"Right as usual," Kelly said, happy to flatter him. He had lived in Paris longer than anyone, without ever finding someone to help him get to the States, and he was growing discouraged.

"You'll get rich in the States," Sophia said, and everyone agreed. But while everyone cheered and talked about what Kelly should do with the money she would make, Kelly grew silent. Her head spun with memories of the Philippines. Even unhappy memories made her heart ache! She remembered when the family, eleven altogether, had slept on one coconut mat covered with a mosquito net. The net was the largest in the neighborhood and all the neighbors were impressed.

With the money they earned from Pan Am they bought a fish pond between a public cemetery and the sea. Half salt, half freshwater, the pond contained some of the fattest fish in the province. Prawns, milkfish—national fish of the Philippines—everything. The family raised fish. Her father thanked God and the pond's proximity to the cemetery for the fishes' fatness. The fish fed and spawned, growing enormous on seepage from the cemetery, so every three or four months her father would harvest them. He would drain the pond, and all the Merida children would run across the mud with baskets, scooping up all the dying, flopping fish.

"Remember when we would drain the pond and catch fish?" Kelly asked.

"You won't be doing that in the States," Jerry said. "There you'll have your own fish market."

"You girls had it easy," Paul Anka said. "Draining the pond, collecting shells to sell to the tourists. You never fished the reefs."

"Don't talk about that," Kelly said. She shivered every time she thought of Paul Anka, Jerry, and Ricky going to fish the reef for tropical fish to sell to pet stores in the States. Five hundred boys— plus livestock, dried corn, and rocks—would squeeze onto a boat and go to sea for two months. They would tie long ropes around heavy rocks. Then two hundred boys at a time would dive into the water, hanging onto ropes that held the rocks, and they would bang the rocks on the coral to scare the fish. When the fish swam out, the captain would drop a huge net over them. The boys would dive down, eighty or a hundred feet, to make sure the net didn't tear on the reef. Sometimes boys got caught and drowned.

Now Kelly looked at Paul Anka, her eyes filling with tender tears. Too many minutes underwater had left him with a slight palsy. He was her favorite brother. "Let me get you some noodles, Paul," Kelly said.

He smiled at her. "Shrimp noodles, okay?"

Kelly felt honored that the family would serve shrimp noodles at a party in her honor. She heaped Paul Anka's plate high with them. Now Marie-Vic was asking him to tell the story of Imelda's snakeskin wallet. Kelly knew it by heart, how Mrs. Marcos had called the ambassador to tell him she wanted a red and purple snakeskin wallet to match her shoes, how the only one Paul could find was a sea snake wallet—from the Philippines.

"Imagine Imelda with a sea snake wallet!" Jerry said, making everyone laugh.

Kelly had dived for sea snakes as a child; they all had. Then her father would boil the skins off them and sell them to shoemakers. He had warned the children to be careful, saying that the snakes were poisonous, but only recently, in a magazine Patrice had given her, had Kelly learned they were even more poisonous than cobras.

She took a bite of chicken, savored the flavor and the sound of her family's voices. The voices wrapped her like a cocoon, and she felt warm and loved. She had never lived without her family before, but she was prepared to try. She had a fantasy of standing in a crowd, swearing allegiance to the United States of America. Sending for the rest of her family, Paul Anka first.

# 20

*Whatever I said I said out of love, out of interest, out of esteem for a name and a house which no one could honor more than I, honoring it perhaps even more than he does.*

—To Françoise-Marguerite, February 1680

Lydie studied a road map showing the way to the Loire Valley, and realized that she had a new appreciation for the precision of maps. Four-lane highways, dead-end roads, scenic routes, public parks, historical monuments: all were marked. In the past, on trips outside the city with Michael, Lydie had relied on road signs and her sense of direction instead of maps; their rate of success for reaching their destination without major wrong turns was about fifty percent.

Reading the map, Lydie thought of Patrice and Kelly. Patrice, so forthright, with her clear sense of loyalty and betrayal, and Kelly, with her single-minded drive to escape poverty by getting to the United States, had inspired Lydie by their precision. They carved out their places in the world instead of taking what was thrown at them. Lydie thought of how she had come to Paris with a vague sense that her marriage was going bad, with a stalled desire to live again—to really live, without always halting to consider the consequence of every small action. To take events as they came, with more pleasure and less apprehension.

She thought it incredible—revolutionary—that she could keep going, surer than she had in years, now that Michael had left her. Every morning she wakened with his face in mind, the blank sense that he wasn't in bed with her. But then she would make coffee, make a mental list of things to be done for the ball, for Kelly. The list would push everything else out of her mind: her troubles with Michael, her father's death, her mother back in New York.

The ball was just a week off. She studied the road map, plotting the best way for the d'Origny entourage to travel from Paris. Police cars raced down the quai, startling her. Then came a knock at the door.

Michael stood in the hallway. Lydie held the door open a crack, regarding him. "Hi," she said.

"I want to talk to you," he said.

The sight of him forced the checklist, the road map from her mind. The satisfying sense of precision was gone. "Come on in," she said.

He held her shoulders at arm's length, easing her into a chair. Then he sat in the chair opposite. She traced the textured bargello pattern on the chair's arm with her thumb, afraid to look at him.

"Lydie," Michael said. She stared at the pattern for a minute before raising her eyes. She felt startled to see his brown eyes, usually so clear, now bloodshot. Lack of sleep? Crying? Neither seemed impossible. "I want to start over," he said.

"Starting over sounds good," she said dryly. "But when? Before tonight, before coming to Paris? When?" She knew the two-parted answer: before Anne, before Neil's death. But she wasn't prepared for Michael's response.

"Eleventh grade," Michael said, deadpan.

"*Eleventh grade?*" she asked. "But why?"

"Why didn't you like me then?"

Lydie frowned. "I *did* like you. I used to love watching you play basketball. But we didn't know each other very well—we were in different crowds."

"I wanted to ask you out," Michael said. "I was dying to, every time I saw you."

Lydie was dumbfounded. Michael had told this story before, usually in an offhanded way, at a party, as in "I was crazy about Lydie in high school, but she had no use for a jock." Now his expression was totally serious, as if he had been dwelling on this for a while and needed an answer. She studied his hands, his wrists, his face. His features were exactly the same as they had been in high school, along with some accumulated sadness.

"I would have gone out with you," she said. "I'm sure I would have."

Michael shook his head. "No, you were in love with the priest."

Lydie was about to laugh, to deny it, but Michael was right. She *had* loved Father Griffin. She remembered the nights she had lain awake, torturing herself with thoughts of what would happen if he broke his vows. She supposed that her crush on the priest had prevented her from dating high school boys, including Michael. "But that was just high school," she said. "I fell in love with you the instant we reconnected—in Washington. For me it was love at first sight."

"For me too," Michael said. "Only my first sight took place about six years earlier than yours did."

Lydie felt thrilled by the notion that Michael had been harboring such a romantic resentment all these years. He rose from his chair and began to pace, a frown on his face. He walked to the window, stared out at the Seine, gave her a sidelong glance. Then he came to her, pulled her out of her chair and into his arms. Lydie said nothing, but she let him kiss her. It was a long gentle kiss, and it tasted so familiar she could hardly believe it.

When they pulled apart, his face was close to hers, and she could see an expectant look in his eyes. "What?" she asked.

"Is this starting over?" he asked.

"I can't forget what happened," she said, giving him a little involuntary push away. "I want to, but . . ." She couldn't think how to finish the sentence. But what? But you've had an affair, but you betrayed me, but I've been a jerk . . .

"It probably can't happen all at once," he said. "I thought maybe it could. You know what it's like when you go over and over something in your mind, till it's all worked out and seems so clear and obvious? And then you mention it to someone who hasn't been thinking about it at all, and you can't understand why they don't accept it instantly."

"Oh, I've been thinking about it," Lydie said. Her heart raced. Michael had been working this out in his mind? And what had he decided?

"I'm sorry for what I did to you," he said. "I'm sorry for leaving. I'm sorry for . . . Anne Dumas."

Even the sound of her name on his lips made Lydie feel cold. But she saw such regret in his eyes that she forgave him. "I know you're sorry," she said. "I can tell."

"You can?"

"Yes. Your voice is shaking. And you look a little afraid—as if you think I'm going to hit you."

"You should hit me," Michael said. "But that's not what I'm afraid of." He made a move toward her, as if he wanted to touch her, but he held back. "I'm afraid I hurt you so badly you won't have me back."

I'll have you back, Lydie wanted to say but couldn't quite get the words out. He *had* hurt her badly. She felt not at all confused, but she wasn't quite ready to start over. She needed time to catch up, to do some of the thinking Michael had done, and, now that she had forgiven him, to forgive herself a little. Instead she said, "It wasn't all your fault. I know life with me hasn't been a trip to the beach."

"That's exactly what it's been," Michael said. Now he did touch her. First he put his hand on her shoulder, and she looked him straight in the eye, daring him to hug her. He did. "A trip to the beach. Some days are clear and fine, and then you have a tropical storm."

"A hurricane," Lydie said.

"A whopper," Michael said. "Hurricane Gloria."

And wasn't it interesting, that he would name this personal, romantic hurricane "Gloria"? "Gloria," to Lydie, sounded so hopeful, exuberant, even exultant. She wondered: was this the eye of the storm? Or had it moved out to sea, blown itself out over water?

"It's been a little wild," she said.

"A little," Michael said, watching her.

"Would you mind if we lie down for a minute?" Lydie asked. "I'm feeling a bit light-headed."

"We wouldn't want you to faint," Michael said. They walked toward their bedroom. Lydie *did* feel slightly dizzy, as it occurred to her, unbelievably, that in all the times she had walked with Michael into their Paris bedroom, this was the happiest she had felt.

"Much better," she said, lying back on the pillow. Her hair must have fanned out above her head because Michael was touching it, tucking it behind her ears. His touch sent a tingle down her spine. She closed her eyes, and the next second he was kissing her.

"Are you still light-headed?" he whispered.

"Much more so," she whispered back.

They lay there holding each other. Lydie kept her eyes closed some of the time. When she opened them, there was Michael, watching her. They touched each other's necks, wrists, hair. She stroked his back, feeling the rough texture of his cotton shirt. Something kept them from taking off their clothes. She felt content, and so did Michael, to just lie still, next to each other. It was perfect, really.

After a long time, when it had grown dark and the pastel lights of the tour boats shimmered along their walls, Michael hitched himself up on his elbows. "Time to go?" he asked.

"I guess so," Lydie said. It was true that she loved him but wasn't ready for him to move back home. That it *was* his home she had no doubt. But she wanted to catch up with her feelings of love—they had come on so strong and suddenly after all that had happened.

"Is there something you want to ask me?" Michael asked.

Lydie considered. "Everything. But nothing in particular right now."

"Maybe I should have said, 'Is there anything you want to ask me *to?*'"

She grinned. "The ball," she said.

He regarded her, saying nothing, waiting for her to go on.

"Will you come with me?" Lydie asked.

"I'd like nothing better," Michael said.

# 21

WHAT IF THE worst happened and the petition was denied? Kelly lay on her bed, trying to calm the thrill that ran all through her body. It was her day off; soon her sisters and brothers would be home, and Kelly had done hardly anything around the house. All she could do was pace the floor, flip through old magazines Patrice had given her, and listen to music. Right now Barry Manilow was singing about love in New England. Kelly wondered what New England was like. Patrice had told her it snowed there, and Kelly knew what snow was. She had seen it at least six times during the eighteen months since she had arrived in Europe.

"Hello, lazybones," Marie-Vic said, interrupting Kelly's thoughts.

"Yes, I'm lazy," Kelly said. Usually she and Marie-Vic had the same day off, but Marie-Vic had a new part-time job cleaning the apartment of her employers' daughter.

"What are you doing? Daydreaming about the States?"

"A little," Kelly said.

"Do you think the fish markets are the same there?"

"I don't know. I don't even know if the fish are the same there."

"I think it is so strange that a country like the States doesn't have a national fish," Marie-Vic said. "Maybe because it is so big and there are too many fishes to choose from."

"I'll miss milkfish in the States," Kelly said.

"I'll miss you," Marie-Vic said, giving Kelly a pang in her heart. Kelly was Marie-Vic's favorite sister. Marie-Vic told everyone that Kelly's christening was one of the high points of Marie-Vic's life. She couldn't get over, especially, the importance of Kelly's godparents: twelve vendors from the market, plus the son of the governor. So what if her parents had never met him? Kelly smiled fondly at Marie-Vic. "Are you the one who cast the spell?" Kelly asked. "The day of my interview?"

"Yes," Marie-Vic said with a solemn smile.

Kelly thanked her. Their mother came from Visaya, a very remote island full of magic, phantoms, and a witch. She had two kinds of powers, Barang and Mankukulam, and had passed them on to some of her daughters. Kelly had never got the hang of it. Marie-Vic, the best at Mankukulam, had a drawerful of dolls that represented people they knew. If she met someone new she wanted to help or curse, she simply made a new doll. Their mother used to be known throughout the province as the best at Barang. She had plenty of bottles of insects, especially beetles, and when someone had an enemy they could visit her, pay her some money to do a ceremony, and the enemy would swell up and need an operation. Barang was the most dangerous. Kelly knew only two ways to protect yourself from it: either curse the witch, which took more bravery than most people had, or carry atis, the delicious fruit with smelly leaves.

"I want you to get to the States," Marie-Vic said, "and to have dignity there. Don't get caught doing what Annette did." Kelly knew she referred to the time their sister disgraced herself in California. In their province it was customary for people to cook foods, then go outside calling out that they had good foods for sale. But when Annette tried that in San Diego, someone called the police. For the next month their sister Darlene had pretended she didn't know her.

"Lydie will tell me what is proper and what is not," Kelly said.

"You are so lucky to have Lydie and Patrice," Marie-Vic said. She sat at the end of Kelly's bed, her legs tucked under her. People thought Kelly and Marie-Vic looked alike, which pleased Kelly because she thought Marie-Vic, with her light skin, big dark eyes, and silky hair, was very pretty.

"You can work for Patrice after I leave," Kelly said.

"Of all of us, you are the only one who has met Americans that let you call them by their Christian names."

"It is true. I am lucky," Kelly agreed.

"Christmas will be very different in the States," Marie-Vic said.

"I know," Kelly said sadly. Christmas in the Philippines was the longest Christmas in the world. The rule was, it lasted through all the "ber" months: September, October, November, and December. All the radio stations would be playing carols, and decorations would appear in stores. That was because the Philippines were a Catholic country, very religious as well as magical. Naturally the States, with its mix of Catholics, Protestants, Jews, Muslims, Buddhists, and born-agains could not have such a long and festive Christmas season. Kelly would have to learn to celebrate it in her heart.

"Do you think Lydie requires extra workers at the ball?" Marie-Vic asked.

"No, she told me there are enough. Lydie wants me to help the photographer." She giggled with pleasure. "Imagine, me working at the very ball I discussed with Mr. Wright."

"It is very hard to believe."

"You should have heard me telling him about the shopping Lydie and I did to get everything ready."

"To shop for a living! Wow!" Marie-Vic said, laughing.

"It's not as easy as it sounds," Kelly said, wondering whether she had sounded convincing in her interview.

"I hope the spell works and the petition is granted," Marie-Vic said.

"I pray for it," Kelly replied.

⁓

Patrice was writing in her diary. She had written twenty pages so far, covering her memories of the first year she had lived in Paris. She figured it would take her all winter to get up-to-date. She intended to fill the notebooks with personal details, including her innermost thoughts, her relationships with Didier and his friends and family, her experiences with Lydie. She would mention the food served in restaurants and at dinner parties; she would describe trips to the Midi, Courcheval, Saint-Lô, Corsica. She would discuss the elections, the tension between the political right and the Socialists, the new spirit of cooperation within the Common Market. She would relate, in detail, the immigration problem. She would weave facts with memories, humor with gravity, legend and predictions, gossip and confession. She knew the world would never see her words, but she found pleasure in recording her impressions, just as Madame de Sévigné must have done three hundred years ago in a house just across the Place des Vosges.

It was Kelly's day off; at the sound of the doorbell, Patrice breathed deeply and lay down her pen. She had invited Clothilde, Didier's sister, to tea. It was becoming a habit, their Tuesday afternoon teas; it was habit, also, the way Patrice's stomach would tense at Clothilde's arrival.

"*Gros bises!*" Clothilde said, kissing both Patrice's cheeks.

Patrice led her into the salon, then went to the kitchen to make tea. When she returned, Clothilde was standing by the window. "The Bretechers are upset about not being invited to the ball," she said.

"That's tough cookies for them," Patrice said, pouring the tea. "They should have realized this day might come when they had their little fête at Longchamps."

"*Mais* Patrice," Clothilde said, "they know Didier hates horse racing."

"Well, I happen to love it," Patrice said. "The reality of the situation is that I have a long memory, and I expect people to do unto me as they would have me do unto them."

"I'm sure it was an oversight that you were not invited to Longchamps . . ."

"You just said it was because Didier hates horse racing. Look: if you want the Bretechers, feel free to include them in your quota. Care for a biscuit?"

Clothilde shook her head. Watching her weight as usual, Patrice thought as she helped herself to an oatcake. She had to admit the d'Orignys really knew how to take care of themselves. Just once she would like to get Clothilde into the bright sun without dark glasses and a hat and check out her hairline for facelift scars. How old was she, anyway? Older than Didier, and she looked barely forty. She claimed to go to the same homeopathic doctor as Catherine Deneuve, and Patrice could believe it.

"Listen, Clothilde," Patrice said. "What I need you to do is suggest two of your friends whom you would trust to wear jewels at the ball."

"But I trust *all* my friends," Clothilde said. A little testily, it seemed to Patrice.

"Of course, of course. But we want only about fifteen people to wear jewelry for the photo session, and not all at the same time."

Patrice had to be a bit delicate; Clothilde, after all, was a major shareholder of d'Origny Bijoutiers.

"My dear, my friends all have their own jewelry. I wouldn't impose on them to model our jewelry for advertisements."

A definite slap in the face! Patrice sipped her tea and felt her cheeks redden. She had the mean, furious thought that Clothilde was the perfect example of what too much leisure and money could do to a woman. Yes, she looked beautiful; then again, she could afford the Fountain of Youth. Clothilde loved saying things like "I had lunch with the Minister's wife." Big fucking deal! What had the Minister's wife done except marry better than Clothilde had? Patrice had to feel a bit sorry for Clothilde, married to squeaky little Fulbert, Mr. Haut-Bourgeoisie 1924, whose only obvious talent was his uncanny ability to work the word "enema" into practically every conversation Patrice had ever had with him.

"Patrice, dear," Clothilde said. "Why don't you like me?"

"What an idea!" Patrice said. "It's you who doesn't like me." She had a psychic sense of talking to her mother.

"You are so huffy with me," Clothilde said. "I always feel I am saying the wrong thing to you."

"As a matter of fact, you just let me know it's pretty tacky of me to let my friends model d'Origny jewelry. I know you think I'm the tacky American."

Clothilde gave her a long look, then smiled. "Well, not exactly. I think of you as the 'young American.' So young, so modern. Really 'with it.'"

Patrice had to smile at Clothilde saying 'with it,' even if she didn't quite believe Clothilde's smooth excuse.

"Didier tells me you are quite sad over the prospect of losing your American friend and your maid."

Patrice really didn't want to discuss it with Clothilde, but at the thought of Lydie leaving Paris her eyes filled with tears, leaving her no choice. "Yes, I am. But he shouldn't worry—I plan to keep busy. I'm working on my own personal history of France."

The sympathetic set of Clothilde's mouth was replaced by an "O" of astonishment. And that alone was enough to dry Patrice's tears and make her smile.

∽◦

The night before the ball, Lydie felt remarkably calm, well organized. Every item on two checklists, "the ball" and "Kelly," was checked off. Her third checklist, "moving," remained wide open, but she would turn to that in a day or so, when she and Michael had had the chance to discuss it. She had time, if she wanted, to do the things she imagined Patrice might do the night before a ball: set her hair, give herself a manicure, place damp tea bags on her eyes. But she felt charged up, full of energy that had no place to go. Twice she stepped onto the terrace, peered down the Seine. She wondered where the Hôtel Royal Madeleine stood in relation to the Grand Palais. Tomorrow morning Michael and the d'Orignys would pick her up before dawn to drive to the château.

She cooked an omelet, then settled down to eat it and drink a glass of Beaujolais. She pulled the soft middle out of a crusty baguette; thinking of the expression "all my ducks in a row." Her mother had said it when Lydie was little. "I have everything I could ever want," Julia Fallon would say. "My Neil, my Lydie, and a wonderful life. I have all my ducks in a row." Lydie had envisioned the ducks, cute baby mallards swimming in a row. Now Lydie thought of her own life: waiting to reunite with Michael, optimistic about Kelly's petition, ready to leave Paris for New York. Yes, all Lydie's ducks were in a row. Then she thought of a carnival shooting gallery, with tin ducks going around on a conveyor belt, waiting to be picked off by anyone who'd pay a quarter. The thought made her gulp her wine, and when the telephone rang, she was ready for bad news.

And those were Dot Graulty's first words: "I have bad news, Lydie. You'll get official notification soon enough, but Kelly Merida's petition has been denied."

"Denied? Are you sure?" Lydie asked in a voice that echoed in her ears.

"All too sure," Dot said. "Someone from Immigration in D.C. called Bruce, and he told me."

"Do you know why?"

"Officially, they'll tell you it's because you didn't make your case strong enough. Between you and me, it's because she's a Filipino."

"But I can try again, can't I?" Lydie asked, the enormity of Dot's words suddenly hitting her. She felt blinded by them, as if they were the bright flash of a star exploding.

"Well," Dot said, "you'll want to try, but I wouldn't encourage you to bother. I'm truly sorry. I'm disappointed myself—I had a stake in this. You know I tried my best. In this place, sometimes it helps, sometimes it doesn't."

"Thanks for everything, Dot," Lydie said.

She sat still for a long time, not hanging up the phone. Then she dialed the number of Michael's hotel. The switchboard put her through.

"You ready for tomorrow?" he said when he heard her voice.

"Something terrible happened," she said, her voice tight and little. "It's about Kelly's . . ."

"Her petition didn't go through?" Michael asked.

"No, it didn't," Lydie said.

"Damn it," Michael said. "I'm sorry. When did you find out?"

"A minute ago. Dot called to tell me. I just can't believe it," Lydie said, realizing that she was numb.

"Do you want me to come over?"

Lydie thought for a moment. She imagined negotiating an evening with her husband, their first in a long time. She believed that the fact she considered it "negotiating"—like a captain negotiating shoal waters or a lawyer negotiating a difficult deal—was a signal that tonight wasn't the night. "No, but thanks. I'll see you tomorrow."

"You sure will," Michael said. "Do you think you'll be able to sleep?"

Lydie felt pretty sure she wouldn't. "I'll try to," she said. Hanging up, she instantly called Patrice.

"Kelly's petition has been denied," she said instantly.

Patrice was silent for a few seconds. "Wow," she said. "Wow. Does she know?"

"No," Lydie said, realizing that her hands were shaking.

"We have to tell her."

"Tonight, Patrice?" Lydie asked, feeling suddenly tired.

"Think about it, Lydie," Patrice said. "Wouldn't you want to know right away? Doesn't she deserve that? Come on—I'll pick you up in Didier's car."

∽

Twenty minutes later Lydie was hunched over the Plan de Paris, and Patrice was speeding around the Place de Clichy. "Hookers, Quik-Burgers, riot police: this is where she lives?"

"Take that next left," Lydie said. They stopped in front of a grimy tenement. Lydie would have liked to sit still for a few minutes, rehearsing what they would say to Kelly, but Patrice was already out of the car.

A young woman who closely resembled Kelly opened the door. Lydie cleared her throat, ready to introduce herself, when the woman called out, "Kelly! Patrice and Lydie are here!"

"We're famous," Patrice whispered.

Kelly came to the door. Members of her family stood behind her, fanning into a semicircle. Lydie looked from one to the other, wondered which was the brother who had smuggled Kelly across the border in his trunk.

"Hello, Lydie, hello, Patrice," Kelly said, twisting her hands. She tried to smile. She glanced over her shoulder, then back. "I wish I had known you were coming; I would have . . . prepared."

"We know you don't have a phone," Lydie said.

"Please come in," one of the older sisters said, smiling brilliantly. "We are honored by your visit."

"Yes, please come in!" Now that they had absorbed the shock, they all began to speak at once.

"Listen," Patrice said, in a voice both strong and kind, "we have some disappointing news for Kelly. It's about, uh, your petition."

Kelly's face fell so hard, Lydie had no doubt that she understood what Patrice was saying. Some of her family took a small step back. "It was denied," Lydie said, looking into Kelly's eyes.

"You can't take me to the States?" Kelly asked.

"No," Lydie said, knowing there was no way to soften the word.

"Don't worry about me," Kelly said right away. Her words were brittle, her smile quavering, and Lydie knew then they had made a mistake to tell Kelly the bad news in front of her entire family. In the first seconds, Lydie had thought they would provide strength, but now she saw that Kelly was ashamed to have them hear it.

"That's the spirit," Patrice said, her eyes shining, taking Kelly's hand. "Didier and I are going to make you legal here: I promise."

Kelly nodded, still smiling but unable to speak.

"I'm glad to finally meet all of you," Patrice said to the others. Several of them stepped forward to shake her hand. "Kelly, I want you to know that you'll always have a place with me, and that Didier and I will look after you."

"Thank you, Mum," Kelly said.

"And if you don't feel like working at the ball," Patrice said, "I'm sure Lydie will understand. Maybe you need a little time to yourself."

"I'm sorry," Lydie said, stepping forward to kiss Kelly's cheek, wanting to close her eyes so she wouldn't always remember the look in Kelly's eyes. Then she and Patrice walked away, leaving Kelly to suffer the disappointment and kindness of her brothers and sisters.

‌⌘

Michael left the Hôtel Royal Madeleine with endings in mind: an end to his time at the clean but impersonal hotel; an end, in twenty-eight days, to the Paris year; and an end to his relationship with Anne. The taxi, a Mercedes with a poodle sitting next to the driver, took him to Anne's building. He held the key she had given him, knowing he wouldn't use it; he wished merely to return it, but she wasn't home.

"*Elle n'est pas là, Monsieur,*" the plump Spanish concierge said with a mean glint in her eyes. Michael had always felt her disapproval. "*Elle n'a pas revenu hier soir.*"

"That's her business," he said, not wanting to give the concierge the satisfaction of seeming alarmed by the fact Anne hadn't been home all night.

At the Louvre, the guard stopped him. "She walks again," he said to Michael.

"What do you mean?"

"The ghost of Catherine de Medici," the guard said. "She was sighted last night, for the first time in seven years."

Michael laughed, tapped the guard's shoulder, brushed past him. He walked straight up the stairs to Anne's office. On the museum's top floor, Anne worked in a small room with a circular window overlooking the Seine. She loved telling visitors that in the days of Louis XIV it had been an artist's studio.

"Anne," Michael called, tapping at the door. He felt divided by worry for her whereabouts and by the wish to put this meeting off. He stood there a minute; he had just turned his back to the door, started walking away, when he heard footsteps down the corridor. Here came Anne in her wig and an ancient dress; although different from the last one, it was recognizably from the seventeenth century. Her smallness made her seem even more vulnerable, more capable of being hurt.

"'I can already notice his absence,'" she said in her Madame de Sévigné voice. "'Yesterday I went to the post office . . . to see whether he had turned me over to someone else there. I find all new faces, unimpressed with my importance.'"

"Anne, were you here all night?" Michael asked.

"That is a question I should ask as well," she said. "Where were you last night? No longer do you visit or call me . . ."

"I was at my hotel," he said steadily, alarmed by her appearance.

"I understand you have a ball to go to."

"Who told you that?"

"You told me about the ball, *chéri*. I have always hoped we could go together. We would be the most elegant couple there . . ."

"Anne, I'm going with Lydie. I'm going back to her."

"I am not terribly surprised," she said.

"I do care about you," Michael said. "Are you all right?"

She laughed harshly. "Did you think I would fall to pieces when you told me?"

"The guard told me he saw a ghost last night," Michael said uneasily. "Did you sleep here?"

She smiled, saying nothing. He thought he detected something dark behind her smile, and it frightened him. For one moment, he saw her as an evil force, now revealing a side of herself no one had ever seen. Like the moon, rotating as she revolved, she presented only one face to those who saw her. Like the moon, half of whose surface is never seen from earth, Anne turned her other face away.

"Don't worry about me, eh?" Anne said. "We had a good time together, and I treasure it."

Michael nodded but said nothing.

"Leave now, Michel," Anne said, in as sane a voice as Michael had ever heard. He obliged.

# 22

*The weather is wonderful . . . I find the countryside lovely,
and my Loire River is as beautiful here as at Orléans. It is
a pleasure to meet old friends en route. I brought my large
carriage so that we are in no way crowded.*

—To Françoise-Marguerite, May 1675

DAWN WAS ABOUT to break and Château Bellechasse stood in
mist rising from its moat and from the Loire River, wide and slug-
gish, on whose banks it stood. Built of smooth stone, asymmetri-
cal, the château had pointed turrets, balconies, massive doors that
could hold back an army. Roses clung to its walls, and perhaps it
was the château's fairy-tale delicacy that made Lydie give the roses
old names: Florizel, Belle Isis, Belle de Crécy. Lydie remembered
telling Kelly the news last night and pressed closer to Michael. All
the way down from Paris he had responded every time she'd
stirred; now he pressed her right back.

"Sleeping Beauty, we've come to rescue you," Patrice said from
the front seat, but in a flat voice. How were they going to accomplish this? How could they stage a festive ball when everyone felt

miserable? Lydie felt like a bundle of nerves: the least thing was going to set her off. She had arranged for several country-house-weekend sort of activities for the photographer's benefit: the grouse hunt, dressing for the ball, and the ball itself. Now all she wanted to do was snuggle under an eiderdown.

Tiny stones crunched under the wheels as Didier steered the car into a lot behind the stable. The other vehicles in their caravan from Paris followed. Lydie, Michael, Patrice, and Didier climbed out without speaking, stretched, looked around. A perfect lawn stretched to the riverbank in one direction, to a dense forest in the other. Lydie and Patrice stood together as Michael and Didier directed the truck, full of props and two borrowed hunting dogs, and four cars, full of servants, photographers, and d'Origny's guards, to park beside his car.

"Did you sleep last night?" Patrice asked.

"No," Lydie said. "Did you?"

"No," Patrice said. "I can't bear to face her today. I wish she'd decided to stay home." Both women looked toward the truckload of servants, Kelly and her sister among them. They had urged Kelly to stay with her family; when she would not, they had invited her sister to come with her.

"Once Kelly says she'll do something, she does it," Lydie said. "She would think that by not coming she'd be letting me down."

"There's a sorry little tone in your voice that tells me you think you let Kelly down," Patrice said. "You didn't. You went to the mat for her."

"We're going to miss our chance, if we don't hurry," Didier said, removing his gun case from the trunk.

Lydie tried to organize herself; they would have to rush to set up the hunting shots in time to catch dawn and the morning mists. Then the entire day loomed ahead, until the ball that night.

Michael came to stand beside her. Although he didn't touch her, his presence strengthened her. Lydie sighed.

"You did your best," Patrice said. "Tell me you know that."

"At the moment I'm a bit distracted. Here we are, photographing jewels at a beautiful château. Doesn't it seem a little . . . unbalanced?" Lydie asked.

"But you'll get through this, won't you?" Patrice asked anxiously. "For Didier?"

At Patrice's concern for her husband's project, Lydie smiled. "Yeah. I'll even do a good job."

Patrice gave her an impetuous hug, then walked toward Didier. Lydie and Michael stood alone. Lydie realized that Michael had never been with her at a major shoot, and that gave her something new to feel nervous about. "Just pretend I'm not here," Michael said. "Or else let me be your flunky and give me something to do."

Lydie laughed. "There's nothing I can think of . . . just watch, if you want."

"If I want? Are you kidding?" Michael said.

Lydie forced herself to concentrate, to explain her ideas to the photographer. "Mysterious and funky, very dramatic," she said. "We want the feeling of modern people carried back in time—a hundred years. You'll want to contrast the magic and timelessness of this setting with anything high-tech or contemporary. Didier's rifle, for example, or his sunglasses. Patrice's hairstyle. Always have the jewelry in focus, but off center. Remember you are photographing a *story*." She tried not to lecture, but she wanted to make sure he understood.

Guy nodded, trying out settings on his light meter. They had worked together often, and Lydie knew he didn't need specific direction. She caught sight of Kelly, standing with other servants.

She waved to Kelly, motioning for her to step away from them so that Lydie could speak to her privately, but Kelly misunderstood, or pretended to. She waved back at Lydie, then turned away. What did it say about Kelly's spirit and drive that she would come to the Loire, having been told she didn't have to, the day after her world was rocked forever?

As Patrice came toward Lydie, Lydie had the impression of looking into a funhouse mirror. Patrice was a tall, dark-haired, identically dressed version of herself. Lydie had borrowed "shooting clothes" from Patrice and dressed at home, before dawn. This was the first time they'd been face-to-face in near daylight. A khaki skirt, rolled at the waist to shorten it; a tawny suede jacket with compartments full of shotgun shells. "Didier is out of his mind with joy," Patrice said. "He's already seen a deer on the front lawn."

"He's not going to shoot deer, is he?" Lydie asked, momentarily distracted from Kelly.

"No, just birds." She looked from Lydie to Michael to the photographer. "We about ready?" she asked.

"As ready as ever was," Lydie said. Her concentration had kicked in, and she discovered that she meant it. Then Didier came forward, followed by a guard carrying a black lockbox, and the hunt was on.

∽

Patrice, Didier, Michael, and Lydie walked four abreast through a hayfield, waist-deep in mist. Only Lydie was gunless. Guy and Marcel, the guard, followed. Lydie listened to the rasp of boots through dry grass she could not see. It was not quite dark, though the sun had not yet risen. The world was pale and gray, the color of a cloud.

Then wings flapped, birds cackled, and shadows appeared on the lightening sky. There were two nearly simultaneous orange bursts: Didier's gun and Guy's flash. Lydie jumped. The dogs, only their heads visible over the mist, raced to find the birds.

"Great shot!" Patrice said. Didier, in his padded green hunting jacket, looked proud and excited.

"Let's see what the dogs bring back before you say that," he said.

Lydie stood still as Patrice and Didier hurried forward to meet the dogs. They seemed pleased by the catch, but Lydie hardly noticed. The shot roared in her ears, and she felt curious about something that had never occurred to her before: what was it really like for her father? She wasn't thinking of the impact on her family or wondering about his last crazed thoughts. For the first time, she wondered whether the shot rang in his ears, whether he had even heard it.

"Four grouse in one shot!" Didier called.

"Still a little too dark for good pictures," Guy said.

Didier stuffed the bloody birds into a leather sack slung over his shoulder. "Let's get a few more before we start taking pictures."

The line formed again, continuing across the field. The rising sun, illuminating the silvery mist and dark forest, made the scene beautiful and eerie, and after Didier shot another bird and Patrice shot three, Lydie told everyone to stop. "You can keep hunting, but we have to start photographing," she said. "Marcel?"

Marcel, tall and dour, came to her, bearing the lockbox in outstretched hands. He wore a pistol on his hip. "Didier?" she said.

Didier produced a key, opened the box. Although Lydie had never seen the actual jewels, she knew what would be inside. Michael said "wow" at the sight of them, but Lydie went about her business methodically, noticing but not distracted by their sparkle. She pinned a sapphire-and-diamond brooch, shaped like a snowcapped mountain, on her own jacket. Didier removed a ring, a giant emerald-cut diamond. He displayed it, for everyone to admire. "For my wife's trigger finger," he said.

"Now, that's my idea of a rock," Patrice said. She held out her gloved hand, wiggled her index finger. "Slip it on."

Didier tried. It didn't fit. "Shit, Marcel," he said. "You know her size."

"Perhaps without the glove," Marcel said.

It didn't fit her bare finger. Lydie's eye was on the sun, which was shining through the forest. Soon it would rise above the trees, and the mist would burn off. "Let's forget the ring," she said. "Give Patrice some dangling diamond earrings, and let's take pictures."

Didier came to Lydie, held her right hand, slid the ring over her brown kid-gloved ring finger. "There," he said. "Now grab your gun."

Lydie froze. The sight of that huge diamond on her finger was mesmerizing, but she looked past it, to the rifle Didier was holding out. "I can't," she said.

"You don't have to shoot," Guy said. "Just pose, holding the gun. It's what we planned. There's not much time."

"You don't have to do this," Michael said, but Lydie reached for it, in a daze. Her fingers closed around the wooden handle, highly polished and engraved with Didier's name. It was the first time she had ever touched a gun. Its weight surprised her; she had no idea of how to hold it.

"Left hand on the barrel," Patrice said, "the stock in your armpit, and your finger on the trigger."

Lydie pointed at the sky, looked down the barrel at the sight. Her father had used a shotgun. Shooting his Margaret Downes, he could have used two hands. But how heavy, how clumsy it must have been to turn the gun on himself, to hold it in one hand, point it at his head, and pull the trigger. "Take the picture," she said to Guy. "Fast." His flash went off three times, in quick succession, and Lydie lowered the gun.

"Excellent shots," Guy said. "With that diamond and the gun metal sparkling, and dawn breaking through those trees."

"Let's take another try for birds," Didier said. "Get some pictures of Patrice in these earrings."

Lydie started to join them in line, but Michael took her hand, held her back. Michael said nothing, only looked into her eyes. The gun had felt so solid, Lydie thought. He would have had to lift it, aim it, pull the trigger. It took some time. Had he been scared of what he was about to do? The phrase "without hope" came into her mind. Lydie thought of Kelly, a young woman with high hopes journeying far from the Philippines. Another journeyer came to mind. She thought not of her mother, but of her father, a young man full of dreams, sailing on a steamer out of Rosslare Harbor, setting a southwest course for New York City.

∽

The day was sunny, hot for September. Patrice and Lydie both wore sundresses. Patrice followed Lydie around. Now they were in search of Kelly and had walked from the kitchen to the salon to the lawn, where they found Michael and Didier sitting side by side in chaise longues.

"It's definitely warm enough to hold the ball outdoors," Lydie said to Didier.

"But why, when we have that beautiful ballroom?" he asked. "My guests would prefer it."

"I'm thinking of the pictures," Lydie said. "The château owners told me about chandeliers in the attic, from when this place was new, made for hanging in trees. Imagine hanging them in those chestnuts over there—" She pointed across the lawn. "I mean, *anyone* can hold a ball in a ballroom . . ."

Michael grinned at Lydie's powers of persuasion. "Sounds good to me," he said.

"Okay—we dance under the stars," Didier said.

"Let's check out those chandeliers," Patrice said.

"We'll need help," Lydie said. "Let's find Kelly, okay?"

Kelly stood in the great kitchen peeling carrots. The sight of her pierced Patrice's heart. Patrice had harbored such mixed feelings about Kelly's going to America, but now she felt only wholehearted sorrow that Kelly's chance was lost. Other workers stopped talking at the sight of Patrice and Lydie. "Hey, there," Patrice said to Kelly.

"Oh, hello, Mum," Kelly said. To Patrice she looked unchanged, untouched by what had happened. Was that because life in the Philippines trained you to face disappointment? Patrice imagined childhood there to be one disappointment after another: no food one day, a swarm of mosquitoes the next, no presents on your birthday. Or were those just a spoiled American's view of what might disappoint a Filipino?

"We could use a hand," Lydie said. "Will you come with us?"

Kelly glanced at the chef, who, Patrice supposed, Kelly considered her boss at that moment. For Kelly, life was hierarchy. The chef was watching them, his arms folded across his chest; he had never met Patrice before, had no idea that she was Madame d'Origny, and for one instant Patrice had the brutal wish that he would put up a squawk about letting Kelly go and Patrice would let him have it.

But Lydie explained to him, very politely, in French, who they were and why they needed Kelly. He smiled graciously and said, "*Bien sûr.*"

The three women climbed a rickety spiral staircase inside the northeast turret. Lydie said, "Precarious." Patrice gasped once or twice. Kelly climbed in silence. All three seemed determined to focus on their task instead of more important matters. At the top they looked around the round room. Piles of hard and ancient bat feces covered the floor. The only window was a small square cut in the stone, overlooking the park, forest, and river. Lydie glanced out, saw they were at least one hundred feet off the ground.

"'Rapunzel, Rapunzel, let down your hair . . .'" Patrice said. Lydie pulled back a canvas tarpaulin, revealing four chandeliers. The three women knelt. "They're wonderful," Lydie said, dusting them off. To Patrice they looked too heavy for chandeliers, stocky, made of wood. Each one was attached to a long woven rope with a wooden stake at the end.

"Aren't chandeliers supposed to be graceful?" Patrice asked. "With prisms to reflect the light?"

"Not if they're made to hang in trees," Lydie said. "It could be windy. Let's see . . . I guess we toss the rope over a tree branch, then anchor the stake in the ground."

Patrice listened to her, noting the flat tone in her voice. Was this her way of suffering over Kelly, to keep herself from taking any pleasure in the ball? Yet Patrice felt the same way. Her own voice sounded sonorous, a dirge echoing through the turret. Absently she picked tendrils of hard candle wax off the chandeliers.

"We'll put candles in the holders," Lydie said. "They'll be lovely."

"I'll go downstairs and locate many candles," Kelly said, leaping to her feet.

"Wait!" Patrice and Lydie said at once. Kelly stood still; with escape impossible, her eyes flooded with tears.

Lydie and Patrice rose, walked to Kelly, and hugged her. "I'm so sorry about the petition," Patrice said.

"It will be okay," Kelly said, a note of panic in her voice. She quivered; sensing that Kelly wished to wriggle out of their embrace, Patrice stepped back. Kelly wiped her eyes furiously, as though she were angry at them for betraying how she felt. Patrice herself felt washed out, and Lydie was crying. She sobbed with such intensity, Patrice wondered what else had gone wrong: could it be something with Michael? "Um . . ." Patrice said to her. Lydie glanced up, her eyes red-rimmed.

"Am I making it worse?" Lydie asked Kelly, taking her hands. "I can't tell you how badly I wanted you to get to America . . ."

"I know you did," Kelly said. "And I am so grateful."

For what? Patrice wanted to say. She felt like snorting, shaking some sense into Kelly. It made her feel impatient, to see Kelly lapse into her old, subservient role. Patrice wanted to believe that Kelly's time with her and Didier had enlightened her a *little*. On the other hand, Patrice realized that she herself was slipping into a familiar pattern: it was easier to feel outrage than compassion. "We do have options," Patrice said, steadying her voice. "I can make you legal in France, my mother can call her congressman . . ."

"I can contact Immigration when I get to New York next month," Lydie said.

"Next month?" Patrice asked.

"Yes," Lydie said, looking at her. "I leave in October. You know that."

"Of course," Patrice said, and she did—but she had never thought of Lydie's departure happening *next month*.

Lydie smiled suddenly, an expression of recognition in her eyes. "You're going to miss me," she said. "Isn't that nice?"

"Wonderful," Patrice said, looking from one friend to the other. "Aren't we a fun bunch to be throwing a ball?"

"Hilarious," Lydie said. There was silence, and Patrice actually held her breath, waiting for Kelly to say something.

"We're a barrelful of monkeys," Kelly said, her shy smile turning into a grin at her successful use of the American phrase.

∽

After that, they seemed to feel better. As the afternoon progressed, Lydie spent more time with the photographer and Patrice began greeting early arrivals. Lydie smiled whenever Patrice saw her, but she acted skittish. Finally Patrice cornered Michael, who was staking a chandelier. He had thrown the rope over the branch of a chestnut tree and was pounding the stake into the ground. Patrice stood above him as he crouched. Sweat glistened on his tan neck; his brown hair had fallen into his eyes, making him look boyish.

"Can you take a break?" Patrice asked.

"Sure," Michael said, laying down his mallet. He tugged the rope, to make sure it would hold, then stood.

"What's with Lydie?" Patrice asked.

Michael gazed at her. "She's upset about Kelly."

"No," Patrice said firmly. "It's definitely more than that."

"I don't know, Patrice," Michael said. "Kelly mattered a lot to Lydie. I think she's more upset than you think."

"Listen, you bozo," Patrice said, realizing that he was patronizing her. "I'm the one who held her hand while you had your fun. I know her better than you think, and I know her mind's on something else."

Michael's face hardened, like a man taking his punishment. But then his expression turned humble, melting a little of Patrice's anger. "She's thinking of her father," Michael said. "She didn't like holding that gun this morning."

"Oh, because of her father!" Patrice said, suddenly realizing what it must have meant to Lydie to lift that rifle.

Then Lydie and Didier came toward them, across the lawn. "I

think we should dress for the ball," Lydie said. "Guy wants to take some pictures at sunset . . ." She checked her watch. "And it's not that far off. Michael, do you know where they put our bags?"

Patrice listened to her sweet, defeated little voice. She knew exactly what to do. A lifetime as the daughter of Eliza Spofford had trained her how to whip a party into a party. "I know where they put your bags," Patrice said, "but that's beside the point. I'm having Marcel switch everything around. Girls dress in one room, boys dress in another." She linked arms with Lydie. "We'll be just like brides—they can't see us till the big event." Lydie smiled at her, but it wasn't enough. Patrice tickled her under the chin. "Come on, honeybunch," she said. "Let's have a ball."

Both Didier and Michael were laughing at Patrice's act; in addition, in Michael's eyes, Patrice saw a fervent wish for Lydie to let her sorrow go.

"Okay," Lydie said, laughing along.

∿

Dressing turned out to be some fun. Patrice said the jewels should be put on last. She had commandeered a bottle of champagne from the kitchen. Weeks ago she and Lydie had decided to wear real silk stockings with garters. Lydie's garters dangled from a rather splendid lace undergarment, and she couldn't get them snapped to the stockings.

"The last time I tried this was in tenth grade," Lydie said.

"They let you wear underwear like that in Catholic school?" Patrice asked.

"Are you kidding? I wore the most demure little garter belt you ever saw," Lydie said. "White elastic, like a bandage."

Patrice glanced down at her own garter belt, shimmery pink silk and lace, and thought it symbolic of the carefree girlishness she hoped to feel with Lydie but instead could only mimic. They were being swept along by what they ought to feel at a ball, but in the background lurked the facts: that Lydie's father had shot himself, that Kelly wasn't going to America, that Lydie was. Patrice sighed.

"What?" Lydie asked.

"Can we do ourselves a favor?" Patrice asked, pushing a glass of champagne at her. "Can we drink a really festive toast?"

"Here's to the d'Origny ball," Lydie said, raising her glass over her head. Light poured through the tall window, making her bare arm look pearly white.

"Here's to you and me. Best friends forever," Patrice said.

"Here's to that," Lydie said, drinking.

From then on, things veered uphill. Lydie used an ivory buttonhook to do up Patrice's buttons, stopping now and then to shake her arm and complain about lactic acid buildup. "My arms feel as if they've just done fifty chin-ups."

"Press on, only a hundred more to go," Patrice said. Their jewels sat across the room in little velvet cases, and as the time drew near to put them on, Patrice felt more excited. She strode around the room, feeling velvet swish over her silk stockings.

Lydie's dress was made of rich green satin; against it, her pale skin glowed like porcelain. When she turned around, stepped back to let Patrice look at her, Patrice could see that she felt beautiful. Her golden hair fell to her shoulders, brushing the satin. Smiling at her, Patrice wondered if this was how a mother felt, watching a daughter dress for her wedding. Yet Patrice and Lydie were the same age, or practically. What gave Patrice the feeling of seniority? She knew, of course: a marriage that had been happy and loving.

"Michael's going to fall in love with you all over again," Patrice said to Lydie, feeling a little sad because in saying it she was relinquishing Lydie to Michael and America. She opened one jewel case and ceremoniously removed Lydie's ruby-and-diamond necklace. Lydie smiled, staring at the necklace. She lifted her hair as Patrice clasped it around her neck.

"It's beautiful," Patrice said.

Lydie touched the stones with one hand. Then, saying nothing, she went over to the bureau and removed Patrice's necklace from its chest. Patrice turned her back, waiting for Lydie to clip it on. It felt slightly unreal, to be decked out like fairy princesses for the d'Origny ball. As the clasp was fastened, Patrice felt the stones' weight tug at her neck.

"This is the real me," Patrice said to her reflection in the cheval glass. "I am never giving these back."

"They're great on you," said Lydie, who couldn't stop touching the large ruby dangling from her pendant.

"And they're great on you," Patrice said, smiling in spite of the superstitious shiver she felt at the sight of her best friend wearing rubies.

# 23

*La Brinvilliers has gone up in smoke . . . her poor little body was tossed, after the execution, into a raging fire, and her ashes scattered to the winds! So that, now, we shall all be inhaling her! And with such evil little spirits in the air, who knows what poisonous humor may overcome us?*

—To Françoise-Marguerite, July 1676

PATRICE HAD ALREADY told Lydie that the name on everyone's lips that night was "Lydie McBride." Patrice said she had intoned it a thousand times, in answer to all Didier's crowd from Saint-Tropez, his business associates, his sister Clothilde, asking who had done the fantastic job. And only about half the guests had arrived so far. Lydie had to admit the ball had an air of glamour and mystery, with an orchestra playing and flashbulbs going off in everyone's eyes. She had lined the château's drive with votive candles, hundreds of them in paper bags. Wooden chandeliers, each full of fifty tall white candles, hung from ropes in the trees. Beneath them was a dance floor bordered by long tables covered in white cloths.

There was Patrice, adjusting her diamond tiara, taking a sip of champagne. She gripped the ebony wand and directed her black-sequined mask to her eyes. She surveyed the crowd. Lydie touched the ruby tiara Patrice had insisted she wear, and at that instant Patrice caught sight of her. "Oh, Your Majesty!" Patrice called to Lydie.

"How do you think it's going?" Lydie asked, feeling impossibly anxious. Wondering why Michael hadn't come downstairs yet.

"It's ugly, everyone's having a terrible time, and it's going to rain—*give me a break!*" Patrice said, hugging her. "It's fantastic. Have you ever seen so many great masks?"

The men wore white tie. Many wore their decorations: war medals, Légions d'honneur, heraldic sashes and medals. Most of the men wore plain black masks, but one wore a splendid lion's head. The women's gowns evoked the eighteenth century; several, including Lydie and Patrice, wore ones Lydie had borrowed from the costume museum. Their masks were feathered, sequined, of silk and satin, trailing streamers. Clothilde wore a special d'Origny creation: a full-face mask of the sun, made of thin, hammered gold.

"You look gorgeous," Patrice said, and Lydie felt it, in her full-skirted green dress and ruby pendant. She could do without the tiara.

"Guy should be taking more pictures," Lydie said. "I wish everyone would arrive so we could serve the banquet." She spoke fast, her eyes flicking across the scene.

"Where's Michael?" Patrice asked. "Has he seen you yet?"

"No, not yet," Lydie said. "I thought he'd be downstairs by now."

"Isn't that always the way?" Patrice asked. "They complain about how long we take, but men are a hundred times worse than we are." She gave Lydie a knowing look. "Listen, any misgivings or *guilt* I had about arranging for you to wear rubies are gone now. You're beautiful, and your night is a triumph."

"Thanks, Patrice," Lydie said, standing on her toes to kiss Patrice's cheek. Both she and Patrice turned, startled, toward Guy's flash.

"Two queens kissing," he said, grinning.

"I want a copy of that one," Patrice said.

"I've come to ask my wife to dance," Didier said, in a formal manner. He stood tall, elegant in his evening attire.

Patrice grinned at him. "Charmed, I'm sure!"

"Listen," Didier said to Lydie, "this is the best party I've ever seen. You're a genius of style."

"Thanks," Lydie said. "I wish my husband would get down here, to hear you say that. I guess he's still dressing."

"I've just been defending your husband to some assholes," Didier said with a glance over his shoulder. "Laurent Montrose hates the Salle des Quatre Saisons, says Michael's design is not innovative. I told him the Salle is fantastic, everyone thinks so." He lowered his voice. "Of course, Laurent hates Americans on *principle*."

"Here comes Didier's World War II theory," Patrice said.

"It's no theory—it's the truth," Didier said, a bizarre combination of innocence and fury in his eyes. "Everyone knows Laurent's family made the Nazis very welcome in their *pâtisserie* at Cabourg."

"What were they supposed to do?" Patrice asked. "Refuse to sell them eclairs and get their kneecaps shot off?"

"I may have been too young to join my father and brothers in the Resistance," Didier said, "but I saw what the bourgeoisie in small towns would do to stay on the Germans' good side. When their *duty* was to refuse them any help at all!"

"Why do you say he hates Americans?" Lydie asked. She had been under the impression that the French felt grateful to

Americans for the part their country had played in liberating France during the war.

"Simply that people like Laurent carry around *tremendous* guilt for helping the Germans, and that makes them hate and envy any American. Cowards always hate heroes."

"He's right," Patrice said, edging closer to Didier. "People in France still judge each other by how they behaved during the war."

"Laurent wants to find fault with Michael McBride's work just because he's an American." Didier smiled. "Of course, so are you, but Laurent cannot find any fault with this ball because it is perfect."

The orchestra playing old-fashioned music, the candlelight, the mention of war, made Lydie feel she was reeling, traveling back in time. She swallowed, stared at a chandelier swaying in the breeze.

"Shall we dance now?" Didier asked Patrice.

"I'd better check the kitchen," Lydie said, glad for the chance to be alone.

Lydie made her way through the crowd, saying hello to acquaintances, keeping her eyes open for Michael. She passed Clothilde with Léonce d'Esclimont, discussing changes at the Louvre. She hung back for an instant, listening for Michael's name, then moved along without hearing it.

Lydie walked into the château, along a corridor, into the kitchen. Kelly, in her black uniform with its starched white collar, caught sight of her, tried to escape through another door. They had already faced each other today, true, but in Patrice's presence, which was another matter entirely. Something about Patrice encouraged best behavior.

"Kelly!" Lydie called, hearing herself bellow. Kelly stopped short, turned shyly.

"Hello, Lydie," Kelly said. She wouldn't meet Lydie's eyes.

"Are you okay?" Lydie asked.

"I am fine," Kelly said. Chefs and servers bustled around them; the air crackled with oysters being opened, vegetables sliced, crab claws cracked, roasts sizzling. Saying nothing, Lydie put her arm around Kelly's shoulders and led her down the long hallway, into the back room where boots and guns and the morning's grouse were hanging.

"I apologize for failing," Kelly said when they were alone.

"But *you* didn't fail," Lydie said, astonished. As she spoke, she realized that neither of them had, that it was a failure, or perhaps, worse, a triumph of bureaucracy.

"I did, Lydie. I failed in my interview. I am not qualified to be an alien of distinguished merit. I am not of the caliber to live in the States." Her face was ashen, her eyes blank.

Lydie thought of what Patrice had said, that Kelly would feel bad tonight, better tomorrow. She stared at Kelly, wanted to believe it was true. "Oh, Kelly," she said, helpless.

"Don't feel sorry for me, Lydie," Kelly said sternly, the same tone Lydie had heard her use months ago, when she had told Lydie the story of crossing the border in the trunk of a car.

But Lydie felt worse than sorry for her. She believed she had brought Kelly to this point in her life, where dreams came to nothing. She felt intense sorrow. What's happening to me? she wondered, panicked, as if the feeling came from an outside force instead of circumstances of the night.

She turned to Kelly, who stared stonily into the distance. Kelly, who had represented hope to Lydie, had none of her own left. Again Lydie thought of the young Fallons, Julia and Neil, leaving Rosslare Harbor, and she knew she had Kelly to thank for making it possible to imagine her parents as hopeful people starting off on a long journey. And feeling tears well up in her eyes, Lydie wished all three journeys hadn't ended in despair.

The open door gave onto the lawn. Lydie had an impulse to run out and not look back. She gazed at the crowd, laughing and brilliant in costumes and jewels. The orchestra struck up a waltz. Hordes of guests poured onto the dance floor. They whirled around, under the canopy of chestnut leaves and flickering candles. She felt hypnotized by emotion, by the movement and music. The area around the dance floor was practically empty, and her eyes took in the few people standing there.

Michael stood apart, whispering to a woman in period dress. Lydie started toward him, but she held herself back. She peered at Michael, in his white jacket, and at the woman, very tiny. The woman wore a wig that might have been lifted from the head of a mannequin in the Louvre and a black velvet dress full of silver thread; Lydie recognized the style as seventeenth-century.

"That's Anne Dumas," Lydie said out loud.

"What?" Kelly asked. She started toward Lydie, but Lydie was backing away.

Lydie bumped right into the wall, stood there for a moment staring out the door. She felt her lips moving, and she knew the words they were saying were a form of prayer. She felt a breeze move her full skirt; it might have been the passage of ghosts. Not eighteenth-century ghosts from the château, but recent ghosts. Ghosts of people she had loved, from two years ago and from today, begging Lydie to lay them to rest. The solution came to her like a gift, in a flash.

Trembling, tears running down her cheeks, Lydie lifted Didier's gun off the rack. She aimed it at Anne and Michael, just the way Patrice had taught her. Her finger was on the trigger. She wedged the stock into her armpit. Her heart pounded like wild horses, and she heard her own breath.

She looked through the scope, saw nothing but darkness. Then she found Michael's head, so close to Anne's that both their faces were in the sight. Magnified, the faces looked angry. They were arguing. But they faded away, and what Lydie saw instead was a cozy Village apartment with family photos on the flowered wall-paper and a young dark-haired woman lying on the bed. Instead of the orchestra, she heard the drone of a television and the voice of a two-year-old girl playing in the next room.

"Lydie . . ." Kelly said. She touched the back of Lydie's hand, so softly she might have been afraid of setting something off.

But the shots had been fired more than a year ago. Lydie lowered the gun but continued to hold it as if testing its weight. She found the spot where it was perfectly balanced in the palm of her hand and let it totter there while continuing to watch Michael and Anne with the avidity of a theatergoer waiting for the final curtain. She felt peculiar, as if she had been given permission to feel joyous. She no longer felt sorrowful; she no longer felt the presence of ghosts—neither the young, dark-haired woman nor the handsome, grinning Irishman. Somehow she had laid them to rest. She glanced at Kelly. "Excuse me," she said. She walked onto the lawn.

❧

"What are you doing here?" Michael heard Lydie say in the calmest voice possible.

He stepped toward her, put his arm around her shoulders. "It's all right, Lydie," he said. "She's just leaving."

"Your decorations are superb," Anne said, dimpling. "And the château, well . . . if only it were not built in such an unfortunate epoch."

"What are you doing here?" Lydie repeated, her shoulders tense under Michael's arm.

"I was invited, of course," Anne said. She tucked a loose curl under the wig, smoothed the line of her skirt.

Lydie looked up at Michael. Her face was blank, as if any expression was suspended pending Michael's explanation. "I didn't invite her," he said.

Anne laughed, a gentle trill; she whipped an ivory fan from her reticule and held it to her face. She gazed into his eyes, seeming to implore him to take her side. "'I conjure you to speak out on what you know about all this. I cannot have too many friends on this occasion.'" She spoke, as she had since Michael had encountered her tonight, in her Madame de Sévigné voice.

"Your name wasn't on the guest list," Lydie said. She turned to Michael. "Did you invite her?"

He shook his head no. He knew there had never been so flagrant a case of bad timing in the history of romance. All he wanted was to be with Lydie: court her, watch her in action at the d'Origny ball, dance with her, kiss her on the banks of the Loire. Yet here was Anne, spoiling it all. Not because of his old feelings for her, or even because Lydie seemed devastated by her presence—she didn't; he felt Lydie press closer to him. But because he didn't know whether Anne was acting or whether she had lost her mind.

"'She has a charming tone of voice,'" Anne said to Michael, tilting her wig toward Lydie. "'She is fair, she is clean . . .'"

"What are you talking about?" Lydie asked.

"I think she's . . ." How to say it? "Quoting Madame de Sévigné," Michael said.

"Where can I find Madame d'Origny?" Anne asked. "I must thank her for her kind invitation."

"Patrice invited her?" Lydie asked, her head snapping around.

"I don't know," replied Michael, who had wondered all along how Anne had learned the ball's location.

"I want you to leave," Lydie said to Anne.

"'The wife of *Monsieur* is outraged. A snag has developed in her marriage. Her tears flow, as from a fountain. Her great boob of a husband is not very loving,'" Anne said.

At that, Lydie's face turned white, and her shoulders tensed. Michael wanted to protect her, to get her away from Anne. He shook Anne's arm. "Shut up," he said.

Anne spit on his shoe and walked away.

Lydie and Michael stood together, watching her go. Michael held his breath, waiting for Lydie to say something. He glanced at her, wondering why her expression was suddenly serene.

Patrice interrupted them, clearing her throat. "I guess when you throw a party at a castle, you have to expect an evil fairy. What's Malificent doing here?"

"Anne Dumas?" Lydie said. "She said you invited her."

Patrice's mouth flew open. "I did not! The most I did was *mention* it to her at your opening, Michael. I can't believe she said I *invited* her—I was keeping her occupied, keeping her out of your hair."

Lydie reached over to pat Patrice's cheek. "I know. Of course you didn't invite her." But Lydie's eyes were distracted, as if she were discussing something as unimportant as cake batter.

"What's wrong with you?" Patrice asked, frowning. She leaned close to Lydie, looking into her eyes like a school nurse checking the pupils of a student suspected of drug use.

Michael felt Lydie swaying, and he held her steady. "Maybe we should leave," he said.

"But this is her big night," Patrice said. "She's the star of the show."

"I'm fine," Lydie said. "Have you ever had a moment when you know for sure your life's about to change?" She backed away from Michael, and from Patrice. She was receding from both of them, from the ball, into some private sphere of her own. "I'm going to check on Guy," she said, giving Michael a last glance that held a tiny smile.

"What got into her?" Patrice asked. "She's my best friend, and I don't have a clue. I should never have let her wear those rubies."

"She'll be okay," Michael said, fascinated by his own wife. He believed that she had just experienced something so strong and private that she had to get away, off by herself for a while.

"It must have been some shock, coming upon her husband and his mistress, then finding out the only reason she's here is because I told her," Patrice said, adjusting her tiara.

"That's part of it," Michael agreed, but he didn't feel worried. He couldn't take his eyes off Lydie; he watched her walk the ball's outskirts. She had her mind on more than Patrice telling Anne about the ball; more, even, than catching sight of Michael with Anne. Any chance for the romantic night he had hoped to have with Lydie was gone, but Michael felt excited by whatever the alternative was going to be.

⁓

At one point it seemed that everyone was dancing. Lydie felt Michael's hand on the small of her back, and they whirled through the crowd. The dance floor was a pillow of billowing, full skirts. Lydie hadn't told him what had happened with the gun; she had had neither the chance nor the inclination. After making sure all the jewelry had been properly photographed, after overseeing the kitchen to make sure the banquet would go off without a hitch, Lydie was loving the chance to dance with her husband.

Every so often Patrice in scarlet waltzed past, and she or Lydie would wave or touch fingers. When the music changed to a cha-cha, Patrice cut in on Michael, leaving Lydie with Didier. But after one dance Michael reclaimed her. His breath on her neck, the pressure of his hand on her lower back, the way he seemed to be watching her every time she gazed up at him: it all reminded her of falling in love.

Anne Dumas seemed to be everywhere. If Lydie glanced over her left shoulder, Anne was dancing with someone near the orchestra. If Lydie looked straight ahead, there was Anne doing the minuet with Léonce d'Esclimont. Yet Anne never seemed to look in Lydie's and Michael's direction. She wore a small intense frown, and Lydie had the wild fantasy that Anne had been plucked from the leaves of French history just for these months, and it required all Anne's concentration to attend this twentieth-century dance. But Lydie had already dispatched two ghosts tonight; even such a hateful one caused her no great anxiety now.

A gong sounded, then sounded again and again until the orchestra stopped playing. Everyone stopped dancing, to wait for something to happen. Even Lydie, who had planned this moment, felt expectant. Two boxwood hedges formed a path to the kitchen, and she focused on the spot where it joined the dance floor.

Here came the parade of food to the banquet table. People lined up to watch servers bearing roasts, salads, *fruits de mer,* and *gratins,* and they exclaimed as each dish was carried past. Kelly carried a tray of spider crabs, red and spiky. She smiled; she looked almost happy to hear the crowd's reaction. With rehearsed precision the chef directed each server where to place each dish. When all was in place, he began to carve the capon. Didier stood aside, grinning, next to his masked sister Clothilde.

"It's fantastic!" Patrice said, running over to Lydie. Marcel helped the guests form a line while Guy took pictures of the untouched food. In this scene the only d'Origny pieces were the carving set, silver and vermeil serving pieces, and sterling silver boars, porcupines, and pheasants decoratively set around the banquet table.

The line began to move. People filled their plates, then went to find seats at white-clothed tables under the chestnut trees. The food smelled delicious, but Lydie wanted to wait until everyone had been served. Clothilde and Fulbert approached her. "*C'est magnifique,*" Clothilde said from behind her gold mask. "*Vraiment,*" said Fulbert. Clothilde leaned forward to kiss Lydie's cheek, but instead of lips Lydie felt only cool metal. She smiled at the mask, an astonishing disk of thin gold with rays that wavered and made Lydie think of Medusa.

"I'm so glad you like it," Lydie said. "Did Guy take some pictures of you? That mask is incredible."

"A roll, at least," Patrice said. "Wouldn't you say, Clothilde?"

Michael tensed. Lydie could feel it even though her back was to him. Then she heard Anne's voice. "'Because out of modesty and lack of interest in his appearance he had omitted to put ribbons on the bottom of his breeches, so that he looked quite naked . . .'" she said.

"Anne!" Michael said sharply.

Perhaps she didn't quite recognize him. She tilted her head from side to side. "'There was some muddle about his wig, which made him wear the side at the back for quite a time, so that his cheek was quite uncovered.'" Her voice rose until she nearly screeched: "'He went on pulling, but what was wrong refused to come right. It was a minor disaster.'" At that she yanked Clothilde's gold mask from her face and clutched it to her bosom.

Clothilde gasped and touched her cheek, which Anne had scratched. Fulbert leapt forward to grab the mask, but Anne kicked him in the groin. He fell to the ground moaning. Michael stepped toward her; Anne stepped back. Her eyes on his, she said, "'But in the same line Monsieur de Montchevreuil and Monsieur de Villars got caught up in each other so furiously—swords, ribbons, lace, all the tinsel, everything got so mixed up, tangled, involved, all the little hooks were so perfectly hooked up with each other that no human hand could separate them . . .'"

"'But what *completely* upset the gravity of the ceremony,'" Patrice said, seeming to quote from the same text as Anne, "'was the negligence of old d'Hocquincourt . . .'"

Anne focused on her. Her eyes were no longer dreamy, but suspicious, as if she was not quite sure of where she was. She looked from Patrice to Michael to Lydie to the mask she held in her hands. Lydie could imagine her balling it up like a sheet of tinfoil. Anne stared down at it for a moment, then looked up at Patrice. She handed the mask to Clothilde, who accepted it, stunned. Fulbert sat on the ground, holding his crotch.

"It's not so lovely, is it?" Anne asked.

"The mask?" Patrice said, slipping her arm around Anne's shoulder. "No. I'm sure you-know-who would have considered it pretty gaudy."

"She had the most exquisite taste," Anne said.

"You remind me of her," Patrice said. "Really. Where did you have that wig made?"

Anne dimpled, patted her hair. "At Monsieur Antoine's, *bien sûr*. He is old and doesn't take many new clients, but if you are interested, I shall introduce you."

"How kind you are to share him with me," Patrice said. She glanced quickly at Lydie, then led Anne away.

"What a shocking woman," Clothilde said, examining her mask for damage. "I think we should call the police."

"I don't think Didier would like his ball spoiled by the police," Lydie said, though she took a certain pleasure in imagining Anne hauled off to the big house.

The orchestra started playing a waltz. Clothilde and Fulbert strolled toward the dance floor, leaving Lydie and Michael alone under the trees.

# 24

*But is it not cruel and barbaric to regard the death of a person one dearly loves as the starting signal for a voyage one passionately desires to make?*

—To Françoise-Marguerite,
Good Friday, 1672

It was nearly dawn before Michael and Lydie reached Paris. With Michael driving, Lydie slept. She, who could never sleep in a moving vehicle, slept through that entire trip, the dreamless sleep of someone at peace. Only the sound of lorries, rumbling down the slow lane from the Rungis market, wakened her. A golden, cloudless sunrise shimmered over the city.

"Good morning," Michael said, glancing over as she stretched.

"We're already here?" she asked, smiling. "Are you exhausted?"

"I'm not tired at all," he said. Instead of driving into Paris through the Port d'Italie, Michael continued along the Périphérique.

"Where are we going?" she asked, as they left the Eiffel Tower behind.

"Let's not go home," he said. "Let's keep driving."

"To where?" Lydie asked.

"Normandy."

He replied so fast, Lydie wondered whether he had been there with Anne, found the perfect romantic hideaway. Was that where he had gotten tan? But, after last night, what would it matter? Her skin tingled with the memory of what she had viewed down the gun barrel. "Why Normandy?" she asked.

"Because we can drive there and back in one day. Because it's on the sea, and you love the sea."

"Oh," she said, still half-asleep, not quite ready to fully waken. She longed to dream, as if further answers could be found deep in her unconscious. While she dozed again, Michael stopped at a *boulangerie* and brought croissants and café au lait out to the car.

They drove north in silence. At one point, Michael reached across the seat, covered Lydie's hand with his. The sun rode low in the sky. Every field seemed full of cows. The flatlands around Paris gave way to rolling hills crowned with poplars. Every so often they drove through tiny towns, blinks of civilization that resembled each other: church, butcher, baker, *café-tabac*. On the open road old men rode bicycles. Workers hoed fields. Laundry flapped on clotheslines outside farmhouses. In every town, stout women and small children walked home with *baguettes*.

"The ball was beautiful," Michael said after a few miles. "You did a great job."

"I think Didier was pleased," Lydie said. Didier hadn't even known about Anne until it was over. Michael had tracked down an aunt, who had called Anne's doctor, who had booked her into a clinic in Anjou. "Didn't Patrice save the day with Anne Dumas?"

"Two people who can quote Madame de Sévigné at the same party," Michael said. "It's bizarre."

"Well, Patrice has read Anne's book about a hundred times," Lydie said. "But why did her quotation snap Anne out of it?"

Michael shook his head. "I don't know. Maybe it was the shock of hearing someone else speak her language." Then, so obviously wanting to change the subject he didn't even bother to pause, he asked, "Where should we have lunch? Which town?"

"There's always Honfleur . . ." Lydie remembered the little port rimmed by crooked half-timber houses, the bar they had visited on their first trip outside Paris.

"That's what I was thinking," Michael said.

The smell of apples came through the open windows as they neared the coast; the orchards were thick with them, and with pears. Lydie felt the breeze turn chilly. "We'll need sweaters," she said.

"Let's drive straight into town and find a place with tables on the quai," Michael said.

"Okay," Lydie said. They parked their car on the hill near St. Catherine's, the wooden fifteenth-century church. A market was in progress, the vendors selling cheeses, milk, live chickens, linens, honey, herbs, apples, cabbages, lobsters, sole. Compared to the ball, it seemed real, earthy; walking through it, Lydie felt something in her had been released. Michael bought a small paper sack full of *crevettes grises,* baby shrimp the size of Lydie's thumbnail, spiced and cooked live over an open fire. They ate them as they walked down the winding street toward the port.

It was just noon, early for lunch. Café proprietors stood outside their premises, smiling and nodding at passersby. Lydie and Michael stopped at each one, reading the menus set in metal frames by the doors. They chose a restaurant overlooking the old port. Across the boat basin stood the houses, ancient and askew, that Lydie remembered from their previous visit.

They sat side by side at a table near the back of the terrace, against the restaurant's façade. Lydie smoothed the white paper cloth as Michael ordered the wine: Meursault.

"Meursault?" she asked, smiling. His choice was festive, significant: they always had it with shellfish.

"Let's have a *plateau de fruits de mer,*" he said. "I feel like cracking shells."

Lydie sipped the white wine, dry and flinty, understood that Michael was waiting for her to talk.

"A lot happened last night," Lydie said, wanting to start off slowly.

"I'd like to hear about it," Michael said.

"I know you would," Lydie said, bursting to tell him, searching her mind for the words. What had seemed obvious, explainable, in the midst of an eighteenth-century château, could sound absurd in modern surroundings. Yet she believed, more strongly than ever, in the power of what had happened to her.

Michael was silent, watching her. "I was surprised you weren't more upset to find me talking to Anne," he finally said.

"I was upset, at first," Lydie said, looking him straight in the eye. "I aimed a gun at both your heads."

Michael said nothing, but held her gaze.

"Kelly stopped me. I wouldn't have shot, but I didn't want to put down the gun."

"Why were you holding it at all?" Michael asked.

Lydie shrugged. Her heart pounded as it had last night. She wondered whether he would believe what she was about to tell him. "I had a vision," she said.

"A vision?" he asked, frowning. "You mean like a religious vision?"

Lydie nodded, trying to keep her hands steady. "Well, I saw you and Anne, and of course I knew she was the one you had been with, and I went a little wild. Then, all of a sudden, I thought of my father. I can't explain it."

"What made you pick up the gun?"

"I'm not sure. I thought if I looked through the scope, I'd be able to see more clearly . . ." She paused, and Michael didn't seem able to stand it.

"Tell me," he said.

"I was thinking of how it was for him, how he had picked up that shotgun, pointed it . . . But Michael—I didn't *aim* at you . . . I was looking down the gun barrel . . . God, this sounds weird."

"At what?" Michael asked. "You were looking down the gun barrel at what?"

And then Lydie felt as calm as she had last night, at the instant she had lowered the gun. "I was looking into my father's soul. As soon as I did, I understood him. I've kept myself from trying to ever since it happened. I had to see it my mother's way—that he just went crazy—in order to be loyal to her. She can't bear to understand that he really loved Margaret Downes. I guess I hate him for that. But he was my father, and I love him. And when I looked through the gun scope, I forgave him."

"You did, Lydie?"

"Just holding the gun made my body feel different, like I had no control over my heart, my lungs, even my eyes. I realize how he must have felt. That second when he pulled the trigger, he didn't have a choice." Lydie heard her voice go up; she could imagine it stopping altogether. "I looked through the scope, and I saw you fighting with Anne. Just seeing you together made me want to kill you for a minute. Even though I could see that you didn't want her there."

"I didn't." Michael sat perfectly still, hanging on every word.

"My father didn't know what he wanted," Lydie said. "He loved us all—me, you, Mom. I know that now. But he loved her, Margaret, too. He couldn't live without her. My mother will never face that."

"I've always known he loved you, Lydie," Michael said. "But he was desperate."

"He was desperate," Lydie said, her voice breaking. "That's so different from being crazy. Mom saying he 'went out of his head' let him off the hook, but it kept me from understanding him. Now I know it was his only way out."

"And you've forgiven him?"

She nodded her head, waiting for her voice to come back. "Do you know? I really believe it was a vision last night. A clear vision. I believe that God showed me, so I could forgive my father. Do you think that's too strange?"

"No, I don't."

Lydie stared into his eyes, silently thanking him.

"But can you forgive me?" Michael asked.

"I'm trying," Lydie said. "You hurt me."

"I know. And I'm so sorry," Michael said, his eyes filling.

Lydie scrutinized his mouth, his gaze, the small lines around his eyes, looking for clues. For what? she wondered. For a reminder of how much she had once trusted him?

"I love you, Lydie," he said. He stroked her cheek with one hand. She covered it with her own, held it steady. "I have an idea," he said tentatively. "What if we didn't go back to Paris after lunch? What if we took a room at some hotel? Would you be ready for that?"

"The old one," Lydie said. "The farm overlooking the estuary, where Boudin and Monet painted . . ."

They sat there for a long time, and then the *plateau* arrived. A battered silver platter piled high with cracked ice and rockweed, it was covered with *belons* and *creuses*, clams, *langoustines*, *crevettes roses* and *grises*, periwinkles, and *torteaux*. Alongside were lemon slices, brown bread and butter, a half-lemon stuck with pins for extracting periwinkles and crabmeat. They gazed at it for a moment, appreciating its beauty, and they began to eat.

∽

The old, famous hotel, whose brochure claimed it was the place where Impressionism was born, stood high on a hill. It faced the mouth of the Seine, beyond which lay the English Channel and the North Atlantic. Ivy climbed its shingled walls, geranium-filled flower boxes hung at every window. The service was correct, even formal. The maid led them to their room on the top floor.

"How many people check into a place like this with no bags?" Michael whispered to Lydie, climbing the stairs.

"Let's hope they think we're up to something illicit," Lydie whispered back.

But when the maid left them alone in the room, Lydie felt shy. She looked out the window, across the garden to the sea. Turning toward Michael, she blinked, thinking of how she had aimed a gun at his head. He leaned on the window frame, watching her. His hand rested on the sill, and she could imagine it tracing the inside of her arm. Then he pulled her toward him and kissed her.

"I hated thinking of you alone in our bed," Michael said.

"But you did think of me?" she asked, brought straight back to the present.

"Yes, I did. A lot. You have to relax," Michael whispered, his breath warm against her ear. "Everything will be fine. Haven't we been here before?"

Lydie laughed at that. "Never *here*," she said, not meaning the hotel.

"That's true . . ."

She watched the tall windows. Although she couldn't see the water, she knew it was near by the quality of light. Shadows played on the ceiling as the sun moved across the western sky. The time had come to trust him or not. She lay on her side, looking into her husband's eyes. She had known him for so long. She had watched him play basketball in high school, she had fallen in love with him in Washington. She had come with him to Paris and nearly lost him.

He was watching her, waiting for her to make the first move. She stroked his cheek, kissed his mouth. One hand closed around his erect penis and the other slid up, grazing his stomach and chest. She felt reluctant desire building as she arched her back against him. Then, as if given permission, Michael came to life. He rolled her onto her back, kissed her soundly on the lips, then moved slowly down her body. Lydie moaned, her throat constricted. She felt as excited, as apprehensive, as she had the first time they had made love. And only Michael's touch, no longer awkward but sure, reminded her that years and continents and lives and one clear vision had passed since that first time.

# 25

*The enemy fired, from a distance and at random, just one wretched cannon ball, which struck him in the middle of the body, and you can imagine the cries and lamentations of this army.*

—To Monsieur de Grignan, July 1675

THREE DAYS HAD passed since the ball, with no word from Lydie; the last Patrice had seen of her she was driving off, into the sunrise, away from Château Bellechasse, with Michael. Patrice felt optimistic, positive that Lydie's silence meant that she and Michael were in blissful seclusion. Still, the calendar on Patrice's desk warned her that only twelve days remained before Lydie would leave Paris, and Patrice resented losing any chance they had to spend time together. The thought filled her with panic and a sort of grief. She knew about vows to stay in touch, and although she believed that she and Lydie could do that, she knew it would be no substitute for their daily phone calls and frequent visits, for simply *knowing* that Lydie was just across Paris.

Patrice filled diary page after diary page with descriptions of the ball. What everyone wore, what everyone ate, what the orchestra played. Somewhere down the line, people would care about the details of a ball in late-twentieth-century France, not that they would ever see this. But it satisfied her, to think that she was recording history. Her mind kept wandering to the personal details: The set of Lydie's mouth when she asked if Patrice had invited Anne. The way Patrice's thoughts kept floating to her mother, wishing Eliza were there—enjoying herself, watching Patrice in her role as hostess. Kelly in defeat, avoiding Patrice and Lydie.

Kelly. The thought of her made Patrice frown. Kelly was off today. Kelly never seemed to lose hope. Yesterday she'd come to work smiling, asking Patrice and Didier if they had enjoyed the ball. Patrice remembered those days, early on, when she had so feared losing Kelly *and* Lydie that she had wished, fanatically, for Kelly's petition to be denied. As if Kelly were just a checker or a chess piece or a tiddlywink, a little plastic counter in someone else's game.

Patrice tried to get Kelly out of mind. She picked up the telephone. She dialed Boston, Massachusetts.

"Hello, Mother," she said.

"Patsy, darling! How was the ball?" Eliza asked. "It was last Saturday, wasn't it? I've had it on my little mental agenda . . ."

"Absolutely wonderful," Patrice said. "All of Paris is talking about it. How are you?"

"Oh," Eliza said and sighed. "The same—nothing much happens to me anymore."

Patrice felt her shoulders tighten. "Why don't you *make* something happen, for a change?"

"If this isn't going to be a *nice* chat," Eliza said brittlely, "I see no reason to run up your phone bill."

"I mean, why don't you go visit Aunt Jane in Cleveland? You'd like that, wouldn't you?"

"Jane's very busy these days," Eliza said in a tone that suggested to Patrice that perhaps her mother and aunt had had a falling-out. The thought did not entirely displease her.

"Aunt Jane and her good causes," Patrice said, inviting some gossip. "But why don't you call her? You know she'd love to hear from you."

"Well . . . maybe I will," Eliza said. "Tell me what you're doing, now that the ball is over."

"I'm keeping a diary," Patrice said.

"You always did, as a girl," Eliza said.

"I did, didn't I?" Patrice said, remembering the locked pink ones her aunt had given her every Christmas. She had regretted the tiny amount of space allowed per day.

"I kept a diary," Eliza said. "All through my childhood. I had— oh, it must have been twenty volumes. I burned them the week I got married."

This was astonishing: that Eliza could do anything as introspective as keep diaries, that she in fact had written them *and* burned them. "Why did you burn them?" Patrice asked.

"I didn't want your father to read them," Eliza said. Patrice heard a tiny giggle her mother had, perhaps, not intended for Patrice to hear.

"I don't care who reads mine," Patrice said. "I'm just jotting down observations—not really personal things."

"Many an American has traveled to France and observed it more acutely than the French," Eliza said. "Hemingway comes to mind. Henry James, Irwin Shaw . . ."

"Well, no one's going to read *my* observations," Patrice said, laughing nervously, flattered her mother would make such a comparison.

After she hung up the phone, Patrice resumed her writing. A picnic was going on in the Place des Vosges, but she ignored the sounds of festivity. *Three Women of the Marais* sat on her desk; every so often her gaze would light upon it. How had she come up with the perfect line with which to answer Anne Dumas? It had soothed Anne, somehow, to hear Patrice speaking the words of Madame de Sévigné. Patrice had never consciously memorized her letters, but they had a distinctive rhythm and style that Patrice had found easy to conjure. She sat there, trying to recall other lines, but without Anne prompting her, she found it impossible. The telephone rang, startling her.

"Hi," came Lydie's voice.

"There you are!" Patrice said. "Where have you been? Never mind—don't answer. I've missed you."

"Oh, I've missed you too," Lydie said, her voice full of happiness. "Michael and I just got back from Honfleur."

"Did you stay at that great old hotel? I forget the name . . ."

"Yes," Lydie said. "It was wonderful. We'd intended to stay for one night. Well, for one afternoon, to be honest."

Patrice put on her Mae West voice. "A quickie at the No-Tell Hotel," she said.

"It didn't turn out that way," Lydie said. "We stayed for two nights. It suddenly hit us—neither of us had work to do in Paris. The Salle is open, the ball is over . . ."

"Don't you feel let down?"

"Not yet," Lydie said. "Do you?"

"Yes," Patrice said. But she knew that was not so much because the ball was over but because it meant Lydie was about to leave. She felt her throat constrict, and she coughed.

"How is Kelly?" Lydie asked.

"Not here today," Patrice said. "I've given her a couple of days off. She seems fairly chipper, I guess. You know Kelly."

"I want to try again," Lydie said. "Michael called some lawyer he knows in New York who recommended someone who does immigration law. I'm writing a letter to him."

"I thought that lady at the embassy, what's-her-name, told you not to bother," Patrice said.

"She did, but she's a bureaucrat," Lydie said. "I want to find a way."

"You know what I'm thinking?" Patrice asked.

"That we should tell Kelly?" Lydie replied.

"*You* should tell her," Patrice said. "You deserve all the credit."

"No," Lydie said. "I'll be the New York connection, you'll be the Paris connection. We're in this together." She paused. "Michael's in it too" she said after a moment. "He's been encouraging me to try again. He explained to me last night what I've been doing all along; I want to pass our luck—our 'good fortune'—on to someone else."

"I can relate to this," Patrice said. "I'm the great-great-grandchild of immigrants. Bishops on one side of the family, pirates on the other."

"So, should we visit Kelly?" Lydie asked.

"We should," Patrice said.

⁓ ✺ ⁓

For the first time in her life, Kelly was taking days off from work. Since childhood she had worked every day—folding Pan Am's laundry; emptying the fish pond; gathering shells; picking fruit; operating the wash cycle in the college laundry; at her first "real," respectable job, as an accountant; now as Patrice's maid. But every day of her working life she had known she was aiming toward something, a good life in the United States. What was there to work toward now? Another day, week, year doing housework, no end in sight? Her brothers and sisters could not disguise their disappointment in her; she could barely stand to pass them in the hallway.

At the ball she had done her best to avoid Patrice and Lydie; she wished she never had to see them again. She told herself this was because she knew she had failed them, having been judged unacceptable to enter the United States. Another thought kept sneaking up and she kept chasing it back: they had failed her. It was, perhaps, the worst thought she had ever had. How foolish she was, how naïve, to think Americans could do everything! How unfair to Patrice and Lydie!

Kelly remembered one moment at the ball, when she was in a parade with the other servers, rushing out of the kitchen with platters held before them. Spider crabs, red and spiky, balanced on her platter. That was the moment when everything turned crystal clear: she was not going to the States, then or ever. The other servers seemed so happy, hurrying past the guests who had lined up to applaud as they watched the food they would eat go by; two other servers told Kelly they had felt like stars at that moment. Stars don't carry food, Kelly had wanted to say. At the same time, she knew: this is our life's work.

Tears trickled down her cheeks. Hearing noises in the hall, Kelly started. She knew she was home alone; perhaps Paul Anka had finished his work early. A knock sounded at the door. Kelly held back, afraid to answer. It was midday: all her family and friends were at work.

Then someone broke the lock, the door opened wide, and two policemen stood there. Kelly edged toward the window. She looked over her shoulder: four flights to the street. She would dive through the glass praying. She rushed the window, but the officer caught her, clipped manacles to her wrists, speaking rough French.

"*Américaine,*" she said. "*Parlez-vous anglais?*" Could she trick him into thinking she was American? Surely they wouldn't treat Americans this way, even illegal Americans. But he did not reply. He pushed her into the hallway while the other officer stayed behind, searching for other illegal Filipinos.

Kelly wished she had made it to the window. She would rather be dead on the pavement than walking through the building in handcuffs. And then the worst thing of all happened: Patrice and Lydie arrived. Patrice moved toward them like a locomotive, all iron and steam. Hands on her hips, black hair framing her face like a corona.

"Put me in the car, don't let them see me," Kelly begged the policeman.

"What's going on here?" Patrice asked, not allowing the policeman to pass.

Lydie came straight to Kelly, put her arm around Kelly's shoulders. "Everything will be fine. We'll get you out of this."

"Leave me," Kelly sobbed. "Please leave me."

Lydie's pale eyes looked so troubled, Kelly knew she understood Kelly's shame. Still, Lydie wouldn't let go. Patrice spoke to the officer in French, her voice rising and rising. Kelly began to be afraid Patrice would be arrested. She heard Patrice saying "President Mitterand," "President Bush," "Minister of Culture."

"Cool it," Lydie said to Patrice in a stern voice.

"They're saying the embassy turned her in." Patrice spoke English now. "We can't just let them *take* her."

Kelly began to hope; she felt it growing inside her, hope that Patrice and Lydie would somehow win, prevent the police from taking her away. But then the officer shoved Patrice out of the way, pushed Kelly into the car. When Kelly turned, to try to catch one last glance of her two Americans, the policeman yanked her around. He made her face straight ahead.

# 26

*This conversation lasted an hour, and it is impossible to re-peat it all, but I certainly made myself very pleasant throughout this time and I can say without vanity that she was very glad to have someone to talk to, for her heart was overflowing.*

—To Coulanges, December 1670

"You've done what you could," Michael said to Lydie. "You have to let her go." They stood in the living room, empty now except for their suitcases and the few cartons the movers would pack after lunch.

"'She came to Paris and learned to let go,'" Lydie said. "How's that for an epitaph?"

"No one's dying," Michael said.

"That is true," Lydie said. "It's also true that there's a difference between letting go of my father and letting go of Kelly. I'm not giving up."

"I know," Michael said. "But she's going back to the Philippines for now, and there's nothing you can do about that." He felt proud of Lydie's determination to bring Kelly Merida to the United States. She was getting ready to go to the airport with Patrice, to see Kelly off. He watched her, standing in the middle of the bare room, changing her clothes. She stripped off her dusty jeans and T-shirt, slipped into her black linen suit. Standing still, she faced him. Michael took her hand, led her onto the balcony.

"Our Paris year," Lydie said, gazing downriver. The Seine was blue today, glistening, reflecting a perfect October sky. Yesterday she told him that she had called Julia to tell her they were coming home—together. It had bothered Michael, that Lydie had waited so long to tell her; he had wondered whether she doubted their reunion would hold. But she had needed to put distance between herself and Julia, to keep her own vision strong.

"Can you believe we're getting ready to leave?" Michael asked.

"Can you believe I came to France and made best friends with another American and a Filipino?"

Michael smiled, slid his arm across Lydie's shoulders. The black fabric had absorbed the sun, felt warm against his bare arm. It was true, he thought: Lydie had had one foot in America when she arrived in Paris. Perhaps that was why her important friends were also foreigners. He, on the other hand, had had an entirely French experience. He had left his mark on the Louvre, found a French lover. Anne. People at the Louvre were saying that Anne had gone to Vichy, to take the waters at Madame de Sévigné's favorite spa.

"I should go," Lydie said, checking her watch. "Patrice is picking me up in five minutes."

"*Bon courage,*" Michael said. "I love you."

"I love you too," Lydie said. She smiled, brushing the hair out of his eyes. Then she walked away.

✑

It was nice of Lydie and Patrice to come to the airport, Kelly thought, waiting to board the plane to Manila. Lydie sat on her right, the police guard sat on her left. Patrice stood in front of everyone. Kelly had told her family that she was leaving but not when, because she did not want them to see her in handcuffs. Kelly felt ashamed to wear handcuffs in public, and she felt grateful to Lydie for covering them with her coat.

"I have your address in Cavite," Lydie said. "I wish you had a phone."

"There is no phone," Kelly said, smiling a little because no one in the province had a phone.

"I'll do what I have to in New York, and I'll write to you as soon as I hear something."

"And I'll keep track from this end," Patrice said. What could Patrice do in Paris? Kelly wondered, but she smiled at Patrice, knowing that Patrice felt very bad for her. Patrice spoke harshly to the policeman; he shook his head. Kelly wished Patrice would quit asking him to take off the handcuffs.

"M.V. is reliable," Kelly said. "M.V." was her code for "Marie-Vic," who would replace Kelly as Patrice's maid. She didn't want the policeman to get wind of the fact that Patrice employed illegal aliens.

"Are you okay?" Lydie asked, squeezing Kelly's hand.

Kelly nodded: a lie. She was not okay. She wanted only to get away from Lydie and Patrice. But she couldn't let them see her true feelings. She had many things she wished to forget: their kindnesses, the nights she had spent in jail. The first one was the worst; she had lain awake all night, waiting for one of the Americans to get her out. Around midnight she had realized that was not going to happen, and she had accepted her fate.

A voice came on the loudspeaker, and in the blur of French, Kelly caught the word "Manila."

"They're calling your flight," Lydie said. She looked pale, so worried. "Be brave about this. You'll be in America in no time. I won't stop trying."

"Thank you," Kelly said, knowing that Lydie would stop trying, even if Lydie didn't know it yet. Once Kelly was out of sight, Lydie could begin to forget her. The guard took away Lydie's coat, exposing the handcuffs to all the other travelers. Two other Filipinos wore handcuffs. So, Kelly thought: the French police had a good week.

"Have a safe trip," Lydie said, throwing her arms around Kelly, pressing her face so hard into Kelly's neck that Kelly felt Lydie's tears trickle into her collar.

"Don't cry, Lydie," Kelly said. "You did all you could, and I will always be grateful."

Lydie stepped away, and there was Patrice, her face grave. Oh, this was the moment Kelly had dreaded, her last words with Patrice. Memories already filled Kelly's head. Learning the computer with Patrice, ironing Patrice's clothes, the smell of Didier's cigar, and, most special: the long talks she and Patrice had had about life in the States. Patrice took Kelly's hands. The expression in her blue eyes was soft. "My friend," Patrice said.

"I will never forget you," Kelly said.

"Let's make a promise," Patrice said, "to celebrate next Fourth of July in New York with Lydie."

Kelly found herself unable to speak, even when the guard began to pull her along. Patrice stared into her eyes and held on to Kelly's tethered hands until the last minute before letting go.

⁓

"Shit," Patrice said, watching the plane taxi on the runway.

"Is she going to make it?" Lydie asked, gulping. She had been crying since Kelly disappeared through the door.

"Yes," Patrice said, sounding stubborn.

It would be so easy, Lydie knew, once the rawness of Kelly's arrest and deportation began to heal, once the strength of Kelly's single-minded drive began to fade, to let her become a memory. But she would refuse to let that happen. The refusal would be an act of will, of faith.

They watched the plane move forward, gathering speed. Lydie caught glimpses of the white tails of scared rabbits flashing through the tall grass. Then the plane lifted off, zooming into the clouds. She closed her eyes, imagined what Kelly was seeing out the window: the patchwork fields outside Paris, brown squares of earth next to green squares, tiny forests, farmhouses and châteaux. Michael and I take off just days from now, Lydie thought, opening her eyes, looking at Patrice.

"It's a good idea," Lydie said. "You and Kelly coming to New York next summer. That leaves us until July to make her legal. Nine months."

"My mother actually has a good friend in Congress. Who knows? Maybe I can convince her to pull strings," Patrice said, shrugging. Then her blue eyes filled with tears. "She was so brave. I really thought she'd get that visa."

"So did I," Lydie said. The plane to Manila was just a speck in the sky. When it disappeared, she and Patrice walked away from the window.

"This is good-bye," Patrice said.

"I *know* we'll see her again," Lydie said.

"No, I mean us," Patrice said. "We'll see each other a few more times, of course. And I'll come see you off when you go, but Michael will be here then, and Didier. This is our good-bye."

Lydie, who had been thinking the same thing, took Patrice's hand as they walked through the airport. "We'll stay in close touch," she said.

"Yes," Patrice agreed. "We'll write letters. Our phone bills will be terrible. You'll take vacations in France."

"And you'll come to America for Christmas," Lydie said.

Travelers hurried past them, laden down with luggage and blue-and-yellow plastic bags from the duty-free shops. Patrice and Lydie strolled along, like two friends wandering through the roses in the Bagatelle.

"Finally I understand what you were saying, weeks ago," Patrice said, "about always calculating the time difference between Paris and New York. I'll be doing it myself now. Subtracting six hours to figure the time in New York, adding seven for the time in Manila."

"And you know Kelly and I will be thinking of you, on Paris time," Lydie said. "We've been on it ourselves. Once you've lived in a time zone, well . . ."

"You set your clock by it," Patrice said.

"When it's dinnertime in New York, it's midnight in Paris," Lydie said.

They walked in silence for a while, out of the airport, into the short-term parking lot.

"What do you say you take us for a spin?" Patrice said, throwing Lydie the keys to Didier's big silver Citroën.

"Great idea," Lydie said. She walked around to the driver's side and unlocked the door.

"We'll drive around till teatime and then sit outside in the Jardin du Palais Royal," Patrice said. "It's warm enough out, don't you think?"

"It is," Lydie said, remembering that that was where she and Patrice had first met. They would sit in the shadow of Richelieu's palace, gazing into the blue, October sky, and they would drink a toast: a farewell, but also a celebration. Lydie would raise her glass to Paris, to visions of forgiveness, to Michael, to Patrice, to Didier, to her father, to her mother, to the Seine, to the Salle des Quatre Saisons, to Madame de Sévigné, to the "Marseillaise" and the "Star-Spangled Banner," to St. Patrick, to Kelly in the Philippines and Kelly in America.

They climbed into the car and Lydie started the engine. She revved it twice. She fastened her seat belt, watched to see that Patrice fastened hers, then shifted into gear. Lydie drove very carefully out of the airport parking lot. At the stop sign she looked both ways. Patrice found a radio station playing a French variety of rock and roll. Then Lydie pulled onto the Périphérique, hit the toggle marked "overdrive," and drove.